Praise for the Book of the Order novels

"A fast-paced ad... *Reviews*

"*Wrayth* has all ... us Order
novels: fast pacir ... f tropes."
... *cape Pod*

"Ballantine is a master at building worlds without letting the
construction get in the way of the story . . . Consistent writing,
imaginative stories and well-fleshed-out characters."
—*View from Valhalla*

"Interesting revelations . . . Red-hot action sequences . . . An
enjoyable romp." —*citybookreview.com*

"A power addition to the Book of the Order series . . . A fantasy
that does not fail to deliver a powerful punch to readers."
—*Snarkymamma*

SPECTYR

"Picks up smoothly from [*Geist*], continuing the fantasy adventure with a mix of romance and power play by the world's
deities . . . Will appeal to the paranormal romance and steampunk crowds." —*Kirkus Reviews*

"*Spectyr* keeps up the series' promise: well-crafted, tightly
packed action . . . Should satisfy even die-hard fantasy fans."
—*Drying Ink*

"A unique, character-driven fantasy that delivers on all levels."
—*Smexy Books*

continued . . .

GEIST

Ace Books by Philippa Ballantine

GEIST
SPECTYR
WRAYTH
HARBINGER

HARBINGER

PHILIPPA BALLANTINE

ACE BOOKS, NEW YORK

THE BERKLEY PUBLISHING GROUP
Published by the Penguin Group
Penguin Group (USA) Inc.
375 Hudson Street, New York, New York 10014, USA

USA | Canada | UK | Ireland | Australia | New Zealand | India | South Africa | China

Penguin Books Ltd., Registered Offices: 80 Strand, London WC2R 0RL, England
For more information about the Penguin Group, visit penguin.com.

HARBINGER

An Ace Book / published by arrangement with the author

Ace Books are published by The Berkley Publishing Group.
ACE and the "A" design are trademarks of Penguin Group (USA) Inc.

For information, address: The Berkley Publishing Group,
a division of Penguin Group (USA) Inc.,
375 Hudson Street, New York, New York 10014.

ISBN: 978-0-425-25655-8

PUBLISHING HISTORY
Ace mass-market edition / August 2013

PRINTED IN THE UNITED STATES OF AMERICA

10 9 8 7 6 5 4 3 2 1

Cover art by Jason Chan.
Cover design by Lesley Worrell.
Interior text design by Tiffany Estreicher.

ALWAYS LEARNING   PEARSON

To Tee Morris, my captain, who made me
unexpectedly believe in soul mates

ACKNOWLEDGMENTS

This has been a rollicking, fun series to write, and I am sad to leave Arkaym, Sorcha, Merrick, Raed and even the Rossin. To all who have supported me along the way, I need to give thanks, so here is the list.

To my editor at Ace, Danielle Stockley, for keeping me honest and on the straight and narrow with large cats and cursed princes.

To my agent, Laurie McLean, who back in 2007 said she liked my prickly Sorcha, and found her such an awesome home.

To my cover artist Jason Chan, who has always delighted and astounded me by capturing my characters in such wondrous detail.

Most especially to all the readers who have embraced the series. May you enjoy the ending, but keep dreaming of the comradeship and bravery of the Order.

The Runes of Sight

Sielu—See from another's eyes

Aiemm—See into the past

Masa—See into the future

Kebenar—See the real nature of a situation

Kolar—Send your sight traveling

Mennyt—See into the Otherside

Ticat—The Last Rune of Sight; for the last moment

The Runes of Dominion

Aydien—The Rune of Repulsion

Yevah—The shield of fire

Tryrei—Open a peephole to the Otherside

Chitrye—Bringer of lightning

Pyet—The cleansing flame

Shayst—Steal another's power

Seym—The Rune of Flesh

Voishem—Phase through walls

Deiyant—Move objects with your will

Teisyat—Open the doorway to the Otherside

ONE

Return of the Wanderer

Smoke blew off the once-admired canals of the capital of the Empire of Arkaym. Several times the geistlord, who wore a coyote shape, had to backtrack as he found bridges broken before him and houses tumbled down everywhere. The Fensena sniffed at the bodies left to rot in the alleyways of Vermillion, but unlike a real coyote he did not pause to dine.

The fact that a five-foot-tall coyote was wandering the byways of the heart of the Empire in broad daylight would have been impossible to contemplate even just a few months before. Yet here he was with the run of the place, and not a Deacon of the Order or a soldier of the Imperial Guard to give him pause. The Emperor of Arkaym had very little care for his capital, and had chosen instead to chase after the Princes who had risen in rebellion against him—and it turned out there were quite a few such Princes.

Papers rustled and blew past the coyote in the sharp wind. He caught one as it spun by him, his lightning-fast paw pinning it to the ground. Through gleaming golden eyes the geistlord read—a skill he had taken pride in devel-

oping. It was the offer of a bounty; one on the head of
Sorcha Faris. She was accused of sedition, treason and
murder. More telling was the title they were giving her.
"Arch Abbot of the outlawed Order" was written beneath
the badly drawn picture of her. The Fensena had no love for
the Deacons, but he knew what awaited him on the Otherside and had no desire to see this world burn.

As these dark thoughts filled him with dread, he moved
on through the city and finally made it to the Bridge of
Gilt. The canal that ran beneath it was clogged with all
manner of dead and decaying things that made his nose
twitch. Someone had tied offerings to one of the small
gods on the railings: fruits, dead birds and something
bloody and unidentifiable.

Still, the bridge was intact, and so he padded over it toward
the Imperial Island. The coyote's ears pricked forward as they
traced running footsteps up ahead among the shops that lined
the bridge. Though most merchants had long since abandoned their businesses for whatever safety they wrongly per-
ceived elsewhere, a few brave held on. He could smell them
huddled in their little shops, and hear them whispering.

A young woman was running along the bridge toward
him, clutching something to her chest. The odor of fear
was overpowering to the Fensena's sharp senses.

It was a baby. She was cradling a baby to her chest as
she ran. In the lowering light of sunset, her eyes were wide
with terror. Finally, she saw the huge coyote standing in the
middle of the bridge and skidded to a halt.

The wind ruffled the coyote's brindle coat, made for
deeper winters and more northerly climates. He felt a
clench of sympathy for the woman and her child. The
Rossin, the great geistlord who wore many shapes and all of
them terrible, would have snapped her in half in an instant.
The Fensena himself could have at least bitten her and
leapt into her body to use her energy to keep his toehold in
this realm for another few days.

The woman glanced behind her, and the Fensena could

feel it now; the swirling approach of one of his kind. A geist eager for a host was sweeping down from the island. It tasted to him like a broken soul, perhaps one that had in life even worn the robe of a Deacon. Certainly, something that had been twisted by the Otherside and chewed into dire form.

The Fensena tilted his head, considering, and then placed one paw before the other to perform a slight bow in the woman's direction.

"Run while you can," he whispered through jaws made for cracking bone and tearing flesh.

That beasts should open their mouths and speak in the language of men had not been so strange in the first days, generations past, when the geists first came into the world—but humans had such very short memories and did not read very much of their own history.

The woman pressed her lips together and took her chance. She darted forward, and past him, so close that her skirts brushed against his fur and the perfume of her skin reached his nose. The coyote did not watch her, but his ears tracked her progress.

The geist was on her heels, and it was indeed as he had suspected. The torn and desecrated figure of a Deacon of the Order of the Eye and the Fist floated down the bridge. Once water would have prevented the geist from crossing, but the Otherside was very close to this realm now.

The geist did not acknowledge the Fensena's existence. It floated on, making even the weeds in the cracks in the pavement wither as it passed. He knew what it would do to the woman when it caught up to her—and it would eventually.

It was not his concern, and he could not let it make him miss his appointment. Moving faster on its small, neat feet, the coyote crossed the bridge and trotted up the hill toward the seat of government. He did not like being in this city. However, just like the last time he'd been here, he was on a mission for the Rossin; the great and powerful geistlord whom he was tied to—like it or not.

The coyote raised his nose and sniffed as he approached

the burned shell of the Mother Abbey. The odor of rotting human flesh was easily discernible here. When the roof collapsed, there had been none about to pull the bodies from under the stone, and now the ruins were a graveyard. This place had been full of beautiful gardens, dormitories crammed with Deacons, and a massive library.

However, what he was looking for was not here. Nothing was here.

The Fensena moved on, his nose twitching. Ahead lay only the Imperial Palace. However, a little caution was called for here. Like the shape he wore, the Fensena knew he had to exercise a care; he had a body, he could be killed, and lose his grip on this realm altogether. Unlike the Rossin, his bond with his host was not a permanent one. So he lowered his head and kept to the shadows of the buildings that looked out onto the Imperial Square. His nose told him that unlike the Mother Abbey, there were living people inside—people who would probably not like a large coyote having the run of the place.

He nosed his way around the large square, which faced the palace, eyes darting every now and then to where the pale stone wall ran. His fellow geists had not let the palace alone, despite the cantrips and protections laid down by Deacons over the centuries.

The coyote stopped and let out a faint yip as the thought occurred to him; those Deacons had for much of Arkaym's history been the Circle of Stars. The newer Order that Sorcha Faris had served might have laid their cantrips over the top, but if the earlier foundation had been torn aside then it was all for naught. He sensed that was what they had done as soon as the Mother Abbey was destroyed.

At last, near the rear of the palace, the Fensena found what he was looking for; one section of the wall and the cantrips that had protected it had given up its structural wholeness. The crumpled heap of red stone was a welcome sight. The Fensena needed to get within and soon, since his master was not the most forgiving of creatures.

He entered the pleasure garden of the palace, and realized that no pleasure was ever likely to be found here again. It looked as though a small whirlwind had passed through the ordered rows of plants and topiary. Everything was ripped up and thrown about, and he suspected that mist witches had once again taken to the Ancient paths that the building of the palace had displaced. Though the island was no longer a swamp, the witches would traverse their old paths, and thanks to the thinness of the veil between this world and the other, their powers would be greater.

The Fensena disliked the lower geists and their chaotic nature. He preferred logic, since it usually meant a greater chance at survival. A low rumble started in his chest, and his brindle tail tucked instinctively closer to his body.

The mist witches were still here.

Robbed of any chance to lead travelers astray, drown them in the swamp and take their essence for their own, they would instead be quite happy to rip apart a human. Or indeed another geist or geistlord. Energy was energy after all.

The Fensena snarled, but the mist witch was a mindless thing; designed only to tear apart and feed. It was no geistlord capable of thought, reasoning and plotting. It was drawn to whatever living thing was about. Before the Circle of Stars, the recently returned Native Order, had done whatever necessary to rend the barrier between the Otherside and here, the mist witch might have only lured people to their deaths, or scrabbled their wits. Now however it was far stronger.

Like a Deacon, the Fensena saw its shape completely; the spiraling patterns that looked remarkably like runes that held together this spiderweb of hunger. When it came at him, howling and flinging its icy fingers at the Fensena's flesh, he snarled and leapt.

He might have been one of the lesser geistlords, but he was still more than a match for a simple mist witch. His teeth connected with the strands of the geist, and his own power was transferred to the knot of runic, shifting shapes. With a jerk of his head, the Fensena pulled the thing apart as if it were the ripe flesh of a caribou that had been sitting out under the sun for days.

It dissolved in on itself howling, leaving only a bitter taste in the coyote's mouth. Regrettably there was no way to get rid of that, and generally why he avoided skirmishes with geists when he could.

The Fensena inclined his head and directed his senses to the building, which lay beyond the gardens. It smelled of death and there was fresh blood throughout every corridor. Whereas once, in his early days in this realm, he had reveled in it, now it disturbed him.

His long pink tongue lolled from one corner of his mouth, and the huge pants that he needed to draw air were quite distracting. He knew why too; this body had not much more time to run.

This was why the coyote geistlord no longer liked to travel to Vermillion; too many bodies were already occupied by other geists. His connection with human blood was tenuous at best, and it was very hard for him to take a host when there was already one of his fellows within. Another reason to dislike recent events.

With a long canine sigh, the Fensena trotted up what had been a well-manicured gravel path. Up ahead there were humans; he could smell them as well as sense them with his geist-sight, but they were in such disarray.

The coyote nudged open a door that should have been barred and guarded, and wandered into the corridors and hallways, where once the business of the Empire had been conducted. His nails clicked on the stone floor, and the smell of piss and desperation filled his nostrils.

As the Fensena moved through the palace, he thought about how it had come to this. The Rossin had been a ferocious force on the Otherside; devouring many of their kind. However, since he had taken up with the royal family he had been much subdued. The Fensena had found he had not needed his protection. Indeed, in this realm, the coyote had been quite free to wander, as he preferred. It had only been the shift in currents, the fractional thinning of the border between this world and the Otherside, that had signaled a change.

That powerful fool Derodak had made this happen when he decided the time was ripe to complete his plan to harness the geists, and take this world finally for his own. That in turn had set in motion a series of events that could bring the realm to an end. It would make the destruction heaped on this palace seem like a drop in a bucket.

It was amusing to the Fensena that the Rossin was now the one to try and save this realm, well . . . save it and cut a slice for himself; a particularly leonine slice. His jaws split in a canine smile. He would see the proud Rossin brought down from his high-and-mighty perch before this was all over—provided there was an opportunity to stop the Maker of Ways ripping reality open.

The Fensena turned his mind away from these dire thoughts and padded on up the hallway in the direction his nose was leading him. A few times he was forced to hide in shadows, and duck into damaged rooms to avoid people, but considering this was the center of the human Empire it was ridiculously easy.

The coyote found the stairwell that lay at the heart of the palace. This was part of the original fortress that had stood long before Emperor's vanity built pleasure gardens and golden rooms above it. The deeper down the Fensena went the cooler and quieter it became, but the less he liked it. The faded murals on the walls were deeply etched and told stories of his kind and the humans that had sought to control them.

Many things had been buried down here beneath the palace; things that the various Emperors of Arkaym had wanted hidden. Some had broken loose over that time, but there were still plenty of others that remained.

The Fensena stopped and paused at a smashed section of wall. His nose told him a geistlord had once been imprisoned here. His memory was not good for names, but he recalled a beautiful winged creature—one that had been very good at pretending to be what she was not.

The floor was now sloping down even farther, and the cavern walls were transitioning to rough from polished and carved. The flickering weirstone lights were also now few and far between. It didn't matter; he needed no lights to see by. He had both animal and geist-vision to guide him.

The Fensena stopped at the place where all pretense at building ended, and the Ancient caverns began. The roots of the palace were down here. His ears flattened on his head as he looked up at an image carved above the entrance. That it stood open was yet another sign that the Emperor was losing his grip. This place had always been sealed as long as Vermillion had an Emperor to sit on the red throne high above. Now Kaleva had gone mad, the locks were all sprung—just as the Rossin had told the Fensena they would be.

The image above the passage, however, would have been enough to scare away any curious adventurers who came down this deep. The Murashev, the bright deadly female-shaped geistlord danced around a terrible figure, one that was very far from human. It towered over the entrance, clasping the edges of it with muscular tentacles. The Maker of Ways had been depicted in the very moment of tearing open the world to the Otherside. It was a cataclysmic event that the first Emperor had warned against. Many thought this was a depiction of the Break, but the Fensena knew that the damage this powerful geist would do was so great that that earlier event would seem but a bruise to this realm.

With his head lowered and his ears pinned flat, the coyote slunk under the terrifying arch and into the Ancient belly of Vermillion. It was a small circular room with a wide sandy floor, unmarked and unpaved by anything made by humans. Yet it smelled old and felt warm. The coyote slunk forward and sat down at the center of the room. In the human realm there were sacred places; some were venerated by the gods and their worshippers, some were home to Ancient legends, and still others were marked because of terrible things that had happened there.

This place was known to very few—but those few were

very powerful. Where the Fensena now sat was the very
spot where the Rossin had come into the human world.
Here was where the first Emperor—who had also been the
very first Deacon—had sealed the pact with the terrible
geistlord and given him a toehold into this realm.

The Fensena looked up at the ceiling. He marveled at
how the rock above was as smooth and polished as glass.
Great heat had bloomed once in this room, and the rock
still spoke of that.

The sand beneath the coyote was special too, and definitely not from Arkaym . . . it was from his home. A deep
chill settled into the great coyote's bones as he recalled the
Otherside. It was either all burning or all freezing, and
there was no rest to be found there. It was why all geists
wanted to be on this side; in the human realm where there
was choice and hope. He had no desire to return there—
nor to see the geists of hunger and revenge come to the
human realm. They would lay waste to it as they mind-
lessly had the Otherside. They feasted on the human souls
that passed through that place, because that was all they
had. The Fensena, and the mighty Rossin, had other plans.

The coyote smelled the arrival of the human and heard
the racing of his heart in his ears long before he appeared.
His golden eyes gleamed as he turned and looked over his
brindle-furred shoulder at the coming of the Emperor of
Arkaym.

In his own way, he was a handsome man, fresh skin and
firm jaw, but the geistlord easily saw beyond that. Kaleva,
the Prince that the leaders of Arkaym had called from far
Delmaire to crown their Emperor, was a broken vase of a
man. All the spirit had been snatched from him—but then
he had never really been strong enough to hold so much.
The coyote ran his tongue over his lip and swept it against
his nose. He firmly believed that all the strength of that
family had been placed in one female vessel. The Princes
of Arkaym had not chosen well.

The Emperor was making a show of striding through

the Ancient cavern, but the truth of the matter was, he had been summoned by the same geistlord that had caused the Fensena to be here.

However, he understood nothing—that was immediately apparent. He looked at the melted stonework and did not blink. When the Rossin had spared this puny human's life at the breaking of the Mother Abbey, the Emperor had promised the great pard something from his palace . . . and he could not leave to continue his personal war until that pact was satisfied.

Kaleva in his smart white uniform reached the part of the tunnel where he could see the interior, and he visibly flinched when he saw the huge coyote crouched at the center of the room—after all he had not had good experiences with the geistlords in animal form. The Fensena's mouth split open into a canine pant that was his best approximation of a human smile.

"You are tardy for a leader of men." He couldn't resist the jibe—nor the chance to make the Emperor jump with his ability to speak.

The Emperor took a step back, and glanced over his shoulder as if he expected some kind of puppet master to leap out of the darkness. The man really was a fool, and Derodak had left him barely holding on to sanity.

"You sent the dream?" Finally the Emperor found his own voice.

"No, it was not I," the coyote yipped, getting to his feet and stretching. He was trying to convey his best impression of not caring. "It was he that we both call master."

"I do not—"

The Fensena growled. He preferred to play the trickster, but when it was called for he could be as vicious as any geistlord in this realm or the Otherside. "He is the Rossin, the scion of the Imperial family. From him all strength comes. I believe when he stood before you in fire and dust you understood that . . ."

The Emperor swallowed hard and turned the color of

parchment. The Fensena was completely sure that the image was flashing in his fractured mind. The Rossin did many things well, but chief among them was make an impression.

The coyote paced forward a step, lowering his head and fixing his golden eyes on Kaleva. "Enough of this posturing. You are here to fulfill your word and give my lord what he desires."

The Emperor looked around at the blasted and empty room. "There are many things in my palace I could have given him, but there is nothing here that—"

The Fensena cut him off again in mid-stupidity. "You really do not see a thing do you? It is as if no story was ever read to you as a child." He whiffed a breath out of his long snout, shaking himself as if foolishness were water and he could somehow dislodge it. He could not believe that this man had come to Arkaym to rule it yet had never taken the time to listen to the old tales and myths. Delmaire was a beautiful land, but it was not *the* land. Not the first. Arkaym was the more Ancient by far.

Still, he had neither the time nor the compunction to waste his breath on telling it now. If the human was as blind as he appeared, then he would have to be shown. Instead, the coyote turned on his own tail and went to the center of the room. He could feel it humming through his bones, and setting his fur on end; the most Ancient of places and also a hiding spot.

Unlike the Rossin, the Fensena could at least come to this place, but even he could not do what the Emperor was required to do. To give him the hint the coyote began digging. His blunt but effective claws made the sand fly, and though the digging set his teeth on edge, he did not cease for many a minute.

Eventually, the Emperor became curious and drew nearer to observe what the geistlord was up to. The Fensena was panting, and his head was ringing, but he had done all he could. Together geistlord and Emperor stared down at what he had uncovered.

It was a doorway—or perhaps more accurately a hatch. The palace of Vermillion had more than its fair share of such hidey-holes, but this one was far more than that. Kaleva dropped to his knees and stared at the perfectly round silver hatch. "What do the words say?" he choked out.

That he could not read them was no surprise; they were in the language of the Ehtia, which had long been wiped from human memory. "Cursed be he that takes this up," was a fairly decent translation, but one that the broken Emperor did not need to know.

"I do not have to answer your questions, boy," he replied, a growl darkening his tone. "It is for you to do as you are told."

To his credit the Emperor hesitated a moment. He stared at the coyote for a long time, his eyes darting this way and that as if he were having a conversation with himself. Maybe he was.

The Fensena's hackles went up, and his lip pulled back from his teeth. "Do as you are bid—as you promised the Rossin when he spared your life—or feel the consequences!"

A line of sweat broke out on the Emperor's forehead, but he leaned down and grabbed a tight hold of the handle. This was the moment where it could all go wrong. The Rossin's blood did not flow in this Emperor, and the powerful cantrips Derodak had placed on the door could turn and grind Kaleva to dust. However, he was the Emperor and had sat on the throne of Arkaym. That should be enough for the cantrip . . . hopefully.

Kaleva gasped, and bent over as if he'd been punched in the stomach. The coyote waited for him to catch fire, burst into ashes or melt away. None of those things happened.

Finally, the Emperor uncurled himself and yanked on the door handle. A grinding, Ancient noise filled the deserted room, and then a rush of stale air exploded from behind the hatch. Both coyote and human turned aside and coughed desperately. The Fensena's sharp senses told him to run; it was not just stale air down there. The Otherside was close, and an Ancient seam ran here. It was closed tight for now, but it still made the geistlord nervous.

Since he did not move, it was the Emperor who leaned down into the hole. He might be nearly as empty of sense as a cracked bowl, but he had plenty of that terminal problem for humans: curiosity. The Fensena let him do what he was doing since there could well be traps in there too.

The Emperor proved the coyote right when he began to scream. Long tentacles, green and a vivid red, had appeared at the edge of the hatch, and the Fensena reconsidered; perhaps that breach was not as tightly closed as he had thought. The tentacles had already wrapped around Kaleva's arm, thick and pulsing with power, and tearing at his flesh until blood pulsed from the wounds.

The Fensena felt a low whine escape his throat and he fought the natural inclination to flee. As the Emperor screamed and tore manically at his arm and the tentacles, the coyote bounded from side to side. He realized that the Emperor's blood must stay in the hatch, above all things, so he lunged forward and clamped down on the Emperor's arm, just about where the other had its grip. The Fensena braced, and made sure the human could not move.

The room stank of the Otherside. What if the barrier breached right here and now? Primitive fear—which the Fensena thought he was long past—rushed through him.

The tentacles held on, and the smell of blood filled the room. The Emperor let out a strange strangled scream, and then there was a tearing sound.

Kaleva was left rocking back and forth, clutching his arm to his body, but the tentacles were gone and so was the blood. It had been accepted. The Fensena let out a yip of relief and darted forward.

When he peered into the hole, he could see his goal inside the hatch, but he was not so foolish as to try and take it himself. He turned to the Emperor. "Reach in. Get it."

Kaleva's eyes were wide and terrified. "No, n-n-no . . ." he stuttered.

Foolish damn human. The Fensena had reached the end of his tether. He was so close to achieving the task the Rossin had set him. Finally, pushed to it, the coyote used his own power.

He charged the Emperor and knocked him down. For a moment he went into a frenzy; ripping and tearing at the howling man. The smell of blood drove him on, and it was quite possible that he might kill him then and there.

Eventually, the Fensena found his cool Center again. When he came to himself, he was standing over the terrified Emperor, who now had many bites to go with what the tentacles had already inflicted. The Fensena's gaze was fixed on his throat, and he contemplated how easy it would be to tear it out. He could also take the Emperor's body for his own—the coyote was close to burning this one out.

No, he could not do that. The Emperor was needed, and the Rossin only wanted what had been promised. He growled, deep and low. "Reach in there, and take it out. Now!"

The Emperor slid sideways, away from the coyote, and toward the hatch. Finally, the Fensena had convinced the human that he was more dangerous than whatever was in the pit. His hands wrapped around a bundle, and he pulled it out.

The smell of it was musty and powerful. The coyote immediately forgot about the human; all of his senses were focused on it. "Open it," he growled.

The Emperor, still shaking, did as he was bid. The Rossin's pelt was distinctive; the fur thick and luxurious and patterned with dark patches. It was wrapped in a bundle, and tied closed with a thin, red rope.

The Fensena's eyes gleamed, and without a word he took the binding in his teeth. The Emperor he left sitting on the floor clutching his wounds. He was of no further concern. Now the coyote had to return to his master and quickly. It was time for their plan to move forward.

TWO

Seeing Through the Veil

It was the nature of all traitors to strike in darkness, and this night—like many others that had come before it—they took that chance.

Sorcha Faris had begun the night sleeping next to her lover, Raed Syndar Rossin, perhaps the second most wanted person in the Empire of Arkaym after herself. They had drifted into sleep after making love and warming the sheets as best they could in the cold northern citadel that had become their refuge. It was a good way to slip off to sleep—even if she was not entirely used to it yet.

The smile on the Deacon's face was not the kind many from the Mother Abbey would have recognized; Sorcha Faris was not known for her smiles. However, since the Order of the Fist and the Eye was broken, and the Mother Abbey lay in ruins, none of them would have the chance to judge her. That was truly the only good thing about its destruction.

When the first scream sounded, Sorcha jerked awake, and her initial instinct was to reach across to shake her lover out of his sleep. It was a surprise to realize that the

howls for help were in her head; however, they also seemed
to echo in the stone of the citadel.

Another shock was that her grasping hands found nothing; Raed was not there. His side of their meager bed was
chill, and even the smell of his skin was absent. He must
have slipped off sometime in the night.

Not that she could really begrudge him any late-night
forays. Only hours before, Sorcha had sat in counsel with
ten of the strongest remaining Deacons until the citadel's
hearth fires burned low. Afterward, she had very much
enjoyed waking up Raed—consequently she had no real
remembrance of falling asleep herself.

Raed's whereabouts were however not the most important thing now, as another muffled yell could be heard, this
time coming from above their room. Leaping up from bed
naked, she threw on her cloak and belted it around her,
along with her saber. Instinctually, her hands reached out
for the Gauntlets she'd grown up with, and then stopped
suddenly. The Gauntlets had been destroyed. She had to
remind herself that every single time, because a near-
lifetime of working with them as her foci had not been
undone by mere months. She still felt that loss. The intricate workings of the runes on her own flesh did not offer as
much comfort as the weight of smooth leather on her hands
once had.

So, as clothed as she could manage, Sorcha bolted from
the room, and ran toward where the commotion was now,
not only in her head, but echoing down the hallway. What
could it be this time? One of the Deacon's dogs had been
dismembered last night, while ghostly messages had been
burned into stone the previous week. She knew escalation
when she saw it; someone wanted them to know they were
not alone and to put fear into their very bones.

This Priory citadel was old, falling down in places, but
also rather large, a fact Sorcha cursed as she bounded up
the stairs two at a time. However, it was not like they'd had
their choices of bolt-holes. This northern outpost had long

been abandoned by the first Native Order, the Circle of
Stars, but was the best they could do. The remnants of the
Order of the Eye and the Fist that she'd gathered here had
scoured the place for cantrips and physical traps before set-
tling in. She'd thought it safe.

The silvery runes carved into Sorcha's flesh twisted and
flexed, as if they were in fact alive, as she pounded up yet
another set of spiraling stairs. They were not as quiescent
as they had been when worked into the Gauntlets, a fact
that she found disturbing, even while she found the knowledge that they would never be taken from her comforting.

The guttering lamps set into the walls of the stone Priory cast unreliable light, but she did not need to trust that;
she had something far better. Another thing they would
never take from Sorcha again was her partner Merrick
Chambers. Even though she could not see him, she knew
when he woke. His presence was a warmth on her back,
like an unseen candle that spurred her confidence.

Her Sensitive slept very lightly—a fortunate trait considering their predicament. His Center enveloped her like a
comforting embrace, but it was more than that. Apart, they
were only themselves, together, they were more than the
sum of their powers and parts. When he shared his vision
with her, she was a hawk, a lion, and almost a goddess.

Now Sorcha raced up the stairs more surely, her feet
striking the stone with confidence. Whoever had come
calling at this late hour was about to get more than they
could possibly have bargained for—whether they were
creatures of this realm or the Otherside.

Up ahead, Sorcha could not only hear people screaming
and shouting but also taste their emotions. Fear was running amok up there; lay Brothers tried to bellow over the
howls of the terrified camp followers in an attempt to
restore some kind of control.

They are dying. Merrick always seemed to deliver news
in the calmest of tones. *We need to be there now.*

She didn't respond, too busy feeling out the shape of the

panic above them. Normal human folk were being driven into blind panic by something not yet identifiable, while the cool, hard Centers of the lay Brother were like anchor stones in the midst of a chaotic storm. They might not have powers, but they had training.

Panting only slightly, Sorcha reached the landing, just as Merrick and Zofiya—once the heir of Arkaym—appeared from another corridor. Their rooms were deeper inside the Priory, closer to the root of the mountain. The Deacon was not entirely sure how she felt about her partner's attachment to the dark-haired and beautiful Grand Duchess Zofiya, who no matter the situation always looked as imperious as her title. Merrick caught Sorcha's gaze, and he didn't need to say anything; she knew now was not the time.

Zofiya was throwing on her bandolier as they ran up the remaining stairs together, but remained thankfully and diplomatically silent. The continuing screams from upstairs were growing louder. Remarkably, she let Merrick and Sorcha precede her.

Perhaps, Sorcha thought sharply, *my friend is making improvements on her.*

Merrick shot her a warning glance from the corner of one eye. The tattoos of the Runes of Sight carved his young face in eerie shadows that it had not been made to wear. It gave her a twinge to realize that she would never again see him as she had that first time in the Mother Abbey. It had only been a few years ago, and yet so much had changed.

Careful. His thoughts formed in her head as easily as her own did. That too had almost been taken from her. Though she'd railed against the intrusion of Merrick's thoughts initially, now she welcomed it. It was the bedrock of the Order. Her Order. Whatever that might come to mean in the future.

Rise together or fall alone.

It was the kind of thing that could be carved on a majestic building and had come to her in a rare idle moment. Perhaps it would be a motto someday.

Strange the thoughts that would not be silent in her head, even at moments like this. Merrick's Sight was giving her much more clarity as he wakened, and they drew closer to the epicenter of the attack.

Yes, attack. That is indeed what it is. Merrick's voice blended into her own mind. No sinister words in stone or dog carcass this time. A blatant attack.

Their shared Center however was confused all the same. Geists were in the room, or just had been, but as they got to the top stair they could feel no more of them.

Merrick and Sorcha shared a glance, and then with an unspoken agreement she thrust open the door to the Great Hall.

This was the room where only hours before Sorcha had sat in counsel with the other Deacons—those strongest of the survivors—to try and find a path for whatever was left. Now it looked quite different. The tables they had so recently occupied were overturned, and the fire in the hearth was blazing like a bonfire. It had been guttering out to scarlet embers when last Sorcha had seen it, warming those without powers who had come to them for protection.

We failed them.

The Great Hall was where many of the lay Brothers and camp followers had settled down for the night, since most of the habitable rooms were taken by couples and Deacons. It was also, she could observe, where the geists had stepped through into the human world. Consequently, it was not a pretty sight.

The rules, such as the inability of the undead to directly hurt the living, that Sorcha had grown up with as a member of the Order's novitiate were nothing more than distant memories; now the undead were more than capable of hurting the living. In fact, they appeared to relish it.

Blood was splattered against walls and on the table she had sat at only hours before. Bodies were strewn about from corner to corner and wall to wall like so much chaff. Through the Center she shared with Merrick, the scent of fear and death in the room was overwhelming. If she had not had so much exposure to similar scenes in her time as a Deacon, Sorcha might have thrown up, or run mad in the opposite direction.

"Stay back, Zofiya," Merrick muttered to the Grand Duchess. "This is not over with."

He was right, and luckily the Imperial sister knew it too. She frowned, her grip tightening on her sword, but she remained where she was.

The stench of the Otherside was still all around them—even those without any abilities could smell it. The survivors who were struggling to their feet gagged on it as they hastened to leave the room. Zofiya guided many over to her and helped them stagger out the door.

Merrick and Sorcha shared another look. The Active flexed her fingers—almost as though they were still encased in tooled leather—and stepped into the room, hands outstretched, and runes ready.

Dimly, she could feel other Actives and Sensitives racing up the stairs toward them, but she would not rely on their ability to arrive in time.

Someone wants us here. Her Sensitive whispered into the quiet parts of her mind, apart from her racing thoughts.

Instinctively, she knew that he was right; she and Merrick were the ones meant to hear the screams of the injured and dying.

This attack on the Order they were building was very purposeful. They had gathered more converts in the months of travel since the breaking of the Mother Abbey, but they could not afford to lose any. If someone wanted to get the attention of Sorcha Faris and Merrick Chambers, then this was the way to do it.

"The rest of you, get out now!" Merrick waited a few feet behind her, effortlessly holding the Center steady for her, and yet still managing to instruct a last knot of followers who were still huddled in the far shadows of the Great Hall. They stared at him, obviously deeply shocked by what they had seen, but then a thin-faced woman with blood trickling down from her hairline led the way to whatever safety the door offered.

Sorcha waited, keeping her breathing even by force of will, and trying to hold on to the confidence she had only recently regained. She hoped it was not too evident how fresh it was. Along the Bond she shared, she whispered her intentions to her partner.

Merrick didn't question her. Once the injured were beyond the threshold, he gestured to Zofiya. "Bar the door."

That the Grand Duchess, the sister to the Emperor of Arkaym, would take orders from a mere Sensitive Deacon would have been a joke only a year ago. It was further evidence that the world was turned on its ear.

Sorcha heard the thick wooden door slab slam shut, and then moments later the somewhat reassuring thump of the bar being dropped. It wouldn't be much to stop the undead, but it was symbolic to those huddled outside.

It didn't need to be said that they had also effectively cut themselves off from the rapidly approaching assistance of the other Deacons. Sorcha frowned as she stepped over the remains of a broken and charred table. She wouldn't let any more of her fellows be killed—not for her sake.

Merrick stepped closer to her, pushing back the hood of his cloak, and pressing the tips of two fingers to the stylized Third Eye now tattooed directly above his nose between his eyebrows. His Strop, the thick leather strap engraved with the runes that had been the Sensitive's focus, had been destroyed like the Gauntlets when the Order of the Eye and the Fist had been broken. The loss of that Pattern had necessitated they create a new one, but had also meant that the Sensitives had been forced to put the Third Eye on their skin. Usually only used with the more powerful of the Runes of Sight, its constant presence on them had made their adjustment much harder than what the Actives had to suffer through.

Merrick, though, as always excelled and was very much

ahead of his peers. He was in many ways a better Deacon
than Sorcha could ever hope to be. Perhaps that was why
she had taken an instant dislike to him when they had first
been partnered.

*I thought it was because I was younger and better look-
ing than you.* His voice in her mind was deceptively light.

Despite the dire nature of their situation, Sorcha couldn't
help smiling just a fraction. *As far as I know you still
are . . . unless I have aged you . . .*

Her partner tugged on one curl of his dark brown hair,
as if to demonstrate some imaginary grays. If stress caused
gray hair, by the time this was all done they would all be
silver.

All levity was abandoned when Merrick's Center caught
just a whiff of something undead; the odor of rotting flesh
rising above the sharp tang of blood and fear. It was among
the first things both of them had learned in the novitiate:
smell nearly always preceded an appearance.

A less clever or attuned Sensitive might have summoned
the rune Aiemm to see what had occurred here. A braver
one might have called forth Masa to peer into the future,
but Merrick knew as well as Sorcha that they didn't have
much time. The blood around them told all they needed to
know about the past, and the future was as reliable as
smoke. Instead, Merrick called on Mennyt and looked into
the Otherside.

Many times both of them had shared a vision of the
undead; glimpses of souls passed, or geists trembling on
the edge of this realm ready to come forth. Never, however,
had they seen what Mennyt showed them now.

Ranks upon ranks of geists were lined up like soldiers
ready to breach castle walls, and every single one of them
overflowed with purpose and hatred. It was a sight that
took both Deacons' breath away, and froze them for an
instant in place.

They waited there; all kinds of dire creatures of death.
Some were the wounded souls of the dead from this world,

now twisted and lost in the Otherside. Others were geists who dwelled there always, desiring the pain of the living. Finally, there were the geistlords who were possessed of terrible intelligence.

So many. By the Bones, so many.

Neither Deacon could have said whose words those were, but it was the sentiment they shared.

Sorcha's eyes watered as she watched through Merrick. Only the strongest of the undead usually were able to find cracks through into the human world. Now as she scanned the room, she realized it was full of the undead lining up to step forward. The veil between their world and hers had never seemed so paper-thin and ridiculous.

Was it the destruction of the Order that had done this, she wondered, or had this always been going to happen?

The Order is not the only one in the world, Merrick reminded her, his words filling her mind with reassurance. *Many other Orders have fallen and blown away in the past, but there have always been new ones to take their place. This . . . this is very different.*

Her partner was the most resolute person Sorcha had ever known—yet she felt the fear in him like vinegar on her tongue. Line upon line of geists waiting silently for entrance to the world would do that to even the bravest Deacon.

Yet there was no pathway large enough for them—not at the moment.

Teisyat, the final rune, the one that every Active learned as their last test, was that what had brought them here? Perhaps all it would take was one Deacon to raise their hand, and . . .

Don't even think of it. Merrick's fingers locked on her shoulder. The close physical contact jolted her back to reality. *If someone had used Teisyat here, then they would all be through, and we would all be dead.*

No, someone had indeed opened a rune, but it was not the Seventh. Tryrei then . . . just a crack—enough to let a single more controllable geist through.

Kebenar washed over her, the Rune of Sight that showed the true nature of things. Now the images of the waiting geists dimmed, and a filigree of faint cracks ran over her vision. This in a way was worse.

So many, Merrick muttered, following her deeper into the Hall. It was like an egg that has been struck against a bowl and just like that egg, any one of these cracks could give. Several had, but the geists had slipped back into the Otherside. Such cleverness was not their usual stock-in-trade.

The citadel was old, had once been a Priory, and there were many dusty corners in it. Suddenly, Sorcha did not trust the place. Even though they had examined it closely, it had been made by the Native Order, the Circle of Stars—the very one that had brought about the destruction of the Eye and the Fist. They were known for their crafty nature. However, the Priory was also the last place the Circle of Stars would have looked for them and was surrounded by water on all sides. Once, that would have guaranteed no geist would enter it.

Sorcha was heartily sick of knowing that all the rules had been broken in the last few years.

Outside, Merrick whispered to her. *Look outside.*

She stepped boldly out onto the stone balcony and was greeted by the sound of plummeting water. The blunt profile of the citadel pushed out from the center of the Avalanche Falls, which plunged off granite cliffs, hundreds of feet down to the lake below. It was a treacherous place, but not nearly as dangerous as the streaming gap into the realm of geists, geistlords and everything malevolent that the Order stood against. Corenee was a small principality largely comprised of stern dukes and the goat herders they ruled over. Far into the southwest of Arkaym, it made a perfect principality in which to hide. Or at least, it had.

Her face was suddenly covered in the swirling, freezing water droplets. Sorcha waited for a moment, her eyes unfocused on the real world but tightly concentrated on the one

Merrick was showing her. The long files of geists were watching her just as intently. It felt as though they were merely a few inches away through flimsy gauze, and if she just reached out her hand she might touch one of them.

Such dangerous thoughts were interrupted when Merrick called her name—both into her head and out into the night. One of the cracks was spreading. Whatever was strongest was coming through.

Twice before, Sorcha had faced a geistlord; the Murashev and Hatipai. The first time they had relied on the strength of the Rossin to give them a chance. The second, without Merrick at her side, Sorcha had won, but had been thrown into the terrible living death of a coma. Now, they stood alone, on the balcony.

Where is Raed? Sorcha thought to herself in an off-hand sort of way. Her lover had still not made an appearance, and she could not feel him in the citadel. She felt along the Bond that tangled her, Merrick and the Young Pretender together. The connection was still there, but nothing else. It was as if the awareness of Raed was wreathed in dark smoke.

She glanced across at Merrick. Under the tattoos of the runes, his brown eyes were troubled. His words, when they entered her mind, confirmed that. *I can't see him.*

Few words could have chilled her more than those. Merrick was not just her Sensitive—he was the best she had ever worked with. The Bond they shared the strongest. If he could not see the Rossin, then she had real cause to worry.

However, now was not the appropriate time. Thinking of her missing lover while the world was splitting before them would have been beyond foolish. It was almost suicidal.

Concentrating on survival meant concentrating on what was before her. Blinding red cracks were now growing bigger, signaling that whatever was ready to come through was near the end of its journey. The similarity to watching a chicken hatch only went so far. This was going to be much more than a giant angry rooster.

Such a stray, comical thought at this moment was not something Sorcha was used to. Discipline and training had been hammered into her, ever since she was a child, and as she had recently found out, she was also the daughter of a powerful Sensitive.

And the daughter of something else too, a small voice whispered in the back of her head.

Sorcha's gaze jerked away from the spreading gaps in reality, toward Merrick. He however was concentrating on seeing more of the situation. He had not spoken into her mind.

Just as Merrick turned his own head toward her, Sorcha had straightened. With careful and precise determination she managed to shift her thoughts away from the momentary terror and concern of what exactly that voice had been, and once more onto the horror that was coming. Sensitive and Active Deacons were tightly bound together in a partnership that had few secrets, but there were ways to hide some little things from one another. Sorcha was not yet prepared to share her darker, creeping fears with Merrick.

First, they had to survive this. Through her partner's Center she could sense more Deacons nearing their position. Once they reached Merrick and herself, they could form a Conclave and then they would have the superior strength.

However, a Conclave relied on physical proximity.

No sooner had that thought escaped Sorcha, than a cold, stinging wind blew fiercely off the chasm. It raced around both she and Merrick. Its scream was nothing that a normal gale could have produced, and it was full of teeth and bitterness. It swirled around them, blowing their capes around them like shrouds, before racing into the Great Hall.

Sorcha heard the sounds of the heavy wooden shutters slamming shut, and if that was not enough to assure the Deacons that this was deliberate, it was soon accompanied by the racket of furniture suddenly being thrown up against the doors. Heavy wooden tables, chairs and their packs acted as most effective barricades against Sorcha and Merrick leaving, or anyone else reaching them.

The rune Voishem that would have allowed the Deacons to shift and phase through the walls had not yet been mastered by the recently tattooed of their colleges. They would hesitate to use it. No one wanted to be stranded half in and half out of an object. Instead, the sounds of shoulders being applied to doors could be vaguely discerned.

"So that's the way it shall be," Sorcha muttered through ice-cold lips, and her words froze in the air. She turned back to the now foot-wide gap and rolled up her sleeves as high as they would go.

Merrick took a step nearer to her, so that he stood in her shadow, which streamed backward into the Great Hall. The light coming from the gap in reality was that bright.

Everything was absolutely still for a moment; even the roar of the waterfall seemed distant. Their shared Center was tightly focused on the long thin figure that was pushing its way through the gap in the world. It slipped free with a sucking pop—but its place was immediately taken by another that was its exact replica.

They were not geistlords, which was an immediate relief, but neither Deacon had a chance to enjoy that, because they identified what had escaped instead.

Wari were greater than the average geist, and known for appearing just before geistlords. Some called them the "heralds," but they carried more than trumpets and banners. A wari could rip a soul from a human body like a man might tear a bone from well-cooked chicken. They were incredibly uncommon, and yet now a third was squeezing its way through the gap.

One would not have been a problem, but as the knife-sharp shapes began to circle toward them, Sorcha raised her hands. Confidence was what she was trained to project, but along the Bond she shared her worries with Merrick. The runes on her flesh did not feel as comfortable as when they had been on her now-destroyed Gauntlets. They were as slippery as fish, and so she hesitated to act.

Through the shared Center the wari gleamed like silver

scintillating clouds. Their long arms were formed into claws perfectly shaped for their purpose.

Sorcha. For a moment she didn't realize it was Merrick's voice in her head. *Sorcha,* he repeated. *They are flanking us. We have to move before they do.*

The Active felt a little annoyed at his goad—but damned if he wasn't right. She was moving as slow as an old man first thing in the morning. The warm shapes of the other Deacons beyond the door wouldn't get in quickly enough. She and Merrick would be soulless shells before then.

Sorcha wrapped her mind around Pyet, the Fifth Rune of Dominion. It felt like it wriggled to elude her, but she bore down on it. The experience of summoning a rune from her flesh rather than from tanned leather was excruciating. Something about the Gauntlet had stood between her and the raw power. Now it felt as though her skin were being flayed as Pyet illuminated and ran down the patterns carved there. It was a stream of molten metal that she had to release.

With a howl of frustration and rage, Sorcha spread her fingers wide on her left hand, braced it with her right, and let the flame boil out of her. Her control was not what it had been, and Merrick had to duck wildly out of the way as fire roared from his partner and scattered all over the Great Hall. He tackled her around the middle, holding her up where she might have fallen. Her eyelids were heavy, and rather than the usual euphoria that enveloped her when channeling the runes, she felt as if she might be blown away on the swirling winds.

"Let it go," Merrick screamed in her ear. "You can't hold it steady and the wari aren't even there."

With his mind and body for support Sorcha was able to close the rune. The wari had been scared off for only a moment. They dropped down from the ceiling to the floor and advanced once more. The heat of Pyet was soon forgotten as the geists' freezing presence enveloped them.

Sorcha was used to pain; what she was not used to was

not knowing what to do. The wari were closing in, but Merrick—still holding her upright—unrolled Kebenar, the Fourth Rune of Sight around them.

Now everything was laid bare to her. The wari were more than just three entities. Sorcha pushed her hair out of her eyes and got her feet under her. Not for the first time she wondered how she had managed without Merrick at her back.

They are a net, sent to take us back. The idea of that was worse than if they had been trying to kill or destroy their souls. To be wrenched through to the Otherside and pulled apart by geists was the most terrible fate imaginable.

A bright memory flashed across the Bond, one from her partner. Floating in a sea of stars, with the indistinct face of Nynnia hovering nearby. Such a feeling of peace and joy filled Sorcha that she began to understand what misery Merrick had been in. No one forgets his first love, and Nynnia, Ancient, sent through time, had been that to Sorcha's Sensitive.

This time however, it would not be Nynnia bringing them to the Otherside—and the geists would have far less generous ways of handling them. As the wari charged, Sorcha reflexively threw up her left hand and summoned Yevah from her skin.

A gleaming scarlet flaming dome leapt to life between the geists and the Deacons. For a moment the cold lifted slightly. It should have been a deep relief, but Sorcha was still frozen down to her bones.

The hand she was holding the shield rune up with had her full attention. The spiderweb Pattern of the rune on her arms was running flame red, gleaming on her skin like colored fire, but now she saw something else entirely.

The light coming from the crack was illuminating something she had never seen before. Now standing before the shimmering gap into the Otherside, she saw the tendril of the rune gleaming on her flesh, and disappearing into it through the space to the realm of the undead.

It makes sense. Merrick's whisper into her mind was like a trickle of cold water over her stunned conscience. *The runes are powers from the Otherside, and it seems the Order stole them from there.*

He was so calm, and yet what he was saying was not in their teachings. In the novitiate they were taught that the runes came from humanity's own psyche; ripped from their souls in order to fight the geists. It was so relentlessly drummed into them that Sorcha had never thought to question it.

The Sensitives . . . had they known? How could they not know? A little worm of distrust bit her deep down. *No, not Merrick. He can't have known.*

Sorcha! His voice battered the inside of her skull as hard as a hammer blow. Her distraction had however been enough.

The three wari were inside the shield. Their long stretched faces charged at the two Deacons while their claws flashed back, ready to strike. Sorcha heard Merrick shout over her right shoulder, but there was nothing to be done, and what could a Sensitive do in any case? She caught a glimpse of the long, sharp faces, the mouths curved open in something that might have been undead delight; macabre joy that surely meant the end for the pair of Deacons.

Sorcha had a moment to contemplate how foolish and weak she had been. Her soul was about to be ripped from her body, and there was nothing at all she could do to prevent it. The three assailants moved. The cold tips of the geists' fingers touched her, and the pain of those touches penetrating her skin was enough to have broken a normal human. However, the claws did not drive deeper to separate soul from body.

Three sets of empty, dark eyes locked on her, and the words that formed in her mind were like pools of ice. *Mistress . . . apologies . . . we did not know . . .*

Unbelievably, she was hearing the geists in her mind as clearly as she heard Merrick. Just when she'd thought that the world could not get any more broken and strange.

Merrick was there, though, and louder than the undead could ever hope to be. *Shayst! Now!*

It was beaten into her to obey her Sensitive when he called. His judgment was not be to questioned. She thrust out her right arm, and the green light of the sixth rune ran widdershins up it. The pain of the wari and the rune combined until it felt like her head was about to turn itself inside out.

The geists were all connected to her; their bodies were inside her, and they had no time to escape the ravages of Shayst as it reached into their very being. They had come from the Otherside to rip her soul free, and instead it was she doing the ripping. Sorcha tore their very substance apart. She did it quickly so that there was no way that they could poison her mind with more terrifying words.

The two Deacons stood there a moment, panting slightly, their minds and Sight tangled together. Sorcha was not sure how much her partner had seen of those moments of chaos, but she hoped he had not caught any of it. She didn't know what they meant and she didn't want to hear—at least straight away—what he might think had happened.

Merrick straightened and pulled back his Center. For some reason, this time she felt bereft. Her partner didn't say anything to her, but strode off the balcony, back into the Great Hall, and began throwing the heavy furniture away from the door. After taking a deep breath, Sorcha went to help him.

The flood of angry and worried Deacons surged into the room. They looked about them, and Sorcha did not need to share Merrick's Sight to know they were horrified. The scene was a little dramatic; blood, bodies and the dissipating fetid smell of the Otherside.

"It is lucky that we hadn't decorated the citadel yet," Sorcha said, motioning to the burned stone and pools of blood drying on the floor.

Then, pushing aside the dark thoughts that had been born in the carnage, she began helping them tidy up. In this new world, they couldn't afford to merely let the lay Brothers clean up the mess. Now, they all had to pitch in.

THREE

The Beast Walks

Raed fled the citadel, holding the Rossin off by only the scantest breath. His throat was choked, so that as he ran up to the sentry at the entrance, he could only manage a few garbled words before shoving his way past him and into the night. Luckily, the man had instructions to keep watch for dangers without—not within. He bowed, and stepped aside as the Young Pretender ran out into the rock-filled valley that was one of only two entrances into the citadel.

Staggering, Raed sprinted as fast as he could, the image of the Rossin running amok in the confines of the fortress burning in the back of his brain. He would not do that to Sorcha. She had worked so hard to bring them to this place of refuge that he could not allow it to become a one of slaughter.

The night was cold and as desolate as his thoughts. His breath, which came in ragged gasps, froze before his straining eyes. None of that registered, though, as he stumbled on, catching his feet in the cracks and fissures of the scree slope.

It didn't matter. What mattered was what was going on inside him. The Rossin, that great cursed Beast that had taken up residence within him, was laughing. At least that was what it felt like.

He had, months before, made a pact with the creature. It was one born out of survival, and a desire to save a sister, now lost to him anyway. The geistlord had given him control over the change, in return for the Beast living closer to the surface. It was an arrangement that had allowed him to pass through some of the most hostile environments in Arkaym, and track his sister to the farthest ends of the Empire.

It had been a ruse by the Beast.

Raed clutched at his throat. It felt as though the Rossin were clawing its way up from down there, an image of ferocious rage that almost dropped him to his knees.

Once, the Beast had been confined deeper in his consciousness and only risen to the surface when the presence of other geists had given him power. Now, it seemed the Beast would have its way whenever it wanted.

He had reached the lakeshore where the iron gray waters of the waterfall pounded into a seething cauldron at the bottom of the mountain. Everything around him was shades of blue and black, and even the moon had hidden her face from him.

It was as if the days he had spent with Sorcha had been nothing but a bright, hopeful dream.

"This wasn't how it was meant to be," he gasped, clutching onto a boulder. "You promised."

You are such a child. Let me take over and the pain will go away.

The Rossin's voice in his head was seductive; a rattle of power and strength that promised it would share everything with him. Raed wondered if that was how the Beast had sounded when he made the deal with the first Deacon, who Merrick had informed him had become the first Emperor.

He slid down the rock and leaned his back against its chillness. From here he could just make out the jutting form of the citadel.

"She will know," he rasped out to the Beast slithering

within him. "Sorcha will know when you come because Merrick will tell her."

They are blinder than you think. Do not place your trust in false Deacons; they will always disappoint.

Raed let his head drop back against the rock as despair welled over him. Exhaustion was overrunning his defenses, and he wasn't sure if he could muster any strength for another fight. He knew the way things were and had been here far too often. Still, it would be a shame to waste his clothing. With numb fingers he stripped off his shirt and pants, and then as fresh pain washed over him, huddled on the ground. He was as weak as a kitten in this moment.

Ever since Sorcha's new Order had come to the citadel the Rossin had been stirring, but at first Raed had been able to ignore the sensation. He had thrown himself into the joy of actually being able to be with Sorcha, even if it was at the worst possible time. When she wasn't wrapped in Deacon business, they had stolen moments together, hungry for each other. It had meant that he was out from under the watchful eye of Aachon, his first mate on the *Dominion* who had brought the remaining crew with them to this place. Aachon had easily taken over the running of the lay Brothers, and for once let his role as Raed's conscience lapse.

It was—quite naturally—the precise moment when he needed a conscience and a friend the most. Yet every time Raed had opened his mouth to share what was happening to him with Sorcha or Aachon, his voice locked in his throat; the Rossin would not let him.

Don't fight it, because you can't.

His body was moving; that horrible crawling sensation that preceded the Rossin taking the reins. Blackness wrapped itself around him, and tore him away from reality.

The Rossin sprang into the cool night with an unrestrained snarl. The great cat looked back over his shoulder at the citadel hanging on the granite rock face like an unnatural growth—which it was. It was full of Deacons, every one of them scurrying about, replete with all sorts of concerns. A small breach was opening up there, and the true nature of what they had unleashed was apparent. The smell of blood and sweat reached his sensitive nose even here.

Yes, the foolish humans were realizing only now that things had changed. Geistlords on the Otherside were stirring, and the hated Derodak, first of everything, was the instigator. The Rossin's jaw, which could crush a man like a fly, opened wide, displaying his saber teeth, and a growl rumbled in his chest.

No, that particular enmity would have to wait for the moment. He turned his thickly maned head away from the citadel and the distant screams of its inhabitants. They had earned whatever came through from the Otherside.

What the Rossin wanted, his former subjects and rivals could not give to him. His freedom would not be brought from the Otherside . . . that would be found elsewhere. The great cat bounded off down the length of the riverbed, leaping over rocks and bushes with speed not even a horse could manage in this terrain.

It felt good to be moving away from the Deacons, their runes, and the corrupt Patternmaker that they had hung their dreams on. The night was chilly and the moon low in the sky—perfect weather for hunting.

The river valley eventually faded away again, and the Rossin stood, head raised into the wind, on the edge of a cliff that dropped away in another series of rapids and waterfalls. The cat opened his mouth and roared. It was a full-throated proclamation of his pride and his strength, but it was meant for one set of ears in particular.

The Rossin did not have long to wait. The Fensena padded out of the low scrub near the river. Humanity called him the Oath Bender, and a hundred other unpleasant terms, but the geistlord admitted they were not given without cause.

The huge coyote with eyes of burning gold looked in his

direction with his tongue lolling out of his mouth, and
began to trot toward him. When he reached a rock just
below the Rossin, he dropped back one paw, and performed
a bow that a circus pony would have been proud of.

Well met, my lord of the great long tooth, the fellow
geistlord offered mind to mind rather than using humanity's
more difficult words. *We are met again in strange times.*

End times, the Rossin replied, his claws flexing on the
unyielding rock beneath. He had come to like the feeling of
this realm—in fact come to rely on it. He would not have it
snatched away. *The moment of the geist is upon us, and I
will not be unprepared for it.*

*Indeed, those meddling priests have woken more than
they could imagine on the Otherside. They wanted power,
and soon it will come to find them.* The coyote looked up at
the stars, as contemplative as the Rossin had ever seen him.
*We must all make preparations for the changes to come or
else be swept away by them.* His gaze when it returned to the
other geistlord was chill and strangely free of humor. *To that
end I bring news. I did not come empty of paw to you tonight.*

He bounded off into the brush and returned a moment
later, something long clutched in his mouth. The Rossin
inhaled the scent of this offering and felt the warmth of
achievement wash over him. His servant had done as he
had asked. His pelt lay on the rock before him—his real
pelt, not the one he formed from his host. It was one vital
piece of their puzzle. The great cat bent his head and nuz-
zled its luxurious softness.

You have done well, the Rossin conceded.

I would say I have. The Fensena sat down and cocked
his head. *Vermillion is a dangerous place to be for man or
geist these days.*

His fellow geistlord survived in the human realm in his
own way; a way that the great cat viewed as more than a
little disgusting. The Fensena was transmitted from body
to body through bite, and he wasn't particular about who or
what he lodged in. He happily jumped from human to dog

and back again, leaving a trail of exhausted bodies in his wake. Possession by the coyote burned through a body's resources, but he most often chose not to wear them down to death. It was a messy, wasteful business, but at least his fellow geistlord was not trapped as the Rossin was.

Linked to one family, one bloodline had seemed like a wonderful way to lock into a focus point in this world. Unfortunately—either by luck, or perhaps by the design of the family that had taken the name of the Rossin as their own—the pool of blood relatives the geistlord could transfer to on the death of his current host was gone.

At least for the moment that is so, the Fensena replied. *This is the answer to your problem.*

My pelt is not the answer! The Rossin tilted his head and snarled. *A thousand years, and you think it can just be fixed by putting this on me?*

Those clever searching eyes of the coyote, fixed on the massive cat. *It is a step, my lord. A step closer to your freedom.*

The Rossin, tired of these games that the Fensena did so love to play, examined the pelt. Through his geist-sight it appeared like nothing more than a piece of luxurious fur. Not one touch of rune or cantrip was on it. However, there was a tug inside him, and an urge to keep it in his sight. When the first Emperor had ripped it from him, and taken it as part of the pact, it had hurt. It was a part of him; his freedom.

The fact that he did not know what to do with it frustrated the great Beast.

Rage boiled inside the geistlord that Derodak had thought to trick him in such a way. He would have bent and grasped the useless pelt right then and there, had the Fensena not put himself between him and it.

Not after what it took to get this!

The two geistlords snarled and snapped, for a moment reverting to the nature of the flesh they inhabited—a dog and a cat arguing over scraps. It was the danger of being so

clothed; it sometimes overcame their greater nature despite
all they might do. After a few seconds, they gained control
of themselves.

The Rossin, huge golden mane of fur standing out from
his body, loomed over the smaller shape of the Fensena,
but the pelt had been saved.

Out with your plan, scavenger, the Rossin hissed.
Before I lose every bit of my temper.

The Fensena tucked his tail between his legs. *The
priests I told you about, they have the knowledge of how
and where the pelt must be attached to bring your whole
power into this world.*

*I need to be free of this cursed family before the last of
their blood dies.* The Rossin bent and sniffed the pelt as if
it might hide a clue.

It is one part of the puzzle. The Fensena licked his own
jowls in a gesture that might have been nervousness. *The
rest of the answers I will hunt the world for.*

There was an ill tone in the other geistlord's words; an
almost leer that the Rossin could not tolerate. He sprang on
the coyote, with such little warning that the Fensena was
knocked off his paws. He tried to scramble away, but the
Rossin slammed one paw the size of a cauldron down on
the coyote's brindle hide, pinning him to the rocky ground.

The Fensena howled in pain, but he was lucky that the
great cat did not extend his claws and do him real damage.
The coyote made to bite at the paw holding him down, but
the Rossin flexed it hard enough to make his point.

*Give me what I want, liar, or there will be a true death
for you, with no foolish beast or man to give you shelter.*

The Fensena looked up at him, and there was a satisfying edge of fear in that gaze. *I promise I will hunt down the
priests with the knowledge you need. Derodak's story is
old and scattered, but it still exists I am sure.*

The Rossin breathed down on him, letting him smell
destruction hot on his face. *If you do not find what I want,
then you will meet the same fate as all my enemies, but*

their suffering will seem like a welcome relief to that which I will deal to you.

The two geistlords stared into each other, and the memory of flame flickered to life in the Fensena's gold-coin eyes. That was when the Rossin knew he had not forgotten the Otherside and the chaos of survival there. Geistlords were snakes that fed on other snakes, and the alliance between himself and the coyote was unusual. Yet they had both profited off it.

When the Otherside tears its way into this world, the Rossin reminded him, *we will need all those skills and more to survive. I cannot be vulnerable with this body. Help me, and I will help you as of old.*

The Fensena's ears shifted back and forth, as if he were listening to distant sounds and making a judgment. The Rossin had some idea of his fellow's powers, and it was possible that was what he was doing. He was hearing the sound of distant battles and the breaking of promises all over the realm. Finally, the coyote closed his eyes and dipped his head.

Even living off your scraps, my lord, has always been a fine way to dine.

The Rossin stepped back and allowed the Fensena to climb back onto all four feet. The coyote shook himself as if he had just emerged from a very dark and cold pool. *I promise you, great lord, that soon enough you will be free of both the family and the troublesome Bond. I must seek out one more detail for you, and then we shall move.*

And these priests that have all the answers, will they die with all their secrets? The Rossin did not like the idea of anyone else finding out his weaknesses or what he was up to.

The bright pink tongue licked once more over the coyote's nose. *I will leave their monastery in flames and their bones scattered in the dust.*

Good. We do not have much time to bring this all about. I feel the Wrayth moving in that cursed Bond we share. They are planning something—probably with Derodak—and it will ill suit this world. You must be quick about this task.

The Fensena dipped his head—for once choosing the safer path of not arguing. *I will travel swifter than thought, there and back.*

Both geistlords stood still for a moment looking up at the stars, judging the turning of the world. The Rossin thought to himself that they were the most beautiful things he had ever seen. Nothing in the Otherside compared to the gleaming ice blue jewels in the night sky. However, in a constant battle for preeminence, he had never had much chance to look up.

The Fensena tilted back his head and let out a wild, screeching yelp. It was not as magnificent as his own roar, but the Rossin understood what it was: a mark on the world. It was a promise that he was going nowhere.

Hold on to the pelt. The coyote's eyes gleamed in the moonlight. *I will bring you news of the rest that is required.*

It is my own pelt! Do you think I would lose it? The Rossin growled softly.

The coyote performed his little routine of making a bow, and then loped off into the underbrush. Alone, the Rossin hunkered down on the rock once more, the pelt still lying at his feet. For once the urge to take blood did not touch the geistlord, and he feared what that might mean. The Otherside was closer than it had ever been since the Break. He recalled the joy he'd felt that last time the two worlds intersected, but he'd been on a different side then.

He'd come to appreciate the joys of this realm, and he would not give them up. For now, he would watch the stars, and muse on what might lie ahead.

The morning sun woke Raed with a start. He was naked, lying on a rock, looking up as clouds skidded across the sky. He shuddered with the chill and, wrapping his arms around himself, sat up. Unfortunately, he had a lot of experience waking in such situations, and now, as in every other time, he felt terrible. The blinding pain behind his eyes and the deep aches in muscle and bone were a particularly favored gift of the Rossin. Reflexively he checked himself over, and was surprised and delighted that he was not covered in blood. It felt damn good to have a mouth that didn't taste like iron and guilt.

As Raed stood up, however, his heart slammed into his throat; not two feet from him lay a bundle. The Young Pretender frowned and cautiously padded over to it.

"Curious," he whispered, even as a deep shudder ran through him. This rock was definitely cold and exposed. He was used to waking up aching and miserable, but the Rossin had never left him a gift.

Carefully, he leaned down and examined it before opening it. It was a large piece of fur, wrapped in red string. After he had checked from all angles, he took a chance, unraveled the fur and spread it on the rock.

It was a thing of great beauty. The sunlight gleamed on the tips of the strange silver fur, and Raed leaned forward to run his hands through it. It had to do with the Rossin, of that he was sure. Despite that, the Young Pretender scooped it up and wrapped it around his shoulders. Instantly warmth enveloped him. He wanted to throw it away because he was sure that there was more to this gift than it appeared. Yet, it was protecting him. The Young Pretender was caught in the middle. The pelt was seducing him, a deep part of his being understood that but could not fight it.

Still Raed turned back toward the citadel, and began walking, clutching the warmth and softness of the pelt to himself. Hopefully somewhere along the way he would find his clothes.

That search however was going to be nothing compared to having to explain to Sorcha where he had been. She was bound to have felt the Rossin appear, and was certain to have questions. Those he feared facing, because at this stage he really didn't have any answers.

→ FOUR ←

A Blown Leaf

In the wake of the attack, there was no time to even take a breath. Zofiya stood in the doorway watching Sorcha and Merrick talking quietly to each other while the smell of death was ventilated from the room. Something had just happened, something that shook them to the core, but she found herself hesitant to interrupt.

While she helped clear the debris out of the Great Hall, stepping over pools of scarlet blood, a lay Brother appeared at her elbow. He was tall, thin and pale faced, but his hand was not trembling as he passed a roll of paper to her. "Imperial Highness," he said, and she managed not to flinch at the use of her title, "you asked if we could find any news of your brother's activities to the north. We have been able to secure this."

Zofiya's hand clenched on the scrap, but she managed to remain calm. "Where is this information from? Can we trust it?"

"Indeed yes! It is from a lay Brother who escaped a Priory to the north of Vermillion." The young Brother dropped his eyes. "Like many others he managed to get out with a weirstone and has been sending in what reports he can."

"Thank you," she managed, while her eyes darted over the short message. It felt like ice water flooded through her veins. What she read there made up her mind immediately—she had to get out of the citadel.

Without a word to anyone, she spun on her heel and made her way back to the room she shared with Merrick.

In the city of Vermillion, she'd slept on a bed carved like a boat and had whatever material possessions she had wanted. In the citadel, they had a narrow camp bed with a thin blanket to cover them both.

Shutting the door behind her, Zofiya leaned on it for just a moment. "I am the Grand Duchess of Arkaym," she whispered to remind herself, before snatching up her rucksack and starting to throw the few items she had into it.

Merrick had saved her, and it had been a relief to give herself over to that fact for a time: to be a follower rather than a leader. However, the appearance of geists tonight had merely underscored what she had already known. Her brother was part of this, and she had to do something about it. Now, she must leave and not think about how doing so would hurt.

"Zofiya?" Merrick had slipped in the door behind her without her noticing. He was capable of great silence when required—certainly, he would have made an excellent spy or assassin.

She looked up at him and into those brown eyes that were the most reassuring she had ever seen in any human. In them, for a few months at least, she had been able to rest and recover. Yes indeed, it had been a dream, but now it was time to wake up.

When she could no longer take Merrick's puzzled look, Zofiya thrust the piece of paper with the dire news on it into his hand. She didn't wait for him to finish taking it in.

"I have to go," Zofiya said, turning her back on him and rolling up the final few clothes. "I am who I am, and I can't pretend I am just some camp follower any longer. I need to speak to my brother immediately. You know I am the only one he might listen to."

She heard him let out a long sigh, presumably after reading what she had. When he spoke, his voice was laced with sadness. "You know that I have never thought of you as a camp follower. You are the Grand Duchess of Arkaym." His hand rested on her shoulder. "You are also not responsible for what your brother does."

Zofiya had been born a royal, taught that human connection—even to her own family—was a danger; however, at that moment she wanted to turn around and take his hand in hers. Her whole being told her to bury her head against his shoulder and stay there. She'd never had anything so good that she feared losing it so badly; lovers had come and gone for her.

She paused, took a breath, and pushed her dark hair off her face. "I didn't mean responsible—at least not to him. My duty is to the people of Arkaym. It is for them I must try and talk sense into Kal."

Merrick walked around her, so that she had to meet his eyes once more. Normal lovers she suspected would have begged her to stay, covered her with hollow promises of eternal love, and thrown themselves against her will. Not Merrick. He saw too much for any of that.

"I realize that," he whispered, folding his hands into the sleeves of his robe. "I understand it too, but I hope you don't think his destruction has anything to do with you?" The candlelight flickered over his face, now forever marked by the runes of his calling. The change in his appearance had been startling at first, but Zofiya had become used to it. It rather suited him she thought—and she would miss it.

Zofiya reached out and cupped her hand against the strong line of his cheek. Even though he saw so much, she couldn't leave without having actually spoken what was inside her. "I have been happy here with you, Merrick. Even with all the running, the awful food and dreary conditions, I have been more content than anywhere else in my life."

The corners of his mouth turned up, as he spoke, "And yet you are still going to use that weirstone that Aachon found here, aren't you?"

Despite the sad moment, the Grand Duchess laughed. "I should have realized you would know immediately." She sat down on the bed they had shared and looked up at him. "Why didn't you say anything about it before?"

Merrick shrugged and took a spot next to her. "I thought it would make you feel better to have it with you."

Zofiya reached into the rucksack and pulled out the swirling blue stone. It was not a large weirstone—not enough to power an airship—but it was enough to contact one. It was also how she had already reached out to several officers in the Imperial Guard whom she trusted implicitly.

Looking down into the weirstone, she commented, "For a person so committed to the old Imperial family, Aachon has been quite helpful. He's taught me the basics of using it for communication."

Merrick shrugged. "I think the death of Raed's sister made him see how little his friend wants the throne. It's been quite a change for him."

Both of them started as the sound of footsteps raced past in the hallway outside. Merrick got that distant look in his eyes, for just an instant, before returning to their conversation; nothing beyond their room apparently required his attention. The Deacon wrapped his hands around hers. "What will you do?"

Zofiya lurched to her feet and shrugged the rucksack onto her back. "The *Summer Hawk* and her captain are loyal to me, and we are not far from their usual route. I will send the message as soon as I am clear of the citadel."

"And where will you go then?" The troubled look on his usually calm face pleased her. He did care.

She shot a look at him over her shoulder as she took up her own traveling cloak. "I will return to Vermillion. It is the capital, the place where everything begins and ends. I will find out the true lay of the land and hopefully be able to save my brother and the Empire."

"I guessed as much, but I've discovered people find it a little off-putting if I lay out the facts before they've given voice to them. Besides . . . it's impolite to presume."

Zofiya felt a sharp clench in her belly, but managed not to rush to his side. "I like that you are not trying to keep me here."

"I wish I could." Merrick glanced down at his hands.

"But neither of us are normal people with normal responsibilities." Zofiya shifted from one foot to another. Now it had come to the moment, she found herself reluctant to leave. The citadel was the most unwelcoming place she'd ever lived in: full of chill drafts, echoing chambers and the remains of furniture. By all rights she should have been racing out of it. Yet, Zofiya knew that once she left, it could be a long time—if ever—before she saw Merrick again.

"I can read you," he said, clasping her around the waist from behind, and pulling her in tight, "but I cannot see what you will find in Vermillion."

Zofiya turned in his arms. "Do not—"

He stopped her words with a finger placed over her lips. Once he would have earned a broken arm for such daring. "The city will be full of powerless Deacons, lost, bewildered, but they will still have the potential." He cupped her face in his hands and rubbed his thumb over the curve of her lips. "Deacon Petav has been recording the works of the Patternmaker, and been learning the art of applying them to the skin. You must take him with you!"

The idea of that particular Deacon journeying with her was not very appealing; as far as she was concerned he was as dry as a stick that had been left out too long on a summer day. However, she understood what her lover was getting at. If she could resurrect at least some of the Deacons at the capital, then they could help bring the citizens of Vermillion some protection from the geists.

Zofiya nodded slowly. "If you think he is up to the task, then yes that would be very useful."

Merrick chuckled. "Deacon Petav has proven himself very useful to me, but he would also welcome the chance to get out from under Sorcha's gaze I think."

"Perfectly understandable," Zofiya replied with a twitch of her lips. Petav had been Sorcha's husband once, as well as her partner. They had come to a working understanding, but things were still a little tense when they were both in the room—you didn't need to be a Sensitive to feel that.

Merrick drew in a long breath. "Then there is another favor I must ask of you, Zofiya."

She loved how her real name sounded on his lips. She so seldom heard anything but titles and platitudes from people. "Of course," she whispered, holding herself as steady and far away from him as she could manage.

"When you reach Vermillion, can you please try to find out what has happened to my mother and brother? Aachon tried and failed to find them in the chaos after the destruction of the Mother Abbey." His brow furrowed, and seeing his pain only made her love him more. "They have been on my mind ever since."

"I will do all I can," Zofiya said, pressing her lips together. She knew full well that he had lain awake many nights struggling with guilt over leaving them behind, so she just hoped that she could send good news back to him, rather than the other darker possibility that could be the reality. How much of a chance for survival could a mother and small child in a Vermillion lost to chaos have? Her skin prickled at the thought.

The world outside of the citadel was tearing itself apart. Her brother and the Arch Abbot of the Native Order had condemned it to be so. Once she and Merrick plunged back into all that, death was a real possibility—tonight's events had reminded them all rather forcefully of that.

Zofiya rushed forward on the wings of that realization. The Deacon and the Grand Duchess clasped each other tight and kissed with the kind of desperation she had never known. It was a terrible thing to care for people, she thought angrily, and now her love for her brother and her love for Merrick were totally at odds. However, it wasn't love for Kal that was taking her from the Deacon. It was her pledge as Grand Duchess.

As Hatipai had said in her holy books, "Each soul is given a purpose to bear." Though the goddess Zofiya had hung her being on had been proven a geistlord, the Grand Duchess still remembered her words. Maybe as goddess and geistlord, she had been able to see the future that lay ahead.

Zofiya steeled herself, remembering that humiliation, and determined not to make a fool of herself again. Merrick let her go. "I will see you again."

He said it with such conviction; Zofiya chose to believe that he had looked into the future with that Sensitive skill of his. It made it easier to step away from him and leave the citadel.

The Grand Duchess' hand clenched tight on the warm weirstone, until her fingers ached, and she took her leave of Merrick and the citadel.

FIVE

Madness from Above

The world had become unhinged and so had its Emperor. Kaleva could tell that was what those around him were thinking. He stood on the deck of the airship *Winter Kite* and kept his eyes on the clouds rather than on the officers that stood on each side of him. The thrum of propellers sounded very much like war drums, and the strong wind at his back was pushing him onward.

Yet even in this moment of power, all he could think of was the open mouth of the Rossin, and the gleam in the eye of del Rue. Those were the images that chased him in his dreams, but haunted him just as much in the daylight.

He shook his head, trying to banish them. Kaleva knew he could trust no one—that had been proven in the disaster of the Mother Abbey. His advisors had been corrupted by runes and the undead—even his own sister had been tainted by association. It was as his father had told him. *"A ruler stands alone, and no one is above suspicion."*

He'd always thought his father was just being cruel, but now the Emperor fully understood he'd been communicating the truth.

However, Kaleva smiled to himself, for a surplus Prince
in a distant land, he had come far. His father, the King of
Delmaire, had supplied him like a sacrificial calf to the
bickering Princes of Arkaym as a figurehead of an Emperor, and he had shown them all.

He would fight the hallucinations of the geistlord and
the unnatural man that commanded them. The Emperor
would not give in to fear.

"General Beshan?" The Emperor shot the name over his
shoulder, and the old man, with his salt-and-pepper beard
and battle scars, snapped to attention.

"Imperial Majesty!"

"How long before we reach Sousah?" Despite the speed
of the airships, they did not move as fast as Kaleva wanted.
It made him more than a little irritable. He wanted to experiment with the tinker's contraption immediately, and it would
be a nice example for the rest of the rebel Princes; when they
saw what he could do, they would scamper back into line.

"Another few hours," the general muttered through his
mustache.

The Prince of Sousah had declared for this Pretender,
this sister of Raed Syndar Rossin. Many principalities—
most in the west—had declared for her. They claimed the
Conclave of Princes that had summoned Kaleva across the
ocean to rule was invalid, and that they had been pressured
to agree to his appointment. Instead, they wanted a scion of
the Rossin house to rule over them. The very thought of
that family made Kaleva grind his teeth together. The Rossins had been tainted right from the very beginning thanks
to that geistlord. They were abominations and traitors to
their race.

If certain of the Princes of Arkaym wanted a Rossin back
on the throne, that did not matter to Kaleva; he had taken the
crown, and he most certainly was not going to give it up. To
spur those Princes that did remain loyal to him onward, the
Emperor had promised that they could add any principalities
they took in his name to their own. It had brought many

Ancient enmities to fresh vigor, as they scrambled to fight over the bones he was throwing on the ground.

"Hold your course, I am attending my wife downstairs," the Emperor said shortly, before striding off the deck and going down the polished wooden stairs to the stateroom.

He could hear her weeping long before he reached the door. Ezefia, Empress of Arkaym was wailing as though her life depended on it.

The Emperor could tell by their pressed lips and pale expressions that the screaming and wailing was bothering the two guards stationed at the door.

For too long, Kaleva had realized, in the burning remains of the Mother Abbey, he had been in everyone's shadow; first his draconian father, the King of Delmaire, then later his martial sister who everyone had feared and respected. The Deacons, with all their twisted, demonic magic, had at least shown him that much.

He had to be Emperor. Alone and singular as it was meant to be. However, he would require an Empress and children to follow. The question was, would it be this one?

Kaleva pressed his hand against the door and listened to just one more sob. When he pushed the door open and stepped inside, her weeping stopped as abruptly as if it were attached to a string.

She was a great beauty even with tears, Ezefia of Orinthal; dark eyes, a heart-shaped face, and warm full lips. She was also a liar and had made him a cuckold.

The man, who had concealed himself in the Imperial Court, called himself Lord Vancy del Rue, and had given Kaleva so much useful advice, had also been the lover of the Empress herself.

Now Ezefia was trussed to the chair she sat on. Tears were running down her cheeks, but she was the daughter of royalty and pride kept her from weeping in front of her tormentor.

Kaleva smiled and shut the door quietly behind him. Ezefia was not gagged, but she did not say a word as he approached. So he spoke instead.

"We shall be over Sousah soon, and then I shall show them the power of an Emperor unleashed." Kaleva tapped the top of her head sharply. "I shall make sure to bring you up on deck for the fireworks. Perhaps, if we are lucky, your lover is down there."

Ezefia's head came up at that. Her stunning green eyes were brimming nearly over, as she stammered, "My lord, it was not by choice. He cast a spell over me, enamored me. It was like I was trapped in my own body, howling to get out. He did things to me, and it may have seemed as if I were his, but in my heart I remained true to you." She paused, and then managed to gasp out the rest of her pitiful attempt to win him back. "After all, my love . . . it was I who told you all, once his spell on me was broken."

Perhaps, if he had loved her as he once had his favorites, perhaps if there were more than just a convenient connection between them, he might have found a morsel of sympathy. Yet now, as he looked down at her, he saw nothing but a duplicitous woman who had committed treason against the crown.

The fact that her belly was just beginning to swell with del Rue's child only added to the offense. Kaleva's face twisted into an ugly set of lines; he suspected that Ezefia might have tried to pass the bastard off as his own if the whole mess at the Mother Abbey had never happened.

Still, it had shaken him loose from his complacency. Everyone had thought the Emperor a kindly man, but kindly men were often taken advantage of.

"You were merely trying to pre-empt the servants' gossip reaching me," Kaleva hissed in reply.

Ezefia hung her pretty head at that—the tears apparently dried up—but her shoulders still shook. "Why don't you simply have me killed then?" she said, her voice low and husky with resignation. History was ripe with tales of Empresses who had betrayed their marital vows as well as the punishments that were meted out on them. Kaleva knew that she was running over them right now in her mind.

The Emperor looked out the window of the airship and formulated an answer. "It was suggested that I seal you up in the walls of the palace, as the third Emperor did to his unfaithful wife. Others said I should have you defenestrated." Kaleva tilted his head, rolling the oddly fascinating word around in his mouth. "I was tempted by that."

He sighed and lightly touched Ezefia's shoulder. "But the truth of the matter is, that by keeping you alive I may bring del Rue back. Oh, I am sure he has no concern for your welfare. No," he said, pointing at her bulging belly, "I know he will come back for that, then he and I have some unfinished business to conclude."

He wanted to show the man that had mastered him that he had no hold on him now. The orphaned Deacons had provided plenty of information on the art of manipulating the weirstones, and it had proved not nearly as difficult as the Order had tried to convey. In fact, the weirstones were very useful in so many ways.

Tinker Vashill had been brought in to consult on some new uses for the power of the weirstones, and his designs would be the hammer that Kaleva would bring down on the unruly Princes of the Empire—starting with Sousah.

The communication horn strung near the window blew a short note, and the Emperor picked it up eagerly. "Your Imperial Majesty, we are drawing over the target, and are awaiting you command."

Kaleva smiled. Now, it was time to show them. It was strange how in all these years he had always believed that his father was a damned tyrant. He and Zofiya had lived in fear of his wrath—even though they were the youngest of his large brood of children. It had been ingrained in their psyche that he was an evil man. Lately Kaleva was beginning to wonder if they had been wrong all this time. Now, the words that the King of Delmaire had instilled in them were starting to surface.

"A ruler cannot afford to have any softness in him. He must play the game of royalty with ruthlessness that looks

*on even loved ones as pawns. Otherwise he will be swept
from the board."*

The Emperor looked down at the Empress, and it felt as
though he were observing her from a great distance; as a
human might contemplate an ant. His feelings had been
amputated by the man calling himself del Rue—and for
that Kaleva had at least something to thank him for.

He strode to the door and told the guards to bring the
Empress up on deck, tied as she was to the chair. Then
without giving her any further thought, the Emperor
climbed the stairs.

The Imperial Guards all stood erect at their stations, but
the gangly figure of Vashill was at the controls of his dire
machine. Kaleva's eyes narrowed on the gleaming square
brass device, and it brought a delighted smile to his face.

It had been installed at the very edge of the *Winter Kite*
and took the place that some cannons had once occupied. All
of the inner brass workings were visible, giving it the appearance of a vast gleaming insect. Three huge pipes ran from the
machine over the side of the airship before spreading into
wide funnels. The weirstones buried within could also be
glimpsed; ink black and swirling. It used the system that had
been harnessed to propel the Imperial Fleet of airships, but
also tapped into the Otherside's vast reserves of power.

Vashill, despite his disheveled appearance, was one of
the greatest tinkers of the age, and by virtue of his skill had
freed himself of the taint of infamy his mother had earned
for the family. She had disappeared with the remnants of
the Order under the control of the Deacon Sorcha Faris.
Apparently the old widow had been giving them succor for
some reason.

Her son had publicly disowned her and turned his skills
to helping his rightful Emperor regain control of outlying
provinces. As Kaleva stepped up to him, he executed a
passable bow. "The machine is ready to do your bidding,
Your Imperial Majesty."

Kaleva tucked his hands behind his back, and stared down

through the breaks in the clouds to the city of Sousah. It was set on a hillside above a river, with the ports clustered on a blue bend. Thousands of brightly polished tiles on all the roofs gleamed up at them, and the Emperor got a visceral thrill thinking of all the citizens below going about their daily lives, not even guessing everything was about to change.

The Imperial Guards finally brought Ezefia up on deck, and at the Emperor's direction placed her down next to him. Under the sunlight, her bronze skin looked remarkably pale. The tracks of dried tears on her face were all that there were to tell that she'd been crying.

Her eyes darted over the edge of the airship to the city below. "My love, you cannot do this . . . an innocent city—"

"Innocent?" Kaleva leaned down and stared into her lying, deceitful face. "I think not. Your lover was from there! Don't think I didn't hear that accent in his voice— and then Sousah's Prince declares for the Rossin bitch!"

Ezefia closed her eyes for a moment, but when she spoke her voice was as calm as his sister's had sometimes been. "Kaleva, I know how del Rue works on your mind. I know how he can make anything seem reasonable, and I surely know best of all how much it hurts when he withdraws his influence. Please don't let all of that warp you into killing innocent people. Del Rue could have come from anywhere. He is far older than you—"

For an instant—just the briefest of ones—he saw her coming off the airship for the first time only months ago, and how beautiful she had been. Even though it was an arranged marriage, they had treated each other as best they could.

Then his hand arched back, and he slapped her hard across the face. The sound of the blow echoed across the deck and it left a scarlet mark on Ezefia's cheek. The Emperor had to squeeze his jaw tight to regain control of himself because for an instant he imagined picking up her chair and throwing it over the side.

Instead, he turned to Vashill and managed to choke out, "Is it ready?"

"Yes, Your Imperial Majesty," the tinker said, not show-ing an ounce of reaction to his ruler's display of temper. If he had not been such an excellent maker, then he might have prospered in diplomacy.

"Then let us begin," Kaleva replied, folding his hands once more behind his back and drinking in the last normal moments of the city beneath.

The tinker jerked his head at the Imperial Guard assigned to the machine. Two on the far side worked levers, while on the side closest the Emperor, another two began to spin a crank. The machine ground gradually to life.

It really was a miracle of the art of tinkering. Kaleva almost forgot his rage watching the pistons and cogs work their magic within. It was no wonder that Vashill had not given it a case of some kind—it was quite a spectacle—but nothing like what was to come.

Rain began to fall on Sousah. The clouds around the airship were light, and stretched; they contained not a drop of water. Instead, rain was coming from the machine that Vashill had created. It poured through the pipes, the rain sieve, then it fell from the *Winter Kite* on the city below.

The inventor's brow was furrowed, his dark bushy eye-brows knitted together. He held out his hand and gestured to the captain, who relayed the order "Ahead, slow" through the communication funnel. The airship engines whined only faintly, and the vessel began to move. All the time the rainmaker chugged on, sending droplets down on the folk below.

The Emperor leaned over the gunwales of the ship and watched like an entranced child. The water droplets looked so innocent, and he imagined all those citizens below glancing irritably up at the sky at this unexpected scattering shower.

Except it wasn't rain. The machine had no reservoir of water; this liquid it made all by itself. Vashill stepped away from his creation for a moment to take his place—albeit a little hesitantly—at his ruler's side. With a wave of his hand, he placed it directly underneath the nearest spout, and then pulled it back.

It still amazed the Emperor; the small puddle of liquid that Vashill held in the palm of his hand was different grades of gray; spilling to inky black in the deepest parts.

"It is as I demonstrated previously," Vashill said, unable to keep the smile from his face. "The weirstone liquid is completely harmless at this stage, it is only when it comes into contact with geist-infested areas that its power is released."

The inventor held his hand over the edge and tipped the contents free, as if he were loath to waste even the smallest drop.

"Kaleva!" Ezefia moaned, twisting her arms against her bonds. "You cannot do this! Releasing geists on your own people when you spent years working with the Deacons to stop this sort of thing!"

The Emperor stared at her, and for the shortest spell her words made sense—like sunlight penetrating fog. He remembered his first footstep on this continent; how happy he had been to begin his great work with his sister, Zofiya, at his side and the Arch Abbot at his back. It had been a glorious time. The Emperor's mouth lifted slightly.

Then however, the mist enveloped him again. It was worse because he had remembered; their treachery was more diabolical when compared to that recollection.

The Emperor held out his hand. "Spyglass," he snapped. One of the Imperial Guards slapped a long brass form into his palm.

He raised it to his eye and trained it on the city beneath. The rain was falling steadily as the airship tracked across the sky, while the relentless hammering of the machine went on and on—almost as constant as Ezefia's struggles.

Through the polished glass, Kaleva watched the folk scamper about. They were moving faster under the unexpected rain. Few looked up, but if they saw the airship it didn't matter. The only one with the airship technology was the Imperial Fleet, so there was no danger of retribution; there was only death for those below.

As the Emperor watched he could feel his impatience rising within him like he'd eaten something bitter. He shifted restlessly, jerking the spyglass from side to side. The only results seemed to be inconvenience for the population.

"Vashill," he growled out of the corner of his mouth, "I didn't engage your services so you could make my enemies wet." He jerked the spyglass from his eye and rounded on the tinker. "You promised vengeance from the sky and all we have done is perhaps wreck any picnic plans they might have."

Ezefia, still tied to the chair, was not doing a very good job of concealing her delight. The Imperial Guards around were all very studiously avoiding looking in his direction; their eyes were fixed on distant points.

Vashill should have blanched, stammered and definitely feared for his life; instead he straightened and looked the Emperor full in the face with his clear gray eyes. "Imperial Majesty, if you would just raise your spyglass one more time, I believe you will begin to see the liquid's effect."

Kaleva paused, contemplating if he should just have the man's head removed, but curiosity got the better of him. He pressed the glass to his eye and scanned Sousah again.

The machine had finally ground to a halt, and all was silent about the *Winter Kite*, but down below something was happening. The citizens were no longer looking up.

With mounting excitement, Kaleva saw a flickering in the streets; a shimmer of color blinking off in one spot and then appearing in another. It started off slowly, but then the gleams of blue color and light began to flash on and off throughout the city. The Emperor found he was holding his breath.

Vashill stood at his side, pressing closer than propriety and custom really allowed. Kaleva did not correct him.

"You see Your Imperial Majesty," the inventor whispered into his ear. "The weirstone energy is now breaking through to the Otherside. Those tiny openings that are like an invitation to those that wait beyond. It won't be long."

The Emperor did not reply. He pressed the spyglass so tightly against his face that his skin ached, but he did not remove it. Finally, his patience was rewarded. He could have sworn that he heard a scream—even from all the way up here.

People were moving on the streets. Doors were being flung open and the citizens were running out of their homes. Soon the roads were filling with people milling about. Now Kaleva could imagine their terrified faces, as nightmares that they had thought conquered were returning in full force.

The Emperor felt as though he was really smiling for the first time in months—for the first time since the ball they had held in Vermillion, back when he thought all was well in his Empire.

No one remained to protect the people of Sousah—there was no Order to stand between the citizens and the undead. They were sheep in the presence of wolves, and the best of it was their Prince had no way to stop the invasion of geists into his city. Sousah would be a fine lesson to all those that thought to oppose him.

"Tell me," Kaleva spoke, finally removing the spyglass from his eye. "Tell me, Vashill, what is happening down there?" He knew, but he wanted to hear another say it.

Vashill's lips pressed together, and he shot a glance at the wide-eyed and silent Empress. "The power of the dark weirstones has been released. The gap between the Otherside and our world has been punctured, and the geists have come seeking bodies and terror."

The Emperor leaned on the gunwales and thought about that. "Shades, ghasts, darklings, and spectyrs will come out to play. No one will be safe."

"Oh, Kaleva," Ezefia whispered, her beautiful face once again marred by tracks of tears, "you have done a terrible thing. There is no going back from here."

He was sick of women telling him what to do. Looking down at the Empress he could have sworn he saw the shape of his sister looking back at him. He couldn't stand it anymore.

Kaleva gestured to the nearest Imperial Guards, and they hurried to remove the Empress back to the stateroom.

Once she was out of sight the Emperor felt much better, much more in control. He turned to Vashill, letting his eyes wander with great satisfaction over the machine that now stood silent on the deck. Kaleva clapped his hand on the thin man's back. "You have earned your fee this day, Master Vashill, but tell me, how many of these machines can you make in the next month? I have many airships and many cities that need to feel the hand of the Emperor around their throat."

The inventor looked up at him, his eyes alight with the prospect. "Your Imperial Majesty, if you give me the workers, I think you will find I can work wonders for you in no time at all."

"Excellent." Kaleva only barely refrained from hugging the man. "You shall have whatever you require once we have taught a few more cities the meaning of terror. Together we shall bring the Empire back to its rightful form."

Then Emperor and inventor stood at the gunwales of the *Winter Kite* and watched the destruction of Sousah. To Kaleva it was a macabre dance solely for his entertainment. After this no Prince would dare to even think of treason.

SIX

Under the Green Cloak

The Council of five tired Deacons sat somewhat uncomfortably in the Great Hall. It had been cleaned and washed by the lay Brothers, but the smell of death still lingered in the corners. Like all the other Sensitives, Merrick could observe the hovering shapes of the recently slain, hanging over the occasion like multiple shrouds. None of those gathered had slept very much since the attack—Merrick had got none at all.

This room was a difficult one for the Council to be in, but there was no other place where they could not be overheard by lay Brothers and followers.

Melisande Troupe, the sweet-faced blonde woman who had been the Presbyter of the Young in the previous Order, cleared her throat and spread her hands flat on the table as if to balance herself. "We cannot put this off any longer. After last night we must come up with more of a plan than just hiding in this citadel." She shot a glance across to her right where Sorcha leaned back in her chair, her eyes cast up at the ceiling.

The Council of the Order of the Eye and the Fist had

been comprised of five Presbyters elected from among their ranks, and who had contemplated the pressing matters of the Mother Abbey. This gathering had none of that gravitas, and there were no elections; instead it was a thrown together collection of the strongest Deacons that remained.

Merrick and Sorcha had no Council experience, and neither did Deacons Radhi and Elevi. This last man was tall and balding, as well as a surprisingly strong Sensitive. However, his gaze darted nervously around the room, and Merrick didn't need to use his Center to know that he was unhappy being on the Council at all.

The only one with any useful experience sat at the head of the scarred table. Troupe was also one of three Presbyters in the old Council who had survived the destruction of the Mother Abbey; however, she was the only one of that group fit enough to join this new Council.

Yvril Mournling, the former Presbyter of the Sensitives, was far too old and frail to offer much in the way of strength. He was being looked after by lay Brothers and getting weaker with every portal they passed through. Merrick had visited him the previous day and knew that death was not far away from taking him from them.

Thorine Belzark was young, but had told them there was no way she wanted to be on any kind of Council again. Merrick didn't think that was any great loss since she had mostly been a puppet of Arch Abbot Rictun.

As for Troupe, the gathering of lines on her pretty face and the circles under her brown eyes told anyone who had sense in their head that this position was not as easy as her previous one. Still, at least she had bothered to turn up, and she did still retain some of the aura of command that she'd had in the Council chamber in the Mother Abbey.

Merrick stared at Sorcha, willing her to say anything, but although his intentions spun along the Bond, she was steadfastly ignoring him. He straightened slightly in his chair. "We are not hiding—what we are doing is gathering ourselves. Every day we're using weirstones to communicate with our scattered Brothers. All we need to do is find a place to gather, and we can—"

"Do what?" Deacon Radhi, a stocky woman with jet-black hair and flashing eyes, shook her head. "We left Vermillion in such a rush that we never took time to think about what the next move was!"

Troupe nodded and waved her hand toward where the blood had been washed from the stone. "Last night proved that we don't have the luxury of time to sit here and regroup slowly. We must act now and find a place to strive decisively against Derodak, or we will be the Order who dithered while the world was torn apart."

"There is no Order. Not anymore." Sorcha pulled from her pocket one of her cigarillos and rolled it in her fingertips. It was unlit, because she had only two left. Merrick knew when she did finally smoke it things would be very, very bad indeed.

"There won't be much of anything else either." Troupe leaned back in her chair and pressed one hand to her forehead. "What just happened has shown that we cannot afford to wait, and that the Otherside is coming close to breaking through in ways we have never before seen."

"I agree, and you are right; we have to move, and quickly." Sorcha placed the cigarillo down carefully. "No proper Order has ever put itself above the good of the realm. We must risk our own destruction and do what must be done."

The rest of the Council sat silent for a moment, absorbing this sudden pronouncement. Merrick felt as though his own heart had grown just as quiet.

"And what is that exactly? Do we even have a clue?" Elevi rumbled from the other side of the table.

Merrick's own faith was shaken as he watched the Council members look at one another. He'd been raised in the confines of the Order and become used to the infallibility of the Presbyters; it had been a much simpler life than this situation.

"We must redouble our efforts to locate the rest of our

brethren," he said calmly. "All the weirstones must be put to this purpose."

Sorcha's eyes caught his. They were a bright blue and more familiar to him than even his own lover's. When he looked at his Active, he felt his pulse slow, and the clamor of fears die down a little. This Bond was—as always—the rock to which they both tied their strength.

"I have another suggestion," Sorcha said calmly, resting her fingertips on the edge of the table and moving them in a calming rhythm. "The Patternmaker."

All eyes darted up to the ceiling, to the one floor that was above the Great Hall, and Merrick noticed the looks were nervous—as well they should be. The Patternmaker was still an unknown quantity, but the first impression had not been altered much. He might have given them back their runes, but they still did not like dealing with him.

The Deacons had found him, dirty, unkempt, and practically gibbering in the cellar of an abandoned house. Derodak had him stashed away there, for a purpose that they had yet to decipher. In those mad hours surrounding the breaking of the foci and the destruction of the Mother Abbey, the survivors had taken whatever chances they could find. A madman that claimed to know how to reinstate the runes to them had seemed the only one available. They had taken a chance.

The Patternmaker had indeed proved able to do all he claimed—but that did not make him reliable. He was now tucked away in the dark attic chambers of the citadel, and everyone who could manage it, kept away from him.

"Our Patternmaker?" Radhi whispered.

"No," Sorcha replied, leaning on her elbows and locking her gaze with his, "the Native Order. They must have one too."

Merrick smiled slowly, even as the others joined him in realization.

"That makes sense," Elevi was nodding. "They wouldn't risk losing their own runes—not at this moment."

"That means they have a vulnerability." Troupe pushed her hair back out of her eyes, and for a moment looked like the lovely woman she had been only months before. "The burning question is how do we find their Patternmaker though . . ."

"We must use Masa and Kebenar," Sorcha said softly and looked straight at her partner.

He swallowed hard but nodded. "If we form a Conclave of the best Sensitives, we can indeed try and see what the truth of it is." He was thinking about the last time he had tried to control a Conclave during the destruction of the Mother Abbey. That had not ended well. Still, he had to get over failure and quickly. Perhaps it would be easier with a group of Sensitives rather than managing Actives as well. He could only hope.

Sorcha got to her feet, walked to the window and ran her fingers over the broken edges of the stone frame. "We also need to know where to strike and how quickly it can be done. Every moment will mean more and more geists are coming through, and every one is a danger to the citizens of the Empire."

"Then we must be as ready as we can." Radhi steepled her fingers, and paused for a moment as if gathering her bravery. "So I repeat the question I asked you last week: Deacon Faris, when will you take up the mantle of Arch Abbot? Our Brothers and Sisters look to you for advice and leadership."

Merrick twisted around in his seat, so better to judge Sorcha's reaction.

Perhaps she had never mentioned it, or thought about it recently, but he knew that at one stage Sorcha had wondered why she'd been overlooked as a Presbyter. She was certainly the most powerful Active in the Order. Merrick knew the answer; the Presbyter of the Sensitives had feared she lacked real control of her power.

Sorcha traced the filigree of cracks that the geists and she had carved into the stonework of the window with fire and conflict. "I know we must be as strong as we can possibly be to manage what is coming."

Even if it is a waste. Merrick managed not to jump as the bitter thought invaded his mind. He surreptitiously checked out the dark corners of the room. They were alone, and he was positive that the thought was from neither Sorcha nor from any of the other Deacons in the room; the texture of it was quite different.

He swallowed hard. Another disturbing mystery that he didn't dare examine right at this moment.

Sorcha turned around and leaned on the stonework. In the morning light it was much easier to see how much weight she had lost—just as everyone else had. The difference was she had been thin already after a long confinement in bed.

She'd taken them through the Wrayth gates several times, often making fresh ones herself. Now Merrick wondered what the toll of that had been on her.

Sorcha sighed, a long deep breath that seemed to come from somewhere farther away than her body, then she spoke. "I will take the role of leader, if that is what you want, but we are making something else here, something that will be different from what has come before." She pulled her blue eyes away from the middle distance and fixed her gaze on their small gathering. "I don't think we should bear the names of those that have died or given up the fight. The naming of things is nothing to be taken lightly—we all know that. We are no longer what we were. We are no longer the Order of the Eye and the Fist."

The other Deacons jerked back as if she had slapped them, but Merrick understood immediately both what Sorcha was suggesting, and why the others were shocked. The Order had been everything for all of them; they had eaten there, slept there, and fought side by side with others of the Order. Many had died for the Order. Of all the things that the refugees had gone through . . . this could be the worst.

Though not a Sensitive, Sorcha nevertheless could read the mood in the room. She placed her palms on the table and leaned toward them. "I feel it too. I loved the Order, but we cannot go forward holding on to the tattered remains of it, like a cloak." In a symbolic gesture, Sorcha removed the pin with the Eye and Fist and slapped it down on the table, letting her cloak drop to the floor.

To see her standing there without cloak or insignia was disturbing and exhilarating; Merrick felt as though his partner was on the edge of something. Perhaps it had only been meant to be a gesture, but he felt like it might be somewhat more.

The chair scraped on the stone floor as he slid it back and got to his feet. He took off the green cloak that signified that he was a Sensitive. He unhooked the pin and laid it on the table. Holding his cloak in his hand, he thought briefly about how hard he had worked to earn it, then, he folded it up and placed it on the back of the chair.

Troupe, Elevi, and Radhi looked at them, and the expression was not quite terrified, but Merrick sensed immediately that they were not ready yet to abandon their own cloaks.

Sorcha nodded and glanced at him with a slight smile. Then she touched Troupe's shoulder, a curiously sweet gesture from a Deacon known for her sharp tongue and no-nonsense attitude. "Each of us needs to come to this realization. I suggest we let the Sensitives examine the next step in our Conclave."

Then just like that, Sorcha ended the meeting. She left her cloak and insignia where they had fallen and walked from the room. The other Deacons watched her like a flock of curious crows. Merrick smiled slightly, as they inevitably trailed after her; he was sure there would be much gossip among the Deacons.

Merrick looked down at his own abandoned golden and gleaming insignia. His fingers hovered a little above it for a moment. It was hard to give up something after so many years of wanting it.

No, he pulled his hand back. It was just a piece of metal, and the cloak a scrap of cloth that had seen too many adventures. Even the name of the Order did not contain what it was really about. Sorcha was right.

Deliberately, Merrick turned away and opened his Center. In the citadel spread below him, he could have picked out and counted the remaining Sensitives and Actives—but he didn't because that would have been direly depressing. Instead he opened his mind to the members of the Conclave.

They were six of the strongest Sensitives that remained; Akiline, Heroon, Khandir, Yituna, Daschiel and Suseli. They had been only passing acquaintances before the destruction of the Mother Abbey, but he had been cobbling them together into a Conclave for the last few weeks. In fact, Akiline and Yituna were far older than he, and had been among his instructors back at the Mother Abbey. Three others he had known only by sight. Daschiel alone had been in his novitiate class.

Now, however, all six were locked in a tangled web that none of them had ever imagined. It was time to take the Conclave out and find out what it could do. Merrick knew that it was their best chance to avoid what had happened to the previous Order they had belonged to. He sent the signal, then felt the Sensitives respond and prepare themselves.

While he waited for them to be ready, Merrick sat himself down at the table, leaned back in his chair and closed his eyes for a moment. It was just a moment.

"You know you will have to do it." The voice was not in his head, and he was no longer in the citadel. Used to visions and seeing the unseen, Merrick did not jerk upright. Instead he slid his Center open and glanced to where the voice addressed him; it was one that he recognized immediately.

Merrick looked up. Nynnia stood before him. Her dark hair blew in unseen winds, and he could see the trees and forest behind her through her body. She was younger than the last time he had seen her, but that was only to be expected. He had traveled back in time to when she'd been alive; before her people had fled to the Otherside. They had wanted to save the world with their sacrifice. It was a pity that they had failed.

"Has the gap between our worlds become so narrow?" he asked, blinking in the light that seemed to have traveled with her.

She nodded, her eyes dropping away from his. "Everything is much closer now. It is all in flux. I needed to see you again, but do not think it was easy of me to send my image to you." Her brow was furrowed, and he noticed her form was flickering slightly.

"I am glad you did," he muttered softly, unsure what to say to the woman he had loved, and still did in a very real way.

Nynnia took a hesitant step forward. "It was not for our sake, Merrick. I had to. The Native Order has worked tirelessly to thin the barrier between our worlds."

"Why would they do that?"

She reached out for him but then stopped herself. Nynnia was as she was, and she had no body to clothe herself with. Merrick flinched inwardly. Despite his love for Zofiya, Nynnia would always be his first, and it would have been good to feel her touch. She took a deep breath, and glanced away to her right. Merrick realized she was examining something in the distance that he could not see. Whatever it was, she did not seem pleased by it.

A breath of chill wind brushed over his skin.

"They think . . ." she paused and locked her gaze with Merrick's. "He thinks he can use and control the power from the geists and the Otherside for his own purposes. He is very, very wrong."

"Derodak?" Merrick frowned. "You mean Derodak." Now she looked away, and he saw a stain of guilt in her gaze.

His people had called Nynnia's the Ancients; lost in the mist of time, builders of fantastical machines, and masters of the weirstone. Merrick had cast them as heroes when he was a child. He had only later learned that through their

actions in trying to use weirstones they had drawn the
attention of the geistlords. They had paid that price however, when they had chosen to flee to the Otherside rather
than sacrifice this world to the geists.

Merrick could not use his Sight in this vision Nynnia
had conjured, but he could still observe, and what he was
seeing from his former lover was indeed something verg-
ing on guilt. He suspected he knew why.

She hung her head. "I was not the first of my people to
be reborn into the human world. Derodak was. The first
Emperor, the first Deacon, and the grandest traitor is
indeed one of the Ehtia."

"I know," he murmured. "Sorcha and I fought him in
the ruins of the Mother Abbey. I used Aiemm, the Rune of
the Past on him. I saw. We all saw." He could hear the bitterness in his own voice.

If he had not been so consumed with sadness, he might
have felt some satisfaction that he had surprised the
Ehtia—that seldom happened.

"He is our greatest shame, among many great shames."
Nynnia glanced away to her right again—but this time her
expression was pained. "At least we brought the geists here
with our ignorance. Unfortunately, Derodak is all of our
own making. By the time we found out his true nature, it was
too late. He found a way back into the world that had born
us." She leaned toward the Deacon. "You shall have to be
careful now, Merrick. You showed him his humanity, again,
something that he does not wish to be reminded of. He will
not like that. He will seek you out to punish you for that."

Merrick could feel a pull in his brain, the tug of the
Conclave drawing nearer to completion. This dreaming
that Nynnia had conjured could not last much longer. She
must have brought him here for something.

"You can do something. You can tell us how we can beat
him," he demanded. He knew that Nynnia and the Otherside was beyond time, so perhaps she could see and understand more than he could—even with the Conclave.

She looked at him, her head tilted, dark hair blowing in a wind he could only feel intermittently. When she spoke again, Nynnia had to scream for him to hear her over the howl of it, "It is not Derodak you have to fear—you already have the tools to overcome him. It is her that you must fear. Sorcha!"

Now the Sensitive could actually discern the voices of his peers coming up to join him, and the pull of the real world was now becoming more and more insistent. Nynnia was making no sense at all. Derodak was the problem—not Sorcha who had worked so valiantly to save them all.

"You can't mean that," Merrick found himself yelling back, as the wind grew louder and louder.

Nynnia was having a hard time standing in front of him as the gale increased. Her hair was whipped about her, and eventually she dropped to the ground to grab hold of it with her fingers. It was an act of pure will for her to remain.

"I do," she howled into the chaos. "Sorcha could rip everything apart. She is the Harbinger of the end of everything. You know what you will have to do . . ."

"Not the Last Rune. Not that." Merrick jerked himself upright in an effort to reach her—but it was too late. The real world grabbed hold of him and pulled.

"Deacon Chambers?"

His eyelids flicked open. For a moment his mind was lost somewhere between reality and dream. The person standing over him was Heroon; the younger man, only just out of the novitiate, had his hand on Merrick's shoulder.

Merrick shook his head, wiped his eyes, trying to separate the real world and the one that Nynnia had taken him to. Once under the palace of Orinthal the Ehtia had managed to take his whole body to the Otherside, but this time it had just been his Center. He swallowed, and reminded himself of the task that still lay ahead.

"I am fine, Deacon Heroon," he replied quietly. "I am just tired is all."

He pulled himself to his feet, feeling his skin prickle

with exhaustion, and tried to size up the six other Sensitives. They did not appear to have caught the strange visitation. Merrick was pleased; he did not want to stain their already fragile trust in him any further. What Nynnia had communicated was something to be digested, alone, and with his senses dedicated to it. The Council—or whatever it was—had asked him to do this, to look ahead and find the weaknesses in the armor of the Native Order.

To step into the future was not a journey to be taken lightly. He gestured to the seats. "Let's set ourselves together, and see what we can find. There is a way forward, and like many times before, the Sensitives shall find it."

The others looked less than impressed with his little speech, but it was all he had to give at this point. Nynnia had left him feeling fractured and disorientated. Her words about Sorcha would haunt him, but he could not let them distract him. For the first time in his life, he did not want to believe what he had been told by Nynnia and pushed what she had told him to the back of his mind. He had more than enough to occupy his time and thoughts with.

Sorcha was his partner, and there was no other reality he wanted to contemplate.

SEVEN

In the Shadow of Love

"Sorcha!" Raed stood in their shared room and called her name, even though it was a small enough space that he could immediately tell she wasn't there. He stood there on the threshold, and let out a long breath. After shedding the fur cloak, he found fresh clothes in the tiny set of drawers, and stripped out of the ones he had recovered by the river. He always thought there was a strange feral scent in clothes that had come near the Rossin.

As he dressed, Raed eyed the cloak on the bed; it disturbed him, and yet it was a beautiful thing. Could it possibly be a gift from the Rossin? The fur was an exceptional silver color, not at all like the ruddy fur of the Beast that he shared flesh with. He'd found tufts of it before and knew the difference well enough. Then maybe it was something from a victim of the Rossin?

Raed pushed one of his hands through his hair in frustration. Perhaps, he should find Merrick and just make sure there was no geist connection. He would have asked Sorcha, but he did not want to add to her worries.

Things might have been terrible; they'd been on the run

for months from the Emperor and the Circle of Stars after all. However, the truth of it was despite all of that these had still been the best months of his life because they had at least been together.

"My prince." Aachon's voice made Raed start and spin around. His friend moved around as quietly as a Deacon; his boyhood training standing him in good stead. The tall, dark man, with the physical presence of a bear, should not have been able to move around with the ease of a mouse. They may have had to leave their ship the *Dominion* behind, but Aachon had not given up on being Raed's friend. "I am glad you were not here when—"

The first mate's words ground to nothing when he took in the Young Pretender's expression. He had hoped that Aachon wouldn't be able to read what had happened. It was—as always—a false hope.

"Again?" Aachon whispered, glancing up and down the corridor, before stepping hastily into the room and shutting the door. "My prince, if the Rossin is finding—"

Now it was Raed's turn to interrupt; he grasped his friend's shoulder. "Sorcha and the Deacons have more to worry about than my curse. I have been dealing with it for the last couple of weeks." When Aachon's eyebrows shot up, Raed forestalled him once more. "However, things have changed; it appears the Rossin has not killed anyone. Perhaps he has found a way to be content with simply running free instead of needing blood . . ."

Carefully Raed angled himself, so that Aachon could not see the cloak on the bed. Luckily, the other man was distracted by this change in the Rossin's behavior. He rubbed his chin and stared directly at Raed. "I find that highly unlikely. The Beast lives on blood and chaos—why would he be any different now?"

"Everything is turned upside down at the moment," Raed replied. "The Deacons feel it—even I feel it." He met his friend's gaze, daring him to contradict him.

Aachon nodded slowly. "Indeed—and that is why I

came to find you, my prince." Aachon's jaw clenched, as did his hands, but when he spoke his voice was considered. "Last night geists broke through into the citadel."

Raed's heartbeat picked up. "Is Sorcha—"

"Deacons Faris and Chambers are safe, but many were not so lucky."

Raed felt a prickle on the back of his neck, as if he was being watched. He cleared his throat. "But this is a Priory of the Order—how could they breach the walls with all the cantrips and runes?"

"This place was long abandoned," Aachon explained, "and none of the Deacons here had the strength to shore up the crumbling cantrips of protection. This is no Mother Abbey."

They both knew that was a rather sour joke; even the Mother Abbey now lay in ruins.

"So what happened?" Raed asked dully, already suspecting the answer.

"A dozen or so lay Brothers and followers were slain in the Great Hall, but Deacons Faris and Chambers were able to close the breach—at least temporarily." Because Aachon had been his friend for years, Raed caught the slight flinch that his friend made, even mentioning Merrick's name. The first mate was a man of real honor, and his failure to find the Deacon's mother and brother cut deep.

In the chaos after the destruction of the Mother Abbey, Merrick had asked Aachon to rescue them from the Emperor's palace, while he and Sorcha wrestled Zofiya from Derodak. Aachon had been unable to and had returned empty-handed. Most likely, the Emperor had already squirreled them away somewhere as surety against the Sensitive. What their fate had been remained a mystery. No matter how often Merrick used the runes to search for them he could not find anything.

"Where is Sorcha now?" Raed asked, hoping to provide a distraction for his friend.

It had taken some time for Aachon not to wince when

Raed spoke of his lover. Their first meeting had been rather fraught, and then just before the fall of the Mother Abbey he had seen her do things in the home of the Wrayth that had underscored her relation to the geistlords. This was not the type of person the first mate wanted his Prince and friend to be connected with in any way.

"She is on the upper battlements," he said in a low growl.

However, before they could get into any kind of awkward discussion, another figure appeared in the doorway behind them.

"Aachon! Raed!" Merrick smiled, and seemed not to notice the first mate shuffling out of the way, his shoulders slightly stiff. "I am glad to see you are both well. Sorcha was worried after she found you missing . . ." His eyes grazed appraisingly over the Young Pretender.

Raed glanced at Aachon, who took the none-too-subtle hint. Since Merrick arrived he had probably been looking for a way to escape the room. He bowed slightly to both of them. "I shall be in the infirmary if you need me, my prince." Then he disappeared back into the citadel's dark corridors.

Merrick looked at the Young Pretender, his head tilted. "Did you . . . did the Rossin find you last night, Raed?"

The Young Pretender gave a curt nod. "But don't worry; no one died last night—at least not under his paws."

Sometimes there was a comfort in dealing with Sensitives; they were very good at telling the truth. Merrick folded his hands behind his back. "That's very good, Raed, but you will still want to find Sorcha. She does worry about you . . ."

"I will," the Young Pretender assured him. He pushed his hair out of his eyes and sighed. "You know, I don't want to make things harder for her . . ."

Merrick patted his shoulder, turned to leave, but then stopped and glanced back at the bed. "What is that?"

It was then that Raed noticed the Sensitive was no

longer wearing the green cloak that had seemed part of him. The Young Pretender opened his mouth to tell Merrick the whole story, but something very strange came out in its place. "I found it in one of the lower floors of the citadel. It's a rather fine old cloak, don't you think?" A warmth ran up his spine, and he knew that he had to do something nice. "I'm not in need of a new one, though, so why don't you have it?"

"That's . . . that's very generous," Merrick replied, already taking up the fur, and running his fingers over it. "It is a beautiful gift." He did not ask if Raed was sure about giving it, but instead unwrapped it and swept it around his shoulders.

"It looks good on you," Raed had to admit. "You'll be quite the envy of the Deacons."

The Sensitive shook his head, even as he wrapped the fur cloak around himself. "Good point . . . I must return to the Conclave." He paused. "Thank you again Raed, it shall definitely keep the cold out."

Once Merrick had left, relief flooded Raed; he felt that he had done something good. The strange circumstances of the fur didn't seem to matter and faded from his memory the more time passed since he had seen it.

By the time he had climbed the steps to the wind-battered upper battlements, he had other concerns to occupy his mind. He knew he'd been pretty lucky to have gotten away with his midnight excursions this long. Sorcha and the rest of the Deacons had been working hard—both physically and mentally—and she'd come to bed late and exhausted. Otherwise he was sure she would have found out before now that he'd been absent from their bed on other nights as well.

Now, with this attack last night, there was no way she would have been able to miss that he wasn't there. When Raed reached the door to the battlements, he paused, took a deep breath, and then unlatched it.

It was a relief to see they were alone, except for the

view. The Native Order had chosen a magnificent spot on which to build their Priory. The citadel stood at the high end of a long river valley, with the waterfall slicing its way over the top of it but under the walls of the citadel. From these battlements Deacons would have been able to see anyone coming for miles, and the running water provided protection from geists. At least it had in the past.

The sound of the waterfall's descent masked his approach, and he was glad of that. Sorcha was leaning against the crenellations, her back turned to him, watching the smash of the water below.

As Raed approached her, he observed the tiny water droplets that had caught in her flame-colored hair, the curl of smoke around her head, and the fact that she too was no longer wearing a cloak. She was smoking a cigarillo, and Raed knew Sorcha only did that when she needed to think, or was feeling particularly melancholy.

He got within a few feet before Sorcha spun around. Given that she had to have discovered his secret outings, Raed expected anything but what happened next. Sorcha threw herself into his arms; clutching him to her tightly with one hand, while the other held the lit cigarillo. Her face and form pressing against him was a welcome distraction.

She pulled back and kissed Raed. Her firm mouth against his tasted of smoke and salt. He wondered if all of the water on her face was from the waterfall's embrace. It would be typical of Sorcha to come up here, where no one could tell, to let some of her pent-up frustrations and fear out.

He decided not to mention it—instead he enjoyed the kiss. He clasped her close, feeling her greatly diminished form under her clothes. Sorcha had always been delightfully curvy, but the rigors of their constant flight had whittled her away—as it had all of them. Still, it just made him want to look after her more and feed her properly as soon as possible.

Finally, even they had to admit defeat though. Sorcha pulled back, giving his bottom lip a final reminder of a nip.

"What has your cigarillo done to deserve this?" Raed asked, gesturing to the sad, damp thing she held in her hand.

Sorcha shrugged. "It was a bit wet already, and I needed it more than I can say." She shot him a look with the faintest hint of a smile at the corner of her mouth. "Just like you."

Raed waited for the inevitable question. It didn't come. Her blue eyes were locked with his, waiting for an explanation.

The Young Pretender wanted to be perfect for her. He most certainly did not want to add to her already monumental list of problems, but neither could he lie to her face. She was the one person in the world he didn't want to deceive.

"The Rossin came," he began, watching for any reaction from her. When Sorcha didn't move, Raed went on. "He didn't kill anyone. I think he just wanted to run, because when I woke there was no taste of blood in my mouth." Something else had happened, but he couldn't quite remember what. It couldn't be that important.

He cleared his throat. "The Rossin has been coming out these last couple of weeks. I can't help it. I'm sorry—very sorry—that I didn't tell you."

Sorcha nodded somberly, but her hands clasped his tightly. "We should have expected that I guess. The Otherside is so close now that the Rossin is much more powerful—all the geists are."

Raed had never heard Sorcha sound so defeated, and he did not like it one little bit. He wanted the fire and passion to kindle in her eyes again.

"And you've been pulling away from me." Sorcha touched his face, a look of fear flickering across her own. "Don't do that. I need you." That those words came out of the Deacon was a precious thing. He most certainly would not have ever imagined them appearing from the woman he had first met, soggy, and trembling with outrage after being fished out of the ocean. He loved that she finally had let him see her softness—though she would never do it in public.

He picked up her hand and kissed its palm. Her flesh felt good against his lips. "What's happened?" he murmured into it, before guiding her away from the edge of the battlements. The sound of the waterfall was a little less loud to the cliff face, and if anyone came through the door as he had they wouldn't be able to see them immediately.

Raed held her against him as he leaned against the wall of the citadel, and she leaned back so that only their lower torsos were touching. It was comforting, but not so distracting that either of them couldn't think.

Sorcha closed her eyes for a moment, raised the pitiful cigarillo to her mouth, pulled the smoke into her, and then exhaled it away from him. She spoke softly. "I don't know what's going to happen to us . . . to the Order . . . or whatever we are now."

They had been running, in danger for their lives from both the Imperial army and the Native Order for months, but he'd never seen her so concerned as she was right now. He squeezed her just a fraction. "With you able to open the Wrayth portals, we can go anywhere we like. We can rebuild the Order with time . . ."

Her full lips twisted. "That is what we don't have, my love. Last night's attack drove home that point very well. The barrier between this world and the Otherside is incredibly weak now. Derodak has done something—something awful—while we have been running, and soon it will reach a tipping point." Raed felt a long-held-in sigh ripple through her body. "Merrick is in a Conclave with some of the other Sensitives right now. They are trying to use runes to see which way forward we must go. I don't like relying on foresight—but what other option do we have?" Her eyes held his, and Raed realized she was actually asking him about the future of the Order.

He'd been at this point much earlier in his own life. Shortly after the Rossin had killed his mother he'd been swept away on a tide of depression and entropy; unable to decide what to do since all options looked equally dire. He'd relied on his role as son to the Unsung Pretender to the throne of Arkaym as much as Sorcha had relied on hers as a Deacon of the Order of the Eye and the Fist.

"You do what you do best," Raed said, cupping one hand against her cheek. "You make something out of nothing. Isn't that what wielding the runes is all about? You use your own strength to make things happen. You see the path with an enlightened eye that Merrick and you share. You defend, just as you always have. Just because the Mother Abbey is gone, and everything torn apart, that doesn't change who *you* are."

Sorcha swallowed hard then leaned into him. They embraced in the moist air, with the sound of the waterfall at their backs. It was the kind of embrace that said this was all of the world—even if for just an instant. It hurt to stop holding her.

After she had squeezed Raed, Sorcha pulled back a fraction. "You're right, but that doesn't change anything much—we can't go back to what we were." She took a final draft of the cigarillo, before dropping it to the ground and grinding it with her heel. "We must make ourselves anew and become something else. The Order of the Eye and the Fist is dead, and we can't pretend differently. We can't shackle ourselves to what was."

"Why do I get the feeling I just said what you were already halfway to deciding anyway?" Raed said, with an uncertain smile.

"Maybe because I am inside your head?" Sorcha leaned over, tapped his forehead, then kissed him lightly on the lips. "I have an appointment. One I've been avoiding for quite a while."

He watched her stride over to the door, as straight backed and determined as on the first day he'd met her.

Raed was just thinking that nothing much had changed, when she proved him wrong.

Hand on the door handle, she paused and looked back at him. "Is everything all right with the Rossin, Raed? You have him under control, right?"

By the small gods, Raed hadn't wanted her to ask that particular question, but there it was. He smiled and replied, "Everything is under control."

Sorcha nodded and left the battlements. It was indeed a sign that things were turning dramatically toward the worse—she hadn't heard his thoughts. The Bond that connected Raed, Sorcha and Merrick had once been so strong that he'd been unable to hide anything from them. Now however, with the combined problems of lost foci, new runic tattoos, and the closeness of the Otherside, it appeared Raed could get away with disassembling.

The thought did not fill him with joy—only dread. He hadn't exactly lied to her; everything was under control. Unfortunately, Raed had the sinking feeling it was not he that had the control, but instead it belonged to the other darker, more primal creature that lurked within him.

EIGHT

Tracing the Thread

Walking away from Raed was more difficult than Sorcha could have possibly communicated; when he held her, she just wanted to disappear into that embrace. She had clenched her fingers into the palms of her hands hard, because she dared not hold on to Raed too long or lose her will to step away.

With what had gone on the previous night, Sorcha had known there was no other choice; she had to visit the Patternmaker. She'd just wanted to think by herself for a moment—just her and her cigarillo and the roar of the waterfall. Raed's arrival had not been unwelcome, since it had put off the inevitable.

However, she hadn't told him where she was going, or what she was planning to do; he'd have wanted to go along with her. This was her burden to bear. She was the one that had taken the Patternmaker's bargain.

As she walked slowly up the steps, she felt tentatively along the Bond. Merrick was there, but there was no support to be had from him; his presence was like the whispering of many distant voices. That was better too. He had enough to worry about, hunting out the future.

The closer Sorcha got to the high, isolated room that the Patternmaker had taken for his own, the more the smell of death reached her nostrils. Her breath colored the air in front of her white, and despite all that she had seen in her time as a Deacon, she was a little nervous.

In the tumult of the foci that had once contained the runes being taken from them, and the Mother Abbey burning, Sorcha knew they had all grasped whatever hope had been laid before them. They had been desperate for it. Even the ravings of a madman had seemed sensible in those times, but now given a little more space to look around, she and many others had begun to wonder who they had allied themselves with.

That was why it was a relief that the Patternmaker had claimed a room in the highest portion of the citadel. Very few went there, even the well-meaning lay Brothers could not find it in themselves to climb the steps she was climbing.

The Patternmaker was something more than human, but not geist—at least that was what the Sensitives had said. However, the days of Sorcha trusting what she had once taken as fact were long gone. She had to find the answers for herself.

Finally, she reached the door and stood there for a moment, like a nervous initiate lingering on the threshold of her Arch Abbot's doorway. She strained her ears to hear what was going on behind that door.

The Patternmaker was talking. It was a language, she was sure of that, but unlike any that she knew of in the Empire or in Delmaire.

Her stomach clenched, and the runes on her arms tingled as if they were on fire. She hovered there, caught between the desire to kick the door in, and the strange urge to knock politely.

In the end, Sorcha compromised, and edged the door

open a fraction and peered in. The rank odor of unwashed human was hardly what one might have expected from a holy man, but as a Deacon, Sorcha had met more than her fair share of filthy madmen who had claimed that title; she had just never imagined one being part of any Order.

If they were still an Order.

Words in her head. Sorcha froze in the act of entering the room. It was not Merrick's voice, nor the rumble of the Rossin. She did, however, recognize the tone. The Wrayth. A chill rush went through her.

Blindly, Sorcha opened her Center. All Deacons had some ability in Sight and Activity, but her Sensitivity was minimal. Still she tried her best to feel any trace of the Wrayth about her. Nothing.

It was a relief though to feel that Merrick's mind was still murmuring into the void, and giving no indication he had been disturbed by another voice in their Bond.

Sorcha looked up through the gap in the doorway. What was the Patternmaker doing? Curiosity and fear warred within her. The Deacon glanced down at her hands and the swirling shapes of the runes that he had carved into her skin. It was done. They had taken his help, and now she would have to find out the cost of it.

With her knee she nudged the door open wider and stepped boldly inside. As the top room in the citadel was buried mostly in the cliff itself, there was only one window, and the Patternmaker had covered that with a blanket. The inside was gray, and the far walls impossible to see. The smell fulfilled the promise it had made outside, and she raised her hand to her mouth to try and muffle it. Only training kept her from throwing up.

Smell was one of the senses that heralded a geist attack—though what that could mean she didn't want to think too hard on. The Patternmaker was not a geist; she held on to that fact as best she could.

Could you see the Rossin in the Young Pretender?

Shock froze Sorcha in midstride. The mocking tone, the

female voice, all reminded her of the time in the Wrayth hive. The geistlord had spread itself over so many humans, taken them as slaves, and made them into a wasp nest for one purpose. Her mother, a raped and tortured prisoner of the Wrayth, had born her in the hive. Her father must have been one of the geistlord's drones. She would probably never know his name.

Though she'd tried desperately not to think about the Wrayth and concentrate simply on using the abilities she'd been given, her heritage made her the only one capable of saving the remains of the Order. For months she'd been opening their portals and leading them from place to place; so fixed on escape that she'd been able to ignore those horrible facts. Now, Sorcha felt a fool. Could she have put the remains of the Order in danger just by being who she was?

"Come in." The voice, actually spoken outside of her own head, made Sorcha flinch. "Shut the door."

Her right hand prickled slightly and drifted to the hilt of her saber that hung at her side. Deacons were always armed, but it was not her greatest resource. Carefully, she reached out and flicked the door shut. The room was plunged into near total darkness, and Sorcha had the real sense that she was trapped in a room with a wild animal—one that she could not see.

Her Center was her only choice—but a very shabby one it was. She could make out the vague outline of the room's walls, and warmth and life near the back of it. "Is this darkness really necessary?" she snapped. "It's a little too theatrical for my tastes."

The Patternmaker—it had to be him, surely—laughed; a strange echoing noise that seemed to come from much farther off than the rear of the room. *He's not a geist,* Sorcha reminded herself, and strode deeper into the room.

But you are.

"Damn it!" Sorcha let her frustration escape her lips.

Something skittered in the shadows. It had to be a rat, even if she couldn't see anything living apart from the hunched form of the Patternmaker. It was strange that this was the man that had helped them, and yet in this moment Sorcha felt more in danger than she had the previous night facing geists that had spilled over from the Otherside.

"Too many voices?" the Patternmaker hissed. "Now you live in my painful world."

Another rattle of feet—this time to her right. Sorcha realized she was being encircled, yet it was ridiculous to feel this way, Sorcha reminded herself; he was an old man. Apart from that, she was in a citadel full of Deacons, and this was the man that had tattooed her skin with the runes, making it possible for them to fight geists and the Native Order.

Straightening, Sorcha stepped more boldly toward the form of the Patternmaker. "I have come—"

"I know why. The Otherside is closer, spilling over to your world."

He spoke so clearly that she paused her approach. When last she had spoken to him, he had not been nearly this coherent. "How do you know that?" she asked and immediately understood it was a stupid, childish question to pose. The Patternmaker was attuned to the Otherside better than even a Deacon.

Now the skittering came closer, and she could have sworn something brushed her boot. She kicked out. That was impossible! She was not so blind with her Center that she would miss something coming that near. Was this how normal folk felt? She'd had a taste of this before and had liked it about just as much then.

"We feel it," the old man's voice slid out of the shadows.

You feel it too.

Sorcha grabbed her head, slapping her hands on each side of it like a child trying to deny reality. The same tiny primitive part of her brain wanted to turn and flee out of the room completely—however she had never really been anything but a Deacon, trained to be a truth seeker. She'd been taught to hold fast, but it felt like there was very little left to hold on to.

Feeling out with one hand, she clasped the wet, dank stone, and slid to her knees. In the deep dark of the room, the only light was now beginning to grow on her own arm. The runes that the Patternmaker had carved on her flesh were shifting and moving. The shapes of the runes—which she knew better than the shape of her own body—were making new forms; ones that she did not recognize.

"Everything is changing, Harbinger." The Patternmaker's voice wrapped itself around her, giving voice to her own terrors. "You are part of it, more deeply than any other person in this realm. You are woven into its warp and weft like a sharp Wrayth-made little thread."

Sorcha's eyes widened as she watched the patterns shift and dance. "What do I need to do?"

His voice hissed from the shadows and was echoed by those now bouncing around in her head. "The Harbinger makes the changes. Only you can decide what those are—that is the joy and the horror of your creation."

That was when the Deacon froze. In her mind she heard again the mother she could not remember but had experienced in the Wrayth's lair. They had been breeding the Deacons they had caught down there. Sorcha had so completely turned her mind away from the horror of that, she had neglected to consider what their goal had been.

In the depths the Patternmaker, Ratimana, laughed. "They made you, but they were not expecting you. They wanted a way to work the runes of the Deacons, without any of that pesky human will getting in the way."

"How do you know all this? What are you?" Sorcha held her arms before her and stumbled forward like a blind person. She had to have those answers even if it meant tearing them from the twisted man with her bare hands.

Her fingers brushed against skin as soft and giving as boiled flesh. Despite her training, she flinched back. The runes on her own flesh sparked to light, casting an eerie glow on the face of the Patternmaker. He looked up at her, a broken and frail old man, but in the light of the runes his eyes burned. They flashed as the Rossin's did.

Sorcha held her trembling arms, burning with light close to him, and realized the truth of it. The Patternmaker was a geistlord—as much as the Rossin was, as much as she was.

His unnerving grin flashed across his lips, exposing teeth that were now far too large. "I am like you, Wrayth. Another portion created as a scout, in the time of the Break, sent into this world to find flesh and home."

Sorcha froze in place. She did not want to howl or move or show any form of weakness in front of this creature. Still her eyes wandered down to her own arm, which now felt like it belonged to someone else; an alien thing that shouldn't have been attached to her body. The runes on it gleamed and twisted.

Sorcha's breath jammed in her chest, as her thoughts bubbled up. She had brought the other Deacons to this place. They had carved the runes into themselves in the exact same way she had, because she had showed them the way and they had been desperate. Instead, she'd contaminated them. She'd made them like she was; filthy with Wrayth powers.

"What did you find?" Sorcha choked out, unable to voice the real questions crowded in her mind.

"I found freedom. I found I did not want to be part of any hive mind. I wanted to be myself and not part of them."

Sorcha needed Merrick, but she was too ashamed to call for him. Without his better-trained Center she was struggling, but she knew he would have been able to get to the truth.

"This is the truth," Ratimana went on. "The truth you have been trying to hide from. You and I are the same creatures. We are survivors."

The sound of him coming closer was like a snake moving on stone, it made her skin crawl. "You hear them, just

like I do—but the difference is . . . they will come for you.
They still want you."

Sorcha stared down into his inhuman eyes and was lost
for words. She had come here for reassurance and instead
had found horror. Her jaw tightened as she looked at the
Patternmaker. If she couldn't find her bravery soon, then
she would just have to fake it. "Not if I find them first," she
replied, clenching her hand, burning with light, tightly
closed.

NINE

An Old Love

A Conclave was a tricky thing; it was easy to lose oneself in the soft morass of the group-mind. A hundred worries, dreams, feelings and sensations wrapped themselves around Merrick. Suseli's fears from last night's horrific dream screamed in his ear, while Heroon's idle thoughts about whether his lover was really the one he wanted were distracting. The tangle of so many muttering voices was a trap for the inexperienced Sensitive, and Merrick had not been that long out of the novitiate—in reality it was only a year and a half since he had left the security of training. However, anyone working with Sorcha got more experience than they had bargained for.

Now, Merrick put that experience to use. He imagined the strands of the different people in the Conclave threading between his fingers, like brightly colored tendrils of wool. He held them apart from each other and more importantly from his own self. He used his will to sort the tangle out, and was surprised by his own dexterity. The Presbyter of the Sensitives, Yvril Mournling, who had trained Merrick in the novitiate, would have been impressed—if he'd

been able to move from his deathbed that was. Few
remained with the skill to hold a Conclave together, and so
there was no one around to pat Merrick on the back. He
sorely missed the community of Sensitives he had taken
for granted in the Mother Abbey. .

With this sad little thought, Merrick began to weave the
threads back together. He took the powers of the Sensitives
and formed them into a pattern. Their Centers bloomed
around him, and he was awash with that combined power.
Now he could see so much more than even his powerful
Center could bring him.

His Sight soared over the citadel, out over the gravel-
strewn valley, and washed farther away into the mountains.
He could pick out scattered people and animals with the
accuracy that even a great eagle could not have.

It was a heady, deadly situation. Sensitives liked to
imagine that it was Actives that were full of hubris and
overconfidence; but they were just as susceptible. If Merrick looked too long into the sun of the Conclave mind, it
would have the same effect, and then all would be lost.

He turned his Center away from the endless possibilities
of this power, and dove forward into the unknown. Masa,
the Third Rune of Sight, was slippery. He'd been taught in
the first classes as a young boy that it was not to be relied
on. Looking forward into the future was somewhat of an
art—compared to the other runes that could be mastered
with training.

Sorcha was asking a great deal of him sending him in
this direction, and it was a measure of her desperation that
she even asked. Merrick knew how she felt, because he felt
it too. They had to find a path and quickly or else be
exposed as frauds. If they could not change what was happening to Arkaym, then they might as well have never had
the runes carved on their skin.

So, holding on to the skeins of the Conclave, Merrick
opened himself up to the future. It was a moment of abandon, and reckless exposure to this world and the Otherside.

The sensation of rushing scared the Sensitive; it was as if he were speeding away from his body—so fast he felt as though he might crash into something.

Luckily, it stopped just as suddenly, as quickly, as it had started. Merrick opened the eyes of his Center and found that he was standing in a long corridor. It stretched away before him with no sign of ending, and off it were an uncountable number of doors.

Silence was sucking on his senses, and he understood behind each one was a possible future. As he had feared, he was finding it impossible to read. A quick glance behind him, and he realized the corridor was disappearing into shadow—the strands of the Conclave were swallowed up by it as well.

After taking a long, slow breath Merrick had to remind himself that this was all a construction of his trained mind; a way to deal with the confusing power of Masa. It could do him no harm, and really all he had to lose was his ignorance. Later, when back in his body and away from the rune, he could examine what he had found.

Strengthened, Merrick reached out and pushed open the door before him. Almost immediately he flinched back. She was there, the creature wreathed in scarlet flame that had given him nightmares; the Murashev, who had stepped through into the world from the Otherside under the city of Vermillion. He, Sorcha and Raed had been melded by the Rossin into a creature of pure rune magic, so his recollection of the geistlord was warped by that, yet she still blazed in his memory.

Something about the slight, snarling figure aroused him in this half-dream state. "Don't you see?" she said with a magnificent smile. "The change is coming."

The room was full of flame and suddenly Merrick couldn't breathe. He staggered back into the corridor and slammed the door shut. As he pulled his hand back from the handle, he stared down at his scalded fingertips. They hurt.

Shaking his hand absentmindedly, he moved on to the next door. This one he opened more cautiously.

Behind it was the geistlord he had been expecting: Hatipai. She was the scourge of Orinthal, and the creature that had set herself up as a goddess in that southern principality. She was also the false goddess that Zofiya had worshipped for years.

Merrick knew that the revelation of her deception had cut the Grand Duchess very deeply. He had never seen the goddess persona of the geistlord, but the smooth lovely face was unmistakably hers. "You cannot stand against the geists alone," she said with a smile. "You do not have what you need." She opened her arms and stepped toward him.

Merrick had the feeling if she touched him he would not want to return to the real world. He tripped over himself to get out of the room, and threw the door shut behind him.

A chill concern was beginning to build inside him. He was in his own Center, and Merrick should have not been so drawn to something that was essentially built from his own mind.

Now he glanced with real trepidation at the next door; however, the Order had never trained a coward in its entire history. Merrick stepped up and this time, in defiance of his building concern, kicked open the door with a snap of his leg.

Sorcha turned to look back at him. Many, many Sorchas who were crowded in the space that represented the future. Some were smiling, others frowning, but all locked him where he stood with their stern blue-eyed gaze. Merrick tilted his head and contemplated what this would mean.

The Murashev and Hatipai had been enemies manipulated by the Native Order to bring destruction to the world. As far as he knew Sorcha had never been a danger to him. Was the rune he'd followed here beginning to unravel?

The Sorchas all stepped toward him and now their mouths began to part. Wider and wider they opened, until they became nothing but flashing jaws full of terrible fangs. Improbably they began to speak, and the words they uttered were the ones etched on Merrick's soul.

> I promise to protect and shelter Imperial citizens from all attacks of the unliving—even to the end of my mind, body and soul. I shall never lie down before the geists and give up a mortal while I have soul or breath.

It was the oath all Deacons made when they left the novitiate, but the way that these creatures were reciting it was not serious and dedicated—it was mocking.

Merrick knew Masa was an untrustworthy thing, but he did not like the way it was getting away from him, nor did he understand what was going on. Sorcha. As he backed away into the corridor once more, he saw what was etched over the lintel.

See deep, fear nothing. The words engraved above the door were the code of the Sensitive. The trouble was Merrick was seeing deep, but he was afraid of what he found.

"Where is your shelter now?" the Sorchas cried, though their voices were now not hers. They were something else. "How can you protect anyone, when you can't protect yourself?"

They charged at him, and he fled the room completely. He raced up the hallway, letting Masa run out of his fingers, and abandoned his Center.

Merrick knew immediately that he had to find the answers somewhere else. He couldn't tell anyone about what he had found—least of all his partner. No, he would say that he had failed to see anything at all. That would be better than the truth.

✦ TEN ✦

On the Hunt

Sorcha sought out Merrick as the evening began to pull in, and even though they shared a connection, he was remarkably hard to find. Along the Bond she could feel his bitter frustrations and disappointments, which only magnified her own. She returned to the Great Hall and found him sitting alone in the chair by the window. He was wrapped in a luxurious fur cloak on which tiny beads of water from the falls had gathered like a scattering of diamonds. It had to be from the storerooms of the citadel; the lay Brothers were still finding all sorts of interesting items down there. The roar of the waterfall was slightly muffled by the stonework, but it still sounded like oncoming thunder.

Merrick's face was set in still lines, and his eyes locked on the magnificent view, yet Sorcha could read him well enough to know that he was seeing none of it. He didn't even acknowledge her presence.

"Merrick?" She finally had to speak and then again. "Merrick?"

He actually jumped a little.

"Is everything all right?" The words sounded ridiculous

coming out of her mouth. They'd been attacked in their own halls and had a madman living over their heads—yet what Sorcha meant wasn't any of that. She cleared her throat. "I mean are *you* all right?"

"I am . . ." He licked his lips and stared down at his folded hands on his lap. "I am here."

Somehow Sorcha got the feeling that wasn't completely true. "Did you examine the cantrips at all?" She didn't add "as I asked," since things were far too precarious right now for her to start throwing her metaphorical weight around.

He shook his head. "No, sorry. I was too deep in the future. The Conclave has only just gone downstairs for some sleep."

The strains of Masa were not something Sorcha could comprehend, but she could see the exhaustion written in every move of her partner. She took hold of his elbow and pulled him to his feet. "And that is where you should be too."

He made a weak gesture, attempting to stave her off. "We have to reach out with the weirstones every day, Sorcha. We have to search the future for a place to strike at Derodak. Choosing the wrong one could be disastrous."

"Indeed it could," she said, smoothly sliding her hand under Merrick's elbow, "but you won't be able to do that if you burn out like a candle."

Giving in to the inevitable, he finally allowed himself to be led back down the stairs. With her hands on the soft fur cloak, his partner helped him to his room. Sorcha tucked him into bed and wrapped him in blankets to keep him warm. She'd been expecting some kind of further resistance, but as soon as his head touched the pillow Merrick's eyes closed. For a moment she stood looking down at him, strangely maternal feelings welling up inside her.

Her partner was not quite young enough to be her child, but the emotions they shared veered everywhere. The relationship of Sensitive to Active was a complicated and unusual one. However, there was one thing Sorcha knew for

certain: Merrick would strive until his body and mind
broke. He had changed a great deal since their first meeting.
His nerves back then had shown in the humor he tried to
force. Now he barely had the energy for words of any kind.

"That lad looks like death warmed up," a voice commented out of the half light of the corridor.

Sorcha turned to see Raed stepping out of the darkness
and nodded her agreement. "He's been pushing himself too
hard."

"I think Merrick would say there is nothing that's too
hard, love." Raed took her hand in his, and his skin against
hers was a comfort. "You didn't come to bed last night, and
the night before that you fought off a geist attack. You
need your sleep. I hope you're not tiring of me already,
are you?"

She wanted to blurt out some of what the Patternmaker
had said, but she was still digesting it herself. Additionally,
she didn't want him to know one more disturbing fact
about herself: she was needing less and less sleep. She'd
spent the night on the battlements of the citadel thinking
hard on her time inside her mother's head. Those thoughts
that they'd shared might contain some way for her to defeat
her heritage. Nothing however had come. All she'd done
was recall the one who had birthed her, and the fear and
desperation that had driven her right to the edge. Sorcha
ended up worrying if she was coming close to that place
herself.

"Don't be foolish. I was just busy." It was much easier to
lie to Raed than it was to Merrick. The Bond between the
Young Pretender and herself was strong, but did not communicate stray thoughts.

"But I am glad you are here," she said, tugging him out
of the room and quietly shutting the door behind them. "I
need your help with something."

He straightened slightly. "You just have to ask, you
know that."

She was playing on one of Raed's principle concerns:

not being of use. Her request might also serve to distract him a little, just in case he saw panic in his lover's eyes. Sorcha knew what she had learned from the Patternmaker was nothing she could fix. She'd been born as part of the Wrayth, and if they came for her then she would have to deal with that. Right now however, there was something far more important.

"We have to find how the geists got inside the citadel's cantrips and runes," Sorcha said as she led him away from Merrick's room and down the steps deeper into the bones of the building. "Even with this weakening of the veil, they should have provided some protection. The citadel is hundreds and hundreds of years old, and has been layered with barriers by every generation of Deacons. I asked Merrick to look into it but . . ." She shrugged.

"How can I help with that?" he asked. "I'm no Merrick that can—"

"You have him." Sorcha cut him short and pressed her hand against his chest. "You have the Rossin, the master of breaching barriers, and . . ." She smiled." . . . I could do with your company, plus I have something that I want to talk to you about."

"I am afraid marriage is quite out of the question without you asking my father first." She caught a glimpse of his white teeth gleaming in the fading light of distant torches.

Sorcha wasn't sure if she should smile back. She settled for a short laugh, and then called on Yevah, just a little. The red fire ran through the designs on her arm, providing a useful if slightly strange light as they descended deep into the roots of the citadel.

The question Sorcha was burning to ask Raed was weighing her down, and it was harder to get out than she had expected. She found her mouth was a little dry since she'd not revealed to anyone—not even Merrick—how the Wrayth had been whispering to her of late. Finally, she choked out, "I need to know what it feels like to have the Rossin inside you . . ."

For a moment there was only the sound of their boots on the stone, and Sorcha worried that Raed was too stunned by her question to reply. She wheeled around in the narrow confines of the corridor and held her arm, burning with red fire, up slightly so she could see his face.

It was not fear or disgust she saw there, though his brows were drawn together and his jaw was tight. Raed's voice, when it came out, was hoarse and strained. "You know, no one has ever asked me that." He swallowed. "It has become . . . easier . . . if that is the right word for it."

Neither of them was happy with this conversation—Sorcha didn't need to be a Sensitive to figure that out—yet she pressed on. "Does he . . . does he speak to you?"

"Sometimes," Raed confessed. "Usually when he is trying to get me to do things, or when there is some immediate danger that he doesn't want his body involved in. Since Fraine's death he's been more interested in keeping me alive."

Sorcha clenched her jaw hard and turned away before whatever feeling was bubbling up could show itself on her face, but Raed's hand pressed against her shoulder. "Is there a reason you are asking, love?" he asked softly.

She didn't want the Patternmaker to be the only one who knew . . . just in case something happened later on. "It has to be the weakening of the barrier," she stumbled out. "The Wrayth like every other geist are gaining power . . . and I am starting to hear them . . . just now and then . . . sometimes . . ."

If the fledgling Council she was creating got wind of this, the remains of the Order would fall apart completely. Merrick in good conscience couldn't keep it from them, and by not revealing her Wrayth heritage he was already lying to them. Raed at least had none of those allegiances.

The Young Pretender stared down at her, his fingers still grasping her shoulder. "Have they asked you to do anything . . . anything that you feel compelled to do?"

She shook her head while choking back the desire to throw herself into his arms. It was an unfortunate truth that

she cared too much what he thought of her to break down—
but it would have been nice.

"Then you can live with it," Raed said, his breath making tiny white clouds in the cold air around them as he
leaned closer to her. "The Wrayth is probably just trying
to unnerve you and sway you from your course. The Rossin does it all the time to me, but neither of us needs to
listen."

They were the very words Sorcha needed to hear. Her
lack of sleep had to be caused by the extreme stress of these
last few months. A long-held-in breath escaped her. "Right,
then," she said, "let's see what is going on down here."

Holding her arm in front of them, she took his hand
with her left. It felt good to be able to do that since they
were down where no one could see. It was almost as if
there was no one in the world but the two of them.

Soon, the light around them was coming not just from
Sorcha's rune. Other twinkling colored lights began to
appear on the face of the rock tunnel.

"Cantrips?" Raed breathed. "I've never seen so many."

Sorcha glanced up at the complex patterns. "I have
heard tell the roots of the palace at Vermillion are also
very complex, but I don't think there is a Deacon alive that
has seen them."

"Except maybe for Derodak," Raed breathed.

Her heart leapt in her chest, but the Emperor had run
mad and was no longer her concern—though she feared for
the people of the capital.

Her lover cleared his throat, and tried to change the subject as quickly as he could. "So, what are we looking for?"

"Changes in the pattern," she said, pointing to the con-
centric rings that rose from the floor upward. "The lower-
down ones are the more ancient, and they get newer the
higher they get."

He frowned as his eyes focused on the tiny inscriptions.
"I feel like I might need eyeglasses for this task, love. How
on earth do you read . . ."

Sorcha wasn't quite sure how to tell him what he was really here for, but it wasn't as if she could put it off any longer. "I read them, Raed. You touch them."

The Rossin was not active in him and thus was not going to be affected by the cantrips; however, direct contact to his flesh should be the only experiment that needed to be conducted. It couldn't be the first time that he'd felt the sting of a cantrip.

"I see . . . it is not just my charm and good looks you were after," he replied with the faintest hint of a sigh. "Very well." He bent down, and touched the first ring of cantrips. The snap of blue power struck his finger.

The Young Pretender leapt back. "By the Blood!" He stared at Sorcha, and she—only just managing to conceal her smile—gestured to the next line of cantrips carved into the root of the citadel.

With a slow shake of his head, he obediently touched the next one. It went on for another hour, as they circled the foundations, testing the lines of cantrips.

"I think you are starting to enjoy this," Raed grumbled in a slightly overly hurt tone.

"Starting?" Sorcha shot back, but applied a kiss to the end of his fingertips. "I promise I will make it up to you somehow . . ."

He stared down at her, those hazel eyes locked with hers, and the shiver that ran up her spine was not at all related to the chill in the foundations. Raed must have felt it too, because he smiled slightly before turning back to his task. "How many more to do?"

Sorcha flicked her eyes up. "I think we should go upstairs. I don't know how the cantrips were breached; perhaps there is something Derodak can do that we don't know about, something not written in any book." That idea had been haunting her thoughts since the attack.

"Perhaps you're right, I can think of—" Raed stopped suddenly, and squeezing past Sorcha in the tight confines of the tunnel walked to where it finished abruptly. The glimmer of the cantrips danced over his skin as he reached out to touch one that gleamed pale green. Nothing happened.

Sorcha hurried to his side, as Raed repeatedly touched the line. Still nothing.

They shared a look, and she dropped into a crouch to examine the cantrips more closely. "It looks like some kind of fissure opened up here," she muttered, running her fingers over the surface of the rock, and feeling a sliver of a gap. "The cantrips here were added fairly recently to seal it, but . . ."

She stopped, suddenly, as her touch found a dip in the rock.

Raed swiftly joined her, leaning down on all fours to see what she had found. He brushed away a layer of gravel and rock that had been piled up along the edge between wall and floor. "Looks like a chisel has been used to knock the last few cantrips out and the damage was covered by loose earth. I would say rather recently."

Sorcha sank back on her heels as the realization washed over her. "Someone in the citadel is a traitor . . ."

With everything else they had to deal with, now they had to watch their backs. She'd thought everyone she'd saved and led through endless portals to this place had shared her determination to preserve something from the shards of the Order.

It was possible here to let her feelings out. Sorcha leaned against Raed. "I don't know what to do," she whispered. "We have to find Derodak and the rest of our Brothers. We don't have the time to ferret out a traitor. Besides, if they can hide from our Sensitives, then how do we even . . ."

"This is a distraction," Raed replied, giving her a squeeze. "Derodak wants to harry you to a standstill. You mustn't let him."

They both stared down at the disturbed earth, which signified yet another problem. Sorcha relaxed into his embrace for a moment, letting the calming sound of his heartbeat become hers.

Then with a jerk, she got to her feet. "You're right. Onward is the only direction we have."

As they turned and walked back the way they had come, she slipped her hand into his. "Just don't tell anyone, Raed. We can't afford to start doubting each other now."

"I know," he said. "But that doesn't mean I won't keep an eye out." He touched her shoulder lightly, almost a stroke. "Don't forget I have more than one set of eyes."

It was a strange world indeed where an allusion to the Rossin served as comfort—yet oddly enough it did make Sorcha feel better.

ELEVEN

A Traitor's Smell

As a Prince of the Empire, the heir apparent, Raed had been taught from an early age to take care of the people of Arkaym. The fact that his own father, the Unsung Pretender, chose to lock himself away on a distant island and behave as if they didn't exist did not factor into it. His beloved tutors and instructors had luckily been far more insightful than the man that had given him life.

Later on he'd been given his first command and then his first ship. Raed had immediately chosen to use them as a microcosm of the Empire itself and had lavished care and worry on both of them. However, in the last year their numbers had dwindled—some had even been killed right before his eyes.

Despite all of that, some echo from his childhood and his education still filled him with a feeling of responsibility for those around him. It was what made the devastation that was the Rossin so much harder to bear. Many times the Young Pretender had wished that he didn't care; that way he'd be insulated from the worst that the geistlord could do. However, as he got older he finally understood he was what he was. He'd learned to live with the curse and learned to run.

When Sorcha went back up the Great Hall to be about Order business, Raed found himself returning to the room he'd spent half his time in this last week. It might have seemed a strange place for a person of Imperial blood to work, but in this citadel of Deacons it was the only aid Raed could offer. He was certainly not going to sit idly by and become known only as Sorcha's lover.

The makeshift infirmary that the Brothers had created in the basement of the citadel was in fact one of the more pleasant spaces in the cursed building. Despite the fact that it was on the lowest level, it actually opened out onto a small inward-facing courtyard, which a sliver of sunlight punctuated for at least a few hours a day. Some very optimistic lay Brother had planted herbs in a container there, and the scent of lavender and mint filled Raed's nostrils as he neared the infirmary. It made him think of his mother's herb garden before he could stop himself. Scent triggered the memory of her down on her knees, in among the plants; nothing at all like the well-bred lady she was. In the garden she'd been the happiest, and thus it was the place he'd been too.

The Young Pretender walked swiftly past the flowering plants and into the infirmary itself. Compared to the scant Actives and Sensitives that Sorcha had been able to find, the number of lay Brothers now in the citadel was well over double what it had been when they left Vermillion.

The people had positively flocked to her, wherever they went. Though most of them had not the talent to become a Deacon, they had quickly offered to take on the cloak of a lay Brother.

Certainly, looking around the infirmary he could have almost imagined that they were in a regular Priory. Brothers in the gray of their profession bustled about, taking care of the sick and injured; though there were far more of the former than of the latter. Something about losing their runes and deprivations of the trail made Actives and

Sensitives more prone to illness, and many were coughing up their lungs in the infirmary.

It was yet another worry that Raed knew had kept Sorcha from a good night's sleep for months. The Young Pretender took up an apron that hung neatly on a row of pegs by the door and put it on without a thought to how it looked. Yesterday he had been learning how to make poultices from Brother Timeon, but he had no idea what was in store today.

"Raed Syndar Rossin," Madame Vashill said, appearing out of a back room, also wearing an apron, "are you back so soon?"

One of the preeminent tinkers of her time the old lady might be, but she was also rather deaf. Raed leaned in close to her. "Can't keep me away. I'd get bored if I stayed upstairs all the time."

She nodded and then thrust a mortar and pestle into his hands. "Brother Timeon said you'd be back, but I didn't believe him."

The young lay Brother appeared as if summoned by the mere mention of his name. His flyaway blond hair looked as though he had been running his hands through it for hours. He probably had. "Oh, Sir . . . Your Maj—" Then he closed his mouth with a snap.

The Deacons had struggled at first to find a proper form of address for him, as their connection with the current Emperor meant they had an aversion to using his family name, title or anything else that might suggest he was who he was.

Timeon cleared his throat and bowed his head slightly. "Captain, it is good to see you again. Are you ready for another lesson?"

"Yes, indeed," Raed replied with a crooked smile.

It was good to spend the rest of the late morning in the simple tasks of cutting and pounding herbs. Madame Vashill learned at his side and seemed glad to do it too. She talked wistfully about her shop back in Vermillion and the work she had been unable to bring with her. What she never discussed was her son and his treachery. Raed knew all about the faithlessness of family and how that hurt, so he did not pry.

However, the same could not be said of Madame Vashill; she wanted all the details of his life, which he felt rather uncomfortable yelling at her in the crowded infirmary.

"I suppose you have heard about the woman in the west claiming to be your sister," the old lady said, shooting him a look out from under her eyebrows. "They say she is causing quite a lot of problems for the Emperor."

The problematic question of the person claiming to be his sister, Fraine Rossin, was one he had not yet dealt with. Raed pounded the tansy under his pestle mercilessly. "The truth of it is, there is not much I can do about her. It's not as if I can stand up publically and denounce her for impersonating my dead kin."

The old woman flinched at that, and he knew she had to be thinking of her son. "Still," she said, grasping his hand briefly, "you did hear that your father had come out in support of her?"

It felt as though his stomach had dropped away and been replaced by a fiery pit. His father was not one for proclamations—but perhaps he thought now was a good time to slice himself off a piece of the Empire while it was in turmoil.

"No," he replied through gritted teeth, "I had not heard that. I am surprised though; my father has spent most of his life doing nothing at all. And he knows very well that woman is not his daughter. I sent word that Fraine had died in Vermillion." Even saying those words hurt. In the end, Raed had not been able to save his sister. In the end, she had still despised him for the Rossin killing their mother.

He smashed the pestle into the mortar so hard the hard stone rocked off its base, spilling the herbs onto the bench. Several lay Brothers started from their tasks at the sudden clatter, and Raed nearly swore at them too.

Madame Vashill's hand came down over one of his; wrinkled, warm and not very strong. It nevertheless stopped him for a moment. "You did not choose to come from your family," she said, her voice low, as if she were speaking to herself. "You cannot be held responsible for their actions, but you can walk your own path that might make up for what evil they have done." Their eyes locked and understanding filled Raed.

"Sorcha always said you were an old bat." The words popped out before he could stop them.

Madame Vashill laughed and filled her mortar with more herbs. "I was when I was in Vermillion. Stuck in a trade my father had taught me, and when he died, a husband I despised made me continue it. I find I like this life better. When you get to my age, you learn to appreciate these little moments." She gestured over her shoulder.

Raed turned and saw what she meant; around Raed and the old woman was a community of people, all thrown together by conflict, but still getting on, doing things, looking after one another. Lay Brothers caring for the sick and the injured while others came in bringing them food and supplies. It was—when examined closely—a well-oiled machine.

A machine. The Rossin's voice bubbled to the surface. The Beast was nearer today than any day before, a consequence of breaking loose and not having fed, Raed assumed. A sharp tang caught his attention, and it was not a natural substance that burned his nostrils.

Dropping his pestle back to the bench, Raed turned as if he were being pulled on a string. "Excuse me," he murmured to Madame Vashill, and he began to circle the room like a dog seeking a bone.

Lay Brothers shot looks at him—mostly annoyed that he was in their domain—but they kept out of his way. The Young Pretender ignored them all. Instead, he began to listen to the Beast inside him. The geistlord was, after all, more powerful than he and had sharper instincts. It stung him to admit that—but there it was.

A strange place to bring her leftovers. The Rossin growled, shifting deep inside Raed, who knew at once he was speaking of Sorcha. He felt the Beast was uncomfortable too. *A bastion of her greatest enemy.*

It was hard for Raed to talk to the creature without seeming like he had run mad. The lay Brothers were eagle-eyed for such things and might whip him off into a bed if he wasn't careful.

"The Circle had all these outposts originally," he hissed as he made a great show of peering at the shelf of ointments and lotions. "She hardly had a choice."

Then she shouldn't be surprised with what happened two nights ago. The Rossin sounded very self-satisfied.

Ignoring the Rossin's barbed observation, Raed nonetheless proceeded with a little more caution. The sense of unease he and the Rossin shared led him over to a rack of shelves on the far wall. At present they were stocked with the lay Brothers' meager supply of liniments and ointments. They barely took up a corner of this vast shelf.

Raed ran his eyes over the rack suspiciously up close and then stepped back to examine how it stood against the wall. His father's rickety palace had been full of hidden rooms and corridors, and he wondered if it was the same in the citadel.

He was certain that the smell and the sense of unease were coming from here. Raed shot a glance over his shoulder, to ascertain that no one was watching him, and then ran his hands over the wood.

The shelves were beautifully carved with all manner of forms that were obviously meant to be various geists; there was the pair of staring malevolent eyes that had to be a darkling, the spinning whirlwind of a vortex, and one he knew very well, the beautiful, deadly form of a Murashev in all her painful glory.

And everywhere on the bookshelf were the stars that were the symbol of the Ancient Native Order. Raed frowned. The fact that the lay Brothers were moving around, ignoring him and this bookcase meant that they had complete confidence in it. Sorcha and her Sensitives had carefully examined every surface of the citadel before they'd moved into it and made it their base.

They would not have missed any kind of cantrips or runes.

That is because they refuse to acknowledge the rest, the Rossin purred into his brain.

"Rest?" Raed whispered under his breath.

You saw the pitiful Sensitive become not so pitiful. You saw it and decided to ignore it. You never questioned what it meant. The Rossin dug up the memory that he had brushed aside; how Merrick had brought a whole street of people to their knees outside the Emperor's prison.

He rubbed the space between his eyebrows and muttered into his shoulder, "What does that have to do with this?"

You will see. Look a little deeper. Remember who you are. Even these Deacons do not come from a lineage as great as yours.

It was the first time he'd ever heard the Rossin call his family great—mostly the Beast just belittled them as traitors and weak. Raed let out a faint snort as he realized that most likely the Beast was talking about his own involvement with his ancestors. Literally, his blood was in the Rossin line.

Putting that aside, Raed leaned forward and examined the shelf. He recognized most of the geists, but one that stood out to him was his own sigil. It was the one that the *Dominion* had sailed under—the rampant Rossin. Without thinking overly on it, Raed reached out and traced the shape of it. Under his fingers it felt sharp. It was a curious thing to see here in the remains of an old citadel of the Order—and what's more, it looked freshly carved.

Raed was about to turn around and inquire if anyone else had noticed this, when the world went cloudy and gray. The hustle and bustle of the lay Brothers and their patients faded to incomplete shadows, while the sounds reached him as muted whispers.

Move! The Rossin was like a sharp burr under his skin,

but one he could not shake or rip off. Hesitantly, Raed took a step forward. He knew about the rune Voishem, but the fact that he was experiencing it firsthand—without an Active Deacon—was terrifying.

You have his Blood, but you do not know that you are not the only one.

He didn't need to ask whose blood. Merrick and Sorcha had told him all about Derodak and the fact that he was the first Emperor. The knowledge settled in his stomach like a stone.

The Rossin remained silent.

The sensation of moving through the wall was every bit as unpleasant as Sorcha had described it to him; every particle of his being screamed to turn and race back to the real world. The image of being trapped in stone by this abrupt appearance of Voishem was foremost in his mind.

However, the Young Pretender did not have time to panic because the stone wall behind the shelves was not thick at all. He pushed through and arrived on the other side. As he reappeared back into the normal physical world, he glanced back at the wall he had just passed through. Even though Raed knew it was true, he couldn't help running his hand over the rough rock.

Someone had made Voishem into the wall itself, perhaps to avoid detection from the Sensitives outside. Raed's jaw tightened as he realized there could only be one group capable of crafting such a thing—the very people who had let in chaos the night before.

Raed flicked his head around, realizing that a faint light was gleaming in the tunnel he now occupied. This, clearly, was how the saboteur had infiltrated the citadel.

That lying traitor, Derodak! The great cat sounded almost as angry as Sorcha had been. The Rossin's hatred of the Circle of Stars was embedded in more than just recent events. It was all because Derodak, their leader, had been both first Emperor and first Deacon, and it was he who the Rossin had made the deal with. Apparently being trapped in the Imperial bloodline was not what the geistlord had envisaged when he had struck the deal with the first Emperor. He still carried an intense hatred for Derodak and anything he had created.

Deep within his host the great cat uncurled and against the back of Raed's eyes everything was suddenly awash in golden light.

You cannot deal with a Deacon, the Rossin reasoned with the Young Pretender, *but I can.*

The Beast spoke the truth; sword and pistol would be very little use against a Deacon of the Circle of Stars. However, if he let the Rossin have his way, there would be nothing left of the traitor but blood.

Think of what they did last night. How many were killed?

Raed ground his teeth hard. He could go back and find the Deacons, but by that time the traitor could have disappeared. And besides, if he was honest with himself, he wanted to do something for Sorcha. She'd carried so many burdens for these last months, and he had felt at a complete loss to assist in any way. It would be good to be able to bring something to her for a change.

Now is your moment then.

In the tight confines of the tunnel, Raed hastily stripped off his clothes, and let the Beast take over. It was getting easier and easier to do that.

The human was correct. It was getting even easier by the moment. The Young Pretender's mind was weakening, which gave the geistlord hope that the Fensena was right. He would soon have his way. However, right now there was vengeance to be dealt out.

The Rossin shook his great mane and crouched down. The corridor was awash in the smell of human, and suddenly his lust for blood boiled up inside him again.

It was strange that the Young Pretender knew very little of his progenitor or the power he gained from both the

Rossin and Derodak. That was the way with humans; they learned so very little in their time. His host had apparently chosen to forget the power they had tasted beneath the streets of Vermillion when facing the Murashev.

The Rossin had not however. He would have that again.

His long, rough tongue ran fleetingly over his nose. For now, there was one Deacon to deal with. He might not be of the line of Emperors, but he still shared the great traitor's blood. The Beast could smell it on him.

Crouching low, the Rossin began to stalk forward. The light grew brighter quickly because the tunnel was not very long at all—nothing more than a bolt-hole really. It was merely someplace where the infiltrator could work his craft out of sight of the other Deacons.

On huge but well-padded paws, the Rossin stalked the human at the end of the corridor. His target was so engrossed in what he was doing that he didn't notice golden eyes watching him from the semidarkness. The great pard was intrigued and for a moment merely observed.

Derodak in his cleverness seemed to have outdone himself. The Rossin had little experience with machines; they had always been the preserve of the Ehtia, the Ancient race that had been the cause of the breach into the Otherside. The geistlord hunkered down and let his senses, natural and preternatural, run over the device the cloaked figure was hunched over.

It was gleaming brass, with many intricate parts that moved over its surface and reminded him of scuttling insects. He did recognize some things about it though; the flicker of three weirstones within its boxlike shape and also the writing carved on every surface. Cantrips were scored in the metal, and he knew immediately that they were not the usual kind, though he'd seen them before.

They were necromantic cantrips, which made perfect sense when the cloaked figure sliced at his own outstretched arm and dribbled blood into the vial at the end of the device.

The Rossin's tongue unconsciously licked over his nose once more. Blood was an Ancient source of power—especially the right blood. It could infuse a geist with strength, let the future reveal its secrets, or open up a little gap into the Otherside. That was why killing was always the last resort of the Deacons of the Order; the path for a geist was easiest when blood was spilled or death was summoned.

Yet now here was this man sacrificing his own blood to a machine; a machine that seemed to grow brighter as the blood trickled into it, and the weirstones began to vibrate. The sound they made was so high-pitched that the mere human could not have heard it, but to the Rossin it was like jabbing spikes into his brain.

Unable to contain himself, he rose to his feet with a roar that shook the rock, and for a moment drowned out the unholy noise the machine was making. The man hunched over it spun around and raised his hands instinctively in defense.

He had no marks of any of the runes on him, but he had a pistol primed and ready. His shot could hardly have gone wild in these tight confines, but its impact on the great pard's shoulder was as effective as a bee sting. The Rossin did not know the man's name or face, but he was so enraged by the machine and the pitiful attempt at self-defense that he sprang forward.

In the small space he could not leap as effectively as he would have wanted, but he still fell on the cloaked man like a crazed storm of teeth and claws. In the struggle, the machine was knocked over, breaking the glass vial that had funneled the blood and cracking the metal case. Two of the weirstones rolled free from their settings and bounced across the floor like a child's marbles.

The Rossin was tearing out the man's guts while he beat with decreasing vigor on the pard's head. Eventually he stopped altogether, and the Rossin gave him a final shake, as if he were a rat. With his jaws dripping in gore, the geist-lord glanced at the machine. It appeared broken, but there was a familiar smell in the air.

It was the fetid air of the Otherside. Something was coming.

Leaving the corpse where it had fallen, the Rossin turned about and bolted back the way they had come. The cantrip doorway accepted the blood on his jaws, just as it had accepted Raed's, and he flew through the stone as if it were paper and he a circus tiger.

Covered in gore, the Rossin landed in the infirmary. To say the lay Brothers were excited by his arrival would have been a grand understatement. They might be men of science and healing, but a blood soaked leonine form in their domain was quite a shock.

The Rossin took little note of the chaos that he caused. He did not hear the cries for help, nor see the lay Brothers rushing to remove their patients from his way. He had his senses locked on something else altogether, and his mind was racing over all the possibilities of what it could be. At best a simple rei, at worse the Murashev.

Gathering his hind legs beneath him, he raced from the infirmary, scattering lay Brothers, patients, and furniture in his wake. No one moved to stop him. He powered his way up the stairs of the citadel, still knocking humans aside. He didn't have the time to stop and see if they were Deacons or not. Finally, he threw the door to the battlements off its hinges and sprang into the open air. Behind he could hear thumps and cries of outrage, but they were nothing.

Farther down the battlements, another door was opened and Sorcha Faris emerged. She looked paler than usual, and there was the stink of the Betrayer on her. The Pattern-maker they called him; a geistlord who had thrown his lot in with the humans and taught them the runes to control his own kind. He would have given much to rid the world of that creature, but the Order needed him—at least for now.

Sorcha's blue eyes, shadowed and bloodshot as they were, met his. Shock would have been an appropriate response, but she had been sharing a bed with his host for months— she had to have guessed that this time would come.

This Deacon knew a great deal more about him than the Rossin liked. Raed had whispered much into her ear, and she had informed him that the geistlord could talk. They had always thought him a killing machine—which he had been in the early days of his emergence—and he liked it that way. He had not wished to reveal any more to them.

The Bond between them had thankfully grown a little thinner, but he still could not be sure if she was inside his head or not. He would have loved to be inside hers. Her gaze flickered over the fresh blood and flesh still staining his mouth and face.

Sorcha opened her mouth, but then she stopped, as her gaze drifted away from his to the far side of the battlements. Only a fool would have missed the stench. The Otherside was here.

The Rossin roared. Perhaps whatever was coming through would think again and return to the Otherside. Unless it was a geistlord. Unless it was the Maker of Ways.

Both Deacon and geistlord stood on the battlements, mere feet from each other, as the tear appeared over their heads. The Rossin glimpsed the Otherside; darkness, swirling clouds, and a plain of endless torture. However, it was not a geist that slipped through—at least none he recognized. Instead it was a fine mist with no particular shape or form. It issued from the Otherside quickly, just before the tear sealed itself closed.

It twisted on itself like a fine scarf thrown into the wind and then moved away down the valley, southward. Strangely, it had not even bothered with the two of them.

The Rossin watched it go and wondered just what the Circle of Stars could be up to. A soft growl escaped his chest. Absolutely no good would come of this. He disliked the smell of it.

He heard the Deacon approach him, and she did so with not a hitch in her step to show any fear or trepidation. He swiveled his attention to her.

She was standing before him, and her gaze was curiously

empty. This endgame was draining her. A mere human could not take all that she was being called on to do—even one as unusual as Sorcha Faris. The geistlord was abruptly worried that she might not survive—and he needed her. She still owed the Fensena a favor.

Her eyes darted over him, perhaps weighing him up in a similar manner. She took in the clumps of gore splattered all over his mane, jaws and throat. Then she reached out to the great cat. The Deacon had dared a similar gesture when they'd been inside the Wrayth hive, but then it had been accidental—this time she was very deliberate. He tensed, his back legs bunching.

Then Sorcha Faris' spread palm came down on the spot between his nose. It rested there for a moment, buried in the fur and destruction.

"You found the traitor," she whispered, and the Rossin flinched slightly. Everything was changing with the Otherside coming closer. How she had plucked thoughts and memories from inside his head, he did not know—but he most definitely knew he did not like this development.

She was very close to him, warm and full of blood. That was not the only thing though. His golden-slitted eyes locked with hers and for an instant he felt what she was feeling.

The Wrayth inside her, long quiescent, was stirring. The whispers of that hive-mind geistlord were a faint rattle in Sorcha's brain, like dry leaves shifting on one another. Along the Bond they scampered toward the Rossin.

The great cat let out an outraged snarl and jerked back away from the human's touch. Indeed, if he hadn't needed her alive, he might have lashed out right there and ripped her to shreds. The Wrayth had been looking for a weapon, some way to draw all geists together under their dominion for generations. It looked like they finally had what they wanted.

The Rossin was now not sure who he should be more worried about: Sorcha Faris or the Maker of Ways. Her blue eyes didn't leave him though.

"You hear them too." It was not a question, and even a geistlord could feel the sadness and desperation in her voice.

The Rossin growled, low and deep, while his ears flicked backward and forward. The voices had subsided, but he had the feeling that they were waiting a very short distance across the Bond.

"Give him back to me," Sorcha spoke to him. "Give me back Raed Syndar Rossin."

He growled. He snarled. He even raised one paw threateningly, but she never blinked or moved out of the way. She simply stood there on the battlements, her red hair twisting in the wind like a banner.

"I will have my way," the Rossin finally spoke, spitting out his rage. "When the Wrayth have torn you apart and made you their blade, I will still remain. I have always remained."

She looked unmoved by his predictions, only watching him out of eyes full of shadows. This Deacon was so nearly lost, and he still needed her. For now, he would let her pretend she was safe.

The Rossin wrapped his power around him and returned to the depths.

Raed uncurled himself, feeling the wind cut through to his very bones. Before he could shake off the effects of the change, a cloak had been swung around him. He looked up and saw Sorcha standing over him, fixing shut the buttons on the clothing she had given him.

He caught at her hands and looked up at her. "How many times have you given me your cloak?" The Young Pretender was trying to make a joke, but her brows drew together.

"Many times, my prince," she said, helping him to his feet, "but I think you have not noticed—this is not my cloak."

He looked down and noticed it was a simple gray one.

"I have given mine up," she said, "at least for now. I got this from downstairs for you though." Looking up at her, Raed understood this was something deeper than a fashion choice.

The Rossin had dived deep, but left him the memories of what the Beast had done—for once it was something that he was glad of. He did not regret the blood spilled. That treacherous Deacon had caused the deaths of many good people two nights earlier. He clasped Sorcha's hands and got to his feet.

Pulling her close seemed like the most natural and most important thing to do. A deep shiver ran through the Young Pretender's body. He loved her so much, and yet he also knew that a dark path lay ahead. For a second he just concentrated on the feeling of her arms around him, and his around hers. Then he kissed her. Not the urgent, demanding kiss they had shared that first time in Ulrich, but one that lingered. He was trying to remind her that she had him—if nothing else.

Sorcha squeezed her hands around his neck, and then slowly, reluctantly pulled back from him. She pressed her forehead against his, making just enough space between them for the wind to enter.

Finally, he spoke. "The Circle of Stars knows we've discovered them. Since I—I mean the Rossin—killed their informant here, we have to move before they do."

She sighed, but nodded. "I guess it had to come. I had hoped to stay here just a fraction longer, but you are right; we must move if we want to live."

And despite it all he did want to live; to be with her and to fight.

TWELVE

Returning on Wings

It felt very strange indeed to be at the head of a force of armed men walking with all speed back to the palace of her brother. The Grand Duchess Zofiya's hand rested on the pommel of her sword, and she dimly felt the weight of her new rifle bang against her back. These things had given her confidence in the past, but now they felt rather hollow.

She knew luck was with her—for the moment at least. The airship nearest the Priory had been the *Summer Hawk* with the redoubtable Captain Revele in command. It so easily could have been another—probably one who would have shot the Grand Duchess on sight.

What was even luckier was that they made Vermillion city in five days. Revele burned every weirstone she had in the airship's engines to make that happen. It was a risky course of action, because with no replacements the captain was entirely throwing the fate of herself, her crew and her ship in with that of the Grand Duchess.

Zofiya knew it and accepted that loyalty gratefully.

Even now, walking through the damaged streets of the capital, she was still not sure what she had done to warrant it though. She was a little afraid to ask. They passed over the Bridge of Whispers to the south of the ruined Mother Abbey of the Order. She did not want to see that broken edifice, nor did she want to draw too close to the new geists that surely must have been created there after the destruction Derodak and her brother had wrought.

The city was revealing her injuries gradually to Zofiya like a wounded animal. The smell was of death and smoke, but there was also a strange tang to the air—something sharp and hot. She had become reacquainted with it after months spent with the remains of the Order; geists left a peculiar scent behind them. It was impossible for a normal human to detect only one being but many could leave a residue like this.

Shooting a gaze out of the corner of her eye, she observed that she was not the only one affected. Revele's eyes were wide with shock, and Zofiya suddenly felt very old—though she could only be ten years older than the captain.

"You don't remember," the Grand Duchess found herself speaking more to give herself something to do as they moved through the streets. "You weren't in the corps when my brother and I arrived in Arkaym. The same smell hit us in the face as we landed for the first time."

"I was there," Petav ventured from behind her right shoulder, "and I hoped to never see it again." She had almost forgotten about the Deacon. It made her feel almost normal to have one with her.

Zofiya was lost in the memory for a moment. "When the Arch Abbot led the charge, he was at the head of the largest Conclave ever assembled by any Order. It was magnificent." Her throat strangely choked for a second. After a moment she went on. "And now that Order is broken, and we have only a small chance of recovering any of their number. With so few remaining, I do not know how any of us will survive this."

The Deacon at her back did not comment, only shifted

slightly and hugged the irreplaceable tube, which contained the Pattern of his Order. As a Sensitive he was probably already searching for his lost fellows—yet he did not share what he was finding. That was not a good sign.

Finally, Zofiya called a brief stop, drew Deacon Petav to one side and addressed him in an undertone. "Reverend Brother—a word if you will."

He followed her obediently.

"What may I do, Imperial Highness?" Petav asked, his gaze narrowing on her face.

Zofiya looked him up and down. "Now we are here, I must ask you to take on a dangerous mission."

The Deacon made no comment, so apparently the training of the Order held better than their Mother Abbey had.

The Grand Duchess still felt like it was a very fragile thing to hang her hopes on, but she understood it was all she had at this moment. "I want you to immediately head out and begin searching for your fellow Deacons. I need you to get them organized and their powers restored as quickly as possible." She spared a look over her shoulder at the smoke-wreathed city. "I cannot guarantee your safety— since I may well be arrested and executed when we reach the palace—but your task is the more important."

The Deacon tilted his head as if she had asked him to bring her a glass of water. "I understand Imperial Highness, the people must be protected at all costs. The Order has always put themselves in harm's way." With that he folded his cloak around him, gave her a faint bow and then strode away down the street. It did not take long for him to be swallowed by the smoke and debris.

Just the idea of not having the Deacons to protect the people from the undead made Zofiya very angry. Being very angry helped. It helped keep off the thoughts that what she was about to do was very, very wrong. She held it before her like a shield. Zofiya turned back to the task at hand and gestured the troops to follow her once more.

As they passed people on the street, she noticed that

they did one of two things: they either cheered faintly, or
fled back into their houses. Whatever protection moving
water had once offered the citizens of Vermillion was long
gone—as had been forewarned at that very first attack Sorcha had stymied right outside the palace. It felt like ages
had passed, but it had only been two years ago.

Still the palace had to be taken—and this time by
Zofiya—if she was to have any chance of setting herself up
as regent until her brother could be brought back to his
senses. Unconsciously, Zofiya lengthened her stride as they
began to climb the hill.

The vast sprawl of the red palace was coming into view,
and she found she was holding her breath, when Captain
Revele spoke, "Your Imperial Highness, look!"

The airship captain pointed to the west side of the battlements; it was as if a great fist had been brought down on
the wall. It lay in tumbled pieces.

The Grand Duchess' thoughts raced to the map Captain
Revele had shown her back on the *Summer Hawk*. A swathe
of cities down the center of the Empire had been struck
out; ugly gray crosses over their names. To the east, sweeping out from Vermillion was a mess of colored markers—
red, green and yellow. The colors she recognized as those
of the many Princes of Arkaym. Now looking down, she
could see the palace had not escaped damage either.

The captain leaned across to her. "It is as you said, your
brother has gone mad, turned on his own people. No
one will deny that you are the next legitimate ruler of
Arkaym now."

Zofiya gritted her teeth; her concerns suddenly going
from how she was going to take the palace, to if there
would be anyone left inside to put up a fight.

"Kal, what have you done?" she muttered softly to herself. It might have been Derodak that had turned her brother's mind, but if he had been stronger . . .

"Follow me," she snapped.

The cobbled square around the palace was very wide,

but there were plenty of homes and shops around the
perimeter. All looked sadly empty, but she had spotted a
public house with a low stone wall around a small garden.
It had fine lines of sight and an excellent view of the main
entrance to the palace. Zofiya and her motley collection of
airmen, marines and soldiers gathered there.

The Grand Duchess clenched her jaw and tried to imagine this was like any other tactical situation—and not the
place that had been her home in Delmaire for so long.
She had to quickly size up what was going on here and
decide the best course of action.

Despite the condition of the rest of the defenses, the gate
was manned. It should have made her fearful, but instead
the Grand Duchess actually found she was pleased. If they
could mount some kind of defense of the gate, then there
had to be someone in charge. Still, despite all that, she did
not want to simply lead her own group within rifle shot of
them—not without knowing how they would react.

Zofiya yanked down on the edge of her borrowed uniform
and gestured to the soldier standing nearby. "Spyglass!"

His cap was missing and the insignia on his shoulder
torn off; he looked like a war victim rather than the supply
sergeant of the Imperial docks. He gazed at her for a
moment, and she could actually observe the clouds roll
back from his eyes. He'd joined them at the airship port
along with a few others, but the majority of their troops
were marines from the *Summer Hawk*.

Recovering himself, he slapped a brass spyglass into her
open palm; she trained it on the soldiers manning the
defenses, running her eye over the squadron. Their uniforms were tidy enough looking, but through the glass she
could see that they were hollow eyed. Some part of her was
proud that the men she had trained had stayed at their
posts, despite what her brother was doing.

Many of the aristocrats had probably fled to the Imperial Palace when geists started appearing once again. However, she had to consider that the palace housed many

artifacts collected over its long history. She could only hope none of her brother's men knew how to use them.

"The cannons, Your Imperial Highness." Captain Revele drew Zofiya's attention away from the men, to where short, snub-nosed cannons had been pulled up on the battlements. "Should we not conceal ourselves?"

Zofiya drew her eyebrows together in a hawklike stare. This was a new addition to the battlements. In the early days of her brother's reign, there had been artillery on the walls, but Kal had ordered them rolled away once it was obvious the population welcomed him. What could have happened here to make him bring them back? Again, she had to remind herself that the last time she had seen her Imperial brother he had been frothing at the mouth like a rabid dog.

She took a deep breath before speaking, "Captain, these are my men. I trained them. They know me, and I want them to see me."

With the aide of the spyglass she determined there were no gunners nearby, so they were probably safe for the moment. Still, she did not want to show any hint of fear. If Zofiya were to pull off what some might call a coup, she would need the appearance of knowing what she was doing.

She could call in the remaining airships to the city and bombard the walls—but that would be what her brother in his current state would do. No, she had to not only take the palace and the city, she also had to secure the goodwill of the citizens. Without that, she would be simply another Pretender to the throne—no better than Raed Syndar Rossin.

Zofiya gestured to one of the aircorp sailors who had joined them from the *Summer Hawk*. "Do you know my bugle call?" She had noted earlier that he had the standard-issue instrument hanging from his belt. On airships and in other branches of the military different calls were played for various activities and events.

The young man's eyes widened at being addressed by the Grand Duchess of Arkaym; they were coincidentally the same deep brown as Merrick's. "Yes, Imperial Highness," he stammered out. "I know all the regulation calls."

Her gaze tightened on him. "Then I need you play it, as loud and clear as you can make it."

The young man swallowed hard and raised the trumpet to his lips. His first notes were halting, but after a few moments he grew a little more confident. Her call blasted out across the square and directly at the palace that not that long ago she had lived in.

The soldier kept shooting a look out of the corner of his eye, until she eventually gave the signal for him to cease. The final notes of the horn fluttered off and died among the rubble. It was not long until results were in evidence.

The first was a shot that ricocheted off the pavement directly in front of the Grand Duchess. She did not flinch, though most of those on each side of her ducked back behind a low stone wall that surrounded the shop.

"A fine shot," she commented to Revele who had jerked a little but remained upright. "At least one of the Imperial Guard snipers is alive." She trained the spyglass in the direction of the shot, and caught a glimpse of ginger hair and a long rifle barrel pulling back behind the battlements. Schling—that was the only sniper she knew that could make that shot and had hair that color.

If he was still alive, then there was still some order within the palace. He was a stickler for protocol and needed a leader he could believe in. If not, he would not act. The Grand Duchess' mind raced over the possibilities of who could have been left in charge of the palace. It had to be Mertle or Gunnine.

Quickly, Zofiya began stripping off her weapons, dumping both her saber and her pistols at Revele's feet. The captain looked at her in horror. "Your Imperial Highness, I hope you are not—"

"We have no other choice," Zofiya replied, retying her

belt around her waist. "I will not kill any Imperial Guards, but I must have the palace and the throne under my control. You have seen what my brother is doing . . . I can't let him . . ." She stopped, steeled herself and looked the airship captain in the eye. "In the end, I don't matter. None of us do, but the Empire and her people do. We must see them through, even if the Emperor no longer can."

The captain stared for a moment—perhaps weighing if she believed Zofiya or not—and then nodded shortly. "The 'Call to Talk' then?"

"If you please." The Grand Duchess adjusted her uniform as best she could, and then waited.

The bugler now had a thin line of sweat running down his face, though it was still chilly. Zofiya could imagine that he was terrified of being the soldier that sent the Imperial sister to her death. However, he raised his instrument to his lips and blew out the solemn notes of "Call to Talk."

Zofiya stepped around the stone wall, and walked toward the guard tower with her arms outspread. She kept her face impassive, but her heart was racing in her chest, and now she was sweating as much as the young soldier.

The line that the sniper had on her—she could feel it like it was a bee stinging her between the eyes. As Zofiya approached the wall, her steps sped up. The sound of the bugle went on, and it was a dull funerary drone to her footsteps. Finally, she looked up and saw there was another uniformed figure leaving from the walls of the palace, keeping the same pace she did.

Zofiya was excited to see that she did in fact recognize the narrow tall form of Gunnine approaching. The major had been the protector of the Imperial Palace for as long as Kaleva had been Emperor—and in fact before then. She had been the caretaker of the palace when it had been empty, making sure to keep looters and fortune hunters from it in those dark years between the disposal of the Rossin family and the arrival of Kaleva and Zofiya. Her scarred and Ancient face made the Grand Duchess feel a little more secure. Now if she could only convince the major of her good intentions toward Vermillion and the Empire itself.

They reached the middle ground between the edge of the square and the palace walls. Gunnine snapped off a salute that was as sharp as any by a solider half her age. Her keen gaze flickered over the Grand Duchess' uniform and presentation, and the Imperial sister was suddenly glad that she had taken some care with it. Such things mattered to the older soldier.

"Nice to see you are alive," Gunnine said, raising one of her eyebrows. "Your Imperial brother has however put a price on your head."

Zofiya had expected it, but nevertheless, her heart sank. "I am sorry to hear it, Major, but my purpose for coming here is not to give a bounty hunter an easy payday. It is to save the Empire."

The old soldier frowned and glanced once over her shoulder. "The palace still stands, the throne is still there, and so are we." She paused. "Your Imperial Highness should know, though, that we remain loyal to the Emperor."

Zofiya would not have expected any less. "I understand that, Major. However, I think you will agree that there are exceptional circumstances to be taken into account."

Gunnine tilted her head, the skin around her gray eyes crinkling as she narrowed her gaze on Zofiya. "It is not for a soldier to judge the merits of the leader that she serves. It is not our job to do so. If we had to stop and think about the value of every order that is given, we could not operate."

It was the usual argument given by any soldier, marine or airman in service, but Zofiya could not simply accept that. "I understand your position, truly I do, but I think that you will agree recent events have changed things for all of Arkaym." She shuffled her feet, looking down at them for a minute and considering how much to reveal she knew. Eventually she decided that she needed to release all the cannons. If Zofiya could not gain entry to the palace, and the trust of its final guardians, then there was no chance to be had.

"You have heard of the bombardments, I take it?" she went on. "The cities in the west have all suffered from them . . . and some of them not very far away."

"Indeed," Gunnine murmured, her voice low and stained with distress, "we are not that cut off that we would miss them."

"My brother, I am convinced, has become quite unhinged." Zofiya looked up, and was not ashamed to show the guardian of the palace her barely held-back tears. "It is not his fault. A lying worm insinuated himself into the Court and poured poison into his ear—it has driven him mad, and that is why I have come back."

"A dangerous tactic," the major commented. "I should really be arresting you as a traitor to the crown."

"I am no traitor," Zofiya spat back, "and you know it. You *know* me, and you know I have only the best interests of the people in mind. That is why you must give me control of the palace in the name of my brother."

Gunnine blinked, which was the only sign that she had heard and comprehended what the Grand Duchess said. "Imperial Highness, I fear you go too far . . ."

The time for politeness had long come and gone. Zofiya stepped forward, using her greater height to force the older woman to look up at her. "You have known me as long as my brother, Major Gunnine. I have served him and this Empire with every breath in my body—putting my own life at risk, time after time. You also know that my brother's attacks on the people of this Empire are completely contrary to the vows he gave when he took the throne."

The old solider swallowed and shot a look past Zofiya, sizing up her small band with a practiced eye.

The Grand Duchess, sensing a weakening, pressed on. "I have the support of the Imperial Air Fleet, because I am not seeking the throne for myself, but merely to hold it for my brother until he returns to his senses." She took a step back and spread her arms to take in the damage to the city. "For all your loyalty and goodwill, Major, you have not been able to keep the city safe—nor its people. Let me in, and I can help you do that."

Gunnine's jaw flexed, and her hands flexed into fists. This was a terrible choice for a soldier, but the major was more than just a simple soldier; she was trained to keep the safety and goodwill of the city of Vermillion in mind. She tucked her hands behind her back, and stared up at Zofiya. "Do I have your word on that, Imperial Highness? If the Emperor returns to claim his throne once more, you will give it up to him? Do you swear on the blood of your ancestors?"

Zofiya swallowed, and for an instant glanced up at the sky. It was clear blue and not marred by a single cloud. It was the kind of day that she and Kal had shared often in Delmaire. Things had seemed so simple then.

"I swear," she whispered, "on the blood of my ancestors, if my brother returns fully capable of taking up his throne and rule over Arkaym, then I will turn it over to him."

Gunnine held out her hand, browned and creased by duty, to Zofiya, and the Imperial sister gave hers in turn. "Then I will place the palace and the city in your care."

The Grand Duchess knew this was a terrible chance that the major was taking. If Kal returned as mad and dangerous as Derodak had left him, then he could well order the destruction of the entire military outpost and city of Vermillion.

Both of the women, young and old, had obviously decided to put such a possibility out of their minds. Gunnine turned and waved a signal to the sniper and the troops on the battlements. Zofiya did the same to her squadron, and they double-timed it over the square to stand at her side. Revele's face expressed all of their surprise, but she handed back the Grand Duchess' weapons without comment.

"Truly," she whispered to Zofiya, "Your Imperial Highness has the gift of the bard. Gunnine is not known for her flexibility."

"Captain Revele," the Grand Duchess snapped back, "you will have to work with the major, and you should know that she has only the best interests of the realm in mind."

The airship captain looked put in her place but nodded. "As you say, Imperial Majesty."

They followed Gunnine in through the gates, and Zofiya took note of the number of troops that remained. It was not many. She understood why the cannons had been dragged up to the wall. Gunnine had wanted to portray a façade of might—even if it were as thin as a piece of paper.

"Report, Major," the Grand Duchess snapped, even as a few Imperial Guard secured the postern gate behind them.

Gunnine drew herself erect. "I have two hundred and thirty-four Imperial Guards remaining at the palace. The Emperor took every other one of them aboard the Imperial Airships."

"Did he tell you when he would return?" Zofiya strode deeper into the palace, taking note of the general disarray and the lack of regular folk in the hallways.

"Unfortunately no." Gunnine matched her stride for stride, while Revele took up the rear. "We have done our best to secure the palace against all attacks, but without the Deacons of the Order, the geists have come back in full force. We are not equipped as they are however and we've been unable to keep them from infiltrating the palace." She looked away. "We have suffered many casualties."

"Major," Zofiya's voice was sharp, "I understand you have done the best with what you have. I cannot expect you to fight geists. That is something that we relied on the Deacons for." She slowed her pace slightly, now thinking of what Merrick had asked her. "How many of the Court are still in residence?"

"A few." The soldier's lips twisted. "Most of the Princes left immediately following the fall of the Mother Abbey, but many lesser aristocrats came to the palace for shelter, since they could not get passage on the Imperial Airships and other travel is so dangerous."

Zofiya nodded and bit her lip. "Tell me, do you know if Japhne del Torne and her son are still here?"

Gunnine's face darkened. "I was going to bring this to your attention anyway. I think you need to see the situation, Your Imperial Highness."

Captain Revele's mouth twitched, but the young woman managed to keep her tongue.

"Very well, Major," the Grand Duchess said with a slight smile, "but while I do, my captain here will ascertain the state of the palace defenses—a fresh eye on the situation may yield much."

It was an insult to the old guardian, but she took it with good graces. While Revele snapped off a salute, Zofiya followed Gunnine through the corridors. The Grand Duchess was surprised, but a little cheered that as they went doors popped open and the residents of the palace appeared. All looked worse for wear; eyes with dark circles under them and haunted gray expressions. However, when they saw her striding down the length of the palace, a spark of hope seemed to catch in them. A few times she had to stop and shake a hand or pat a back. Not one of them questioned what she was doing—and none of them mentioned her brother.

"Imperial Highness?" Gunnine had stopped at the stairs leading to one of the round towers. They were in the oldest part of the palace now—the section where in fact she had found the liar Hatipai—the section where she had made her greatest mistake. It made Zofiya very uncomfortable, even though they were on the second floor, and nowhere near the underground caves that had been the prison for the geistlord.

"Is this the place you wanted me to see?"

"He's been waiting for you." Gunnine gestured up the staircase. "He said you would come."

Zofiya raised one eyebrow, and her hand went instinctively to the hilt of her saber. However, the major was not talking about the Emperor, because Revele had confirmed he was with the fleet. She reminded herself of that a few times before she set foot on the first step. If Gunnine wanted her dead, she could have shot her right outside the palace.

So, the Grand Duchess climbed the stairs with determination and knocked on the door that was at the top.

It opened, and she was staring into the face of an old man. For a second she didn't recognize him, because he was most certainly not whom she had been expecting, but then her mind processed his creased face and piercing gray eyes. He was a Deacon—or had been. Her gaze flickered over the cloak he still wore, the same color as his eyes. A lay Brother then—a retired one. She had seen him at the Mother Abbey, but she could not put a name to his face.

"Empress," he said, and gestured her inside.

Zofiya's skin crawled at the title he used, and it felt as though ice-cold water had been poured down her back. Her reaction to that abrupt fear was just as suddenly anger. She shoved the door open and pushed her way past him. "You must be a madman if you think you can call me—"

Her words died in her throat. Japhne del Torne was standing by the window wrapped in a fine purple dress with a sturdy baby wriggling in her arms. Zofiya had never really noticed how much her lover looked like his mother. He had inherited her thick dark hair and the line of her jaw. They were a handsome family.

Japhne made a very proper curtsey, all while balancing her son on her hip. "You Imperial Highness, it is so very good to see you again."

In truth, Zofiya had imagined that she would have to tell Merrick the sad reality of his mother's and brother's deaths. After all, how could a woman and a baby survive in so much chaos, surrounded by geists and tumult? The Grand Duchess felt a soft smile curl her lips. Perhaps, if this could happen, then all was not lost.

It was not her usual way, but she rushed over and hugged

Japhne tight. The baby wailed while waving his tiny fists at her, and she observed how his eyes were now the same brown as his half-brother's. Zofiya kissed one of the hands wriggled in her direction and laughed. It felt like the first laugh in a very long time.

When Japhne had first come to the palace, she had been a stranger, but after so many nights sitting up with her, Zofiya dared to count her a friend. She wondered how to broach the subject of her love affair with her grown son . . .

"Joyful reunions will have to wait," the Deacon rumbled as he shut the door behind the Grand Duchess. "There is much to do and not much time left." She noted that he had a saber readily at hand by the bookcase, and despite his age, looked as though he could handle it. He too sketched a bow, but his was considerably less practiced and less deferential.

Zofiya tucked her arm around Japhne's waist, and narrowed her eyes on the man. "I have only just arrived here, and—"

"It does not matter how tired you may be, daughter of Delmaire, people of your Empire are dying as we speak."

That he dared interrupt her, Zofiya did not mind—she had her fair share of that from Sorcha in these last few months—but that he did not even introduce himself was quite unacceptable.

Japhne slipped free of her and stepped over to the old man. "Please don't mind Garil Reeceson, Imperial Highness. We have been many months here waiting for your return. In that time, confinement and a baby's fussing have robbed him of his manners."

The old man stared at the woman for a moment, but it was impossible to become angry with Japhne del Torne. His shoulders slumped as if all the energy suddenly drained out of him, and he allowed himself to be led to a nearby chair. Japhne put her young son on his lap, and a smile sprang to the old man's mouth. Yes indeed, his roommate did know how to handle him.

"Forgive me, Imperial Majesty," Reeceson said, slumping back in the chair as the baby pawed at his face. "Prescience is a difficult burden to bear, especially in these times."

Zofiya swallowed back his continued impertinent and far too presumptuous use of the wrong title; instead she tucked her hands behind her back and waited. Prescience was something many claimed to have—both geistlords and various Deacons. You could also apparently find it in wizened women at fairground attractions—Zofiya gave all of them the same amount of credence.

Behind her, a chill wind from the garden whipped in through the open window and ruffled her hair playfully. She was in no mood.

Reeceson glanced up, smiled and shook his head. "Yes, that is the look most folk give me, but the wild talents are not appreciated as they once were—before the Break."

"Tell me what you see, and I will be the judge of how much I appreciate it," she snapped back.

"The cataclysm is coming," the Deacon replied bluntly, dandling the baby on his knee as if he were merely speaking of the weather. "The Circle of Stars have found a way to weaken the barrier between our realm and the Otherside. Soon enough they mean to destroy it entirely."

Merrick had told her as much before she left, but she was surprised to hear it from this old Deacon. He had no markings, nor his Strop—so how could he possibly know such things?

She swallowed hard. "And what do you think I can do about that, old man? I am the sister to the Emperor, not your Sorcha Faris. I look after the Empire, Deacons look to the Otherside."

He flinched slightly. "I have a message to send to her, that is for certain, but it will be your task to become what you were always meant to be . . . the Empress."

"That will do!" Zofiya snarled. "I am no Empress. I am merely regent until my brother returns and takes his place again!"

Reeceson tilted his head, his eyes closing for an instant. "I can see you are not ready for my words yet, so perhaps I will offer something more certain." He handed the child back to Japhne and levered himself out of the chair.

He was older than he looked, the Grand Duchess guessed, just by the way he moved. When he gestured to the carpet in the middle of the stone floor, Zofiya helped him roll it back. A door in the floor was revealed with an elaborate series of carvings in it. They were not runes but cantrips.

Reeceson smiled to himself. "Do you know that cantrips are actually far older than the runes? They are examples of the earliest form of reaching for power in this realm. It was only with the arrival of the geists that they came into their own. Now we consider them lesser . . ."

"For a man determined to hurry up you really are taking your time about it." Zofiya could feel her patience waning with every breath. The palace at Vermillion had many secrets, and a protected entrance into the depths of the oldest tower in it was certainly a juicy one.

Reeceson laughed and leaned down. He touched his finger to where a lock form was etched on the red stone. He whispered a word to it, and a sharp crack echoed in the chamber.

"Impressive," Zofiya muttered despite her best intentions to remain unfazed.

The once-Deacon shrugged. "We have been in this tower for quite a while. I have had a great deal of time to work on it." A set of hinges had emerged from the stone, slicing upward along with a circle of metal that had to be a handle. Together he and the Grand Duchess pulled.

When finally the hatch gave up and swung open, it was without noise.

Reeceson gripped her arm. "What you are about to see you can never reveal to your brother. He would use it to cause even more destruction to the people of this Empire."

Zofiya had no idea what he was talking about, until she

spun on her heel and peered down into the pit they had opened. She needed no light to make out what was in there, because the weirstones were stacked high and gave off their own eerie glow.

"With these," Reeceson whispered at her shoulder, "you can start to save lives, and stop your brother taking any more."

Her mind raced over the possibilities. She thought of Deacon Petav and those he must be gathering. She would have to tread very carefully or fall into the dangerous trap her brother had. Too much power could be a heady thing, and she felt she was teetering on the very edge.

Still it was a start. Her luck was still holding. She turned and smiled uncertainly at Garil Reeceson. "I will do my very best."

THIRTEEN

Girding the Order

Sorcha felt as though she'd been drifting along a gentle forest creek that had suddenly and abruptly turned into a tumultuous white-water ride. In the beginning she'd been so busy fleeing the Circle of Stars that she hadn't thought of turning to fight. Now it felt as if she was being shoved that way. It was useless to dig in her toes now—better to dive in and go with it.

Merrick's visions, the thinning of the barrier, and now the revelation of the traitor told them all that they could no longer afford to hide. Before the deaths in the citadel, all of the Brothers had been merely scattered survivors hanging on to their scars and memories. The revelation of an infiltrator among them had given the Order something to rally around. Now they had a mission and that seemed to make all the difference.

Without Zofiya, Sorcha worried that her partner would never sleep again. While Sorcha felt stronger than ever, she could see the toll it was taking on Merrick. It was not just the lack of sleep—it was what he was doing.

Two days after the exposure of the reason the cantrips

had failed, he had locked himself away with his Conclave and the rune Mesa. That was all the time Sorcha had felt comfortable giving him. When his partner caught a rare sight of him, she observed his pale look and deep shadows lingering around his face. However, she did not chivvy him about it, knowing full well that all of them were under strain, and all close to breaking.

Sorcha and Raed busied themselves by stepping up the search for lost brethren. While Merrick and his Conclave worked in a small room off the Great Hall, Sorcha found herself on the battlements, freezing cold, with a contingent of Brothers skilled in the art of weirstone.

"How does it go?" Raed asked as he carried up the last of the weirstone supply. He'd committed himself to splitting his time acting as general dogsbody for the searchers, and working to get the infirmary and its patients ready to move. Given the choice Sorcha knew which task she would have preferred. The infirmary was at least warm and not lashed by the chill winds that howled regularly down the valley.

She gestured to the line of Brothers, sitting cross-legged, with their various cloaks wrapped around them, clutching weirstones. "As you can see, hard at work, but it is a strain to keep searching. I have to make sure the Brothers don't fall at their posts from exhaustion."

Raed cocked an eyebrow at her. "Not using the weirstones yourself?"

"Believe it or not, there is a skill to it," she shot back, knowing full well he'd heard her complain about the stones before. "Besides, I have another mission."

Leading him away from the line of concentrating Deacons, she took him around the corner where Deacon Troupe sat at her work. Raed's eyes took in the swirling weirstone at her lap and widened slightly. Troupe was too deep in study to notice either of them.

"What is she doing?" he asked Sorcha in a whisper.

"Tracking the portals," she replied. "I finally managed

to key a weirstone to their power, and Melisande and I have been watching where they are going. It should give us some warning if Derodak tries to make a portal to the citadel. Even though we've repaired the cantrip on the foundations, they could still appear in the valley somewhere."

"Good idea," Raed said, shooting her a sideways look. "I'm sorry, I heard Mournling passed away last night."

Sorcha looked down at her world-weary boots. "He was a good man and a good Presbyter. He tried to hold on to see us through our task, but perhaps it is better he didn't." Mournling had been in the Order longer than she could remember. His passing was rather like losing an aloof grandfather. "He lived long enough to pass the torch to Merrick as the strongest Sensitive, and he will feel his passing most strongly."

Raed opened his mouth to say something, but just at that moment Melisande jerked backward and dropped the weirstone onto her lap as if it were burning hot. She looked around and for a moment her eyes weren't focused on them. The Young Pretender offered her his hand, and clasping the weirstone she rose to her feet.

"How are things, Presbyter?" Sorcha said, wondering at the other woman's wide eyes.

Her pretty pink mouth twisted. "Nothing coming our way, but I detected a lot of activity to the west of Vermillion. I could feel people moving to and from there. I couldn't tell if any of them were Derodak or the Circle of Stars."

Sorcha's mind raced. Could it be that there was some kind of assault on Vermillion planned? Or perhaps it was Derodak's base? He must be working from someplace.

Just as that was all sinking in, the door to the inside of the citadel opened, and Merrick stepped through—though a more apt description might have been staggered. However, there was such a look of triumph on his face that Sorcha held back on admonishing him for driving himself too hard.

"I know the place!" Merrick said, his voice cracking as

he stood there trembling in the cold air. He pulled the thick fur cloak tighter about himself, and the Bond between he and Sorcha fairly sizzled with delight.

Along it, she saw a devastated wreck of a town. *Waikein,* Merrick's voice whispered. *One of the first places attacked by the Emperor, overrun with geists. That is where we should go.*

"You have a target?" Raed asked, glancing at the Deacons. Once again he was excluded from their sharing.

"Waikein," Merrick spoke for his benefit. "All the paths of the future start there, and it is where we must strike our first blow if we are to have any chance."

Melisande's white blonde hair was tossed by the wind as she whispered, "A town to the west of Vermillion. Within a short distance." She shared a questioning look with Sorcha as if wondering how much she was willing to bet on Merrick's sight.

The answer was of course, everything.

"I will send word then," Sorcha said, already turning toward the line of weirstone wielders. "All Deacons who can manage it will meet us in Waikein at the full moon. It's only a week away, but . . ." She paused and turned on Merrick. "How much do we know about this place?"

His smile was victorious. "I can tell you a great deal about Waikein. You see, I have a friend on the inside."

Her smile broadened. "That's why I love you, Merrick. You make friends wherever you go, and many places you have not."

FOURTEEN

A Waking Dream

The Emperor had come in his airships and nothing was the same. Eriloyn stood in the shadow of the building where he had once apprenticed a blacksmith. The roof, along with the blacksmith, had been destroyed the day of the attack. Coincidentally, that had also been the last time Eriloyn had seen food.

He'd always been a tall, strong boy, but since the destruction of Waikein he'd been whittled away to painful thinness. His stomach had ceased to bother him, but his brain had been enveloped in a fog that was just as dangerous. In this state, he knew he could easily make mistakes, but he was desperate. Only the day before he'd been drinking from a dirty puddle of water in the street, mad for some kind of moisture, and had nearly been run over by a carriage.

Some small instinct of self-preservation had jerked him back out of the way, and the dark shape had rattled and bounced past him. He'd only caught a glimpse of the crest on the door; the mayor of Waikein's pair of crows holding a massive yellow wedge of cheese. It seemed cruel with the current state of affairs.

Even now, Eriloyn's mouth watered at the recollection, his tongue circling around the cavity that felt as dry as wool. The image of his mother knitting by the fire drifted up from his memory, and along with it the recollection of the warm milk and honey bread she brought to him when he was ill. It was a cruel jab from his own treacherous brain, because it drove his stomach, which had been silent for so long, into a knot of wrenching hunger. That was why he had followed the carriage and now stood huddled in the gently falling rain, looking toward the town hall across the square. The mayor had to have food.

The boy glanced up and down the street, searching for any movement, human or otherwise. Nothing stirred—as it had not for days. The terror of the geists had sent many running for the hills, while others had taken their own lives or fallen into madness from it all. Those that remained kept themselves hidden—which was the sensible thing to do.

Except now that the wind changed, Eriloyn's senses brought another terrible blow. It was the smell of baking. It pierced the boy through and made any sensible thoughts impossible. The primitive needs of the body overrode anything else.

Wrapping his arms around his middle, the boy darted across the road, borne aloft by the tempting smell that promised food of unparalleled delight, scuttling from spot to spot like a rat that dared not be caught in the light. His first sanctuary was an overturned cart near the edge of the town square. It was not a food stall, but rather a toy display. Broken wooden dolls lay scattered about where citizens had trodden on them in their mad dash to escape some horror.

The second refuge he scampered to was the remains of a carriage. Once it must have been very grand, because the cerulean paint on the side was a sign of nobility—his mother had taught him that much. The boy dared a peek inside, and had the ravages of the geists not already beaten him into a wreck he would have screamed. The perfectly preserved head of a woman was turned to him from her seat within the carriage. Whatever geist had come upon these travelers had turned their flesh to the consistency of jerked meat. The shriveled eyeballs of the woman seemed to regard Eriloyn with disdain.

If it had been only a few weeks earlier, he would have lurched back screaming for his mother, but in the decimated and unrecognizable town that his home had become, he'd learned to control such instincts. His hands clutched the edge of the carriage, but he stayed where he was, pulling his gaze from the woman and toward the town hall. The smell of warm bread baking thrust itself into his nostrils and made all other thought impossible.

Abandoning all attempts at covert approach, Eriloyn leapt up and sprinted for the door of the Council building, the smell of bread luring him on, as if he were a hungry trout and there was a hook jammed in his snout. The huge oak doors of the building loomed over him but were slightly ajar. Eriloyn looked over his shoulder, but the street was silent.

The town had not been silent for a long time: screams, wails and people begging for their lives. He'd prayed for silence during those horrible days, and yet, now it was here, he was terrified by it. He turned and slipped into the building.

As a young boy, Eriloyn had gone with his father to pay his taxes in this building. It had seemed huge and beautiful back then: high oak beams, blazing fires, and people bustling around on important matters. Now only the oak beams remained. Chairs were overturned, books ripped from the shelves, and the remains of the fire from the great hearth scattered everywhere.

Eriloyn walked on haltingly, feeling his breath choking in his throat, and his heart beating in his ears. As terrified as he was, the hunger was greater.

He stumbled and staggered through the broken room, down hallways smeared with blood and other terrible things. Maybe it was his imagination, but he could hear voices; and not the voices he'd been used to in recent weeks. These were not screams; they were of genuine laughter . . . maybe even children like him.

Eriloyn's feet began to quicken all by themselves. He slipped and slid down the stairs of the hall into the lower floors. Now the smell of fresh baking was overwhelming, and already in his mind's eye he could see other orphans playing, both hands full of warm bread.

The tread of a stair broke under his foot, trapping his leg for a moment. With a sob Eriloyn tore it free. The pain of the wood ripping into his flesh was a distant thing to the hunger. He was almost passing out from both of these by the time he made it down to where the kitchens of the town hall were. It had once produced bread for the poor and the needy, now surely it was doing it again.

For a moment the boy was confused. He stood there in the wreck of the kitchen, blood pouring down his leg, stomach cramped with hunger, and looked at the broken crockery lying on the floor. Everything was turned over and rotten. The hearth itself was snapped in two, the great stone smashed as if by an iron fist.

"Quite the sight isn't it," a voice hissed behind him.

Eriloyn spun about, but he couldn't see anyone there— only the shadows in doorways he was too terrified to enter. His skin was crawling, and the darkness was now creeping into the edges of his vision. Fingers were creeping over his skin, and he couldn't find the strength to rip himself away from them. Terror that he had been fighting off for weeks flooded over him, like an ice-cold tide that he could no longer hold back.

"Give in. Give up. It's all right to surrender," the voice at his back whispered into his ear. "You're tired. Rest for a while."

It made complete sense to do so. He'd been running and terrified for a very long time, so he listened to the voice and fell into its cold embrace.

For the longest time that was all there was, but Eriloyn could not hide in unknowingness for long. Slowly, his eyelids fluttered open. He hurt everywhere, but his leg ached worst of all. Suddenly the need for food was not as important as he had thought it was. Survival now loomed large.

All of this flashed through the boy's mind even before he took in his surroundings. He'd made a promise to his dad to survive, and he had to keep that promise. So slowly he levered himself upright, feeling the grind of hard metal and straw under his palms. He looked straight into the eyes of a girl. She couldn't have been any older than he was, and she had long matted dark hair, blue eyes and a massive bruise that covered half of her face. Her gaze, when it locked with his, was empty, though, as if the light had been snuffed out behind them.

Eriloyn would have smiled in normal circumstances, but here and now he merely nodded. Looking down, something caught his eye, a gleam of metal. Shackles. He and the girl were shackled together by the ankles. Tilting his head, the boy saw that they were not alone; other children, silent and huddled, ran in a line behind the girl. They were in the basement, and there was no longer any smell of bread in the air; there was only the odor of frightened children.

Eriloyn pushed his hair out of his eyes and tugged on the chain. It was pointless, he knew that, but he had to try.

"Don't bother," the girl whispered to him, her voice hoarse. "He'll be here soon enough. You're the last they needed."

A little voice in Eriloyn's head was screaming in horror, but somehow he stuffed it down with a hard swallow. He turned his head and saw that night had come on while he'd been wrapped in unconsciousness. The night was the worst. Something about the darkness gave the geists bravery.

While that thought possessed him, a very real man made an appearance. Unlike those men left in Waikein, he appeared well fed, well cared for, and with not an ounce of pity for the children. They began to sob, but quietly, as the man unhitched the chain from the wall and began to lead them away.

Eriloyn however would not go quietly—not with his father's last words ringing in his head. *Promise me . . . survive.*

As the man wordlessly swung away to tug the captors upstairs, the boy dashed forward, throwing himself at the stocky man's legs. He was young, small and poorly fed, so the adult swung at him, knocking him down as if he were nothing more than a fly. The tunnel seemed to spin, but Eriloyn felt the nameless girl's hands on his shoulders, guiding and holding him up.

"It'll be over soon," she whispered. "Don't worry." Her damp hand clutched onto his. It seemed to be her mantra.

Eriloyn tried to clear his head, struggling to hold himself up. The town hall flashed past him in a series of blurry images. The chain between the children dragged them onward.

Now they were outside. Night was about the city, but there were lights. By the time Eriloyn came back to himself, their captor had reattached their chain to one on the side of the town hall.

They were not alone. Eriloyn swallowed hard. He had not seen so many citizens of Waikein since before the geists came, and now they were all here. It should have gladdened his heart that so many of his living fellows were in one place, instead it only filled him with an abiding dread.

Once he pulled his gaze away from the assembly, it traveled naturally to the man that stood before them. He knew him, though he had seldom seen him this close. It was the mayor of Waikein. A tall man, still well dressed despite the situation, his red and silver hair immaculately styled as if barbers had somehow survived the chaos. The mayor stood on a raised platform, and from where he stood Eriloyn could see that he was smiling. However, it was not a smile that would soothe any fears. When he pulled back his lips, he revealed rows of sharp, pointed teeth—as if they had been filed to a predatory gleam.

The girl holding his hand squeezed it once more, her

empty eyes following the mayor as he waved at the crowd. Eriloyn tugged at the chain, but it was tight and strong.

"Survivors of Waikein"—the mayor's voice carried over the heads of the citizens and echoed off the hollow buildings that surrounded the square—"I am here to offer you salvation, and a way to keep yourselves alive."

Eriloyn tilted his head; there was something strange about the air around the man's head. It was bending slightly, and there was an odd smell coming off him, something sharp that hurt his nostrils.

"Do you smell that?" he whispered to the nameless girl, but she shook her head.

The odor overwhelmed him, and the boy gagged on it, not understanding how she could be so lost to the world as to not be affected by it.

No one else in the town square seemed able to smell it either, because they were actually drawing closer to the mayor as he spoke. Could they not see his teeth?

"We have to live with the geists now." His voice was soothing and sounded reasonable. "The Order is all gone, and we must make our own way. All the undead want is small sacrifices, little offerings, and they will let us live in peace."

Again Eriloyn knew that only a few weeks earlier would have made a world of difference; everyone knew that you didn't make deals with geists. They always turned on the humans eventually—it was written in every legend and myth ever spoken to a child anywhere. Yet, these were people who had seen their loved ones ripped from them, who had lived in abject fear for weeks, and so were willing to reach out for any tiny sliver of hope.

When the mayor turned to look at the line of children ranked behind him, Eriloyn was not surprised to see that he had a long knife in his hands, and a weirstone gleaming in his fist. Blood magic and the gleaming orbs went together like snow and winter.

"Small sacrifices, that will take but an instant," the mayor said. "If anyone objects, speak up now."

He wanted their complicity—he needed it—Eriloyn realized. Gleaming in the mayor's jovial eye was something undead, and it required something from the people assembled. The boy's stomach twisted, and he bent over for a moment; fearful that he was going to throw up whatever little remained in his stomach. When he finally regained control, he stood up tall, and looked not at the mayor who was approaching, but at the girl who still held his hand.

"What is your name?" He whispered the question to her, suddenly consumed by the need to hear it, even as he was aware of death's approach.

Deep down, there was a small spark in her. She hesitated only a moment. "Aloisa," she replied, a tiny smile on her mouth.

The mayor's shadow now blocked out the tiny lights that the people held—the people who were silently watching events unfold. No sound or protestations came from them.

Then, just as the mayor was coming into striking distance, a voice did rise from among the crowd. It was none that was familiar to Eriloyn, though he did recognize that it was a woman's voice. Somehow it carried and caused even the mayor to pause. "You will want to be moving slowly, and carefully away from those children."

From his vantage, the boy saw the thing behind the eyes of the man flicker. Was it possible it was recognition, or could it be panic? Everyone in the crowd strained this way and that to find who had spoken.

The children in the chained line shifted. Little sighs and sobs escaped them. Eriloyn shook his head, blinking; he could swear that the air around the crowd was moving to a strange pinkish hue. The boy wondered if fear was driving him mad.

These worrying thoughts were set aside however when she stepped out of the crowd. The boy found himself stumbling toward her but was caught up short by his restraints.

It was hard for him to see any details of this woman. All he could make out was that she was not particularly tall and was wearing a plain black cloak. It was what his wavering eyes saw, though, that brought him almost to his knees. Whatever madness it was that had wrapped him up, he saw other things about her; silver threads swarmed around her, and they twisted themselves into patterns his eye could not follow.

Yet, unlike the smells and visions he saw around the mayor, these did not fill him with fear. Instead, something like hope welled up in his chest.

The mayor took a step back—so perhaps he did see what Eriloyn did. If that was true, he was a great deal less heartened by it. Still the darkness within him drove him on.

"You are but one," he hissed.

"You do not see so well, geist," the woman said calmly. "I am not alone. I am one of many, and many more to come. We will be the Enlightened who stand against you. I am merely the Harbinger of those to come."

Her words struck Eriloyn hard, and he looked around at those that filled the town square. They knew it too. They all did. This moment was important.

"Harbinger?" The mayor's face turned in on itself, revealing the undead thing beneath. A maw of teeth and coiled hatred wiped away any illusion of humanity. "I see what you are; a weapon left lying to rust. They should never have tried to make such an—"

"An abomination?" The woman unhooked the clasp of her cloak and let it slide from her shoulders to the ground. Beneath she wore a simple pair of trousers, a thin sleeveless linen shirt and a wide leather belt. The light of the torches flared brighter, and they all saw what was carved on her arms. She laughed at the geist who wore the mayor like an overlarge robe. "A weapon may be created for one purpose, but that doesn't mean it can't be reforged into another."

Effortlessly, she raised both her hands and they flared to light; one was clenched on a shimmering globe of green energy, while the other ran with scarlet flames that danced up and down her outstretched hand.

Eriloyn had not seen the Runes of Dominion for a long

time—not since he was still a tiny child, clinging to his mother's skirts—but they were his first real memory. Something had happened in his father's barn, and Deacons had been fetched. He could not recall the faces of those who had come, but the recollection of the silvery blue fire they had summoned was as clear as the day he'd seen it.

Now, here was a woman standing in his ruined city, facing the undead calmly, while the runes burned on her actual skin. This moment was not one he would ever forget either.

His gaze traveled over the crowd, and now he could pick out others among the citizens; all wore simple black cloaks, and stood completely still in the sea of confusion. They were like rocks dropped into a churning stream and that made Eriloyn smile—though he did not understand why this woman called herself a Harbinger and not a Deacon.

The mayor moved toward her and even his footsteps were no longer human. His gait was twisted and awkward as he neared her. The citizens of the city shrank back from him, so that the cloaked figures in their midst were revealed, as when the river dried up, making plain the rocks within it.

The mayor's head swung from side to side, and an ugly laugh welled up in him. "Is that all you bring, *Harbinger*?" His voice cut sharply on the title she'd given herself. "This is our city now, and even if you should drive me from this world, you will never triumph over the many to come."

Eriloyn's heart began to race and that dreaded fear trickled over his skin once more. Even as other cloaked figures appeared out of the crowd and ran to free the line of chained children, he strained his head left and right to see what would happen next. His eyes were fixed as completely to the Harbinger as any rivet his father had ever secured.

"So many?" The woman said with a note of sadness in her voice. She shook her head. "Yes, there had been so many of your kind unleashed here; so many folk who have been twisted by the undead and made into geists themselves. I can see them, feel them. More than that." She raised her hands, still burning with red fire, and now Eriloyn gasped.

Even as kindly hands undid the restraints on his injured ankle, he was entranced by what he saw. From all over the city they came; chill winds, spinning shapes of the undead, and lost souls still crying for their lives. They gathered in the town square, just as the rest of the citizens had, but bound together. In short order the air above the Harbinger looked like a shimmering spiderweb of geists. They darted about, and while Eriloyn was sure the survivors of Waikein could not see what he was seeing—else they would have fled in horror—they did appear to feel the presence. Some people shivered and clasped their coats and cloaks tighter, while an odd few bent over double, afflicted by nausea at the undeads' presence.

The mayor made a choking noise, dropped to his knees, and then to his elbows. Some kind of war seemed to be raging inside him, because he crawled forward, howling, and twisting—it was as if he were being dragged like a mad dog by some unseen leash.

The Harbinger did not take any notice of any of these things. She was the calm center of this mad storm. However, when she spoke, her voice was heard all over the square. "I see you all—every *one* of you. I draw you together. You belong to me."

Eriloyn knew immediately she was talking about the strange, undead shapes wheeling above the humans. However, at the same time, the cloaked figures also came together behind the Harbinger and shed their cloaks.

All of them wore their runes directly on their skin as she did. As one their hands clenched around the flames and claimed the eerie green glow. The light was so bright it eclipsed any meager lanterns that the citizens of Waikein had with them.

The mayor howled, and his cry was echoed by the wind that whipped around the town square. The Enlightened—since that was what she had called them—raised their hands wreathed in the green, and it flowed out of them. It encompassed everything from air to cobbles.

Eriloyn felt it wash over him and pass by. The mayor however was not left alone. To the boy's ears it sounded as though something was being ripped free of him. The Enlightened seemed to straighten taller and, from his point of view, grow stronger as the light whipped around the square, turning back to them.

The mayor sagged, almost falling to the cobblestones that he was crawling on. Briefly, he managed to lever himself upright. His mouth worked on words that he would never say, because the other arm of the Harbinger came down, and this time the flame did not stay on her own flesh.

Eriloyn did not look away as the mayor and the undead creature within him was consumed by flame. He made sure to take in the sound of flesh and clothing burning and inhaled the odor. He wanted to remember this.

Around the Harbinger, the other Enlightened raised their hands into the air, and fire arched up into the sky. Some of the citizens looked away in fear, but many—if not most—watched the display of power above them.

It kindled hope in Eriloyn and a sort of grim determination that survivors all shared. It shall not happen here again.

Aloisa stood at his side, and her eyes were haunted but no longer empty. Long streaks of tears flowed from them, leaving paths in the dirt on her face.

As the Enlightened fanned out through the crowd, moving to help the injured, and comfort the grief stricken, Eriloyn found himself staring at a figure just behind the Harbinger herself.

The man's eyes were locked with the boy's, in a kind of shock. He was a tall man with dark curly hair and wide brown eyes. Something hung around his shoulders, a stain of power in the ether that might not have been as noticeable as around the Harbinger, but it still drew him.

In the ether? The boy shook his head. *What did that mean?*

The Harbinger was speaking to the crowd, but it was no longer she that was important—it was the man and those eyes that saw too much.

Then the world was spinning, and Eriloyn was wrenched away.

Merrick took a staggering step back and found he was staring at the boy with the haunted eyes; the one that he'd ridden in the head of. The runes that he had summoned had drawn him here, to this boy at the very edge of death. He'd been locked in the boy's head for a week, so that they all might be drawn to the correct place and time. The rune Sielu had shown him this for a reason, brought him here for this moment. It was indeed the perfect place and time for Sorcha to reveal her plan.

Eriloyn had provided the information on the city the Deacons needed.

Such an experience was one he would never forget. Merrick had never before considered how the geists would look to everyday folk, or indeed how the Order would. Now he knew. They were hope and salvation.

He looked at his partner's back, tall and straight before him, and knew she had done what she set out to. She was now the head of the Order that she'd given a new name: the Enlightened. The city of Waikein would be remembered for this moment—if any of them survived the coming destruction that was.

The future and his vision had melded and caught up with each other. He wondered what else lay ahead and what the Wrayth power Sorcha had just unleashed could mean. Even he could not see that. They could only go forward as bravely as the boy had.

FIFTEEN

Uncertain Partners

The people of the city were acting as if the fire that had cleansed the geists had also been lit beneath them. They surged into the town hall and set about reclaiming it with vigor that even the lay Brothers could not possibly contain. They grabbed up buckets and mops, began tossing ruined furniture into the streets, and pulled down the curtains to let light stream into the building.

As Merrick stood in the receiving hall with Sorcha at his side, he felt like a rock in the middle of a maelstrom of released human activity. Brooms were being shoved around with tremendous vigor, blood scrubbed from walls, and everyone was darting up to the newly announced Harbinger for a piece of advice or commentary.

Perhaps his own folded arms prevented them from involving him in this frenzy. Sorcha seemed calm, and even smiled when a lay Brother told her excitedly that another twenty former members of the Eye and the Fist had been found alive in the city. Apparently they would have their runes recarved as soon as the implements could be readied.

Sorcha turned and looked him in the eye with a grin.

"See, we are already stronger, and once word spreads of what we have done here—"

Merrick could not let her get any further. Grabbing her arm unceremoniously, he dragged her into a side room and slammed the door shut behind them—thus forestalling at least a dozen more inquiries.

"What are you doing?" He felt along the Bond, but her thoughts and moods were slippery like eels in the darkest part of the river, and he could not get ahold of them. That scared him more than anything else. Her blue eyes were too bright, her smile too fixed for him to like it.

As Sorcha took in his stormy expression, the façade and the smile faded. She had finally taken a cloak, declaring that all could choose which color they would rather wear. Merrick found he preferred the thick fur one Raed had given him. Sorcha found a black one in the abandoned buildings of Waikein. Many of their colleagues had simply ripped the colors from their old cloaks and wore the reverse side of brown or black. It had been her first action as leader of the Enlightened, but he could hardly tell if it was a good one.

The collar of the dark cloak that Sorcha had taken up obscured her eyes from him as she turned away. Merrick could only see her in profile. "I am protecting the people of Arkaym as I was taught to since childhood—just like we were all taught in the Order."

Merrick shook his head slowly. "But not *as* we were taught. Sorcha, you were inside the geists. You were almost part of them rather than destroying them." He paused, took a deep breath and said the words that had been haunting him since he'd seen the display in the town square. "The rest did not see, but I felt it; you were like one of *them*."

"But I did destroy them." Sorcha's reply was so distant that he had to strain his ears to catch it. "You were right— this was the place we needed to be."

Another chill went up his spine. The curious double nature of the event, the way it had been twisted by the runes Masa and Sielu, set his teeth on edge. He disliked everything about it, and yet his partner seemed immune to his concerns.

Sorcha should have been able to sense how much time he had lost and the walking dream he'd been tangled in. Obviously, she had not.

The Bond that had carried them through so much was unraveling and could no longer be trusted. Merrick felt afloat in a dark sea, and he did the only thing he could: he reached out and took Sorcha's hand. Maybe the physical connection would reignite the Bond.

Her fingers were chill, and she looked up at him with the kind of expression he had seen many times on the faces of those who had escaped possession by a geist: shock and distance. Sorcha was coming back to the world, but she was not the Deacon she had been. When she glanced down at his hand holding hers, it was with the detachment of someone who did not fully comprehend her own body.

Merrick squeezed her fingers, as if by that he could pull her back. "Yes, you destroyed them. Yes, you made the population believe—but at what cost to yourself?"

Sorcha swallowed, and her blue eyes, for the first time since her demonstration of power, met his. "They are inside me, Merrick. The Wrayth made me, and I was foolish to think that they would let me go so easily." Her voice making this confession was that of a frightened child, and the flood of her memory ran along the Bond. For a moment he was swept away by it.

Sorcha stood at the gates to the Mother Abbey in Delmaire, the warmth of the summer sun on her back. Her hands were pressed against the ironbound wood, and they were the chubby, soft ones of a child who could be no more than two. To her eyes the cantrips and runes carved there were complex scribblings that meant nothing. However, there was someone whispering to her; a voice, faint and far off. The child could discern no words, but there was an infinite kindness to the voice that promised cuddles and love.

"Sorcha!" Another voice, this one much closer and

louder, caught the girl's attention. She looked up into a beautiful face with a smile on it; a familiar face. The Presbyter of the Young, Pareth, with deep gray eyes, and a fine spider's web of lines around her eyes and lips. She always smiled and always hugged Sorcha when not so many of her fellow Deacons did.

Sorcha didn't see it as a child, but Merrick discerned concern in those eyes. Even secondhand, he noticed how her gaze lifted quickly left and right, trying to see if anyone was observing them. "Let's go back to the garden, sweetling."

Her hand on the girl's shoulder guided her around, away from the door that had so raptly held her attention. The voices faded somewhat when in the presence of the Presbyter, and Sorcha lost interest in them, instead staring up at Pareth in adoration. She had a love in her that she needed to expend on a mother.

"Mother," Pareth said, squeezing Sorcha's little hand just a fraction. "Yes, your mother." She paused and looked down at the girl at her side. "She was a good friend to me, your mother. We grew up in Jhou together, though I don't suppose you can understand that yet." Her frown made Sorcha fear that all was not well.

Pareth bent and kissed her face. "I risked much to get you into the Order, but you are worth it, sweetling." Merrick understood then, how Sorcha had passed the deep search the Order had done into her past—the one that should have rooted out any taint of geist. As Presbyter of the Young, Pareth must have conducted such an investigation and distracted others from looking deeply.

Sorcha's mouth puckered up, and she would have cried if Pareth had not swept her up hastily into her arms. The Presbyter bounced Sorcha high into the air, making her cry transform into a giggle of delight. The blue sky above seemed full of infinite possibilities—and all of them happy ones.

Pareth held the girl aloft there for a moment in her outstretched arms. Sorcha felt like she was flying, and she stared down at the Presbyter, full of love and joy.

"You are so like her," Pareth whispered to her friend's daughter. "Please hold on to that for as long as you can. By all the small gods, may none of your father ever touch you . . ."

With a jerk and a gasp, Merrick pulled free of the Bond. Sorcha's blue eyes still bored into his.

"You see," she murmured to her partner, "I could not remember anything from my childhood when you met me, but since I went into the Wrayth hive, everything has been coming back. They shook something free inside of me, and worse, I think they want me to know what I am. They want me to fear it."

If he had not been her partner, Merrick would have attempted a lie—it would have been the kindest thing. He swallowed hard. "Yet, Sorcha, you would never be able to do what you just did without your Wrayth heritage."

He observed her flinch and understood. The concept that a Deacon would have anything to do with being geist was an anathema—they had both been taught that. In the Order of the Eye and the Fist, such a Deacon would have been at best locked away in the infirmary, but it was far more likely they would have been given a swift death.

Merrick locked his hand around her elbow, holding her face-to-face with him when she might have turned away. "You are still yourself, and you can use what they have given you."

She shook her head. "You don't understand, dear Merrick." Sorcha had never called him such a thing before, and it terrified him to hear her use it in this bleak moment. "I've been listening to their voices, and I understand now. The Wrayth were looking for a weapon—one that would link all geists together and then pull them into the mind of the hive. They realized that the powers that the Deacons control could be the bridge—that is why they started their damn breeding program."

Now along the Bond Merrick saw the many despairing faces of the female Deacons who the Wrayth had taken and forced to be brood mares for their experiment. He was glad not to have seen that firsthand, but tasting Sorcha's horror now gave the memory a particular sting.

"Never fear," Sorcha whispered, placing her hand on his shoulder, "I have you as my anchor. We have done great things before, and I trust you."

The words struck him so deeply that for a moment he couldn't reply. Looking deeply into Sorcha's eyes, he realized that she meant what she said; she had wrapped her sense of self tightly around him. His partner was relying on him to keep her from slipping completely into whatever geist heritage the Wrayth had given her.

Merrick looked back at her and replied as calmly as he could. "What if I am not enough, Sorcha? I'm not as strong as you think I am . . . not like the Wrayth is. It is Ancient, whereas I am . . ."

Her fingers tightened on his shoulder, her gaze going glassy and distant, but when it returned to him, she shook her head. "You are the Sensitive who traveled to the Otherside, who stood before the leader of the Circle of Stars and retrieved your mother from his grip. You have never really acknowledged your own strength, Merrick."

He swallowed on that. All that she said was true enough—he was proud of those accomplishments in his own way—but he was not sure any of that had any bearing on this situation. Still, he knew this conversation was best abandoned—at least for now. They had a city to reclaim and not long to do it.

"Very well," Merrick said, turning toward the door and breaking the gaze with his partner, "I will send word to Raed it is safe to enter the city." They had not thought it a good idea to bring the Young Pretender into a city occupied with geists. Even if the Rossin had been very quiet in the last few days, they could not risk him running riot among the traumatized survivors.

Sorcha sunk into a chair, as if the strength had suddenly gone out of all her limbs. "Once you have done that, come back here. I have an idea for our next move."

Merrick did not dare ask her further questions. His partner had been working without sleep for two days, and considering her recent performance, he just wanted her to get an hour's rest.

The mold was cast, and they were well on the path now. Still, despite her exhaustion, Merrick had one final thing to ask. He had not forgotten the visceral fear of the lad whose head he had ridden in.

"Eriloyn," he said firmly, "the boy who brought us to this place; he had the gift of a Sensitive in him. I will send Melisande to find him. Many of the survivors have the latent gifts, which make them excellent candidates for us to swell the ranks of our Deacons."

She nodded. "I was thinking the very same thing."

"Then I will get those who can test moving among them." Merrick's hand was on the door handle, when he turned back. "The Enlightened, Sorcha? The Harbinger? Where did they come from?" She had mentioned nothing of her decisions to rename the Order to him—or to take up a new title.

She stood a little straighter, and against the rising light of dawn coming in through the window her hair seemed as red as fire. "We must be more than the Order, Merrick. Better. We have to share what we know, because ignorance has not helped one citizen of the Empire. Things will be different if we survive all this."

She did not explain her choice of Harbinger however, and she didn't need to; the intent was written on her face. As Merrick set off about his tasks, the understanding settled in his belly like a heavy stone. Sorcha was indeed what she had named herself: the herald of things to come.

The Orders throughout history had many schisms and changes, and he just had to hope that Sorcha knew what she was about. History was also littered with the broken remains of Deacons whose reach had far exceeded their grasp.

SIXTEEN

The Lost Prince

From the outskirts of the city, Raed saw the lights in the sky, and deep in his belly he felt the pull of the geists. Aachon, who stood at his side, rested one hand on his shoulder and let out a long sigh.

Raed shot him a look out of the corner of his eye. His first mate—even though they had abandoned the *Dominion* on a lonely eastern beach, he still thought of him as that—had something on his mind. The Young Pretender knew the signs and wondered what was holding him back from speaking his mind. Usually it was he, not Aachon that tried to keep his thoughts to himself. It had always been Raed that had the problems; always Raed that had been worried, running, afraid.

It hurt a little—even in their current predicament—that Aachon felt he could not unburden himself.

"My friend," the Young Pretender finally spoke up, finally unable to take the silence between them, "we are surely heading toward a conflict we have little chance of living through. Even Sorcha"—he gestured futilely to where the horizon streamed with green and red light—"realizes this. I know something has been weighing on your mind since we left the citadel. I really need to know exactly what it is."

Aachon looked at him with dark eyes from under his furrowed brows, and his hands flexed around something that had not been there for some time: a weirstone. "My prince," he finally spoke after a few heartbeats, and his voice was heavy with guilt, "I fear I must break my oath; the one that I made before your father, so many years ago."

Raed would have had to be a fool not to hear the pain and effort it took to wrench out those words. "You mean the oath to protect me?"

A muscle flexed in his friend's jaw. "Yes, that is the very one. It has become obvious that if every man, woman and child with an ounce of ability does not take up the runes, this realm and all that live in it will be lost."

Deep within Raed the Rossin stirred, listening with real interest, Raed knew, to the next words. "Go on," the Young Pretender urged.

Aachon held up his hands, looked at them for a long moment and then held them before Raed as if they were sacrificial offerings. "I have that ability, my prince. I am in fact fully trained in its use, so I am asking your permission to join Sorcha's Deacons."

Raed blinked at him. Ever since he had known Aachon he had heard nothing but how corrupt and blinkered the Order of the Eye and the Fist was. His friend had even finally revealed why and how he had been turned away from them, for his love of Garil and the weirstone power. Now, here he was standing before him, asking for Raed's blessing to go back and serve. Things were in a pretty state indeed if it had come to this. The Young Pretender was at a loss as to what to say.

Aachon must have taken it as a slight. He cleared his throat. "You, more than anyone, know what the geists will do if the way to the Otherside is opened. You have faced the Murashev, the Wrayth and Hatipai. The Beast inside you still gnaws at your soul, my prince, I know that."

Raed raised his hand and shook his head a fraction. "I am sorry, Aachon. Please—my silence is not a judgment on your decision. I am just . . . surprised . . . but you are right. Sorcha will need every person that can wield a rune in the coming days."

Aachon opened his mouth, as if to say something, then closed it with a snap. He looked once more over the devastated streets, to where the red and blue lights had now subsided. "I will go to her then, ask to be marked and take my place among them. It is time to forget old grudges."

Now it was Raed that clapped him on the back. "I feel the geists lifting from the city, but I must wait until they are all clear. Still, go with my blessing." His eyes drifted to the flaring lights on the horizon. "I don't know how she did it, but there you are. Perhaps we have some hope after all."

"Indeed, it is a strange world in which I find hope in the Deacons," Aachon commented. "I will see you there, my prince . . . and thank you." They clasped each other's forearms, and then Aachon began to pick his way down the hillside to the road.

The Young Pretender watched and felt a heaviness descending over him. Aachon had always been there, always watched over him, and now he too must be lost to Raed. Just like Snook. Just like Fraine.

Maybe that was the best way to be; hollow. When the end came, perhaps it would not hurt as much if there were only a shell where Raed had once been. And yet . . .

Raed sighed. "I have been reading far too much poetry," he whispered to himself. She was still there. Sorcha. As twisted by all these events as he was—he still loved her.

All the rest was burned and floating away on the winds of circumstance, but that remained.

Not much to hang your life on, the Rossin muttered. *A Wrayth-Deacon half-breed just clinging onto her sanity.*

Raed determined not to listen. The Beast was not to be trusted—least of all in this chaotic time. "Don't worry," he replied lightly, "there will be plenty of blood for you to feast on before this is all over."

The Rossin became ominously silent.

Raed was just about to climb down and make his way in Aachon's footsteps, when he spotted someone else moving at the edges of the city. Merrick had told them there would be a gathering at the town square—one that no surviving human for miles would be able to resist. However, as Raed watched, a gray-cloaked figure was picking its way through the ramshackle and smoking houses. The way it kept to the shadows, and hurriedly crossed streets made it immediately apparent it did not want to be seen.

A Deacon—but not one of hers.

The Rossin's vision was laid over his, a new development that he had previously been too worried to tell Sorcha about, but which he was very glad of now. This figure gleamed in the moonlight; the aura around it flickering silver.

The Circle of Stars had shown its hand with the destruction of the Order and the Mother Abbey, but it had not been seen since. Like Sorcha, they made use of weirstone portals to travel about Arkaym and even the more distant continent of Delmaire. Yet now, here was one scuttling around this devastated city.

The Circle had been responsible for twisting his sister's mind, thinning the barrier between worlds and tipping the Empire into civil war. It was not just the Rossin whose anger had begun to kindle, yet he hesitated for a second to go after this creature. He glanced once more toward the center of the city and thought of her there. Alone.

She is never alone, the Rossin snarled in Raed's head. *She has much to do, and not much use for you. You know that.*

The Beast's barbs were getting sharper and more accurate—as if he was really making an effort. However, there was inescapable truth in the Beast's words and one fact: they did share a hatred for the Native Order that had caused so much destruction.

Without consulting each other they had reached an accord. Raed started walking down the hill toward the cloaked figure, but within moments he was running. The black smoke that still hung over the city would have made it impossible for any mere human to keep track of this fleeting figure, but he had the Rossin's sight, smell and other geistlord senses at his disposal.

The thought crossed his mind that if it were not for the horror that the Beast had inflicted on his family, and the blood of countless others it had spilled, then it would have been a useful alliance.

It was meant to be an alliance, but I was tricked. You hate the pain I have caused you, but your family has become a prison for me. You cannot understand all that I am.

Raed would almost have preferred not to hear the curse of the Imperial family speak. His words of late had become confusing and more terrifying than his former blood rages—so that the Young Pretender almost wished he would go back to that. As he stumbled through the wreckage of a city torn apart by geists, he tasted soot and smoke in his mouth, but none of it could distract from the fact that the Rossin was becoming more real to him.

He did not want to feel an ounce of sympathy for the geistlord. He was far more comfortable with the Rossin he had grown up fearing; one mad for blood and with no shred of desire for anything more than that. The changes in the Beast of late had made no sense, and yet he feared if he could figure them out they would not be terrifying.

You let me in.

Another uncomfortable truth. The deal he had made with the Rossin after the incident with Hatipai had been one he'd made for survival's sake—not his own, but his sister's. However, he was growing more and more sure it had been a mistake.

Concentrate! the great pard snarled in his head, flooding his body with heat. *The Circle of Stars is not to be underestimated. Derodak, the first Emperor, the first Deacon, is the one responsible for you and I.*

Raed slid to a stop behind a burned-out building on the intersection of a ravaged street. He peered cautiously around the corner. Not far off, the cloaked figure was striding quickly out of view.

If that was a Sensitive of the Circle of Stars, then he or she was the worst in the Order.

An Active then.

That made even less sense, but Raed knew if he tried to find logic in this damaged Empire he would be a long time looking. As quietly as he could manage, he followed.

At least there were no geists in the area—the Rossin's senses gave him that much—but there was still a thick stench of death on every street. He choked back bile many times as he followed in the figure's wake.

Finally, they reached one of the ward towers along the city's now scarred walls. The Emperor had not only unleashed a storm of geists on the population, he had also dropped fire to complete the job. The walls here were scorched black, but had managed to stay upright—a testament to their builder's skill.

His prey entered the block tower and without glancing behind, disappeared. Carefully Raed picked his way over the broken road toward the door. This could well be another situation where he would lose his clothing—but history had taught him not to place too much importance on pants. If the Rossin welled up inside him, then there would be bloodshed as well as the destruction of his clothing. He fished around trying to get the Rossin's answer in his head, but the Beast had subsided into his unconsciousness like a monster into a river of darkness. Yet Raed could not be sure he wouldn't leap to the surface again.

Still, he could not afford to head back to Sorcha now—whatever the person he was following had planned could be important. While the Deacons were dealing with the town, he would find some way to be useful.

Raed let out a long slow breath, and opened the door the figure had passed through just a fraction. The air inside was even colder than it was outside, but he could make out the sound of voices. They were too far away for him to discern any words, but it sounded like a conversation rather than chanting. In his recent experience, chanting was always a very bad thing.

Perhaps, some small gods were smiling on him, because the door didn't creak as he nudged it the rest of the way open and slid inside. A set of spiral stairs was the only way forward. He was grateful that it was lit by small yellow fires flickering in sconces, since the Rossin was no longer sharing his senses, for some reason. With his hand on his saber, Raed crept up the stairs, staying as much in the shadows as he could manage.

The voices grew louder as he ascended, but it didn't seem to be in any of the archaic languages, which was good since he had only learned to read them as a boy, and never had learned to speak them. It was in Imperial common, a man's voice, and the tone was rather warm . . . until Raed finally made out the words.

". . . The arrival of the heathen was expected, and you have no need to fear. We protect those who are important to us. With the devices we have given you, there is no fear of discovery by their Sensitives. We have been working hard while the whole world thought us gone. During that time, we learned many things, but one of them was how to remain hidden, and you are now benefitting from that . . ."

Raed felt his mouth grow dry; he knew that voice. He had not heard it a great deal, but the one time he had, it had made quite the impression. Derodak, the apparently immortal leader of the Circle of Stars, had stood in the Mother Abbey and commanded attention.

The Rossin stirred slightly, but did not urge him to stop, and the itch of curiosity gripped Raed. He did not turn

back. Derodak had fully shown his ability to escape at a
moment's notice, so this could be his only chance to
observe him and learn what he was up to.

Still, the voice sounded strange. "We will protect you as
the great chaos begins. When the veil to the Otherside is
finally torn down, this place will give you protection. The
Circle of Stars will wrap around you, as it was always
meant to be."

He had to ignore those words and see what was going on
in there. Raed climbed higher, glad of the soft boots he'd
managed to find only a few days before in the citadel's
stores. Ahead, he saw the stairs finished, and there was a
wide landing lit by larger torches. The floor he observed
was covered in dust and rocks from the bombardment, but
showed signs of very recent and frequent passage of feet.

Derodak's voice continued, and now it sounded even
stranger—as if echoing off a distant mountain. Raed
frowned. How could that be? They were in a confined
space. Ducking his head, he put one foot on the landing
and, keeping himself tight against the wall, slid up next to
the open doorway.

"You are the chosen ones, the faithful who have never
forgotten your true protectors, and it is you who will reap
the rewards."

Raed, keeping his head low, dared a look around the
corner of the door. What he saw made him quite confused
for a moment. The small guardroom was full of people,
some seated on the floor, others lined up around the walls.
He found that he had been wrong; there was not a single
Deacon among them. They were cloaked sure enough, but
none of them were green, blue—or even gray. These folk
looked like normal citizens, from elderly to small children
on their mothers' hips. Certainly there was no chance that
any of them were going to notice the Young Pretender
stealing a glance, for all of them had their eyes fixed on the
device in the middle of the floor.

Derodak had spoken true—it looked as though the

Circle of Stars had been most productive during their time out of the sun. The device on the floor was a work of art; brass like an open basket held a weirstone aloft as if it were an egg in its nest, while beneath spun a collection of gears and cogs that snickered to themselves.

The Order of the Eye and the Fist had thought themselves the masters of weirstone power, keeping it from the general population and setting it to work for their Emperor. However, it appeared they were rank amateurs compared to their predecessors.

The image of Derodak was hovering in the air a foot above the machine. It was the very same as he had appeared at the Mother Abbey, but only three feet high, and curiously flat. Raed was reminded of the shadow puppets the people of Irisil loved so much. They used a flat, pale piece of cloth to act out their local legends, and entertain their children. This device of the Circle's was something far more complex. It didn't need anywhere to project the image.

Raed Syndar Rossin, as displaced heir to the Empire of Arkaym, had been given an extensive education by many of the greatest minds to be found anywhere, yet he had never seen or read of such a thing. However, much had been lost since the time of the Ancients—the ones that Merrick now called the Ehtia, after his little sojourn into the past.

Emboldened by the fact that the leader of the Native Order was not physically present, and that there were no other Deacons, Raed crept closer while Derodak rattled on, edging his way into the group as the person he had followed here had obviously done.

This was the kind of information that Sorcha had not been able to discover. No matter how her Sensitive Deacons had searched and searched, they had been unable to use any of the Runes of Sight to spy on what the Circle of Stars had been doing. How they had been able to conceal themselves was a real mystery.

The idea that he might be able to find out some things that none of Sorcha's colleagues had been able to excited

Raed. He would put whatever he could find out before her and finally feel better about being with them. He'd be back to being a useful member of the community his lover was constructing.

He had already learned many interesting things, but perhaps this was the greatest one: the Circle of Stars was trying to build a base of adoring public. They had learned from history; when they had fallen it was because they had been toppled by angry and fearful citizens.

"Sar," a grizzled old man said, raising his hand as if he were still in school, "the Heretic who calls herself the Harbinger has taken the town hall, and her Sensitives are already spreading through the city . . ." The man paused, and stared down at his feet.

Even as a projection, Derodak demanded respect and could instill fear over distance. "Do you think we do not know that? Do you think we would abandon you?"

Though he offered no violence, the target of his outrage dropped to one knee and bent his head. "No, Sar. We know you keep your lambs safe over all comers."

Derodak turned in midair, his image flickering only slightly. "You will come to us, and join the rest of our beloved followers." He raised his hand and pointed. The people who had been standing against the wall in the spot he was gesturing to scattered like fish when an eagle dived. When he saw what was revealed, Raed's heart raced. He recognized the circle of cantrips and runes; the portal device that Sorcha was the mistress of—the only one of her Deacons that could use them. Even Merrick, when he had tried, had been baffled by it.

The space described by the circle flickered and changed; now it was a corridor, and where exactly it was, no one said. It could be anywhere in Arkaym, or even Delmaire. That was what made the Circle of Stars so very dangerous.

The people in the room—including Raed—got to their feet and began to line up to pass through the doorway.

They did indeed resemble gray sheep. The Young Pretender was just considering if he should and could shuffle unobtrusively out of the room, or if he should actually pass through with them and find out more.

Before he could come to any real decision, it was made for him. He found that he was surrounded by children, and they did not appear to be normal children. Their eyes when they looked up at him were curiously blank, and it felt as though there was something else looking out from them. It was just a split-second realization, but he didn't have time to act. Even the Rossin, swimming so deep in his unconscious, could not reach the surface quickly enough to stop what happened next.

The children threw themselves at Raed, but this was no sudden rush of infant glee. Their hands wrapped around him, and those little hands were not empty; they carried weirstones. They jammed them hard into his skin, just before he could contemplate how to fight back against children. Where the dark weirstones touched, they burned like lava.

The Rossin howled in pain and outrage as the agony reached him. Rendered mindless, the Beast dove deep, prevented from being able to reach Raed in time. That problem taken care of, the adults rushed Raed and knocked him to the floor.

While his mind reeled at this attack, they bound him tightly, keeping the weirstones still pressed against his skin. The pain rendered him both speechless and immobile.

Dimly, he heard a heavily pregnant woman yell at one of the men finishing tying his feet. "Quickly, before the Heathen feels this and comes for him."

That these people knew anything of the Bond between himself and Sorcha was another surprise. However, they couldn't know how the Bond had weakened considerably between them, else they would not have been so afraid. The Circle of Stars was mobilizing a section of the terrified citizens of Arkaym, and it seemed a most successful ploy.

Trussed up like a game hen, Raed found himself carried through the doorway, and far, far away from Sorcha and her new Order. He guessed that his attempt at information gathering was about to become a lot more intense—and quickly.

His last thought before passing the doorway was how ironic it was that the Rossin had been brought low by children.

SEVENTEEN

Alone with the Whispers

Sorcha sat in the dark, on a splendid chair that was not hers, and listened to the voices. Much as she disliked it, she had very little choice in the matter, since they had grown so much stronger. Awakening her Wrayth powers to use on the mayor and his fellow geists had apparently opened a door she couldn't shut.

Merrick was about the work of organizing those that had come forward to take up the mantle of the Enlightened—including the rather surprising addition of Aachon.

The Harbinger of the Enlightened sounded rather grand when shouted to a crowd while wielding runes. Now, sitting alone in the room that had once belonged to the mayor, it felt like a cloak made of gold—a beautiful but terrible burden. The worst of it was the words she had spoken had not been her own; someone else had forced them from her lips.

Harbinger, the voices had whispered into her mind, and at the same time the words had escaped her. She had not shared that particular fact with Merrick, and the knowledge that he had not found that out only compounded her fear. They had once been as close as two Deacons could be.

Now—though she had called him her anchor—she could feel him drifting away from her.

Come to us, and all fear will be assuaged, the little voices, layered upon each other, repeated.

In her sleep they called her "beloved" and "special." They sang to her to return to the hive mind where all was safe and all wrongs would be made right. Her mother had taken her from her proper home, and she need only return to make everything as it should be.

Sorcha's hands tightened on the carved arms of the chair, and her teeth pressed together. She knew what Merrick was afraid of, and it tormented her too. She was fully aware that she was teetering on the edge of a vast abyss, and feared if she even moved an inch she would go over.

Her thoughts darted toward Arch Abbot Rictun. It was strange how she had not thought of him for many, many months and now his face came back to her in the darkness. He had always been at her shoulder when they were growing up, not as a friend, but as a pair of eyes to spot weakness in her. He'd reported Sorcha to the Presbyter of the Young more times than she could count. She'd always thought it was jealousy, but now that the Wrayth had released her memories, she knew that was not what had driven the Arch Abbot.

She recalled a day when the foundlings of the Order, still too young yet for the novitiate, had been set loose to play in the herb garden. It was one of those stifling summer afternoons where the air was heavy with moisture. The more sensible adults had long since retired to the shade and cool of the Abbey's stone buildings. Sorcha had been eight years old. Her long dark red hair had come loose from her ponytail and was sticking damply to her neck. She was playing chase with all the other children, glad to be free of the hawklike watch of all the grown-ups. For once they were able to be young.

She hid behind a tall stand of lavender, stifling her giggles as three other foundlings ran past, oblivious to her absence. When one of the older boys came close, she clambered into the garden bed and, despite the bees, crouched down among the long purple flowers. The smell was overwhelming, and after a moment the heat and the sweet scent overcame her.

She rolled back until she was lying on the bare earth and just staring up at the bright blue sky. The warmth of the day wrapped around her, and the sound of the lazily buzzing bees put her into a half-awake, half-asleep state. It was this that the older Sorcha knew was very close to the state of reaching for her Center. The smells, the sights and the sounds were acting on her like one of the lay Brother's drugs.

As the young Sorcha lay back in the garden, she began to notice that the cloudless sky was not entirely cloudless. Tufts of white, like glimpses of smoke, flickered and danced across the perfect deep blue. She watched them idly, but as she did so they began to form into something that was not so formless. She could make out faces, some long and stretched out, others coming very close to being familiar. One even seemed to look like her own face, but older.

In this drowsy state, the young Sorcha did not panic, because she did not know—did not have the training to know—that what she was seeing was not just idle imaginings. The older Sorcha, sitting in the darkness of the broken and desecrated hall, bit her lip as the memory unrolled.

Now the sound of the bees was not just some chaotic, soft rumble, it too began to take shape. The buzzing began to form words. They were voices calling her. They spoke of a warm welcome. They whispered that she did not belong with the Order. She had to leave. Pareth didn't want her. Pareth was in danger every moment she was in the Abbey.

Suddenly the feelings seemed very wrong. Pareth was the only one who loved Sorcha. She knew that!

The young girl clawed frantically at the side of the trance the sensations had brought her to. It was like being trapped in an awful dream that was struggling to hold on to her.

"Sorcha?" Ernst Rictun's face, handsome but concerned, appeared in her line of sight. He pushed his shaggy golden hair out of his eyes and then offered her his hand. Sorcha was gagging and screaming on the inside as the voices pounded inside her head. She had to get away from them.

Green flame flared at the tips of her fingers as she lurched upright and snatched at Ernst's wrist. The moment her skin made contact with his, she felt some of his strength flow into her. It let her pull free of the soporific effect of the bees, the sky and the scent of the lavender.

The boy that would grow up to be Arch Abbot of the Order in far-off Arkaym was not so lucky. He must have felt the energy being sucked away and out of his body. He let out a muffled yelp that would have become a scream—had it not been for a hand that wrapped firmly around his mouth.

Pareth, the Presbyter of the Young, yanked him close, even as Sorcha lurched up from the warm earth. She was gasping as if she had just dived too deep, and she was too young and inexperienced to realize the terrible thing that Pareth did next.

Older Sorcha did however—and was horrified. The woman she had idolized and loved above all others in her life had broken every rule of the Order just to protect one little girl. She also did something that Sorcha hadn't even known Sensitives could do.

Sielu, the First Rune of Sight, was meant to see from another's eyes, but somehow Pareth corrupted it. She bent the rune opposite to what it was supposed to do. She forced a new vision on Ernst Rictun, one that didn't involve a young and inexperienced Sorcha using something close to the rune Shayst on him. When he staggered away, there was a look of confusion on his face.

"Get inside, Ernst," Pareth barked, and the young boy rubbing at his face in dazed bewilderment did so.

The young Sorcha looked up at her heroine but couldn't find any words. Pareth grabbed her fiercely, and hugged her until the youngster thought her ribs would crack.

Dimly she heard the Presbyter mutter, "We'll have to get you into the novitiate immediately . . . no time to waste . . . none at all."

The older Sorcha shook herself free of the memory with as much difficulty as she had escaped her first experience with her own Center. She licked her dry lips and eased herself back into the chair slowly. It had been a very bad day for Rictun, and she certainly felt sorry for him—something she never would have believed possible. That buried memory explained much.

She wondered where he was now. Was he even alive for her to apologize to? The old Sorcha, the one who had stood before Merrick and scoffed at his age and inexperience, would never have contemplated doing such a thing. Now, she realized she had, by accident, done something terrible, but Pareth had done something even worse—deliberately.

So will you, the Wrayth crooned. *You will go back to Vermillion.*

The geistlord within her was yearning for the Maker of Ways to tear open reality, to allow the geists full access to the human realm. And once the geists started pouring into this world, the Wrayth could draw them into its hive mind. It wanted her to stitch them into itself, making it more powerful than any other geistlord.

While Sorcha shivered at the prospect, the busy little mind of her father's master delighted in it.

For a long moment she imagined what their world would be like. The Circle of Stars, the geistlords and the Wrayth would fight for control of the ravaged human population. The people left alive would be just farmed animals for all of them. It was the grand catastrophe that the Ehtia had feared so much they had sacrificed their own lives in the human realm. They had fled in the face of it.

Sorcha smiled grimly. Derodak's followers in the Circle of Stars could not imagine the horror it would unleash and how unlikely it was that they could control it. Derodak had spent centuries growing arrogant and more self-assured—it would all come undone when he finally experienced a breach in the worlds.

So all that stands against it is you and your little band? the Wrayth voices, dry and hurtful, murmured. *You can't even control yourself, how can you possibly imagine stopping all this?*

Sorcha closed her eyes, hearing the voices but trying not to listen. Instead she summoned up the memories of her mother—scant as they were—to give her strength. Still, what little she had been able to see when she shared her mother's mind, she used as a goad on herself. Sorcha's hands clenched on the arms of the chair, and the wood ground into her flesh. If she did not pull this new Order together, then that would be all humanity's fate: nothing but breeders and food for the undead.

She had to find out what the Circle of Stars were doing. Their hunt for the Patternmaker of the Native Order had come to nothing. None of the runes seemed able to pierce that particular mystery. Merrick's prescience might be terrifying, but not exactly helpful when it came to specifics. His use of runes had brought them to the right place to make a spectacle, but that could not be relied on in the next step.

Sorcha Faris, Harbinger of the Enlightened surged to her feet. It was time for a hunt.

She shoved the doors of the mayor's office open. They swung far easier than she had thought and slammed into the walls on either side with a tremendous crash. The people who had been bustling to and fro in the hallway jumped. Sorcha saw not just respect in their eyes but a little fear as well. Deacons and folk she had known for years now looked at her differently. The new title she had chosen had not apparently been a reassuring one.

Merrick, who had been sitting across from the mayor's office, got abruptly to his feet. He pulled his silver fur cloak around himself and walked over to where she stood. His brown eyes were troubled, but his mind, which she felt along the Bond, was as stalwart as ever.

"We need to find a geist," Sorcha said, taking him by the elbow and guiding him down the hallway and toward the front door—not allowing him to argue in front of everyone. Perhaps pulling her partner out the door wasn't good for their new image, but after the night before's display, Sorcha thought she had some leeway on that.

"Very inconvenient then," Merrick said, shooting her a thin smile, "considering that you just destroyed all of the ones in the city."

"Yes, well, I didn't have much time to stop and think." The blur of the confrontation outside the town hall was something that she still had to sort through. Reaching out to the geists had seemed so very easy. Like a sword removed from its sheath, she had known just what to do.

Sorcha cleared her throat, and jerked her mind away from contemplating that at present. "But nevertheless, we need a geist."

They stepped out into the sunshine and blinked at its brightness. Sorcha even tilted her head back and enjoyed the feel of it on her face. The damage to the city was intense; everywhere broken buildings poked from among the untouched like scorched trees in the forest. While the smell of death would take much time to clear, it still smelled better than it had yesterday. A kindly wind had wafted away much of the stench.

"You and I need to travel," Sorcha said, as firmly as she could manage. Now it was his turn to lead her.

Somehow, remarkably the public stables had survived, and it was here that the Order had brought the Breed horses. When they entered, Sorcha's gaze traveled over the remains of that bright creation of the Order of the Eye and the Fist. Seven stallions and twenty-three mares were all that remained. Much like the Deacons, they had been badly damaged.

Still, her heart lifted a bit when a familiar long nose poked over the stall door and snuffled at her cloak. Shedryi, the tall black stallion, as old as he was, had come away from the scourging of the Mother Abbey with not a scratch on him. A young lay Brother had ridden him out before the flames reached the stables. Melochi, the mare that Merrick favored, was in the stall next to him.

Merrick fished out a sugar cube and fed it to her. That simple pleasure of a horse's gentle mouth on his open palm made him smile. Her young partner had precious few reasons to really smile of late.

Shedryi turned one accusing dark eye on Sorcha, since she had brought no treat. "Here," Merrick said, reaching across and dropping one into her hand. "I found a few down in the kitchens."

Shedryi gobbled his treat and then threw his head up with a snort. "Yes, indeed, we are going on a little ride, you wicked boy," Sorcha said, rubbing his smooth neck. Glancing across at Merrick she asked, "Any sign of Raed yet?"

Taking a bridle down from the wall, Merrick shook his head. "Aachon said he wanted to be sure all the geists had gone before he came back. He should turn up soon."

Sorcha shrugged. She was not worried about her lover, he was no dog on a leash, and besides any who threatened him would feel the wrath of the Rossin. She understood that sometimes the Young Pretender needed his space— he too had dark shadows to wrestle with.

Unlike in the Mother Abbey, the Deacons saddled up their own mounts—lay Brothers were far too busy to tend to the whims of the Active or Sensitive. Sorcha didn't mind. In fact, she thought this new Order of Enlightenment would be better served if the Deacons of it knew a little of what the Brothers of the gray cloaks went through.

Merrick mounted up with alacrity, once again making Sorcha's bones feel very old. "So, where to?" he asked.

Her partner looked positively elated to be on horseback again, so he was not going to like her reply. "Any direction . . . we just have to get out of the city to find a geist. It shouldn't take long or far."

Merrick rode Melochi out into the yard, while Sorcha

saddled the stallion. Shedryi turned and tried to nip at her as she tightened the cinch on him—however when she slapped him on the rump, he settled down. Soon she too was mounted, and with a little nudge of the stirrups, they trotted out of the stable and into the city.

In the dark of the previous night, Sorcha had been given precious little time to examine the city of Waikein they were saving. It was dreadful now to ride through it, but the people that they met along the way seemed positively happy. They looked up at the passing Deacons with soot-stained faces, grinned and waved. They were clearing the streets, gathering up the unburied corpses for proper ceremonies, and repairing those houses that could be salvaged.

"You would hardly know them as the same people from last night," Merrick commented, pushing the reluctant Melochi past lines of smashed barricades.

Sorcha nodded but kept her eyes averted from the gaze of the grateful citizens. She was afraid she had given them false hope. The geists were not beaten back. Countless numbers of them still waited.

Sensing her tumult, Merrick reached across and squeezed her hand. "It was a demonstration, Sorcha. It had to be done, and word of it will already be spreading throughout the Empire."

"Not that there is much of an Empire anymore," she muttered in reply.

"Zofiya will be helping with that," he shot back, and then effectively ended the conversation by urging his mare into a quick trot.

Sorcha needed to feel the wind in her hair and grab a little joy too. She kicked Shedryi into a gallop in response, and soon they had caught up and passed him.

The two of them were quickly out of the city and on their way to the rolling hills that bordered it. It was a wonderful thing to be beyond the stench of death and destruction. They rode the horses up through the velvet green hills punctuated by pale gray rocks, and along the banks of the river. Merrick

was being sensible, though, keeping his Center open as they
went. All the time they felt no geist presence.

Sorcha knew that most of the undead in the area would
have been drawn to the city to feed on the concentration of
humanity there.

She took a long deep breath. At this stage the natural
world was still untouched; she saw rabbits moving on the
hills, and a flock of birds overhead against the bright blue
sky. However, should the Circle of Stars achieve their aim
then eventually that too would be ravaged.

Shedryi snorted and tossed his head, but that was only
when a fox darted across their path. He was a small one,
and definitely not a coyote, but Sorcha nonetheless shivered; it reminded her too much of the Fensena. She knew
he and his favor were waiting somewhere for her—as if she
didn't have enough to worry about.

They came to a looming series of waterfalls, sliding
their way down from the mountains to the east, and the
partners began picking their way up the side of the cliffs
through a series of goat tracks. The roar of the water and
the cloud of spray around them was deeply refreshing. Sorcha took the chance to wipe her face in the chill dew and
rub her neck with it. She'd learned to take enjoyment in
whatever moment they could.

With that thought, she turned Shedryi around and
waited for Merrick to reach her. He kneed Melochi up the
rise and then pulled her to a stop next to his partner. He
looked out over the beautiful scene of nature's power, and
then also tilted his face into the sun. A few of the shadows
gathered in the corner of his eyes seemed to lift slightly.
"This was a fine idea, Harbinger." The way his mouth
formed that title said that he was still not happy with it.
"But which sort of geist do we need?"

Sorcha considered his question. It could not be one of
the lesser ones like a rei, but she did not want a geistlord
either. Finally, she settled on one. "A revenant would be
ideal, but if you could manage . . ."

As Merrick abruptly opened his Center and shared it with her, her words dried in her mouth. Every time he did so she was reminded how lucky she was to have been partnered with him. The hills and grassland that had seemed pretty enough suddenly exploded into life. It would have been overwhelming in the hands of a lesser Sensitive, but Merrick balanced it so effortlessly that the only information she got was the important facts.

Like the blur of red and gold along the ridgeline; a twining undead power that flickered in and out with tormented faces in its midst. A revenant—a geistlord that gathered the tormented souls of humans as they died, and trapped them within—just as she had asked for. Perhaps her luck was going to hold out.

"Well done, Merrick," she said, digging her heels into her stallion's sides, "you have found our informant." A wicked and dangerous grin spread on her lips. Perhaps as Harbinger she was going to have different luck than when she'd been merely a Deacon.

EIGHTEEN

Sensitive and Wrayth

"Right back where we started," Merrick found himself muttering under his breath, but it was not with any true distress. The few times that he and Sorcha had hunted geist on the way to Ulrich had been invigorating. It was, after all, what Deacons were trained to do, and when they did engage with each other to exercise their abilities it was a glorious thing.

The sly smile that his partner shot him now suggested that she felt the very same way. Along the Bond the whispering of the Wrayth seemed to subside, or maybe it was the sheer power of the moment that simply drowned them out.

Both Deacons slid from their mounts and walked together up the hill. The earth was springy underfoot. Now, the revenant would usually have tried to escape them, seeing as they were its natural enemy, but lately the undead had learned more than a little bravery. The weakening of the barrier between the human realm and the Otherside was giving them much greater strength.

Merrick caught the subtle gesture of Sorcha flicking back her cloak. It would have been the moment when she went to pull her Gauntlets from her belt, but of course they were no longer there. A gesture learned over a lifetime could not so easily be put aside. Realizing her mistake, Sorcha cleared her throat and instead pushed her sleeves up, flexing her fingers. That particular gesture worked just as well without Gauntlets as it had with.

The runes trickled and ran through the marks the Patternmaker had carved, and Merrick marveled how she didn't even seem to need to think the words for the runes before they were there. Blue fire filled the lines and flooded down toward her fingertips.

Merrick's own power was just as second nature as his partner's. His Sight filled the landscape around them with life and death; but he narrowed it in on the revenant that had just begun to whirl about on itself.

"You really expect to get information from a geist?" he asked as they neared the undead and tried to sound more positive than he felt.

Sorcha shrugged. "Well, if there is anyone more likely to know when and where the barrier will be torn I cannot think of it right now." She spun on her heel and stared at him hard.

He hated it when she was like this . . . bad and dangerous things happened when his partner threw her hands up in the air and just decided to try some madcap scheme. She might have put on a good show in the town square last night, but she was not fooling him. She was still the same Active that had so casually created a strong, maddening Bond between them.

Sorcha's lips curled at the corners, but there was a hint of sadness in her face. "Oh, so now you are regretting being my Sensitive, are you?"

"I . . . I . . ." Merrick opened his mouth, and then shut it with a snap. *Just get on with this.* He pushed his words along the Bond.

They had both come to rely on the link between them and, in fact, with its recent weakening, he had begun to miss it. Still, they remained partners, and Merrick would cling onto that fact until he was spent and done with life.

The revenant was dancing toward them, twirling and strangely confident. It looked like it had captured quite a number of torn souls, thanks to the devastation of the city. Merrick's stomach turned over in a sick knot. No one had ever discovered the true extent of a revenant's power, and it had been speculated that there could be no limit to it. If the geist could find enough souls, it could possibly rival a geistlord.

Sorcha had to feel his concern, but it did not stop her. She stepped lightly over the ground toward it, as if they were two dancers—and only they could hear the music.

Merrick strained his senses, both ethereal and physical, but it appeared that they were the only living things of any consequence nearby. By the time he looked up, Sorcha's whole arms were glowing red with the flame of Pyet, just as the snapping skeletal heads of the revenant spun and threw themselves down on her.

The swell of voices filled Merrick's head, but he knew they were actually coming from his partner. The Wrayth was never too far away from her now, and the Bond suddenly felt very, very frail. Merrick wrapped himself around it, like a sailor holding on to the rigging, praying for it not to break.

If he was, as she had said, her anchor, then he was damned well going to act like it. She seemed to have even less regard for her own safety than she had when Merrick first met her. He knew what had done it. Sorcha didn't need to smoke those damn cigarillos to tell him that she didn't expect to live much longer. In fact, she seemed like she was rushing toward extinction with both arms spread wide.

"Not today," Merrick muttered to himself. The Third Eye, carved in the middle of his forehead, began to glow white hot and burn on his skin. It was usually reserved for the last few runes in a Sensitive's arsenal, but something about this revenant was bringing it out far more quickly.

Through his Center he watched as Sorcha wrapped her

arms around the snarling faces of those who had been prematurely wrenched from life. They were so angry that it felt as though they might rip her skin right off.

Why are you not doing anything? He screamed along the Bond because it was true. Sorcha was merely standing there, not using a single of her Runes of Dominion—even though they were nearly bursting out of her skin.

A flash of insight burned like lightning in his brain. He suddenly understood what she was doing. The powers of the Wrayth had been proven useful last night, and she was endeavoring to use them in more subtle ways. By twining herself into the fabric of the revenant she was hoping to see what it saw—to understand what it wanted and what was coming.

Merrick felt like a total fool. He had thought she would trap the revenant with the runes, drain it of its power, and demand it show her what she wanted to know. It was yet another mark of the weakening of the Bond that she had been able to conceal her true intentions from him.

The trouble was in the nature of this geist. It, like the Wrayth, was a creature of twined souls, but the revenant contained no single core of intelligence. It was as mindless and muddled a creature as could be imagined. Sorcha was letting it wrap itself around her, and Merrick knew that she would be lost in that chaos very quickly. Revenants were responsible for more Deacons with permanent addled brains than any other kind of geist. Sorcha knew that just as well as he did, but she had become a little too sure of her own power. Lost in it almost.

Merrick raced forward, ready to attempt to pull her bodily from the revenant's embrace, but the Wrayth and the revenant turned on him. He heard a scream that threatened to cut through his bones and was actually shoved physically backward. The breath was knocked out of his lungs, and he could hear Sorcha's howls only dimly. Her mind was unreachable.

The barrier was so thin at the moment that this tumult

could draw other geists from the Otherside. A new invasion could begin here and undo all the good work they had done last night.

Yes, the barrier is very thin. Merrick shook his head. He heard the words against his skin; a physical presence of one he knew was not in the human realm—one that had given up her body to save the world once already.

Yet when he saw her form, smoky and gleaming as it was, his heart gave a little jump. Nynnia was here with him now. Until this moment he'd not considered all the implications of the thinning of the veil. It was not just geists who lived on the other side of it; the Ehtia and their Ancient knowledge resided there too. He had loved one of the Ehtia—probably still did if he cared to admit it. Despite Zofiya, that ember still burned.

He caught himself speculating. They were in a war for survival, and that meant there was a real likelihood that he would join Nynnia on the Otherside for a brief moment, before being swept away to whatever awaited a Deacon beyond.

Merrick! Sorcha's voice jerked his attention and his Center back toward her. She was standing within the revenant. Two skeleton heads were clamped on each of her arms, and her pain was burning along the fragile Bond. He had to concentrate . . . but it was very hard with the image of Nynnia drawing nearer—and there was something different about his lost love. He tried to split his attention as best he could.

The geist that was bearing down on Sorcha was stronger than any revenant they'd encountered, but it was as he had warned her; the closeness of the Otherside was giving them more strength and power. He was terrified of his partner burning away under the strain.

Don't be. Nynnia was now at his shoulder. He could tell because the smell of summer roses came with her, along with a comforting warmth. *Sorcha has also become stronger; the Wrayth has at least given her that.*

The image of his Active wrestling with the Wrayth seemed to retreat a little, as if he were watching it through a spyglass. He could see her nature now. Long, spiraling, blue white connections ran from her and into the geist twisting above her. Pulses of power ran down these connections, but he could not tell in which direction they were going. He was frightened of the implications.

If any of their Sensitives, old or their newly made ones, saw this, they would be terrified. In the old Order they had a name for it: contamination. At the very least Sorcha would have been confined to the infirmary—at worst she would have been put down like a rabid dog.

The final rune. It had been created for a situation like this and kept secret from the Sensitives. The one secret they never shared with their partners.

When it comes to it, will you have the strength to do what is necessary? Nynnia looked at him with infinite kindness. She knew what Sorcha was to him and how deep their Bond was.

Merrick shook his head, and for the first time felt real, deep anger toward the formless woman. "She is all we have! She just pulled off the greatest feat of geist exorcism that has ever been seen. Even the First Deacon could not have done what she did."

Nynnia seemed to blow back and forth. *And you know there is only one way that is possible. She is becoming one of them. Her humanity is weakening . . .*

Merrick didn't know what to say to that. Sorcha had experienced her own mother's final breakout of the Wrayth's prison. He knew she had been tormented when she saw that, and by finding out her father had been one of the Wrayth. He also knew that she was deeply afraid of becoming one of them.

However, right now, with her arms outstretched, channeling or destroying the revenant, she was magnificent—and definitely not tormented.

Nynnia looked at him, and he felt stripped bare under

that gaze. *Remember your vows, my love. That is all . . . remember why you became a Deacon. Your father died at their hands, and—*

"Merrick!" Sorcha's call snapped her partner's head around. She was calling him, and despite everything he followed his training.

"Your Center," she cried, as the revenant bent toward her. He had pulled back his connection to her, and now it was barely discernable. She could see no way to hold and bind the creature without his Sight.

When he shot a glance over his shoulder again, Nynnia was gone.

"Merrick!"

The Sensitive stumbled as he turned and ran to his Active's side. For a moment Merrick could not discern who was feeding off whom.

Neither can I. Now Sorcha's voice in his head was small and frightened. Nothing showed on her expression, but within he could hear the voices of the Wrayth beginning to rise out of the darkness. He didn't know how to combat them, since they were inside his partner—much as the Rossin was inside Raed.

We will deal with it, he replied to her. *They are not as strong as us. Nothing is as strong as us.*

It was a bold claim.

A Sensitive must always hold up their Active; he had been taught that in the novitiate. His instructor's voice, Deacon Rueng, came back to him on the winds of memory. *It is they that will stand in the center of the storm, and they will feel unequal to the task. We are the anchor that gives them the strength to hold against it.*

Merrick ran and stood beside Sorcha. Physical presence did not really matter; as long as they could see each other, the Bond should be strong enough. Yet part of Merrick wanted to stand at her side, share in the danger.

"It is too much," Sorcha screamed. She was holding the shield of the fire rune, Yevah, in one hand, with the green flicker of Shayst ready in the other fist. Merrick immediately saw the problem. If she used the active rune to draw away power while she was still entangled with it, then she could end up killing herself.

Surely there was some way to free herself from the geist? Merrick's mind started to race over the possibilities, to offer something to his partner.

Sorcha sank to one knee as the shield of fire was thrust downward. Parts of the revenant were traveling along their connection, piercing the shield.

"Whenever you are ready," the Active howled, turning her face, white with shock, toward him.

Thinking! he shot back through the Bond. This was no normal case. No Deacon he had ever heard of had linked herself with a geist and still remained sane. Yes, she was still sane.

As sane as ever. She gasped as a tendril of the revenant reached into her body. The sensation of ice-cold flooding communicated itself very well along the Bond and Merrick cried out too.

Faster, he had to think faster. So it was not a case of a functioning Deacon . . . how about a case of an injured one? He had to think like a lay Brother—those that tended to the ill. He had to contemplate what they dealt with: the geiststruck, the contaminated, those that had delved too deep and been lost within the undead's embrace. All of the initiates were taught something of the work of the lay Brothers, the better to appreciate it . . . however most paid little attention.

Merrick was digging deep now. He'd stood in the back row, the infirmary had been hot, and the drone of the lay Brother had put many of his fellow students to sleep on their feet. However, Merrick was not one of them.

"You are very lucky I was such a damn good student." He grinned at Sorcha. She simply stared back at him in stunned disbelief.

Now is not the time. And remember we want to capture

this geist, not destroy it. We have to keep some small connection to it.

She loved piling on the problems, that was for certain. He opened his Center wide. The geiststruck were often able to be pulled back by repetition and reminders of their past. So he dived down deep into Sorcha's memory and plucked out something that would remind her of her humanity. A face was staring back at him; very like that of his partner but with long dark hair.

Her mother. Merrick knew that instantly. She looked at him with an expression of such sorrow that he distantly felt a tear break free from his own eyes.

She'd been a Sensitive like he was, and she had given her life to get the child forced upon her out of the grasp of the Wrayth. That was the ultimate blood pact, and the Bond that was formed by it was strong and deep.

Sorcha feared what she was, but she was part of this woman too. A powerful Deacon had birthed her, and Merrick thrust that reality toward his partner. It cut her deep, slid between the tangled connection of revenant and Deacon.

Sorcha let out a scream that almost sounded like a laugh. The rune Shayst flared green along her arms, yanking the power of the geist into her core. Then, flush with it, she turned the Yevah around. The shield of fire bent and flexed as Merrick had never seen it do before.

His breath caught in his throat, and he watched as she wrapped Yevah around the geist. It was drained, exhausted, and hovered within the bubble of flame like a child's decoration.

Merrick couldn't help the first thought that popped into his head, nor could he stop it racing along the Bond he had with Sorcha. *This must be what Derodak wants to do to geists.*

Sorcha winced, as if he had struck her, and her blue eyes closed for a second. However, she didn't make any comment—instead ignoring his unfiltered words.

"We have our informant," she said, and despite the circumstances there was a note of triumph in her voice. Sorcha had done what many said was impossible.

She began to stride down toward her partner, and the trapped revenant, still surrounded by flame, bobbed along behind her. The flicker of power ran along her arms, casting her face in odd colors. Merrick felt his stomach clench with sudden pain, as pride, with a healthy dose of fear, washed over him. He mounted back on his horse and thought about how quickly they could get their prisoner back to the city.

Sorcha was smiling. It was going to be all right—until the moment that everything flipped on its head. Merrick had only an instant to cry out.

He saw the side of the hill, right next to where she was standing, ripple and fall away. He recognized it in an instant; one of the Wrayth's portals. The opening appeared not a foot away from her. Merrick opened his Center desperately, clinging to the Bond so that she might draw strength from it.

She only had enough time to release the revenant from her activity, and then the Wrayth were upon her; or rather in her.

Merrick pulled out his saber and flung himself down off his mount. Yet he knew—he could tell without any rune—that he was not going to be fast enough. The rattle of voices in Sorcha's head had become a clatter and Merrick knew—this was not an attack by Derodak. This was the Wrayth come to claim their own.

Merrick caught a glimpse of Sorcha's eyes rolling in her head, just before the energy poured out of her body. She slumped to the ground, while the revenant whirled away. Most terrifying of all, however, was the draining away of all that made her Sorcha, seen through his Center.

They were coming through the doorway now, lines of tall, pale people, marked by the Wrayth, and no more individual than an ant. He wasn't going to be able to make it to her, but he was damn well going to try.

As Merrick scrambled up the remaining rocks, he felt Sorcha in the Bond—the merest of flickers, *Go! Please, Merrick, go!*

His foot slipped on the rock. The Wrayth had gathered Sorcha up and were taking her back through their doorway, but a few of them turned his way; the gray eyes, devoid of emotion, suddenly fixed on him. These were no shambling undead; they were racing toward him.

Too fast. His mind processed that in an instant. Too fast and too many for Merrick to get back to Melochi, whose distant whinny seemed to be the only sound that reached above the thunder of the water. He saw at once what they would do to him; he had, after all, shared Sorcha's vision of her mother. Deacon Merrick Chambers would become their puppet just as she had been.

It wasn't really a choice. Without hesitation, Merrick ran toward the edge of the cliff. The thunder of the waterfall pounding over rocks filled his ears. He had no time to think—only to act. It had to be the last thing he heard, as he leapt forward into its embrace, expecting to see Nynnia very soon.

NINETEEN

The Touch of the Sea

Raed woke with a pounding headache that threatened to blind him before he had even opened his eyes. He lay still on the ground for a moment, using the tactics he had come to rely on when dealing with the Rossin: sit still, take in details and assess the situation.

The ground underneath his hands was smooth, and when he dared to crack an eye open he realized that they were tiles, beautifully crafted and decorated tiles. Then his nose brought him a very strange scent, and one that was totally unexpected but very familiar; it was the salt of the sea.

Raed ran his hands over the tiles for a moment, then he shook his head, and levered himself upright. If they were near the ocean, then maybe things were not that bad; Mother Sea had always looked after him.

The only days of his life that had been any good—at least before he found Sorcha—had been accompanied by the rocking of the waves. He held on to that knowledge until his eyes were able to adjust and focus. The room was dimly lit but startling. He was once more in a cavern, but where exactly that cavern might be was the real question.

As he looked around and made out what was lighting the space, his mind did a quick turnaround. He saw windows, thick gleaming windows in the cavern, made of something that he suspected was weirstone, since it shone and occasionally shot through with blue, as those dangerous stones were wont to do. However, they were opaque enough to make him realize where the smell of salt water was coming from. Beyond the glass were floating strands of seaweed, thick castles of coral and shoals of brightly colored fish. This then wasn't merely an underground cavern where secret doings were accomplished, but an underwater cavern.

As Raed leaned on his knees, all thoughts of his own danger were washed away by this amazing sight. He had always loved the sea, but had never had the pleasure of observing it like this. He leaned closer. Truly it was a wonder.

After a moment, though, someone breathing and moving fractionally in the dark made Raed aware that he was not alone. The figure that finally emerged from the shadows was not unfamiliar to him either. Derodak, the Arch Abbot of the Circle of Stars, stepped toward him with a disconcerting smile on his lips. "Welcome, Young Prince. I hope your journey didn't leave you feeling too unwell?"

The effects of traveling through a weirstone portal were unpleasant, but livable—but it seemed that they were compounded when forced to do so with extra weirstones touching his skin.

In what he hoped was an insulting gesture, Raed remained seated on the floor and looked up at his captor. From what Zofiya had told them of her imprisonment by this man, he was both unpleasant and quite happy to apply pain when it was needed. However soldierly the Grand Duchess was, Raed had endured more pain and torment than she could imagine in his role as host to the Rossin. It gave him a shot of confidence.

So he got to his feet and dusted himself off. "I've felt worse after a hard night out with my crew members. How

are you feeling? The mad Emperor and Deacon Sorcha
Faris are people I wouldn't want to have at my back . . ."

His eyes darted around the rest of the room; he saw
nothing that he could use as a weapon. In fact, the room
was entirely barren—just the eerie light of the weirstones
spread out over the floor.

Derodak drew closer, and Raed observed that the man
was wearing a cloak very much like Sorcha's, but it was
held closed by a jeweled circle of stars brooch. The material was also far finer than any he'd ever seen the Order of
the Eye and the Fist wearing. It shifted and gleamed like
some exotic fish skin with all the colors of the rainbow. It
reminded Raed of the way the people of his father's small
Court dressed like peacocks. It was desperate and flashy.

His jailor came close, but not too close. He ended up
perching himself on the edge of the weirstone window. The
strange blue glow illuminated him well enough, but
revealed nothing of his emotions or plans.

The man looked to be in his later years, with gray staining his dark beard, but his eyes gleamed with vigor and
arrogance. Raed had seen that look many times when he
was growing up. His father, the Unsung Pretender, had
plenty of it—though he had never done anything about
pursuing his claim to the Imperial throne. He generally
assumed that the Princes of the Empire would come crawling back to him, howling that they needed him. Now the
Unsung was more irrelevant than ever in this warring
world.

Perhaps his father and this man shared more than just
arrogance. After all, Derodak had exposed the everyday
citizens to the predations of the geists. Raed guessed soon
he would sweep down and show them how he had the
undead under control. Naturally, many would die in the
process, but he would be able to play the role of savior.

As Raed examined Derodak, he was in turn being examined. Finally, it was the older man that broke the silence.
"Quite a disappointment," he said, adjusting his odd cloak

around himself. "Generations of breeding, and yet so very little of me in there."

Raed clenched his jaw and only just managed to hold back retaliation. He wanted to smack that self-satisfied smile from his face, but years of dealing with the fear and the dangers of the Rossin had taught the Young Pretender restraint.

"I hardly think after all these generations there can be much of you left in my blood," Raed returned. "It is the mark of a desperate man to think—"

"Yes, that would be the case," Derodak said, inclining his head, "except of course, every now and then I just popped back to keep it topped up."

The Young Pretender closed his mouth with a snap as a shudder ran through his body. He had a horrible vision of the first Emperor sneaking into the bed of his female ancestors. He would bet good money that they hadn't known or had a choice about it.

"Yes, I believe it was your grandmother that spread her legs for me . . . of course she thought I was your grandfather." Derodak's eyes never left Raed's face. "And like a good gardener I came back now and then to do a little pruning. I couldn't let the family tree grow too large and thin the bloodline."

Raed began to understand what Zofiya had said about this man. His joy in applying pain . . . it obviously included emotional torture.

"By the Blood . . ." Raed swore and then stopped. He said that so often that he hadn't really thought about what it meant. The Blood. His blood. The Young Pretender took several unwitting steps away from him. "You sick twisted bastard!"

"Perhaps by your mortal standards." Derodak stood and tucked his hands behind his back. "But I am far from mortal. The rules do not apply. When my people fled to the Otherside, only I was brave enough to come back. I saw another way that they did not agree with."

He swiftly covered the distance between them, until he was only a foot away from Raed. His eyes darted over the Young Pretender's face, still searching for something. "Your father was a mistake in the line, and your grandfather a traitor to it, but you may be useful."

Where was the Rossin? Raed tried to plumb the depths of his soul, screaming for the Beast to rise and slice this evil thing that wore a human face from throat to crotch. Yet there was no answer; nothing seemed to be there but a distant memory of power.

"I won't help you," he gasped out, desperate to gain some time.

His captor laughed, as if they were discussing a change in the weather. "That is what that impostor of a Grand Duchess said to me, and you saw how well that worked out for her. And don't think the Rossin will help you. I have many, many centuries of experience handling that particular geistlord."

He poked Raed's shoulder with one finger and let out a small laugh. "I took care of everything. I made your line, and I made Vermillion itself. It was a hill, but I brought the water, and wound it around, making the canals and rivers to protect it from the geists. And what thanks do I get? They throw down my Order. Your own grandfather helped them . . . but he learned humility . . ."

He was so smug, so sure of himself, that Raed couldn't take it. He lunged forward and grabbed Derodak by the collar of his cloak. The fabric was slick under his fingers, but he had enough of a grip to swing him about. He connected with the rough stone wall with a satisfying smack, but his expression didn't change. Raed punched with his left fist, aiming to connect to his chin, but his opponent's hand moved quickly, blocking the strike, and then bringing his right around. When it connected with his jaw, the Young Pretender felt as though an anvil had hit him.

He staggered back, the room dipping in and out of focus. He found himself on his knees. At this stage even staying upright was an achievement. How could he be this strong? Dimly he saw the gray shadow of Derodak move closer.

"You don't see what he is doing, do you? You really have been blinded . . ."

His voice came from a long way off, and the sense of it was hard to grasp.

Derodak leaned down and whispered into his ear. "The great pard is looking for his freedom, and he is ever so close. You and I know that will never do . . ."

He was making no sense whatsoever. Raed reached out and grabbed hold of his ancestor's cloak. "You . . . you . . ." he muttered, "it was you that shackled him to my family. It is your fault."

"I did need him at first," Derodak conceded. "When I was first born into this world, I was not as I am now, and I feared death. I wanted to create a family to take my seed into the future. The Rossin's power promised that. It was also a way to control them if necessary—as it happened they turned on me, and you have had to bear the brunt of that."

His hand clenched around Raed's jaw and squeezed. The Young Pretender struggled for breath, clawing at the fingers that threatened to destroy him. He might as well have been pounding on a statue with bare fists.

Still however Derodak talked on; apparently quite happy to converse after so long in the shadows. "So I started another family, and this time I spread my seed a little farther afield. I made my own army over the generations."

As Raed's vision trembled on the edge of vanishing, his eyes locked on the brooch around the cloak. The circle of stars gleamed so brightly, and he understood. All those Deacons were his—and not just in the normal way of an Arch Abbot and his Order. They were as much his children as the Rossins were. Apparently there was no end to his craziness or his fecundity.

"Still, your blood will be of use. The last of the Imperial

line will help summon the Maker of Ways—after I have killed just the right one, he will come." Just like at the White Palace, Raed realized.

Desperate, Raed reached out and grasped the brooch with both hands, tearing it from the cloak. The diamonds in it cut into his hands and the pin pierced the palm of it deep. The pain was intense, and it felt as though he had hit a bone with it. Blood squirted out from the wound.

Now it was Derodak's turn to curse.

The grip around Raed's throat loosened, and he found himself abruptly dropped to the ground. The sudden flood of air into his body was a blessing, though the pain he had caused was not the only consequence. Blood. It was always about blood. The deepest and oldest magic that Ehtia and geist used in combination with cantrips, runes and weir-stones. In the end, it was blood.

Deep within Raed, the Rossin finally stirred. The Beast was uncurling and unfurling, enraged by the presence of Derodak as he had not been by anything else for a very long time. Blood summoned him from the torpor that their enemy had put him in.

Surging upright, Raed dealt an uppercut to the surprised Derodak. Something about the bloodletting had given the Young Pretender a tiny advantage, and he had to take it. Everything slowed, and even Raed's heartbeat felt labored.

Unlike Sorcha's Deacons, he had no access to cantrips or runes—but there were the stones. While Derodak was momentarily distracted, Raed ran forward and slammed his injured hands against the weirstone windows. He had no idea if it would do any good, but he was rewarded when the clear blue stone flared bright enough to burn eyes.

"Fool!" was the only word his captor had time to voice, before the Rossin flooded upward.

He took Raed over in an instant, but they shared the blood this time. Raed had called on him, and there was nothing else to be done. His mind was locked with the Beast's, and he had no chance of escaping the events that would unfurl after that. Actually, Raed found that he didn't want to miss a moment of this.

The Rossin ripped clothing as he molded flesh into his cat shape, but it was only a momentary change. The pard struck the weirstones that the first Emperor had molded with all the impact of a charging warhorse—and something else. It was always about blood, and blood powered something deeper. The weirstone took the geistlord's rage and magnified it.

The stone screamed and shattered around him. The ocean roared like another, even greater beast, and thrust itself through the breaks; finding the weakest points unerringly and pushing the Rossin-shaped hole even bigger. The ocean thrust itself deep and invaded Derodak's kingdom easily. If the Rossin was lucky, the water would carry the infestation of the Circle of Stars away altogether.

The abrupt change to water made necessary another transformation. The Rossin bent the flesh once more, pressing it into one more of his forms: the mer-lion. It was the shape he wore in his depictions on all the Rossin flags that had once flown so proudly over the palace at Vermillion.

The back legs of the pard merged and formed a thick powerful tail, while webbing sprang into being between the toes on his front paws. He still had the claws within though. Now the cold water that entered his body was expelled through gills on the side of his neck, which had also become thicker and more muscular.

He swam with as much ease as he had once leapt— though his roar was now silent in the murky depths. The water around the Rossin brought him information, just as the air did in his favored form.

They were not that far from shore; the ocean here tasted of river water and dirt. It was a taste he knew well; the Vermillion estuary that ebbed and flowed through the capital was not far off.

The ocean here was very deep though. Below, he could not see any rocks, only the untouched blackness of an endless trench. Derodak had made his foul lair on an underwater cliff that dropped away very suddenly. Moving water had helped keep him hidden from the Order of the Eye and the Fist, as well as protecting him from interference from the Otherside.

The Rossin swam with ease, but did not go too close to the room he had burst from. He had enough experience with the first Emperor to know that even in the direst circumstances, he could still be trusted to pull off some daring escape. Only when his head was removed from his body would the Rossin believe he was dead.

The truth was uncomfortable: Derodak still had enough power to overcome the Rossin. The pact they had made together all those hundreds of years before still held. It stung to admit that, and Raed, floating somewhere near the conscious world, was horrified.

In response, the Rossin circled angrily, scaring off a group of gray sharks that had come down to investigate what was going on. Much as it irked him, he knew that the Deacons were the answer to Derodak. Combined they might have the power to stand a chance, but then there was the Circle of Stars to consider.

The geistlord's baleful eye fixed on the cliff face. He could sense them in there . . . the children of Derodak's depravity. Each one of them touched by his blood, and each one of them looking up to him like he was a god. They fed Derodak, much like the Wrayth's various human additions did. Maybe he had even gotten the idea from that vile geistlord.

Just as the Rossin was readying to swim to the surface and see which shore he had been flung to, he felt something stirring below him. His sensitive skin tingled as pressure reached it, pressure that indicated something was rising from below.

Images of the last monster from the deep Raed had encountered flashed across the gap to the Rossin. His host had seen a whole ship destroyed by it; summoned by Derodak to kill Nynnia. It was a blunt weapon, but Derodak had never had much finesse with these things.

Peering down into the darkness, even the Rossin's sharp eyes could not quite make out what was rising toward him. His geistlord's pride wouldn't allow him to flee without at least seeing what he was facing, even though Raed was howling at him to get moving. It was an odd turnabout indeed.

The darkness at the bottom of the trench twisted, and tendrils of shadows clutched at the rock walls. Water was now rushing past the Rossin's streamlined form. Bubbles and fleeing fish raced by him as he struggled to remain upright and not be swept away by this unnatural current.

A sound made its way through the water, a keening, high-pitched noise that struck him almost like a blade. Baleful eyes suddenly appeared in the gloom, slitted and gleaming orange. Now the tendrils of shadows were not merely shadows . . . they were tentacles, pulling and wrapping around the stonework, as the massive body they were attached to rose nearer and nearer.

For a brief moment the Rossin was struck motionless; thinking this was it, the arrival of the Maker of Ways. The realm would be torn and geists of all shapes and kinds would come pouring in. Then, however, he could finally make out the body. It was long and tubular, and had a waving frill around the edges that might have been beautiful if it wasn't so huge. The tentacles were far thicker than the geistlord's body, and they were reaching out to him.

Now he understood fear. It did not matter if he were geistlord or Young Pretender, this thing had been brought out of the depths for the specific purpose of hunting both of them. Derodak had certainly developed an inflated dramatic flair over the centuries. The Rossin wondered if he should be flattered.

The sea beast was not fast, but then it did not have to be. The tentacles shot out for him—and there were many of them.

With a flex of his tail, the geistlord darted away, weaving this way and that as a forest of them descended in his direction. Up close he observed there were large and small ones, and it was the thinner ones that were harder to get away from. They flung themselves at him like a series of slimy pink nets. As a few touched him along his back, his flesh burned with sharp stings.

Pain was not a sensation that the Rossin had much time for, but he was getting a full taste of it now. He roared—though the ocean swallowed much of the effect—and batted at them. Many he cut free, but the water around him was beginning to turn into a veritable soup of them. The geistlord twisted and twisted on himself, trying to cut a way free.

However, the tentacles, large and small, were guiding him closer to the dark center of the monster. Now he caught a glimpse of the beak of the thing: curved and pale, it was three times longer than his body. Tentacles curled and flung around him, cutting off escape routes and shepherding him toward doom. That beak would snap him like a twig.

Raed Syndar Rossin and he would share the same broken fate. The line would die with him, and he would even miss the Maker of Ways. His last thought was how bitter it was that Derodak had won.

TWENTY

The Blood Will Out

Sorcha dreamed that her mother was holding her. She cradled her daughter, pressing her head in tight against her shoulder. Sorcha felt warm, safe and happy. Her nostrils were full of her mother's scent; roses and strength. She planted the lightest of kisses on her daughter's head and whispered, "Remember who you are."

Sorcha held tight to that gentle admonishment.

"Mother," she murmured into the thick dark hair, "why did you leave me?"

It was a foolish question, but it came right from the heart of the little girl lost in the Order, whose sole loved one had been the Presbyter of the Young. She'd only been able to give Sorcha so much attention and care. In the lonely times in the Abbey's garden, before she'd been taken into the novitiate for training, she had whiled away long afternoons wondering what her mother was like. Did they look the same? Sound the same? Did she miss her?

Sorcha did not need to wonder any longer. She was safe, missed, loved.

Just as she pulled that truth close, her mother pushed

back from her. Sorcha screamed in horror. It was not the face she had seen in the vision in the Wrayth hive—it was the Wrayth itself. The thing that was holding her was a bubbling mass of faces, all screaming for mercy and release. The form of the Wrayth held them bound and pressed together.

"I never left you," the creature growled, its hands tightening on her. "I have always been right here with you."

Eventually Sorcha's screams woke her, and she almost immediately wished they had not. Imprisonment of another kind waited.

Sorcha did not recognize the woman peering down at her, but she did recognize the type; long pale hair, and eyes that gleamed with something unnatural. The Wrayth was in the waking world too and looking out at Sorcha. She was being examined exactly as someone might when choosing a puppy from a litter.

The Wrayth woman straightened up, and Sorcha finally noticed that she was tied to a table—one that seemed to come very close to being like the draining table in Ulrich. Luckily, it did not have the spikes, but Sorcha was held at a tilted angle; not quite on her feet, not quite on her back.

At least they would have been unable to take her runes from her. Glancing down at her shackles she called on Seym, to fill her body with strength. Nothing happened.

Her captor let out a soft chuckle. "Do you really think that we have not mastered how to keep Deacons quiet, even if," she said, gesturing to the marks on Sorcha's flesh, "you have found a remarkable way to ingrain runes on yourself."

A cold, hard realization came over Sorcha. She was right where her mother had been. The dire feeling of helplessness was the very same as her mother must have felt when she'd been snatched all those years ago. Sorcha, just like her own mother had been, was not used to the sensation. She was a Deacon—no, more than that, she was the Harbinger. They couldn't do this to her!

However, that didn't seem to matter. The Wrayth woman pressed a hand on Sorcha's head and stared into her eyes.

The voices in her mind grew more insistent now, clamoring for something. Sorcha tried to not listen, but one voice grew louder and louder the longer the hand remained there. It was screaming over and over, *Obey, Obey!* It was painful, and terrifying, yet when it receded she was left panting, but still herself.

Apparently this was not the result that the Wrayth woman had been hoping for. She flicked Sorcha's head to one side with an impatient growl and walked away. The Deacon dared not consider what this might mean—that was until the Wrayth spoke.

"You are a deep disappointment, Sorcha Faris." Her voice was sharp and laden with venom. "You are so very close to our goal, and yet you fall short." Her hands clenched together while her eyes darted left and right. The Deacon had no doubt that the screaming voice was totally in control and letting out its frustration and anger inside that human skull.

"Really?" she gasped, licking her lips in an attempt to make her voice not come out as a dire croak. "You cannot know how much that pleases me."

The Wrayth seemed not to hear her, as she began to pace back and forth. "You have all the makings of the final weapon, and yet you remain aloof from us. We cannot connect with you." She stopped pacing and stared at Sorcha. "The fault lies not with your father, so it has to have been your mother who—"

"It is too late for recriminations now," a familiar voice spoke. He had stood out of Sorcha's line of sight, concealed behind the table she was strapped to. As he walked around into view, Sorcha felt her anger begin to boil, rising over the dull ache of helplessness.

Derodak, Arch Abbot of the Circle of Stars, stood next to the Wrayth and watched Sorcha rage. She strained against the bonds, calling out a stream of profanities that would have earned her stern retribution in the Order.

He was the maker of all Arkaym's misery . . . all this death and destruction. He had brought down the Order of the Eye and the Fist, the only protection for the people of Arkaym. He had caused the Empire to fall into civil war, and now Sorcha saw that he was working with the Wrayth. All these things he had done for his own profit, so that he might rule the world as his Ehtia race once had.

He waited until she was done before turning to the Wrayth. "So, since she is of no use to you, I take it our agreement still stands?"

The pale woman raked her eyes up and down Derodak, her face now devoid of any emotion. "If there was time, we would try again by breeding off her . . ."

Derodak raised a finger and wiggled it at her as if the Wrayth were a recalcitrant child. "Now, now, we all know there is no time for that. You have failed to make your weapon, so our original agreement remains; I shall give you the west to do with as you please. Raise the humans as cows for all I care, but this thing you made is now mine."

The woman's eyes said she would have murdered him if she had the chance, but eventually she nodded.

Sorcha tried to think of anything to say to stop what she was witness to, but what could be said to two immortal geistlords intent on the destruction of her whole world? He would enslave the geists that came through from the Otherside and rule the humans, while the Wrayth would have the western edge of the Empire to harvest.

Instead, Sorcha tugged on her bonds for a time, and offered no words for them to enjoy. Even the Bond was a dark, empty thread; nothing came along it to comfort her. She was alone again.

Yet her whole life she had tried not to be alone. In the embrace of the Order, she had found peace, purpose and friendship. Her partners and her colleagues had filled her life. Her mission to help those endangered by geists had given her something worthwhile to strive for. Now, she was watching the destruction of all of that from captivity. It was enough to break her. Hopelessness rushed in, and she had no Merrick to save her from its icy grip.

The Wrayth woman left the room, head held high, not acknowledging Derodak or Sorcha again. Now it was just the two of them in the room.

Sorcha turned her head away. She had no desire to see the triumph on his face. Could it really be just yesterday that she had driven the geists from the city and claimed the title of Harbinger? It felt like a lifetime ago.

She raised her head slightly to glare at Derodak. "Why are you really doing this? You are causing so much pain and misery to everyday folk—"

"My people ruled this world before the coming of the geists." He stared down at her for a moment, then bent and clasped her chin hard in his hand. "We were mighty and terrifying, because no one else could do the things we could do. When we fled, this place became as a wasteland of insects scrabbling to survive. I will show all of them the way to live. Show them all how to harness the geists and become mighty once more."

Sorcha realized it was worse than she thought; Derodak was no madman—he genuinely believed in his course. An immortal life span had not taught him anything but the value of control.

When she remained silent, he smiled, a slight lifting of the corner of his lips. "The first Order was my Order, and all that you have tried to build here was but a reflection of what I had already done." He flicked her chin aside and stepped back. "You may not be the weapon that the Wrayth hoped for, but I think you will suit my purpose very well."

Something about the way he said it, lingering over the words like each of them was a ripe fruit, sent a shock through Sorcha's system. She had not fought so damn hard to pull together the new Order just so that he could destroy it. Her mother had fought for her, and now she was going to fight for the rest of it.

"We shall be on our way," he said, bending and unlatching her bonds. "Vermillion is waiting for her leader."

Derodak could not be all that good of a Sensitive,

because he did not expect his prisoner to throw herself up and on him. She grabbed him around the head and neck, throwing her whole weight against his throat. Her vision was dancing with black spots, but it felt very good to finally have her hands on him. All of the dangers she had faced—the Murashev, Hatipai and the Wrayth—could not compare to this man. He had made it happen. It was an easy thing to let all of that flow through her. She was going to choke this man out and then beat his proud head with a rock until it was pulp. Let him show how immortal he was then.

They struggled together; Sorcha's one arm wrapped around his throat from behind, while her other hand sought out the knife on his belt. Her addled brain would have been happy to slit his throat. If he had taken the runes, then she would do it the old-fashioned way.

However, apparently Derodak didn't need the runes as much as she had expected. He jerked, and the back of his head connected with Sorcha's nose. The sudden explosion of pain disorientated her, but she held on. So he slammed her backward against the rough stone wall. The wind was knocked out of her, and her grip on his neck loosened just enough so that he was able to get a hand under hers. In one smooth move, he dumped her off his back to land on hers in the dirt.

The green flames of Shayst enveloped her, sucking away the strength from her muscles. In the flickering green light, Derodak smiled. "We have enough time yet, so that you may learn a lesson, Sorcha Faris. I am rather afraid it will be a painful one."

She struggled to rise, but nothing was working.

Derodak took his time, putting on a pair of fine leather Gauntlets. "The Patternmaker is a turncoat." He tilted his head, reconsidering. "Or rather he is the ultimate survivor. When he was in my possession, he created some new runes for me . . . and now I think I will show them to you."

He bent and clamped his Gauntlet on her arm. As she spiraled into agony, she knew that as an immortal, Derodak had learned a great deal about the application of pain.

TWENTY-ONE

Sibling Reunion

"There he is," Deacon Petav said, pointing out to port. "Your brother is indeed waiting for you as agreed."

Zofiya hoped the clenching knot in the pit of her stomach was not reflected on her face.

Captain Revele appeared out of the bridge of the *Summer Hawk*. She snapped to attention in front of the Grand Duchess and offered up her spyglass in one hand without comment. Zofiya saluted and took the brass instrument from her.

She trained it toward where the sun was progressing toward the horizon, and saw the *Winter Kite* ahead of them just in front of the mountain known as the Sky Tower. It was not alone either; twenty or so airships floated nearby. They gleamed and fluttered in the light breeze.

The Grand Duchess wouldn't have minded that so much—since she had brought her own fleet—but they were not tied up together in the usual way for airships suing for peace. They circled behind their flagship the *Kite*, but looked like at any moment's notice they might go into a more combative formation. Yet, from the prow hung the white banner of truce, and all of the cannons were rolled back from their positions.

Captain Revele took the spyglass when it was handed back to her. "Are you certain this is the correct course, Imperial Highness? We could communicate with weirstones instead from the safety of the *Summer Hawk* . . ."

"No," the Grand Duchess shot back and then immediately realized her rudeness. "I am sorry, Captain. It is just that I must see my brother, face-to-face. Weirstone communication is very limited, and I must make my point very, very clearly to him. A great deal rests on that."

The captain nodded, but offered up another suggestion. "At least take a platoon of marines with you. I would feel . . ."

She shook her head again. "One platoon would not be enough if things go badly, and it would only give the impression of a threat. I do not know how broken the Emperor is, so I can take no risks upsetting him."

Zofiya understood that none of those around her were comfortable with what she was doing. They would have preferred she retreat to Vermillion and begin approaching the rebel Princes to join her side. They had said as much in the days after she'd returned to the palace. The pretender who claimed to be the sister of Raed Rossin was losing battles, and many now suspected her for what she actually was.

However, that would do no good; the fighting would rage just as long, and then Zofiya would be waging war on her own brother.

So seeing that her commander's mind was made up, Captain Revele did as she was bid and instructed the pilot to draw the *Summer Hawk* up to dock with the *Winter Kite*. She did not look happy about it though.

As they came within twenty feet of the other ship, Zofiya decided now was the time that she would drop the bomb on her other companions too. "Deacon Petav, I must insist you stay here on the *Hawk* while I converse with my brother."

Part of her was amused by the look of shock on his face.

He certainly hadn't seen that one coming—and it must have been quite the sensation for a Sensitive Deacon.

When his mouth opened to let out some pointed argument, she held up her hand. "My brother is trembling on the very edge of sanity, but Derodak has infected him with an utter hatred of any kind of Deacon. If you set foot on his flagship, then there is a very strong likelihood that he will kill us all."

The hooded heads of the Deacons turned slightly to each other, but after a moment Petav spread his hands. "Very well, Imperial Highness. We will make sure to keep ourselves out of sight, but we will be watching." He leaned in close to her, his hood almost touching her face. "Just remember, at some point you may have to come to terms with the fact that your brother is a lost cause."

The audacity of his words caught Zofiya by surprise, yet she could not offer a rebuttal in the open. Instead, she glared at him. He had only spoken her deepest fears, but she wouldn't acknowledge them.

"I could expect no less," she replied for all to hear. The Deacons quickly glided below, and then all she had to think about was the approaching meeting.

The *Winter Kite* was the very first airship that the Imperial Air Fleet had started with. She was impressive, with her scarlet envelope and long lines of cannons running from prow to stern.

Zofiya frowned, suddenly wishing she had not already dismissed the Deacons, because there was an odd square, squat machine sitting right next the gunwales of the *Kite*. It looked ugly and out of place on the deck, and what's more, she had no idea what it was.

As head of the Imperial Guard she had been in charge of armaments. She racked her brain to try and shake out any memory of the experimental weapons they had worked on, but still there was nothing to be had. She had not seen her brother for many, many weeks—he could have been up to anything.

The two airships gracefully slid together, and a board-ing ramp was lowered between the two. The *Winter Kite*'s deck was full of people, mostly Imperial Guards in scarlet uniforms and a scattering of councilors, but there were a few others out of uniform that she did not recognize. One of the Guards whistled her announcement on a tin pipe, and Zofiya stepped forward until she was poised suspended between the two ships. "Permission to come aboard, Impe-rial Majesty," she called out.

That was when her brother emerged from among his soldiers for the first time. Kal looked better than when she had seen him last, fleeing from the Rossin with the Mother Abbey falling down about their ears. He wore a golden helm and breastplate as if he were off to war, though neither looked much more than decorative. He could have been the brother that she had thrown to the ground to protect from a sniper only a season before—except for the look in his eyes. No warmth gleamed in them, and he did not hold out his arms to her.

"Permission granted," he said, his voice ringing between the two airships.

It seemed as though everyone was holding their breath, as Zofiya took her fateful step forward onto the *Winter Kite*. Out of the corner of her eye she caught sight of a couple of the Imperial Guards shifting fractionally. Among their ranks were faces she recognized, and each one she filed away into memory.

While part of her noted such things, another sectioned-away part wailed that she had to do such a thing. However, she had built walls around that vulnerable portion and would not let it out—especially not here.

Kal was watching her approach, and it was impossible to tell what he was thinking. Previously, she had always been able to read her brother's moods. He had been a kind child and a ridiculously kind Emperor. Zofiya's jaw clenched as she thought of a hundred painful things to do to the one who had brought this all to pass, Derodak.

Finally, she stood six feet away from him, and after a breath to steady herself, sunk into a low curtsey. Perhaps much of the spectacle of doing it was marred by wearing a uniform and not a Court dress, but that was not its purpose.

A low bow meant her head was exposed to whatever the Emperor wanted to deal out. She stayed down for a long time—or at least it felt like a long time—and the back of her neck itched. At any moment she expected to feel the kiss of steel, or maybe a pistol barrel placed against her head.

"Welcome . . . Sister." Kal's voice broke the tension of the moment, and she straightened back up to her full height. This meant that they were looking eye to eye. The Grand Duchess' gaze flickered to the right. She spotted Ezefia among those standing behind her brother, and had to stop herself from making comment. Her brother's wife had a large swollen belly and eyes hollow with horror and misery.

Zofiya had never had cause to spend time with the Empress, because they really shared only Kal in common. Ezefia liked to dance and gossip and make merry. Her sister-in-law liked more serious pursuits. Now however, Zofiya wished that they had spent more hours together, because it looked like both of them could use some support in this moment.

"You have not offered your congratulations." Kal's tone was light, and yet strung through with a hint of menace. "Look," he said, grabbing Ezefia by the arm and yanking her forward. The woman—or rather the Empress—stumbled and nearly fell. Zofiya instinctively stepped forward to catch her, but Kal pulled her upright and away from his sister. "Can you not see we are blessed? What do you think it will be . . . a boy or a girl?"

It was worse than she had imagined. The crack in her brother's voice went all the way into his soul. She knew that within just a few moments—she'd been with him every day of his life.

Yet, she couldn't afford to put a foot wrong. She'd heard

nothing about the Empress' pregnancy and felt ill prepared when confronted with it. So much for all the Sensitivity of Deacons! "I . . . I am just—"

He waved his hand. "It doesn't matter anyway—whatever it is, it shall be a bastard!"

Silent tears were now rolling down Ezefia's face from her peerless green eyes. Her sister-in-law knew how she felt. She'd been in a situation where she had been afraid to make noise, to draw attention. Every part of the Grand Duchess wanted to grab her and hustle her off this cursed airship and onto the *Summer Hawk*. Yet, she could not. More was at stake than the Empress' fears. So she remained still and tried to merely distract her brother from Ezefia as best she could.

"Then take another to wife, dear Brother," she said as calmly as she could. "Denounce her before the Court and choose again. There are plenty of Princesses still aching to be your Empress." It remained unspoken that the field had undoubtedly narrowed since last time they had searched, but there would be some Princes that would willingly fling their daughters at Kal even at this juncture.

Her brother gave his wife a sharp shake and then threw her down. She landed on the deck with a thump and kept her eyes riveted to the deck of the airship.

Just who exactly had bedded the Empress—or even if it was a crazy delusion of the Emperor—Zofiya could not tell. She did not want to ask and risk inflaming the situation.

Kaleva began pacing back and forth between his wife and the lines of Imperial Guard at his back. He was like some mad puppet darting around, with the rest of the people present merely the backdrop to his performance. Zofiya had her answer confirmed. Her brother was indeed mad, and not just angry.

Derodak had broken him, and if he could be fixed remained a mystery. The fate of an Empire with a mad Emperor was well documented, and though Zofiya might not like it, she would have to do what others in history had done:

take the throne for the benefit of its people. She decided in her head in that moment she would indeed be regent.

The fact settled in her mind like a stone. Yes, she would be regent, and she would have the best lay Brothers of Sorcha's Order examine her brother. Perhaps they knew a way to heal him of his grave mental injury. After all, they had been dealing with hurt Deacons for centuries and—

Her thoughts were jerked back to the here and now when she abruptly realized that Kal had stopped right in front of her and was examining her with the intensity of an eagle looking at an injured lamb.

"It was Derodak," he hissed to her, "in case you were wondering. Derodak and my Empress conspired together. She fell into his bed and spread her legs for him like the whore she is."

Never in her whole life had Zofiya heard her brother use such words; he had always been a gentle and soft-spoken man. It made her want to weep to see him like this.

She cleared her throat and picked out every word carefully. "If that is true, then she must indeed be put away . . ."

Behind him, Ezefia raised her head finally, looked directly at the Grand Duchess and shook her head vehemently. She only mouthed her denial. *He forced me to.*

Zofiya's heart sank. She knew intimately that the Arch Abbot of the Circle of Stars could indeed make people do and say things. In fact, Derodak had done that to Kal, so why couldn't he see that? His cruel indifference now only showed how deep he had fallen into insanity.

"And the Princes?" her brother asked her, tilting his head, and raking her with an appraising gaze. "What shall we do with the traitorous Princes?"

She was aware that in front of her, some of the Imperial Guards were making direct eye contact with her. Flickers of tension and fear ran across numerous faces. Zofiya felt their silent urgings for her to do something . . . anything. It was time to be daring, because now she knew any way she jumped would be the wrong way with Kal in his current state.

Zofiya took his elbow and tried to guide him away from the press of people, toward the gunwales. To the port, there was a clear break of sky; endless white clouds drifted across that beautiful blue expanse. Zofiya couldn't be sure about Kal, but it certainly made her feel a little calmer. Perhaps, being out of the direct gaze of so many would soothe him a little.

She hoped so, as she began. "Remember our father, Kal?" He nodded, but the thunderclouds were still gathering in his eyes. It was now or never, so Zofiya proceeded. "Do you remember how he used to beat the dogs?"

A long breath seemed to go out of him. "Yes," he ventured in a small voice.

A flicker of hope kindled in Zofiya, but she dared not examine it to closely. "You and I used to hate it when he did that, but he said it was to teach them a lesson when they had done something wrong."

Kal nodded again, his eyes fixed on her.

"And do you remember what he said, when the dogs came back after being beaten?"

The Emperor leaned back against the gunwales for a second. "He said, 'Give them some meat, so that they learn to like the taste of the whip.'"

It was a cruel and totally wrong message, but Zofiya hoped that it might reach her brother. Their father had certainly beaten the Princes mercilessly, so now maybe Kal would understand. She wasn't sure about giving them some reward, but she just wanted him to come back with her to Vermillion as calmly as possible.

After a moment's pause, she dared put a hand lightly on her brother's forearm; she could feel his muscles tensing. "You've used the whip enough, Kal . . . Let's go back home. Please . . ."

She hardly dared to breathe. It was hard for Zofiya to be gentle and supple. He did not move, and for a moment there was hope. At least for a heartbeat or two.

Then with a twist, he flung her hand off him. "You are

with them," he snarled, as his fists clenched at his sides. "I know what you've been doing, conspiring with the Deacons to take my Empire. I know," he went on with a wicked smile, "that you have sat on my throne in Vermillion, hiding behind the word 'regent'—like I am some child."

Zofiya's heart began racing. "No, Kal. No! That's not it at all. Vermillion was a mess, the Empire is a mess, and I only wanted to assure them that I was there to protect them. That is what a regent does when the Emperor is not well—" She lurched to a halt, suddenly realizing what she had said was completely the wrong thing. Diplomacy had never been her strong suit.

Kaleva's eyebrows drew together in a dark bow, and his mouth pressed into a hard thin line. "That's what they said when they took the last Emperor off the throne!" he snarled. "They tried to install a regent at first. I think, Sister, you will find it not so easy to take *my* throne from me."

Zofiya was caught between wanting to smack him in the face or to sob and plead for the return of the brother she loved. That indecision nearly cost her life.

"Imperial Highness!" One of the Guards behind them with a very familiar face broke ranks and held out his hand to her. "Run! They—" His warning was cut off by one of her brother's soldiers effectively running him through with his saber.

However, the warning had triggered the Grand Duchess' instincts. She sprang backward just as a long string of blue white lightning struck the space where she had been standing. She caught a glimpse of a man—not in any kind of uniform—standing by that curious machine. He was grinning, even though he had almost hit the Emperor as well as her.

Madmen! They were all madmen! Rifles were raised and pointed in her direction, but in the mass of Imperial Guards, chaos broke out. Brothers in arms, all clad in the red uniforms, began to wrestle and fight with one another.

For a moment, Zofiya contemplated tackling her brother

and taking them both over the edge, but that would solve nothing for the Empire. Besides, the cracked-looking man at the machine was turning the narrow barrel of it in her direction again.

She ran, pushing off from the deck while hearing rifle fire begin to start up between the marines on both the *Winter Kite* and the *Summer Hawk*. The path to the gangway was blocked, so she grabbed hold of the rigging, cut a piece of it loose with her saber and then pushed off madly toward her airship. She had the impression of clouds wafting by, while bullets flew in her direction. For a second she was elated, and then Zofiya crashed into the deck of the *Summer Hawk*.

As soon as she was back on her feet, Zofiya realized it was not just her brother that had gone mad—so too had the situation.

The Deacons emerged from the depths of the airship, just as the crackle of her brother's machinery was firing again. With capes fluttering in the growing breeze, the Deacons held up the flaming red shield, providing protection for those on the *Summer Hawk* from the mad machine. It became hard to see as red and blue energies sparked and flew everywhere. Bullets were, unfortunately, not stopped by the shield. Soldiers on both sides were falling.

Zofiya snatched up a rifle from a nearby marine and dropped into cover behind the wheelhouse. She found Captain Revele there, who despite bleeding from a wound in the leg was firing back enthusiastically.

She shot a glance at the Grand Duchess. "So it didn't go quite as you thought then?"

Zofiya cradled the rifle against her shoulder and returned fire. "Unfortunately this is exactly how I imagined it going. I think now would be a good time to leave."

Revele nodded and yelled orders over the rumble of battle to her crew, some of whom had managed to take shelter against the gunwales. "Cut the damn plank!"

While bullets flew and lances of power careened

between the two airships, one spry lad wriggled his way to where the moorings were and sliced the rope that bound them to the *Winter Kite*.

It was by no means an escape. They were now twisting away from the other airship, but all it meant was that the form of the attack changed. No one on the *Winter Kite* wanted to set the *Summer Hawk* ablaze while it was tethered to the flagship. As the *Hawk*'s engines caught, and they turned to port away from their attacker, they also escaped out of range of the bullets. However, the cannons and whatever that damned machine was now came fully into play.

Zofiya raced to the Deacons, while Revele screamed for the *Hawk*'s armaments to be rolled out. Deacon Petav stood at the head of his little group, the light of the runes flickering on their now exposed arms. The Gauntlets and the Strop had been impressive enough, but there was something far more primal about seeing the runes in action on their flesh and skin.

The air smelled tangy and sharp, as if just after a lightning storm. It was something that had to have come from Kal's new machines, because Zofiya had never encountered that odor before.

"Can you hold them off like that?" she demanded of Petav. Zofiya was certainly grateful to the Deacons for their protection, but she needed to know that it was something they could continue to supply. If they couldn't, then this would most likely be the last flight of the *Summer Hawk*. The gasses in the ship's envelope were not susceptible to flame, but the fine material could certainly be punctured.

Petav looked gray, which did not give her much cause for elation. If a Deacon could be shaken by what had just happened, then she hated to think what that might mean.

"A weirstone tinker machine," he muttered, shooting a glance over his shoulder at his colleagues, who nodded in mute confirmation. "What fresh madness is this that—"

"Look," Zofiya snapped, "we can discuss this horror later . . . say when we are safely back in Vermillion."

The Deacon nodded, and his eyes grew glassy. The Grand Duchess knew that look very well; Merrick had worn it often when using his Center. "Go up." His voice was slightly slurred as if he were drunk or had just woken up. "Take the fleet into the clouds."

Up sounded like a fine idea, since getting hammered by their cannons and nameless machine was not something to be wished for.

Revele appeared at her side. Even in the midst of chaos her hat and uniform were still immaculate. Zofiya contemplated how strange it was the little things she noticed in a crisis.

"Deacon Petav says make for the clouds," the Grand Duchess barked at her captain.

Zofiya and Revele turned and quickly scanned the scene. Their vessel was nearest the barrage from the *Winter Kite*, but the other airships in the Emperor's Fleet were positioning themselves so that they too could bring their weapons to bear.

Revele quickly gave the circular spinning motion to her first mate, who was standing at the door to the bridge; he then ducked back in to give the order. The *Summer Hawk* began to rise sharply beneath her feet, so that all on her deck had to crouch a little or be thrown down. Zofiya felt as though her stomach had been left some hundred feet below, but at least the dire machine of her brother's could not apparently fire upward very well. The blue white light spat beneath them, narrowly missing their hull.

They had, it seemed, bought themselves some small amount of time. Zofiya raced to the gunwales and grabbed hold of the rigging, leaning over to observe what was happening. The rest of the airships were following the flagship's lead and rising into the clouds in pursuit, but they had to keep out of range of the mad blue lightning.

Deacon Petav joined her at the railing, his eyes scanning

the scene with a slightly glazed look. "They seem to be having some trouble with their technology," he said, with a slight twist of his lips.

"Good," she replied, clenching her hands on the rail. "That gives us some time."

The blue lightning finally flickered off, and now her brother's airships could maneuver without restriction. They were angling upward, heading swiftly after the *Summer Hawk*. The other ships in the Grand Duchess' smaller fleet were turning about after the pursuers, but it was hard to tell which would catch up with her first.

The Emperor's machine could quite possibly rip the *Summer Hawk* apart before they could engage them. "Reverend Deacon, I suggest you put your mind to coming up with a way for us to fend off that machine, or this could be the shortest regency in Imperial history."

Deacon Petav reached into his robe and withdrew a small weirstone. It did not seem like much against all that was arrayed against them. "I think I have an idea that just might work."

That smile was rather off-putting, but the newest regent of Arkaym had to trust he knew what he was doing.

TWENTY-TWO

Coyote's Call

"Whatever gods you pray to, they are indeed mighty," said a voice filled with infinite sarcasm.

Merrick's mind locked on it. Consciousness swam toward him, but there was icy-cold water filling his lungs. By the Bones, he was drowning!

The Sensitive turned his head and coughed spurts of frigid river water onto the stony bank he was lying face-down on. Once he was able to suck in mouthfuls of air instead of liquid, his mind was able to focus on where he was and just who was talking to him. His complaining body, as it warmed, was telling him that he had been beaten like laundry on a stone.

Carefully, Merrick slid his hands underneath his chest and with an effort of will rolled over. The sun was still high in the sky, so it could not have been long since he leapt into the void.

"It must be nice to be able to be so idle while the world is ready to tear itself apart." The voice came again, and just as cutting in its delivery.

Merrick closed his eyes for a second, gathered his
strength and craned his neck to see who was speaking so
rudely to him. When he took it in, for a moment he wondered how badly he had been struck on the head.

Upside down, it looked like a huge coyote was addressing him. He rolled over and managed to get to his knees.

"I am afraid you have lost your weapon," the Beast
commented, as the Deacon's numb hands fumbled at his
waist for his saber.

The Sensitive opened his Center and saw the unfortunately familiar silver blaze of a geistlord. Considering its
shape he knew immediately who it was.

"The Fensena," he groaned, pulling himself to his feet.
"The Broken Mirror, the Master of . . ."

The coyote's eyes narrowed. "Yes, yes . . . all that and
also, since you were asking, your savior." He shook himself, sending spray all over Merrick as if to make a point.

"Thank you," Merrick stammered. He felt he should be
polite considering his predicament—even more so since
his life might depend on it.

As the weak sun's rays warmed him a little, he was trying feverishly to recall what he knew about the Fensena.
Apart from the fact he was a geistlord and not to be trusted,
Merrick had never heard that the beast was a killer. He
usually left his victims alive, though exhausted. Was this
what the coyote was planning now?

The geistlord bent his front paws in a strange copy of a
human bow. "My Lord Ehtia, it was a pleasure."

"Ehtia?" Merrick asked, trying to surreptitiously locate
where he might run. Above him on the cliffs, he could see
the dark shapes of Melochi and Shedryi making their way
down to him. Breed horses were especially loyal and intelligent, and luckily also remarkably unafraid of geists.
However, they would not reach him before the Fensena
could rip his throat out. "I am not Ehtia."

The coyote tilted his head and sat back on his haunches.
He did not look worried about the approach of horses in the

least. "Humans really are the most stupid creatures," he remarked. "How do you think Nynnia of the mists found you? Do you think she can rip just anyone through time and space? Only blood will out."

Merrick's attention snapped sharper all of a sudden. The fog of his descent lifted from his mind. "How do you—"

"I am the Fensena." The coyote's pink tongue lolled out of his mouth before he licked his nose. "I gather secrets and knowledge. The Scavenger of Wisdom, the Order of the Golden Spider once called me. I don't suppose you remember them?" He looked expectantly at Merrick.

As he slowly shook his head, the Deacon tried to come to terms with the fact that a geistlord knew so many of his secrets.

The Fensena let out a strangely human sigh. "It was a very small order that died out three hundred years ago in Delmaire, so I don't suppose I should be surprised. Ehtia used to train their young better."

Merrick had grown up hearing rumors and gossip that there was Ancient blood in his family on his mother's side, yet he'd always assumed it was just a way for them to make themselves seem important.

"Is that why you saved me?" he asked cautiously.

The Fensena made an odd yipping noise that Merrick though might be a kind of laughter. "The Ehtia brought us here with their meddling with weirstones . . . but that is because the Maker of Ways sent the weirstones in the first place. It knew that curious humans could not leave them alone. Yet still that is not the reason I saved you."

Merrick had seen the Ehtia fleeing when he'd been transported to the past by Nynnia. They had told him about the weirstones—but to find out they had been tricked cut deep. He wondered if Nynnia knew. Something told him that they had discovered this fact when they reached the Otherside; it would certainly explain why Nynnia always looked so melancholy.

Merrick sat back on a large riverbed stone and took in

a long, deep breath before asking, "So what is the real reason?"

"You have a purpose." The Fensena's gold eyes flickered, as if he too were examining Merrick with his Center.

"I don't believe in the little gods or fate, geistlord. I find it strange that you do."

"I do not, but I do believe there is only one person in this realm who can help Sorcha Faris halt the Maker of Ways and stop this world being ripped apart." The coyote twitched his tail sharply.

Merrick stood and began wringing out his silver fur cloak. It seemed to be water-repellant, but still he didn't want it ruined. His suspicions were up, but through the lens of his Center he could see no suggestion of deception in the geistlord. It was certainly an unusual situation for a Deacon to be in. He could not recall many conversations between his kind and the Fensena's. Usually there were runes, fire and screaming. If he had not just seen his partner ripped away by another geistlord, he might have been interested in discussing many, many things with the Fensena.

However, he had just lost Sorcha, his friend, and his Bond. He could feel a faint flicker of her life in his perception, but it was receding.

"Then help me find her," Merrick asked, desperately. "I almost lost her once to the Wrayth without even knowing it. I can't let them have her." Sorcha's fear of the voices in her head and the image of what her mother had endured filled his mind. He could only imagine what a nightmare she had been taken into. They could not want to breed off her; there was no time with the Maker of Ways coming soon.

"It is too late to stop that," the coyote said, getting to his feet, his brindle fur gleaming with droplets of water. "We must rely on her strength or all is lost. Do you think she has enough within her?" Those golden eyes pierced him through.

"Yes." He answered without contemplating for a moment.

"Then we must assume that she will be where she needs to be." The Fensena rose to his feet, so Merrick scrambled to his. The horses had nearly reached them, and Shedryi was already tossing his head in dismay at the smell of a geistlord.

"We need you to be where you need to be," the Fensena said, showing absolutely no fear of the large stallion trotting menacingly in his direction.

Merrick staggered over and grabbed hold of Shedryi's bridle. He calmed the horse as best he could, and it gave him an excuse to gather his own scrambled thoughts. A geistlord wanting to help was a curious thing. "Why should I trust you?" he muttered softly.

The Fensena however had the best and sharpest ears. "Because Sorcha Faris does." When Merrick spun around in shock, he found his gaze locked with the gold eyes of the coyote.

"Use your little rune Aiemm, if you must," the Fensena said mildly, "but it was I that took away the curse of immortality that Hatipai's foolish son gave her."

It was such an outrageous claim that Merrick had to know; the swirling lines of Aiemm flared and ran like silver across Merrick's forehead. He saw Sorcha's face, her blue eyes gleaming with despair, and felt her words in his mouth. *"You will take this mantle of impermeability from me as a favor?"*

His partner had made a deal with a geistlord. The world had become a mad place, so he was not shocked by that, it was the fact she had not told him about it. At the time of their reunion, they had been without the Bond, and after, with all the confusion of the breaking of the Order, she had never mentioned it again. All those months between had been full of simply trying to stay alive. Merrick tried to justify Sorcha's actions in his head before he spoke.

"What . . ." He stopped, cleared his throat. "What favor did you ask in payment?"

The Fensena tilted his head, his ears twisting this way

and that. "I have not yet asked my boon, but remember I could just have easily left her there. I think you are starting to understand the position she was in. No partner. No Young Pretender. Just me."

Merrick's head jerked up, and he threw his Center wide in a mad attempt to feel out Raed Syndar Rossin. He could not. He too was gone from the immediate area.

The Sensitive swallowed hard. He could sense no deceit from the geistlord, but then one of his names was Oath Bender. The uncomfortable truth was that he was alone.

"It is hard," Merrick spoke softly, "to believe in gods at all, when I am left at the end of the world with only a geist-lord for company."

The weight of despair was pressing down on Merrick. Though it had been with him in their months of flight, at this moment it felt crippling. Merrick Chambers bowed his head and wondered if it were best just to lie down and give in to it.

The wetness of a damp nose was pressed into the palm of his hanging hand. Everything that the Deacon had been taught should have made him jerk his arm away, but for some reason he did not.

When he glanced up, the Fensena was holding him pinned with those golden discs of eyes. "There remains some time, human, and the blood of the Ehtia still flows in you."

"Will they come? The Ehtia?" Merrick asked in a rush, suddenly wanting to see Nynnia more desperately than he had in a long time.

"Do not look for their help," the Fensena said, with a low growl in his voice. "The Ehtia have spent their power on surviving the Otherside, and not all of them are as car-ing as the one you loved. You however have more than enough strength to do this. Let me show you."

The coyote led him away from the water, to the cliff edge where there was a fine view of the distant mountains.

For a moment Merrick wondered if the geistlord meant to knock him over the edge to his death.

"Use Mennyt," the Fensena said, sitting down. "Look to the sky for your answer."

The Deacon hesitated; the last time he had looked into the Otherside the parade of geists waiting to enter had given him nightmares. Nothing could have changed since that time.

The Fensena said nothing more, merely looking at him steadily with those eerie gold eyes. So Merrick reached up and traced the Pattern of his Third Eye that was carved into his skin. The world of Arkaym grayed away. The rush of power made him giddy for an instant, because now when he called on Mennyt it filled all of him. The loss of the Strop had not been a bad thing.

The landscape below faded and was overlaid with the dark symphony of the Otherside. It was as Merrick expected; many of the geists were close enough that he felt as if he reached out he would touch them. It was a sight to send him tumbling back into despair.

Then the Fensena's voice reached him. "Your scholars were right; there is an ebb and a flow to the Otherside. Our worlds perform an odd dance, and the perihelion of that dance is coming . . . but it is not yet. Look to the distance."

Dragging his attention away from the frightening closeness of the geists, Merrick did as bid. He tore his gaze away, up to the mountains, and a frown formed under his Third Eye. A faint silver light was leaking from them, as if a tear had been made in the fabric of reality. He had never heard or read of such a thing . . . except in the descriptions of the Break. The first time the geists came.

Merrick's heart began to race and his throat seized up. "Is it coming already?" he croaked out.

"It is near"—the Fensena's voice now seemed almost soothing—"but it is not yet here. The timing is important, and as predictable as this world's seasons. Dérodak has been waiting in the shadows for this for a thousand years. His one moment when he may gain control of all the geists."

Merrick cleared his suddenly barren throat. "How long do we have?"

"One cycle of the moon, and then we must be there to stop it." The Fensena turned and angled himself back in the direction of the city. "You do not have long to prepare."

"What of Sorcha and Raed?" Merrick asked, letting Mennyt slip from his grasp.

"Dérodak will not kill them . . . not yet at least. He will hope to harness their blood for the opening, so he does not have to risk his own life." The coyote was now standing close to the Breed horses, which they did not like in the least. "Every moment you waste is a moment you give him advantage. You will need every Deacon and every weirstone you can gather in that time."

Merrick realized what the geistlord was saying: he was not really alone. He had lost Sorcha and Raed, at least for now, but he was the First Presbyter of the Enlightened. It had only been birthed the night before, but it was the only and best chance of stopping Dérodak. If he did not take the reins now, it would all fall apart. The Deacon did not consider himself particularly brave, but he had training and experience to assist him.

Quickly he climbed onto Melochi and took up Shedryi's reins. Once there, he looked down at the Fensena. They called the geistlord many things—one of them was Widow Maker. It seemed a fragile thing to trust him, and undoubtedly there were more motives at play than were immediately apparent, but one thing was clear: he was all the guidance Merrick would have.

However, there was one thing that the geistlord did not need to tell the Sensitive: where they had to be when the barrier was thinnest. The capital of Vermillion, where the Break had been and where it would come again. Merrick might not believe in fate, but there was a certain tidiness to events.

As the great coyote looked up at him, Merrick felt the weight of that settle on him in almost a comfortable fashion. "A fine fur cloak you wear, young Presbyter. Let us see if you are worthy of it—and the name of your new Order."

Before Merrick could ask him anything further, the Fensena broke into a trot, forcing the human to follow in his wake.

TWENTY-THREE

Ending Loyalty

The unnerving thing about the sky was that it was so quiet. As the *Summer Hawk* rose through the air like a cork released from the bottom of a lake, they quickly left the screaming and noise behind. The wet kiss of the clouds on Zofiya's face almost convinced her that everything was going to be all right. Perhaps it would have, had she been a different person.

She stood at the gunwales, while sailors scurried around and Deacon Petav consulted with his weirstone. The Grand Duchess, in this moment of peace she knew couldn't last for long, found her thoughts strangely drifting to her father.

Her mother had been the thirteenth wife of the King of Delmaire. An inconsequential nobody, who had been swallowed by the harem of wives and had never played any part in the life of the Princess she had birthed. Her father however loomed large; always ready with the harsh counsel and harsher punishments. He looked on Arkaym as the hellhole of the world; the place where geists had come from and still controlled. It contained no civilization and no worth—that was why he had happily sent his leftover Prince and Princess to it.

However, as she stood on the precipice of horror, Grand Duchess Zofiya thought of some of the lessons that he had thrashed into his multitude of sons and daughters. With her eyes closed she could see him sitting on the throne of jade, addressing them all with a riding crop tucked under one arm.

"A leader must always be ready to spill blood—no matter whose it is—there are no loyalties or boundaries when you sit on a throne."

That day when Zofiya knelt on the floor with all her brothers and sisters, it was Kaleva's little hand that had stolen into hers. Tears squeezed themselves out of the corners of her eyes, and she tried to tell herself that it was the wind that was doing it.

Captain Revele cleared her throat, and Zofiya dashed them away while her back was turned. "Yes, Captain?"

The master of the *Summer Hawk* showed no sign that she had seen anything like weakness in the regent. "I thought you should know, Imperial Highness, I've had word from the rest of our fleet. Your brother's ships are pursuing us and not engaging them. Rather than a battle he seems intent on capturing you above everything else. Should I send word for them to engage?"

Zofiya thought about it for an instant. It was not that she had any wish to die, but she also could not afford to lose those precious airships either. "Tell them to hang back. Deacon Petav says he has an idea."

The captain raised one eyebrow but did not question. She moved sharply back to the bridge. The *Summer Hawk* was flying in the clouds now, but this would only be protection for a while. They had Deacons who could see well enough, but her brother's fleet was not without its own resources. They had navigational weirstones and the wherewithal to use them.

Petav was coming toward her holding out the weirstone as if it contained the answers. When he stopped before Zofiya, a slight smile lurked on his lips. "I have made contact with the others of my Order."

"Can they come pull us out of this cloud? Perhaps give my brother back his reason?" Zofiya found she was snapping just a little. The truth was, she was heartily sick of promises and hope. She needed real help. In a voice laden with sarcasm, she snapped, "Can they magically transport themselves onto a moving airship?"

Petav's smile faded a little, but he did not back down. "I thought I recognized the man on the ship, the one standing by the machines. Vashill is his name, once a tinker of Vermillion." He paused, and the creak of the airship was the only sound.

Zofiya hated people who grew silent merely to increase their own importance. "Well?"

"His mother helped the remains of the Order escape Vermillion, and she has been traveling with us. I was able to speak to her, and give her a description of what her son has created."

Zofiya stared hard at him, and he cleared his throat somewhat nervously. "She has given me ideas on how to combat the machines—maybe even destroy them."

The regent closed her eyes for just a second. When she opened them, he and the idea were still there. "How close do we have to be?" she asked.

Petav pressed his lips together in a white line. "Very," he replied. His voice and his hand holding the weirstone were both very steady. Like her, this Deacon would do what needed to be done.

"Send one of your Sensitives to the bridge then. Find me the *Winter Kite* in this cloud." The regent turned her head and called, "Captain Revele!"

The officer appeared immediately; in the gray fog she might have been waiting not that far off.

Zofiya flicked her head in Petav's direction. "We have a plan, but you are probably not going to like it."

When she had told the captain what it was, she turned a little pale, but she quickly left them to make the arrangements needed.

After that, Revele took her place with the marines who were arranged at the aft deck. Zofiya knew there was little worse than waiting as a soldier—except of course for battle itself.

When she stood before them, she explained her plan to them in slightly lesser detail, and then took her place beside the captain. Deacon Petav appeared again, but this time with a wedge of Deacons. He took up position to the rear of the marines. Then all of them waited in silence, while the airship creaked gently around them as if they were not about to be very foolhardy.

The *Summer Hawk* lived up to her name, swooping and turning, the deck alternatively rising and falling under their feet as the Deacon on the bridge helped angle them just so. Zofiya did not like relying on Deacons so very much, but this seemed to be the way of things. Her brother had chosen eldritch machinery over sense, so she had no other choice.

Captain Revele knew her vessel and said it was ready for the task, but nonetheless Zofiya had never heard of such a maneuver. The Imperial Fleet was still young, and had never fought against itself like this. As they began to dip again, the regent felt her heart thunder.

"Remember," she called above the flap and creak of the airship, "no one is to touch the Emperor but me!"

The *Summer Hawk* dropped out of the sky from above like her namesake. The cloud's mist made everything gray, and their descent was so rapid that when they did see the *Winter Kite* finally emerge from it, there was scarcely a second to process it. One moment it was a deep gray shape in the cloud, and then the next the *Summer Hawk* was on it.

It was quite shocking how close the Sensitive had
brought them—but then that was what they had asked her
for. The *Hawk*'s forward cannon fired at the *Kite*'s propeller. The retort made Zofiya's ears ring, but she was heartened to see the chain shot hit true. The propeller jerked and
tangled just as it was meant to.

"Brace yourselves!" Zofiya barked to those that waited
with her.

The rumble of the impact was loud enough to knock out
all rational thought from a person's brain. The bow of the
descending airship struck her brother's ship in the stern,
just behind where that dire machine was mounted.

This was the best place to board another airship without
risking it plummeting to the ground, Captain Revele had
claimed, and no one knew ships better than she. The *Summer Hawk*'s bow was the strongest piece of her, just like in
a battleship of the ocean. Luckily they did not have to
worry about water suddenly rushing in.

Zofiya waved her saber. The marines followed her
charge across the deck and onto the slightly tilted one of
the *Winter Kite*. They had apparently done something
unexpected. The first soldiers they encountered were still
engaged in forming themselves into defensive lines. Skirmishes were soon breaking out all over.

Zofiya threw herself into the battle, allowing the ebb
and flow of battle to keep her mind off what lay ahead. She
was able to put away her knowledge that she was fighting
men she had trained. Instead, she concentrated on keeping
herself moving forward, cutting down those that stood in
her way with a bloody determination. She called out, "For
Arkaym," so that they might know this was not a coup she
wanted. However, By the Bones, she would not stop.

Then something curious began to happen. It started at
the front, where the forces were clashing, and soon it was
like a wave among the Imperial Guard. Several of her
brother's troops began to lay down their weapons. They
held up their hands and surrendered to their brothers. The

idea that Zofiya wasn't going to have to kill any more of her fellows was an uplifting one. Still, not quite all of them were surrendering.

As if to make up for this change in fortune, out of the corner of one eye, Zofiya caught sight of activity around the machines. They looked as if they were attempting to maneuver them aft so as to get a good line of sight on the invaders.

"Petav!" Zofiya screamed, while ducking a wild swing by a young guard. Her brother wouldn't care if he cut down his own troops—that was absolutely certain.

The Deacons, who until now had been keeping back from the fray, stepped forward, and threw back their cloaks. Zofiya wiped blood out of her eyes and watched them. She had to admit, they made an impressive sight. The carvings of the runes on their bodies crackled with silver light, giving them a rather terrifying appearance. More guardsmen, seeing this, dropped to their knees and surrendered then and there.

The soldiers of Arkaym were used to trusting the Deacons of the Order. These ones had not seen one for many months, so their coming must have been extra impressive. Zofiya pushed the surrendered out of her way and strode boldly down the deck toward the huddle of remaining troops. The Deacons followed at her back, silent witnesses to what was coming. Except, they too had their part to play.

The square, squat shape of the machine was indeed being turned in the invaders' direction, and the muzzles of it were already alight with blue lightning. A man was bent over the controls, his fingers flying over its surface. Zofiya could feel all the hair on her body begin to rise the closer she got to it, and every instinct in her was screaming to run away as fast as possible. Yet, past the machine she could see her brother's face. No emotion tarnished it, so she copied him.

Just as the machine began to shake and get ready to spit forth its death, the Deacons spoke. Zofiya could not see what they did, but she felt it at her back. It began as a warmth—and then it became a blinding heat. It took all of her strength of will not to turn and look at it.

The flames flowed over her head, not touching a single hair on her Imperial head. They struck the machine instead, and it seemed to absorb the power for a while. By the Bones, she thought in one terrible moment, were the Deacons feeding the terrible thing? Had they turned against her?

She was committed now. The regent kept walking, though to her death or not, she could not have said. The flames went on, pouring against the machine and seeming to disappear within. Then, some sort of maximum containment was reached. The first sign was a slight creak from the machine. The mad Vashill—it felt good to have his name—was howling something at his creation, as if he could somehow urge it on.

It did not want to work however, since the brass casing bulged slightly. That was the only warning the thing gave. Then it burst. Blue flames poured out of it for an instant, and the younger Vashill was set alight like some horrific offering to terrible gods. He screamed and flailed about . . . then running in blind panic, leapt from the airship.

His machine, meanwhile, raged blue for a split second, and then a deeper part of it burst apart further. It made a very curious rumbling noise, as if something was passing from the world—or rather being sucked from it. The huddle of the Court screamed in unison and scattered from the Emperor. They were as loyal as field mice and just as useful.

Only Kaleva and his bride remained. Ezefia did not have much choice in the matter. Now that the crowds had cleared, the regent saw what had been done to her sister-in-law.

Her belly had been slit as well as her throat, and rivers of scarlet stained her white dress and dripped from her fingertips. Now she stared at Zofiya through the blankness of death, slumped on the chair that she had been strapped to. Apparently being pregnant was no protection.

It was this final action that made Zofiya finally see it; there was no coming back from this for her brother. The Kal she had grown up with and protected loyally for so many years would never have done such a thing. Never.

The regent's jaw tightened. She had wanted to believe she could save him. Zofiya had wanted to have some hope that she could get him back. Now she understood that she had been fooling herself, and people had died because she couldn't see it.

Her brother was standing behind his dead wife, and his fine white clothes were stained with her blood. A grin rested on his lips, which had once smiled far more beautifully and always seemed ready to laugh.

The Emperor Kaleva was as much a victim of Derodak as the Order of the Eye and the Fist. The Kal she knew had died in the breaking of the Mother Abbey, along with all those Deacons, and the person standing before her wore his skin, but was not him.

If she did nothing, then this would go on, until the whole world was torn apart around them, or until there were no more people in the Empire for him to kill. Everyone was an enemy to him now.

Her hand tightened on her saber and fierce tears threatened to break loose in her eyes, but she understood. She had pledged herself to Arkaym, and that pledge ran deeper and further than even brotherly love. She had a duty.

Behind her the Deacons and the marines waited. She could almost hear them holding their breath, as they waited for her to say or do something. It felt like she was poised on her own blade. Finally, she found the will to do what she had to.

"Kaleva, Brother," she began in a sad, but strong voice that carried easily across the deck of the *Winter Kite*, "I demand you surrender the throne to me, your royal sister, and allow yourself to be confined for your own well-being until your sanity is restored to you."

It was a lie. Even if somehow he could be recovered, the Kal she had loved and supported would never be able to bear the guilt of what he had done.

So it was out there now; she was now and forever to be the sister who had taken the crown from her brother. Zofiya imagined the rage and fury her father would go through when he heard of it.

At first she would be regent, then after a short amount of time to satisfy convention, she would be Empress of Arkaym.

Her brother did not look outraged. Instead, he moved from behind the chair, waving his bloody knife idly at her as if lecturing a child. "I know what your plan is, Sister," he said, his voice cracking now and then. "You'll tuck me away nice and quietly in a dungeon somewhere, tell all the citizens of the Empire you are so solicitous of my health, and then later in the night you'll have someone steal in to murder me." His eyes darted across the troops behind her. "Maybe one of these fine soldiers will do you a favor so that your pretty hands don't have to get dirty."

"Kal," she replied, her gaze following his footsteps, in case he got close enough for her to grapple, "you are my brother, and you are not well. I would never do such a—"

"Then"—the Emperor broke in—"you will put it about that I caught ill or some such and bury me in a hidden grave." He jabbed his knife in the air for effect. "I know you've always wanted my throne."

At her back, Zofiya heard the crowd shift a little; their Emperor displaying his insanity so openly was unnerving many of them.

Her brother, though, was now completely ignoring them, lost in his own imagined plots and schemes. "All the women in my life have always wanted to take from me." He darted back behind his wife and laid his head on her shoulder. It was a macabre and disturbing sight. "Ezefia here, she was conspiring with Derodak, that treacherous Deacon, to steal my throne. He even put a child in her belly!" He placed a hand on the bleeding gash just under her breasts, covering his fingers in her still wet blood. "But obviously he did not care for her that much, since he never came back for her as I had hoped he would."

For just a second, Zofiya's determination wavered. Kaleva had never been betrayed by anyone in Arkaym, but he could not appreciate that. Ezefia, if she had been unfaithful to him, had not done it willingly. From what Zofiya knew of the Empress' past, her father had been a true Prince to his people, and though she had always seemed sad, the regent had never detected any falseness in her. Zofiya also knew firsthand that Derodak had ways of manipulating people and bending them to his will. She could only be grateful he had not demanded anything more intimate from her while he had her under his control.

"Now you, Sister," he said, straightening and fixing her with a slow grin that made her skin crawl, "you want to take what is mine directly. You have always been jealous of my rule. Tell me, how long have you been plotting to take it from me?"

This could not go on. The more he talked, the more poison he was infecting the people around her with—people who she was going to have to rely on in the months to come. That was if there were more months to come.

Zofiya drew her saber in one practiced motion. She knew her brother was no match for her; not in sanity or skill. It was almost certain she could drop him to the deck without having to kill him. Her gaze raked over the few people that stood behind him. All were members of the Court, and as far as she could tell, terrified by the Deacons and not capable of standing as seconds to their Emperor. Now all that remained was for her to make the move.

However, before she could get herself to the point of action, something curious happened. It was not on the deck, and it took only a second. Between one heartbeat and

the next, something opened in the mind of the Grand
Duchess Zofiya. A crack of understanding that had been
levered open by the geistlord Hatipai, who had occupied
her brain. It was the same curious something that had
alerted her that all was not as it seemed with the new aris-
tocrat in her brother's Court months before. The same person who, it had turned out, was Derodak. Merrick had seen
that glimpse of potential in her, and now, under pressure, it
sprang open again.

She was, in that instant, terribly aware of Deacon Petav
standing beside her, his Center wide open. She was aware
of it, because she was suddenly seeing what he was seeing.
The world flared a whole range of colors that she'd never
known existed. Everything around her was now not only
beautiful, but also packed with meaning that none could
see. Emotions, Bonds and intentions were all swirling
around her, and the regent had no way of interpreting what
any of them meant. It made her feel sick and exhilarated all
at the same time.

Deacon Petav, the Sensitive was seeing something,
something that was about to happen but had not yet come
to pass. A sickly green light danced around her brother's
form, rendering him into an eerie figure that she barely
recognized. However, Petav saw what was coming.

The Emperor Kaleva was going to shoot his sister in the
head, and then himself. He would end this line of Emperors before it was even really begun. *Cut out the contamination before it spread.*

Zofiya snapped back to reality and felt all the cool air
rush abruptly back into her body. She had been holding her
breath for that long moment. Before she could think on
what she had experienced, she moved.

Sheathing her saber, she tucked and rolled across the
deck. Kal had only time to pull out the pistol concealed in
his jacket, before she was on him. The Imperial siblings
crashed into each other, sliding across the tilted deck and
colliding with the gunwales on the other side. Zofiya had

her brother pinned with one knee and grappled with him for the pistol. He might not have the skill she did, but he was much stronger.

Everyone else on the deck ceased to matter, as for a time, Kaleva and Zofiya were pressed against each other, as close as if they were twins in their mother's belly. Face-to-face, the Grand Duchess wrapped her fingers around the weapon and pulled mightily. "No, no, Kal!" she screamed at him, hoping to get him to loosen his grip.

"Yes," he hissed back, even as his greater strength began to win out. "We were never meant to be in Arkaym, Sister. The geists are coming and neither of us should be here to see them." His eyes were wide as they stared into hers.

Suddenly she realized that he was not struggling to aim the pistol at her.

The Grand Duchess Zofiya flicked her gaze away only a moment before her brother put the barrel under his chin. All she had time for was a strangled "Kal!" and then the pistol went off. Blood and gore sprayed all over the deck and Zofiya. The bullet exploded through the top of his skull and took away any chance of his recovery.

Dimly, she heard the screaming of the Court and the shouts of her troops, but they were a very long way off. Zofiya knew if she turned back she would see Kal's mutilated face. She wouldn't do that.

Before anyone could reach her, she stood up, drenched in her brother's scarlet blood. The Imperial color. Silence swallowed up the chaos, and those on the *Winter Kite* formed a circle around her. Carefully, she took off her jacket, and without looking down draped it over her brother's body. Then Zofiya pushed aside her hair, mopping scarlet drips from her face as best she could.

She had rolled across the deck of the airship a regent, but she arose as an Empress. Zofiya could only hope that her reign would not continue as it had begun—in blood and death.

She stood there, locking gazes with all of those around her: people who had only a short while ago been enemies. It was Deacon Petav who broke the silence when he called out, "The Emperor is dead. Long live Empress Zofiya!"

Soon the cry was taken up and echoed down the airship. As she looked around, the new Empress noticed that even on the faces of the Court, who had been her brother's only moments before, were definite looks of relief. She would bury Kal in the vault under Vermillion, and make sure he was remembered, not as the mad Emperor, but as another victim of Derodak and the Circle of Stars.

It had not been meant to be like this when she and Kal had set off from Delmaire. She thought of the moment that they'd first set foot on Arkaym soil, a bright blessed time that seemed in memory to be surrounded by golden light. As she walked forward and became Empress, she would hold on to that. It was something even these events could not tarnish.

Both brother and sister were gone now. Only Empress Zofiya remained.

→ TWENTY-FOUR ←

Vision of Battle

For a coyote, the Fensena would have made a better sheep-dog than Merrick could ever have imagined. The young Deacon might have thought Sorcha was a hard taskmaster, until he fell under the tutelage of the geistlord.

Word of the success at Waikein spread from city to town to village. Soon the outpost they had wrestled from the geists was inundated by as many people as could find their way there. An airship, a commandeered vessel from the Imperial Fleet, had even arrived within a week. It was damaged beyond the repair of anyone in Waikein, but it had been commandeered by a brave contingent of Deacons from the west, who had answered the call Sorcha had sent out from the citadel. An extra hundred Deacons put a strain on resources, but also made Merrick feel a little more confident.

Then there were the throngs of normal folk who poured into Waikein asking, pleading and sometimes demanding to be tested. Merrick snatched what sleep he could from time to time, but all of the trained Deacons found themselves working every hour they could keep their eyes open.

However, there was one problem: getting all these Deacons to Vermillion. Certainly without Sorcha they could not make use of the Wrayth portals. So Merrick thought of another woman who was just as powerful as his partner.

She did indeed come when he called.

Merrick stood on the hill just outside the city of Waikein and watched as the ships of the air appeared from among the clouds. They were very beautiful, too beautiful to be part of the world that seemed to be falling down on itself. The sharp wind from the east made him blink his eyes and draw the cloak of silver fur closer.

It seemed to be the right thing to do to wear it. With Sorcha gone, the Order needed someone to follow, and the cloak distinguished him from everyone else. He was First Presbyter now, after all. Young as he might be, he was all they had now.

"It suits you, boy," the Fensena, who lounged at his side, commented while his golden eyes remained fixed on the approaching airships, "but those better not be tears in your eyes."

Merrick pressed his lips together and chose not to answer. The coyote kept quiet when in earshot of other Deacons, but all of them knew what he was. It was disturbing how none of them questioned the fact that their de facto leader had a geistlord at his side. They swallowed his statement that he and Sorcha had quelled and tamed the Fensena, and it was he that had given up the information that would lead them to victory.

The world had become such a hardscrabble place that any little hope—even from a geistlord—was eagerly grasped. Merrick turned his head away from the oncoming airships and spared a glance behind him.

The Order may have grown in the weeks since Sorcha's abduction, bulging to almost three times the size it had been in the citadel, but he wondered if it was going to be enough.

It was not the Order that Merrick's previous Arch

Abbots would have recognized—there were not enough cloaks to go around, so many had provided their own. Consequently, the group waiting below him was a variegated patterned quilt of a gathering. Their lack of proper training was the thing that still haunted him though.

Merrick's bleak thoughts were interrupted by a sharp nip on the ends of his fingers. Merrick jerked back from the Fensena, who had drawn blood with his sharp fangs. The coyote's gold-coin eyes were narrowed and fixed on him.

"You must not think of things you cannot have," the beast growled. "You cannot give proper training without time—and you do not have time. What you have is what you have."

Merrick pulled his cloak tighter with a frown. He didn't think the coyote was inside his head, but he very much disliked the impression the beast gave that he was. "It does not seem much to take on Derodak and his Circle of Stars—let alone the Maker of Ways . . ."

The Fensena did not deign to reply, but raised his muzzle as the three airships approached. "You have transport to get where you need to, that should be enough."

It was the *Summer Hawk*. The First Presbyter smiled; even in these dark times something as familiar as that airship lit a small fire of hope in his chest. This had been the very airship he and Sorcha had first commissioned to take them back to Vermillion. Afterward they had defeated the Murashev. He could only hope it was an omen of things to come.

Captain Revele—if it was she, still in command— maneuvered the airship down to a hundred feet off the mountaintop and secured her position with landing ropes. Finally, a sturdy, yet swinging ladder was dropped. Still, apparently someone couldn't wait.

A person, dressed in white, slid down one of the ropes to land only a body's length away from him. For a moment Merrick was caught completely off-guard. Zofiya had come to meet him, but he knew immediately something had changed.

She was dressed in a white jacket and Imperial scarlet trousers, with her dark hair braided up at the nape of her neck. On her left ring finger she wore a thick strap of silver, surmounted with a massive sapphire. It was the Imperial Ring he had last seen on her brother's hand. Encompassing her forehead was a band of gold decorated with a strand of silver leaves. Each of those leaves represented a principality of Arkaym. It was not the Imperial Crown, but it might as well have been. Merrick knew the only thing this all meant.

The Grand Duchess was no more. The person standing beside him was the Empress Zofiya of Arkaym.

Merrick's throat was suddenly dry, and his hands dropped to his side instead of wrapping around her. Automatically, he stooped into the deepest bow a Deacon could give.

"Rise, First Presbyter Chambers," she said softly. Their eyes met and he saw with some relief that she was still herself—though there was a deep, abiding hurt hidden in there. She had said nothing of her change in status in the brief weirstone missives she had sent.

A frown darted across her Imperial brow. "I wanted to tell you myself," she whispered, for a moment looking very vulnerable.

He swallowed before answering. "That is entirely your right, Imperial Majesty. May I ask . . ."

Zofiya looked about, and seeing that they were alone except for the silent coyote, threw herself into his arms. Suddenly she was just his love: warm, soft and hurt. She whispered the horror of it into his neck. "I had to take the throne, Merrick. Kal . . . Kal killed himself in the end. I couldn't stop him . . ."

The feeling that she had been holding all this in for weeks was immediate.

Merrick let her hold him for a little while, but there was no time for much more. Eventually, he pulled back and wiped her tears with the sleeve of his shirt. By the time he was done, no one would have been able to tell that the new Empress had a heart.

"You did what you had to," Merrick said, holding her quite still in his grasp. It was entirely inappropriate for a man—even if he was Presbyter—to hold the Empress in any way at all. "When Derodak worked on your brother for months, he got his claws deeply into him. You cannot blame yourself for that."

Her jaw tightened slightly as she straightened. "I spent all my life looking out for Kal, Merrick. I thought I was doing a good job, but I didn't move quickly enough when I suspected something was wrong with that man. I'm not ever going to forgive myself for that. Never."

Zofiya would hold on to that until her grave; it was what she was like. "Then you must learn to live with it," he replied softly, "because it is not just your brother who has endangered the world."

"We have no time for this," the Fensena, who had been mercifully silent until this moment, said, getting to his feet. His ears pricked forward. "You need to tell the Empress about all this, but we must be off immediately."

Zofiya's saber was out of its sheath and in her hand in a flash. "What is that? Another talking beast?" Her gaze fixed on Merrick accusingly. "Another geistlord?"

The coyote did not help his cause by folding one front leg and performing a bow like some well-trained dog. "Indeed. The Fensena."

Her brother would most likely not have recognized the name, but Zofiya had spent hours learning about the dangers of Arkaym. "The Broken Mirror? The Widow Maker?" She turned slightly on Merrick, but kept her eyes and weapon pointed at the coyote. "Are you the new Derodak then, Merrick? Would you make pacts with geistlords as he did?"

A headache began to form itself at the base of the First Presbyter's head. He'd known that this meeting would not be easy, but he did not want to argue with the new Empress. "The Fensena is not to be trusted—"

"I am right here you know," the coyote broke in dryly.

Merrick shot him a dark look and continued, "But he is as invested in this world as we are. On the Otherside he was one of the weaker geistlords." The coyote growled but held his peace. "He knows more of this than even a Deacon can, and he says that Derodak is planning to contact the Maker of Ways."

The Empress blanched and reluctantly sheathed her saber. "Why would he do that? If the Otherside came through, there would be nothing but chaos and death."

The Fensena answered before the Deacon could. "Derodak has lived in this realm for hundreds on hundreds of years. He was both the first Deacon and the first Emperor. He thinks his knowledge and power is limitless, so when the Otherside spills into this world he imagines that he will control the geists as he has the ones here."

"He is a fool!" Zofiya spat, kicking a rock out from under her boot.

"Indeed," the coyote said, shaking himself as if he'd received a sudden dunking, "but he thinks he knows best. All will look to him, and he will be their father. However, when the Maker of Ways comes, Derodak may have cause to remember the true horrors of the Otherside."

Merrick watched his lover out of the corner of his eye, because he did not want to interrupt her thinking. When she spoke, there was more than a touch of weariness in her voice. "I have spent the last weeks fighting and negotiating my way around Arkaym. Even the false Rossin woman has been dealt with. I think I have mended much of what my brother did, but now you tell me it is all in vain—that the geists are coming and there is nothing I can do about it?"

"Nothing." The coyote sat up tall, his brindle head at the height of her chest. "Nothing except get those who you can to Vermillion." He regarded her with his tongue lolling out of the corner of his mouth. "I expect you remember the tunnels and vaults under your palace?"

Zofiya looked for a moment as if she might strike the beast, but eventually she nodded. "Yes, I remember very well. Is that where the breach will happen?"

"It was where it happened before." When she looked aghast, the coyote made that peculiar yipping noise again, his version of a laugh. "Humans forget so easily! Important things too, like the fact Vermillion was built by Derodak in his early days as protection against the geists."

Zofiya took the scolding with good graces and nodded slowly. "Then let's get your new Deacons aboard, Merrick. You can tell me the rest while we make all haste back to the capital."

It was not easy work to do. The seasoned Deacons that had survived the scourging of the Order were used to airship travel for the most part, but the newcomers were not so comfortable to climb up a swaying rope ladder. Merrick made sure to be the last to go up and held the bottom of the ladder as steady as he could manage. Several times it looked as though there might be a dreadful accident—but eventually they were all aboard. Most looked as unhappy as Raed Syndar Rossin on his first trip during their ascent though.

However, it was only when they had all climbed away from him that Merrick considered what was to be done about the Fensena. He was a large beast. Perhaps they could throw down a net?

He need not have worried. By the time the First Presbyter had held the rope ladder for the last of his Deacons and turned around, there was a naked man standing on the stones next to him. He was older with gray in his hair and beard, but he did not look ashamed of his state of undress.

Merrick blinked. So did the man. For an instant it looked as though a shiver of gold passed through the stranger's eyes.

His voice croaked a little when it came out. "As you see, Presbyter, I am true to my word, the folk I travel with do not burn and die when I can help it. As you can see, it is sometimes most useful to be able to use hands rather than paws."

While Merrick was still bemused, the Fensena used said hands to climb the rope ladder as quickly as a monkey. The First Presbyter did not look up for obvious reasons, but once the rope was clear, climbed up to the *Summer Hawk* himself.

Captain Revele was standing next to the Empress talking to her in an undertone. Merrick felt a surge of awkwardness; he knew Revele had harbored some feelings of attraction toward him. However, he only knew it because Sorcha had pointed it out to him in no uncertain terms. The little flick of her eyes toward him and then away made him realize that his partner had been right.

And now Revele had presumably found out from gossip about his relationship with Zofiya. Still, these were petty, childish things when laid next to the arrival of the Maker of Ways.

The captain of the *Summer Hawk* gave a snap of a little salute. "Reverend Presbyter, it is good to see you well." He knew he looked different from last time they had spoken. The warmth of the fur on his back reminded him of that.

"Thank you, Captain. It is good to see you and your ship have survived the recent tumult."

"Captain Revele has been a loyal and valiant servant of the Empire," Zofiya said. "She and her ship have been invaluable in the fight . . . but now it is time to return to Vermillion."

Revele took the hint, saluted her Empress and retreated back to the bridge of her airship. Soon enough, sailors were setting about their tasks, reeling in the ropes and starting the propeller that would power them on their way.

"I would talk with you, First Presbyter," Zofiya said loudly, and spun on her heel. The Fensena looked up at

Merrick with burning gold eyes, and the Deacon could have sworn that there was a hint of amusement in them.

Still, despite the look, Merrick really had no choice but to follow Zofiya. In the captain's cabin, Merrick had just closed the door before the Empress in all her finery was slamming him against the door.

As her mouth pressed against his, Merrick barely had time for surprise. That he was now embracing the Empress—though not yet crowned—of Arkaym was an event he had not foreseen. Zofiya pulled back from him and stared him in the eyes. "Do not think of it," she whispered. "I am the same person, and this crown means about as much as one made of paper at the moment. The geists are coming, my love. We do not have much time."

When he looked at her, Merrick knew she was right. The breach could be opened in a matter of days, and then there would be no Empire for her to rule, just a lot of terrified people. Everything would break down after that. Airships, and all the trappings of civilization would be lost as the world descended into the grip of the geists.

So Merrick kissed her back, because it was all he had to offer. Her mouth was soft and sweet—just as he had remembered it. In all that had happened, he had still managed to miss her.

Zofiya unbuckled his cloak, letting it fall to the floor, and then pulled apart his shirt. The jacket she wore was stiff and covered in braid and military honors. It scratched his skin, but her mouth soon followed to act as balm.

A fine swinging bed occupied the corner of the captain's cabin, but the Empress seemed to have no thought of that; she instead pulled Merrick down with her onto the fur cloak that she had only just crumpled there. Outside, he knew that there were soldiers, Deacons, and members of Court that would all be waiting for them, but there were also days to go until they reached Vermillion.

As Zofiya's hands unbuckled his belt, Merrick abandoned worry, or rational thought. Just for a little moment. Just to remind himself what the struggle ahead was for. Life was precious and could be remarkably short.

When they finally had spent themselves on each other, Zofiya rolled over onto the fur cloak. Her fingers idly traced through its lushness.

"A beautiful animal must have died for this," she said, resting her head on Merrick's shoulder.

He nodded, for a moment content not to move. In fact, he was afraid if he did that the tiny bubble of time they had stolen would be whipped away. "Raed gave it to me," he replied, kissing the top of her head, "so most likely it did."

Zofiya sighed. "The Rossin Emperors were not a kindly bunch." She wriggled her head back and forward like a child trying to get comfortable. "Do you think I shall be remembered as Kind Empress Zofiya?" Her tone was deliberately light.

Merrick knew that unless they stopped Derodak there would be nobody to remember anyone, but he also knew that was not what his love wanted to hear in this naked, intimate moment. "You shall be as kind as you can be. You will do all you can to be a good ruler because that is your nature. You are a good person, Zofiya. Remember that." He placed a kiss on the top of her tousled head.

They did not have time for more, and considering all that had happened, not much energy for it either. So they slowly climbed to their feet, washed off with water from the pitcher hanging from the chain, and got dressed once more. They shared a moment of unintentional laughter when they had to untangle Zofiya's gold braid on her jacket from Merrick's shirt buttons.

"That wouldn't do, would it," she whispered to him. "Imagine the gossip?"

It remained unsaid that their world was narrowing to one where gossip was a luxury. He smoothed back her hair and kissed her lips once more before they left the cabin. In the meantime, the Deacons had all been tidied away into cabins and to temporary accommodations in the hold.

Sailors were about their business and even Captain Revele was not on deck.

"It is a beautiful day," Zofiya remarked, and she was right. The *Summer Hawk* had the wind at her back as she traveled east, and there was nothing to indicate, in either the sky above or the rolling green hills passing below, that they were flying toward death and danger.

"Vermillion is three days away?" Merrick asked.

Zofiya nodded slowly. "Yes, but only if we burn precious weirstones to get there." When she looked up at him, a slow smile dawned on her face. "I guess in this world they are really not that precious . . . after all we could all be dead in three days."

It was not a happy thought—but perhaps a profound one. Merrick chose not to answer it, instead clasping the Imperial hand as covertly as possible as they sailed toward the end.

TWENTY-FIVE

A Necessary Spectacle

When Raed took back the flesh that he'd been born with, it was a shock to find himself, leg to naked leg, with Sorcha. The only warmth and comfort they had in the cell was each other—which had always done good service for him. He nestled down and drew Sorcha as close to him as he dared. There was no pillow on this cold stone, but they had lived with much the same before.

The truth of it was, he wanted more time with Sorcha . . . he was greedy and only regretted that they had not met sooner. When the end came, in whatever form Derodak had planned for them, that would be his only regret.

"Raed?" Sorcha's voice came out muffled as she turned to him, naked skin dragging against naked skin. "How are you here with—"

"Just lucky I guess," he said, and in many ways it was true, he needed to be with Sorcha—and even in this situation he was glad of it. He would not have wanted her to go alone into this darkness. "Either that or Derodak wants both of us just as much."

He felt, rather than heard a sigh go through her. "I

imagine he thinks once he has control of the other geists he will be able to take the power of the Rossin too."

Raed nodded. He'd already thought of that. "But what does he want from you?"

Sorcha licked her lips. "It has something to do with the Wrayth. They were trying to breed a person . . . a thing really . . . that could connect all the humans to their hive mind. Apparently they came close with me—but not close enough. So Derodak thinks he can use me to help the Maker of Ways."

They both shivered in the darkness and contemplated that possibility.

Raed rubbed Sorcha's shoulder; a blind human gesture of compassion that he knew was little to hold up against the dark. She snuggled in closer.

"You won't do it," the Young Pretender whispered to her. "You won't do what he wants."

Her breathing became, for a moment, very ragged. "I can say that all I like, Raed, but how can I stand against the whole geist world—against all of the Otherside?"

His mind raced. She had done amazing things, helped destroy two geistlords and mend the shattered remains of the Order, yet he knew that every person had a breaking point. So he lied to her to fill the gaps where uncomfortable truth resided. "You can. I know you can." Raed wrapped his arms around her. "Perhaps you can do that trick with your fingertips so we can have some light."

She held up her arms, and he saw that some kind of silver paint was covering the runes. "I've tried rubbing this off, but it won't budge." She swallowed. "I can't reach the runes at all."

They didn't say anything to each other after that. Huddled in the darkness, they kissed softly, to reassure each other that they were still human and still alive, more than anything else.

Sorcha might not have her runes, but the Rossin was still inside him. Raed tried to hold the waves of despair at bay with that thought. It might have been amusing that he was pinning his hopes on the Beast when most of his life had been spent terrified by it.

Eventually they drifted off into a shaky sleep. When they were jerked awake, it was impossible to tell how long they had actually been unconscious. Cloaked Deacons of the Circle of Stars were kicking them, apparently unbothered by the threat of the Rossin. Sorcha was dragged away, and he could hear her swearing and lashing out as best she could at these newcomers, but it didn't last long.

"Sorcha!" Raed howled, unable to see her through the press of people in the cell. No reply came.

Their captors turned on him, and he too struck out, blind with rage. It felt good for his fist to connect with a few stomachs and a couple of jaws. Deep down he called to the Rossin, demanded he rise to the surface and rip these people into bloody little shreds. The Beast was reluctant for some reason, but Raed could feel him swimming toward the conscious world.

The Deacons did not seem to understand the danger that they were in, and Raed was glad of it. He let go and dropped away, like a child falling into a cool pool where there were no responsibilities. Let the Rossin do as he would. Let him kill them all.

The Rossin twisted and took form once more. The back of his throat was dry with the desire for flesh and blood, and it would be sweet to take them from the cursed Circle of Stars. However, as he reworked the body of the Young Pretender to his pard shape, there was a moment where the Circle Deacons made their move.

As he straightened and roared his renewed anger into the tiny dungeon cell, he felt something dropped over his head. A thread of weirstones, but it felt too light to hold him.

They did not have time to work the stones on him. He flexed his back legs and made to toss his head to free himself. That was when the device tightened on him. The Rossin had forgotten the deceitful makings of the Ehtia. Derodak had never been a machine maker, but he had apparently found one in this time that knew some of the lost tinkering arts.

The links of the collar they had placed around him tightened, burying themselves into his fur and cutting into his muscles. The pain that went with it was not just physical, it also flayed itself deeper still, in the dark places the Rossin lived. This was the between state, where he kept the kernel of his self, the bit that persisted when his host held the body they shared.

The pain of it was exquisite, as if he were being torn and shredded.

Derodak's voice was the last thing that he wanted to hear, but it did intrude through the pain. "It is good to hear your howls, old friend. It reminds me of the beginning of these things. It pleases me to know that you will be there at the end of it too."

The Rossin shook his head, climbing back from the agony, and realized that he had collapsed on the floor. The mighty cat leapt to his feet—he found he could do that—and snarled. His voice echoed impotently in the tiny room. None of the cloaked figures seemed moved—least of all Derodak.

The loathed Arch Abbot looked him up and down, before bending and taking up the trailing leash attached to the metal and weirstone collar. "Come," he said and turned, before waiting to see if the Rossin followed.

At first he set his paws against the stone, but then the collar twitched and tightened on his muscular neck. It was a momentary reminder of his position, and it was a bitter, humiliating one. It spoke to the Rossin too much of the horrors on the Otherside, and that in turn reminded him that they were not done yet. The geists might be waiting, but the Maker of Ways had not yet been summoned. So, there was still time . . . even if it was just a little.

With a slight growl, the great cat allowed himself to be led from the dungeon cell.

Out of the corner of one eye, the Rossin saw that Sorcha Faris was being bundled up by Circle Deacons and carried with them. The Bond between them was so fractured he could not tell if she was conscious or not. He hoped she wasn't, because then at least she would be spared some of the coming humiliation.

Derodak led this sorry procession to a tunnel on which was drawn the familiar braid of the Wrayth portal. Last time the Arch Abbot had tangled with the Rossin he had not had this trick up his sleeve. It was disturbing that such an Ancient human could still learn new tricks.

When Derodak pressed his hands against the stones and began to shift them, the Rossin flinched. He already knew where they were bound. A scene began to resolve itself in the area described by the circle, and he knew it well. The sun was just rising over the gleaming canal, and with the flat-fronted buildings directly placed against it, it could be nowhere else but Vermillion.

The Rossin had not spoken yet, but he could not resist it now. "No way to take us straight to the palace and the rift then?" he growled low in his chest.

Derodak's gaze darkened. They both knew full well that he might have been able to make a portal from the palace to wherever he liked, but because of the cantrips and the water, he could not make one go the other way. "I built Vermillion too well," the Arch Abbot said, tilting his head. "The islands and the swamps I created now work against me. Never mind. It will be good for the people of the city to see who is the true master of the Empire now. With their Emperor gone and the geists overrunning them, they will turn to me."

The Rossin was not terribly knowledgeable as far as human emotions and actions went; mostly he was used to the taste of their flesh. However, he had the terrible feeling that Derodak was right. It was after all how he had risen to dominance in the first place—and used the Rossin to power the Imperial family.

The great cat hung his head, and did not reply. Instead he was led through the portal and into the city where it had all begun. The show would begin soon enough.

❧ TWENTY-SIX ❧

Back in Chains

Sorcha emerged from the darkness of unconsciousness and was unhappy to do so. She was being shaken back and forth, so that her head felt as though it might break. It seemed to take a long time for her to lever her eyes open. What she saw was dreadfully familiar.

Vermillion. It was the capital city and her former home. Even more frightening, she could identify the part they were passing through: the Imperial Island. She was strapped onto a wagon lurching its way up the hill toward the palace and seemingly hitting every rutted cobblestone on the way.

The next thing she noticed was how everything hurt. She was bent over at the waist and pinioned in a stock, such as might have once been found in a village square for the display of criminals. Sorcha rattled her hands back and forward but they were securely fastened. Not a good thing. The silver paint remained on her skin with the burning sensation digging into her and still denying her the runes.

As Sorcha strained her head to the left, she saw the rubble of her former home. With impeccable timing she had managed to return to the waking world just as they passed the Mother Abbey.

Despite all the pain and fear that filled Sorcha, she still could not look away from the tumbled ruins that had been the center of her life. The devotional building that had once soared toward the sky now resembled nothing so much as an Ancient hand clawing at it.

The Order had promised so much to her: a place of sanctuary, fellowship and training. It had been able to give her some of those things for some of the time, but eventually her blood and history had claimed her. Deep down a small voice whispered that she might have helped destroy it.

Perhaps it was the Wrayth having the last cruel jab.

Wind whipped down from the top of Imperial Island to counterpoint her bitter contemplations. Before tears could fall, Sorcha jerked her head away, instead concentrating on what else was happening around her.

On examination, she noted the wagon she was on was being pulled by two animals, two creatures that should never have been shackled to such a mean creation. They were Breed horses—thankfully not Shedryi or Melochi, but other of their kin.

As she turned her head to the right, she saw that she was not alone. Beside the cart, Derodak and three more of his Deacons were riding. They were also on horses of the Breed. She hoped savagely that the animals would toss their passengers and trample them.

They did not.

Around her, Sorcha could now make out the sounds of a crowd. Darting little looks on each side, she saw that the procession she was so unwillingly part of had drawn attention from the citizens of Vermillion. They stood in near silent lines on the street, watching Derodak's triumph. Sorcha recognized their hollow-eyed and beaten looks. Geists had certainly worn down the arrogance many had previously accused Vermillionites of possessing.

She thought of the procession the Emperor had taken to

Brickmakers Lane. It seemed a long time ago and wonderfully festive in comparison. It was horrible to consider that those had been her best days.

Though Sorcha worked her mouth a few times, she could not find enough moisture. Her voice would undoubtedly come out a ragged croak. What exactly she had been going to say, even she did not know.

It was when Sorcha dared another glance to her right that she spotted a dark, shaggy form moving between the horses and standing nearly as tall as they.

The Rossin, wearing a brass collar, walked alongside Derodak, and the leash attached by the collar was held by another Deacon. If the use of the Breed horses was outrageous, the sight of the Rossin, head bowed, being led like a puppy through the street was terrifying.

It was over. No sight in the world could have convinced her better than the great cat padding along next to Derodak. Sorcha could not feel her Sensitive or the runes that now ran like welts on her arms. She knew where they were going, and her death beforehand would have been preferable.

The end had to come at the same place as the beginning.

Somehow in the darkness of that thought, Sorcha had a moment of light—just a glimmer. It was a rune. Cautiously, so as not to draw attention, she glanced at her left wrist. A trickle of power, like Raed's finger brushing on her skin, was what had alerted her.

Sorcha averted her eyes quickly, but she'd seen what was happening. Where her skin there had rubbed against the locks, blood had dribble out, and the strange silver paint that Derodak had coated over her rune marks had been cleared just a fraction.

As the wagon lurched on up the hill and toward the palace, Sorcha sawed, as covertly and quickly as possible, at her wrist. The wound stung, but as more blood dribbled from it, she could feel the rune it was exposing grow clearer in her mind. It was Seym, the Rune of Flesh. It was a lucky thing because it was the rune she was most likely to be able to control without Merrick at her side.

Derodak was watching the crowd, and actually waving as he rode past, as if he were some kind of hero. Perhaps immortality made a person immune to normal human interactions, because he didn't seem aware of the effect he was having on the people. It was like a dark wave; expressions on the citizens tightened and grew angry. They knew a tormentor when they saw one.

The Circle of Stars might have been able to wipe away much of the memory of what they had done in the past, but something residual remained. If this was Derodak's attempt to win over the population, he was not doing a very good job of it.

Sorcha determined to give the crowd something more impressive. A few more quick, hard rubs of her arm on the wood and the rune Seym suddenly bloomed in her head. Her body—which had felt beaten and exhausted just a moment before—was flooded with strength. Sorcha's head buzzed, and suddenly a little vengeance did not seem an impossible thing.

Planting her feet, Sorcha pushed hard. Her muscles, filled with runic power, bulged and flexed, ripping the stocks apart as if they were made of string. The snap of metal and wood attracted people's attention. The citizens standing and watching the depressing parade showed signs of life by screaming and scattering.

The Deacons surrounding the wagon did neither of those things, and the Breed horses didn't even shift under their riders. Sorcha knew she didn't have much time; they would be on her in a moment—so she did the only thing that made sense.

She leapt down from the wagon and struck the Deacon who was holding the leash of the Rossin. The impact of her fist striking his jaw was most satisfying. Even better was that he was thrown clear across the street.

In a frozen instant, it was just the Rossin and Sorcha,

eyes locked—then she grabbed at the golden chain of weir-stones with both hands. The pain was instant and blinding. It was as if she were grabbing molten iron—but, breathing through her teeth, she hung on.

Derodak, though, had done her a favor; she was used to pain from her time with him. Ignoring the agony, she yanked as hard as Seym would allow her. The brass links snapped and pulled apart, showering over the street in sharp metallic shards.

Sorcha fell to her knees and gasped out one word: "Run!"

The Beast did not need her encouragement. Bunching his legs together he sprang away, even as the Deacons around him spun in his direction. Sorcha watched through blurry eyes as the great pard disappeared into the streets and alleyways of Vermillion.

Then she saw nothing but green, as the power of the rune Shayst enveloped her. All the power that had fueled her body was drawn away with a searing pain in her bones. One of the Deacons stepped toward her and drew more of the power over her runes.

Severed from everything, she sagged like a puppet with its strings cut. Derodak's hands wrapped around her hair, and she was dragged upward. Sorcha scrambled, but it was a fruitless, weak gesture. They tied her hands behind her back and threw her over the saddle of the Arch Abbot's Breed stallion.

When he got up behind her, he patted her on the back like she was some kind of pet. "That really was a waste of time; by the end of today the Rossin—in fact all the geists and geistlords—will be under my control."

Sorcha hated the sound of his voice and hated to think that he was right. "You reach too far," she gasped, tasting the sweat of the horse and his rider in her mouth. "The geists are much too powerful for you. You cannot control them all at once—no one can."

His hand now rested on her head. "That is why I have you."

She had no answer for that, because he did have her, and

she knew what she had felt from the Wrayth. That connection was what he meant to use. If she could have wriggled free and dashed herself against the cobblestones, she would have. However, Derodak had left her with no opportunities for self-sacrifice.

Blood . . . it was always about blood. Sorcha did not want to die, but she was grateful that if she did, she would not have to see what would come after. Though, if the Otherside had direct access to this world, then would human souls still travel there? Or would they be caught and used by the geists?

She needed Merrick. She needed Raed. Yet Sorcha was very glad they were not here.

Finally, they reached the walls of the Imperial Palace. Hands grabbed at her, uncaring about any hurt they caused her, and bundled her down off the horse. Sorcha's feet were unsteady under her, but she made a great effort to remain on them.

Derodak and his Circle of Stars stood around and smiled. They were looking at the palace with the expressions of zealots, as if they were coming home. Through her hair, Sorcha saw the cannons and soldiers on the wall. Human defenses gave her no hope, even as the soldiers lowered their weapons and made ready to fire.

"Prepare the way," Derodak ordered his Deacons. His children hustled to obey him: some faded away into Voishem, phasing out of the world and dashing toward the walls, while others claimed Pyet and walked toward the walls wreathed in flame.

The screams of the palace defenders were the only sounds to be heard in the palace square for quite some time. It was a macabre music, accompanied by the occasional gunshot.

Then when all grew silent again, Derodak and the ranks of his Deacons marched toward the palace. Two of his Circle pushed open the main gates and let them in; thus was the palace taken, in a matter of moments.

Sorcha could not help but think that if the Order of the

Eye and the Fist had not been crushed, things would have been very different. However, that was why Derodak had made sure to dispose of them first.

The sounds of more gunfire gave her some hope, but they were distant and up ahead of them in the depths of the palace. Sorcha could only guess that some doughty souls were fighting a rearguard action in there.

They had to step over bodies as Derodak led them deeper into the palace, but it was not to the throne room he was aiming—which surprised Sorcha. His grip on her arm was now firmer. "We must hurry. I am about to show you something very special," he whispered.

Sorcha made no reply. They were on the central staircase now. Above, many flights of stairs went up, or to different wings of the palace, but again that was not the direction that they went. Derodak directed them down.

They had to step over one more body on the way, and it was the one body that could have reached Sorcha. Garil lay on the first landing, half of his face burned off and his hand clenched in agony. He might have been afraid of Sorcha and what she was, but he had been her friend for many years before that. She was not surprised he had died defending the palace.

"You are so proud of yourself," Sorcha screamed, twisting around and spitting her words in Derodak's face, "killing old men and women! How does that make you a leader of men?"

She got no answer from the Arch Abbot; he merely pushed her down the stairs more quickly. Sorcha wondered if her old friend had seen his death coming. She also wondered if she was really about to be the peril that he had warned Aachon about months ago. It was looking more and more likely that he had been right.

That thought gave her pause. She swallowed back tears for Garil and all the rest to come. Sorcha would not let Derodak see her cry.

As they went, the trail of Deacons following them diminished as Derodak posted more and more of them as guards in the corridors or landings they passed. Eventually there were only five of them, plus Sorcha and the Arch Abbot.

Though she'd never been down this deep into the caverns, she made the connection to what Zofiya had told them had happened when she freed the geistlord that had caused so many problems in Orinthal.

In fact, they passed a section of a wall that had been brought down in one of the side corridors. Derodak paused. "Hatipai would have made a fine sacrifice for this . . ." He sounded almost regretful.

Then pulling her on, they continued deeper down. The walls went from carved to smooth rock, until they came to a doorway. The carving of the many-tentacled creature guarded this doorway, and she knew immediately who it was: the Maker of Ways.

She planted her feet, struggling for a moment, but Derodak summoned the Rune of Flesh and yanked her forcibly in. The rest of his Deacons remained outside. It was just Sorcha and him in a small cave. Her eyes were drawn to the strange little door in the middle of the floor. It looked like it had been hammered out of some kind of silver material.

Derodak did not seem at all pleased by this. "By the Bones!" He forgot all about her for a moment, dropping to his knees to examine the hatch. Strangely however, he didn't touch it.

Something displeased him, because he began yelling at no one in particular in a language Sorcha did not understand. She watched him curiously wondering if he might fall dead of apoplexy right there and then. It could only be hoped.

Unfortunately he recovered after a few minutes, pushed his hair out of his eyes and turned on her with a smile. "Don't worry, my dear, everything is still on track." He grabbed her by the arm and pulled her close. "I know you are not a Sensitive, but you must be able to feel it!"

Sorcha hadn't wanted to mention it, but she did. Even to her weakened and damaged Center the pulse of the place was unnerving.

However, what was even more so was his grip on her arm. She had already seen the runes he had made for himself. When she glanced down at the marks on his arms, she saw the silvered forms were shifting on the surface of his skin like undersea creatures. Her breath was stolen as they crossed over to her flesh.

Where he touched her, she felt as if hot irons were being applied, and she screamed. Derodak shoved her down against the floor, and Sorcha found her legs couldn't hold her. Now Derodak wrapped his arms around her, until they were pressed as close as lovers. Worse than these new runes on her was the sensation of him drawing something from her.

Sorcha's voice cracked in her throat and then died. The real world no longer mattered. Derodak was guiding her Wrayth heritage, pushing it out into the world, wider and wider.

Sorcha felt as though she might crack under the pressure, but somehow she did not. Her mind blurred, struggling to hold on to some vague sense of self as she became a vessel for human experience. She was being forced to take in the whole world of humans. Women, men, children, young, old, the newborn and the dying; she reached out and touched them all.

Though Sorcha could not control them as the Wrayth had wanted, she could draw a tiny portion of them into herself. Derodak fed on that piece, fed on it and then used it in his own way.

Dimly she realized he was speaking in the language of the Ancients, the language of the Ehtia. The Otherside was so close now. The room plunged into icy chill, the kind that even Sorcha, floating and distant, could feel in her bones.

Then he began to cut her, spreading her blood on the sand. It didn't hurt because she was barely there, but Sorcha understood now. This sand was here for a reason, carefully protected. This was the front door of the Otherside. The sand was from there, not from this world.

As she managed to look up, Sorcha saw the thing that was written about in all the history books. The Break.

The moment when the Otherside opened was the greatest terror of all people—the one event that all cultures, all civilizations had felt the agony of.

Now Sorcha began to appreciate what those ancestors had seen; the world was ripping apart and beyond it was the Otherside. She and Merrick had traveled there once, but their mind—at least hers—had forgotten the details.

Flames, emptiness and eternal hunger waited there. Linked with her Sensitive they had flung their souls into it once, but their minds had carefully hidden it from them. Now it was displayed in its full glory and horror. She recalled all the pain, flames and danger they had risked. It was no place for a human. It was the realm where the Ehtia had their very bodies ripped from them. None could survive there. She felt the alternating cold and heat on her worn-out body.

That was not her greatest fear anymore, because something else was coming. As Sorcha lay back in the sand, bleeding, a giant gray tentacle was pushing apart the breach, ripping a hole through the roof of the cavern and into the world.

Sorcha wanted to scream, to do something to release the pressure, but she had nothing—no choice but to experience the true horror of it all. Derodak was laughing in triumph, sure that he was about to become the greatest being in any realm.

Then he lowered his gaze, pulled out the knife and began to slowly dissect Sorcha Faris on the sands of the Otherside as fuel for the Maker of Ways.

TWENTY-SEVEN

A Predator's Decision

The Rossin ran through the streets of Vermillion like a creature maddened. Its citizens scattered screaming, as he bounded past them. He knocked many over, but he did not turn to devour them. His only thought was to get away from Derodak and what he was about to unleash. All his plans to gain his freedom seemed to have come to nothing. The Fensena had not come back, and his pelt was on the back of that cunning Sensitive partner of Sorcha's who was hundreds of miles away. Still he would take what he had.

Yet, what was it he had?

Soon, the Maker of Ways would arrive and then there would be no going back. The Otherside would swallow this realm, and he would be in dire danger. He had many enemies in that realm, and time did not matter to them.

As his great padded paws fell on the last bit of paved road in Vermillion, he stopped. He had reached the Edge—the most unfortunate patch of swampy ground in the city. Here the marshy ground supported only the poorest of the city, before giving way to wetlands that stretched for miles. He would have to swim, and then get as far from

Vermillion as possible. Hiding was not in the Rossin's nature, but he would have to learn it quickly if he wanted to survive.

He'd just placed one paw onto the wet ground that was the beginning of the wilderness, when a voice whispered in the back of his mind.

Do you really want to run? What will that get you?

It was his host. Raed Syndar Rossin was near the surface, listening, and now speaking, and that was highly unusual behavior.

The great cat shook his mane, breathing hard.

The great geistlord does not run! Raed continued, his voice growing stronger by the moment. *The Rossin stays and fights.*

The cat turned and glanced over his shoulder. From here, there was a narrow view of the Imperial Island in the distance. He knew what would be going on there. It wouldn't be long now.

You wouldn't let them put a chain on you again, so why do you need to run?

The Rossin growled deeply, his claws flexing into the ground for an instant.

Raed's voice didn't seem as weak and foolish as it had in the past. *You are the Rossin, and this is your world. You must fight for it.*

It was true. This was his world, and it had weakened him too much—if he went back to the Otherside it would mean certain destruction. If he did not fight, then there was no hope.

The great pard roared, howling his frustration into the wilderness, and then he made his decision.

The Rossin wheeled about, and this time sprang back toward the palace. His paws hit the cobblestones with rhythmic thumps that sounded like battle drums in his ears. He roared, tossing his head and snarling at the challenge to come.

Soon enough he had eaten up the distance between the

Edge and the Imperial Island, and was barreling along the
Bridge of Gilt. Inside, he felt Raed Syndar Rossin share his
determination and strength. It was an odd sensation since
both of them had spent years battling each other. Now,
feeling the human's strength of will, the Rossin wondered
at it. Had he underestimated his host all this time? What
might they have achieved if they had worked together?
What might they still do?

They sprang onto the square and bounded toward the
castle wall. The human defenders had all been slain by the
Circle of Stars and replaced by Deacons. These Deacons,
Raed let the Rossin hate.

He saw fire, green and red, flash at him from left and
right as Deacons on the battlements threw their runes at
him. None had any effect, flowing over and through him. It
was exhilarating more than anything. When the great cat
leapt at the postern gate in the palace doors, they cracked
and broke under him. The Vermillion palace had not been
made to stand attack in any real sense. The city was protection enough for the palace of an Emperor, but the Rossin
was not a normal foe.

He was full of pride and arrogance as he ran through the
pleasure gardens and toward the main rooms. His goal was
the main staircase. When he had been there last, it had
been the only staircase.

Behind, the great cat could feel the Deacons forming a
Conclave, but even for Derodak's children that would not
be an instantaneous thing. He smashed through another
door, and filled the palace with his roar. It had been generations since he had been here, and the building was much,
much grander than it had been then.

However, there was one thing that had not changed. The
cat turned his head and snarled. He could feel it under his
paws like a hot piece of metal. The breach where nearly a
thousand years ago he had stood with Derodak and pledged
his allegiance to the Rossins—giving them his name and
his power—still existed.

It was the weakest point between the Otherside and the human realm, and even after it had sealed, a scar remained on the fabric of reality.

Now it was screaming once more.

The Rossin knew that there could only be a few more moments. He flicked his head in the other direction and felt another presence appearing near him, a familiar one. It should have been upsetting, but in fact this new arrival gave him hope.

However, there was no time to waste on waiting for re-inforcements. The Rossin wheeled about and bounded down the steps—moving much faster than any human could ever hope to. He passed quickly from the newer parts, through to the Ancient mosaicked walls, and finally into the bare caverns. Along the way he found Deacons waiting for him in their dark cloaks. They held up their foci and tried to use runes on him. When that failed, they tried to use swords. The Rossin sprang on them and snapped them as easily as twigs. They had not expected his return, and the one of their number who could stop him was otherwise engaged.

By the time the Rossin reached the final chamber, he was soaked in blood and flesh, though the blood did not please him as it once had. A terrible sound split the air just as his paw was on the threshold. The great cat looked up at the carved Maker of Ways and saw it was crumbling away. Then the whole ground shook, forcing the cat to spread his paws and brace as it rumbled under him.

Then he smelled it; the hot, fetid odor of the Otherside; something that he had hoped never to experience again. His roar of outrage was lost in the tumult. He bolted through the door toward it.

For a moment all he could see was the geistlord, the Maker of Ways. He towered in the tiny cavern, because above it was more than just a cavern now. The huge form of the Maker was holding apart the breach, two large tentacles in the human realm, while his wide black green shoulders were braced in the Otherside.

Eyes like red lanterns were fixed on the new world, and behind him were all the host of the undead. Closest burned the Murashev, Herald of Doom, ready to burn brightly. For a heartbeat, the Rossin saw nothing but those dire figures. The Maker was pressing on the breach, his strength alone holding it open.

The power to summon the Maker was beyond anyone in the human realm, even Derodak. Thinking of him made the Rossin capable of pulling his eyes away from the looming geistlord.

Below, near one of the writhing tentacles, he saw Derodak and Sorcha Faris. The Arch Abbot was leaning over her, pressing his hand against her collarbone, his eyes boring into hers. She was limp and pale, but her eyes were focused somewhere else.

It was the Wrayth in her. The Rossin saw with all the accuracy of a Sensitive. She was being forced to use those powers to connect with all of humanity. They could not feel it, but she was their conduit, gathering their wills to make the breach and the summons.

Yet still the Arch Abbot had time to spare for the Rossin. He looked up, full of power, and then held out his leather-clad hand. The shield rune sprang up between them, burning scarlet and unbearably hot in the room. It was Derodak, and he was like none of his lesser children.

The Rossin paced back and forth before the burning flames and contemplated the end of the world that had been his home. His frustration burned as brightly as the fire between them.

To have come so close and then be stymied by his old enemy was beyond frustrating. Still as much as he roared and raged, the shield of flame still held him.

Merrick, Zofiya and her army, on board the *Summer Hawk*, reached Vermillion on the wings of the coming storm. The weather had turned against them, and it had taken much longer to make the capital than usual. Still the Empress drove them on, urging her captains to burn whatever weirstones they needed to get them there in time.

When they first saw the city, Merrick rushed forward and saw immediately the damage that had been inflicted on the great city. The streets were full of panicked people, and the palace was burning with a flickering light, the like of which he had never seen before. Screams and prayers to little gods wafted up from below borne on smoke.

He took his place with the Empress, the Fensena and Aachon on the prow of the airship and none of them spoke. Zofiya had told him the state that she had found the capital city in and that had been enough to shock him—this was something else.

The coyote pressed against the Sensitive. "Look with your real eyes, youngster."

He was almost too afraid of what he would see to try, but Merrick finally opened his Center and spread it over the city. What he saw sickened him. The lovely capital full of life and commerce was a fractured and injured animal. Robbed of peace, it was descending into anarchy. The air was stained with the terror of her people for not all of them were dead. That would happen when the barrier to the Otherside was gone and they became fodder for the geists.

"Look toward the palace," the Fensena's remarkably calm words intruded on Merrick's contemplation.

At first he thought the center of the city was on fire, but then he realized it was something else. Indigo colors stained the sky over the palace, while tumultuous clouds flickered with barely contained lightning. "The breach is opening," Merrick whispered under his breath. He had read about it over and over again in his studies, but he had never thought he would live to see it happen again.

Behind him he could feel the rest of the Sensitives—his Sensitives—reacting with horror as their knowledge brought the reality of the situation home.

He turned to Zofiya. "We need to get down there,

now . . . we can't go to the port. We must go there." He pointed down toward the palace itself, though he wished to point only to the horizon and demand to flee.

"And then?" the Empress asked him. "What shall we do?"

They were hidden from the people behind them. He slipped his hand into hers and gave it a squeeze. He would much rather have taken her in his arms and kissed her.

"I will take the Conclave into the palace," he replied. "It will be Deacon on Deacon fighting in there. You must do what you can to help your people."

Her eyebrows drew together in an expression he recognized immediately, but he had no time for her demands. "I should be fighting at your side—that is my palace—"

"Darling," he whispered to her, so that only the Fensena could have heard him, "if this does not work, you must be free to lead the people in whatever way you can against the geists."

His brown eyes locked with hers, and her expression softened even in this dire moment. Since she was Empress, it was her choice to throw her arms around him and kiss him then and there. As always Zofiya made him breathless, but this time he most especially did not want to let her go. The taste of her in his mouth was like life itself, and death was not that far away.

When they moved apart, Merrick glanced over Zofiya's shoulder, but none of the Deacons or soldiers at their back were looking at them.

"I will do as you ask," Zofiya said clearly, "but only for my people."

"No one doubts your courage," the Fensena broke in, his golden eyes gleaming with the not-so-distant lightning, "but this is the way of things. We will either stop the Maker of Ways, or the rest will be flames."

Merrick might have wanted the coyote to couch it in better terms, but it was true. The Empress did not attempt to deny it.

The *Summer Hawk* dropped lower and lower and everything began to come into dreadful focus. They could now see the blood on the cobblestones, and make out every little tragedy as it played out below.

The broken bodies below them were now visible as not only soldiers, but also Deacons of the Circle of Stars. Merrick recognized the spectacular damage immediately; the Rossin had been here before them. He could not decide if that thought cheered him or not.

Regardless, they had to go down there. Quickly, Merrick wrapped his mind around the prepared Conclave. He had arranged his ragtag group of Deacons into groups of twenty, with one foci holding them together into Conclaves. It was the best way to shore up their forces, which were not all that experienced or well trained. This way, those that were could use their strength without losing control of the situation.

Merrick took a deep breath and led the way down the ladder off the airship. The naked human form of the Fensena scrambled down after him and took back his coyote shape as soon as his feet touched the ground. On his heels, the rest of the Deacons scrambled down. Among them were Aachon who led one of the Conclaves, and even the boy Eriloyn from Waikein who had insisted on using his new runes to fight. Most of them still wore their cloaks, though the newcomers' ones were patchwork, or leather.

It was strange to feel the closeness of the Conclave without the presence of Sorcha in it as well. He felt for the first time really like the First Presbyter. Merrick could only hope it would not be the last time he experienced this sensation.

Just as the people disembarked, shots rang out. Two Deacons in Merrick's Conclave fell, their places in the Conclave becoming sucking maws, but he reorganized the pattern of the Conclaves quickly. Terrible as it was, he'd expected it.

Somewhere up in the towers a few Imperial Guards still

held on, and they were shooting at whatever cloaked figures they could, mistaking them for Derodak's Deacons.
As bullets zipped around them, Merrick shouted for his
colleagues to get to cover, while above them riflemen on
the *Summer Hawk* returned fire.

Merrick was holding his portion of the Conclave
together, moving his remaining people in a cohesive group
into shelter, while he stood still, concentrating very hard.
That was until a huge bulk of a man threw himself on him,
knocking him to the ground. For an instant he didn't know
what had just happened. The next thing he realized, it was
Aachon that had barreled into him, and that there was
blood everywhere.

Quickly, Merrick ascertained it was not his blood.
Aachon lay atop him, and it took three Deacons to lift him
up. They dragged him into one of the hallways of the palace, as bullets zipped around them, and used the big man's
cloak to staunch the blood as best they could.

The tall man grinned at those carrying him. "I've had
worse." Merrick checked him over quickly and saw that the
wound had passed through his shoulder cleanly. "But I can't
hold my portion of the Conclave, you'll have to take it."

"Of course," the Presbyter said, getting to his feet, glad
at least the big man was not dead. He'd been gruff with
anyone not Raed, but he had a powerful spirit.

Merrick felt Aachon's blood on his skin, warm and
vital. His anger flared suddenly that a good man—one of
his own—had been targeted by those who couldn't tell
the difference between Deacons. His Center sped toward
the group in the tower, and he felt their heartbeats like fluttering moths in his hands. So many things he could have
done to them, but instead of the runes, that wild talent of
his chose this moment to rise up. It was a lucky thing too;
he did not want to kill anyone who might be saved.

Instead, Merrick hit the survivors with the hammer of
regret. He made them fall to their knees weeping for what
they had done, clawing at their faces in horror. None of

them could lift a weapon or shoot another Deacon, so there would be no more mistakes.

"Go," Aachon said, taking the compress and holding it there himself, "I'll wait here and see how things go. Strange . . . I always thought I would take a bullet for Raed Syndar Rossin. Life is a funny thing."

Merrick clasped his hand. "Then hold tight to it, we'll be right back."

Five lay Brothers were helping the wounded and, under the circumstances, that was the best that could be done. The Conclaves had lost seven Deacons, but the groups had a flexible pattern, though they did lose strength with each member gone.

Merrick now realized that he needed more power to finish the task at hand. The solution meant treading on ground that he had warned Sorcha off only weeks before— and that had not ended well—but there was little choice. Everything rested on these moments. As First Presbyter he would burn all of his Order, all of the new recruits to keep the world from suffering another Break.

Wrapping his silver fur cloak about him, Merrick opened his Center as wide as he could, taking the leaders of the other Conclaves into his own control. He was the spider at the center of the web. The master puppeteer. The heady sensation of so many minds, so much power, almost pulled him apart. It had to be the largest Conclave in Order history.

Now their true enemies could be seen. The Native Order had always been excellent at hiding itself, but they could no longer do that—not with the beam of the grand Conclave on them.

They too were knitted in groups, but something had passed through them and weakened them considerably.

The Rossin. The smell of him and the tang of his passing were now visible on every surface. Much blood had been spilled, but there were still many of Derodak's children in the palace, and they were drawing together with every moment.

Heat enveloped Merrick, rage such that he had never really let out before. Sensitives were taught to be calm, controlled—but now all of that was washed away. He saw again his father murdered on the steps of his childhood home by a geist. Experienced once more the piles of dead he and Sorcha had uncovered on the way to Ulrich. And finally he saw Derodak stealing his mother into the tunnels under Orinthal. It was too much.

With the silver fur cape flowing around him, Merrick set off. His own personality felt very fragile as he held it before him, like a dim light that he could drop at any instant. The chatter of so many voices in his head, even as they tried to remain quiet, was still nearly overwhelming.

The Native Order had regrouped farther into the corridors of the palace, and they came at him again; the Runes of Dominion turned on them in floods of green, blue and red. Flames poured out of the corridors toward the advancing Enlightened, and Derodak's children appeared out of the walls, with swords and spears.

The palace became a heaving battleground in an instant. Battle was joined, and it was Merrick who stood in the center of it all. Blood trickled and ran from the corners of his eyes and his nose as the pressure of holding the Conclave together took its toll. He couldn't move to defend himself, but he was not without a protector. The Fensena was there, apart from the Conclave, snarling and ripping out unsuspecting throats in the corridors and rooms.

Merrick began to use the parts of the Conclave like a body. His arms flashed out, defending with the shield of fire, while the limbs of others called Chityre into being in the corridors. Shayst, the green fire, took power where it could, while Deiyant threw furniture to block oncoming advances. He saw all and killed all.

Soon enough Merrick realized that he had the upper hand and why. Derodak was not in the Native Order Conclaves. He was not present to hold them together in a grand cohesive union, as Merrick was doing.

And they were frightened. In the whirl of moving his people, the Sensitive had not much energy to use his Center to see beyond the current fight. Yet, now as the grand Conclave felt more seamless, he could sense their opponents' fear. The Rossin had run among them, and their runes had no effect on the Beast. He had torn them down and left them in ruins, yet their leader was not here.

Derodak was below. He was making the ground shake, and anyone with ears could hear it, and anyone with humanity could feel the presence of the breach. However, Merrick could not reach Derodak, the Rossin or even Sorcha. They were sealed off in a bubble created by the widening breach.

You have to end this. You have to be there. Nynnia's breath was on his neck, cool in the heat of battle. It was an instant of clarity in the tumult, and he knew what he had to do.

The talent he carried came from the Ehtia. It was how they had been able to work the weirstones and ruled the world for generations. The Order he had been raised in had hated and feared them because they were not measured and controlled. They were wild and unpredictable.

Merrick needed chaotic and unpredictable right now, so he opened the conduit. His body disappeared. It was not just the wild magic of his heritage—it was everything he had ever learned. He let it all flow out into the Conclave.

You are wrong, the talent bellowed at the Native Deacons. *You are bad, evil and wrong. Look what you are doing!*

No one ever thinks of themselves as evil, but Merrick's wild talent made them see what they really were. They had been used and twisted. Their Arch Abbot had no care for them. They were fodder for his madness and had been bred as such. They were nothing more than sheep farmed for his use.

It was too much, too much for his targets and too much for the Conclave. The voices of the Native Order in Merrick's head screamed in horror at what he had done and what he had shown them.

When he came back to himself, he was standing in a room full of bodies. Some were dead, some were howling and crying. The part of him that he'd lost in the Conclave would have felt something about this, guilt he supposed. In this moment he had nothing but emptiness.

Merrick wrapped the cloak about him, stepped over the bodies and strode to the main staircase. The sound of claws on stone was the only thing that made him turn.

The Fensena was trotting in his wake, blood staining his muzzle black, and his gold eyes gleaming above the filth. It was the kind of image that could have come from the dark times when the Break had happened: a wild animal intent on death in the halls of humanity.

It seemed fitting to have such a creature as an escort. With the Fensena following, Merrick went down into the depths of Vermillion to find his partner.

TWENTY-EIGHT

Where All Things Must Come

Sorcha felt everything—not just her own physical distress. The pain of her blood pouring out onto the sand that was apparently welcomed by the Otherside. The thousands of voices and concerns of the humans everywhere in the human realm rattled in her head endlessly. She was just a tiny mote in the middle of it. Bleeding out on the very doorstep of the Otherside appeared to be her fate, and even she found it difficult to care.

Hovering over everything was the Maker of Ways. The red eyes sweeping over it all, his shoulder pressed against the edge of existence, and his great tentacles sliding forward out of the Otherside. Already thin geists, rei and mist witches were wriggling their way past him into the world. When he entered completely, there would be nothing but death and servitude to follow.

Sorcha's mother had not birthed her for this, but there was nothing she could do about it. She was alone and the void around her roared.

At least until she heard the roar of the Rossin. It was loud enough to rise above the screaming sound of the

Otherside. Once that roar had caused fear in her heart, but now she felt her tiny mote of reality flare at it.

Derodak was still above her, still letting the blood flow, still forcing her to hold on to all of humanity. Dimly she saw his gaze flick away from her. He called on the shield of fire to hold the Beast off. As it burned, he screamed at the Rossin, "You cannot harm me, Beast. We made the pact, my blood is your blood. You cannot enter."

The Way is open! Arise Ehtia! A familiar voice called. Sorcha had the fleeting impression of a sweet face pressed against hers, cool and calming.

Then Nynnia and a thousand ethereal forms darted past the Maker. Derodak howled and swore as they collided with him, but he was forced off his perch on Sorcha.

The Ehtia had no bodies, but they had some little power still. They pressed the Arch Abbot against the far wall of the cavern opposite from where the raging Rossin snarled and roared. Their ancestral voices were like dead leaves rustling on cobblestones, but she could make out nothing of their words. It must have meant something to Derodak because he was howling. She was glad of it. Wanted more of it.

The shield of fire dropped away.

Sorcha levered herself up on her elbows, feeling the blood running from many cuts on her arms and body. Her vision dipped in and out. The Maker of Ways was scream- ing his song of destruction and moving forward. He had no need of her power or blood now; he was nearly done with his task. All was chaos and pain, but standing in the door- way, she finally saw them, and understood.

Merrick, pale and calm was beside the Rossin. He had his hands buried in the fur of the Beast's mane. They could have been a statue dedicated to wild beauty. Both of them were looking directly at Sorcha, ignoring everything around them. There was nothing else.

Three bodies, four minds in agreement. Sorcha smiled slowly. No, not four minds. Hundreds of minds. She still held humanity inside her, while Merrick held the grand

Conclave lightly in his mind, as if he were a child with a string toy in one hand. Sorcha cradled the tiny sparks of the rest of humanity in her. As it had been in the ossuary, one of them was dying.

Gasping, choking on her own blood, Sorcha held out her hand. "Come."

The minds enveloped her, the flesh followed, and once more they fell into the Merge.

The Beast made of everything was flayed into existence on the very doorstep of the Otherside, but it was not the same Beast as had been born in the White Palace. It had grown huge on so much power. Its tawny hide shifted and moved to the eddies of the runes and power within it. It was the lost children of Waikein. It was the desperate Deacons of the Enlightened. It was the hopeless Empress defending her people above. Each hurt and barb of the living made up its essence.

Sorcha, Raed, Merrick and even the mighty Rossin were merely tiny parts of this great creation. They might have caused it to come into existence, but they could never grasp what it was.

When it opened its eyes, they flared every color.

If there was to be a god in Arkaym, it would be the Living Beast, and it would be brief and glorious. Unlike the creature four souls had made in the darkness of the ossuary, this one was not proud. It was something else entirely; it was the beauty of life. And life was brief, but powerful.

The Maker of Ways still towered above it, the scion of the undead. Its tentacles had pushed aside the breach, and one of its clawed feet was already on the sand. It could not be allowed to enter.

The Living Beast sprang forward, but the sound that issued from its throat was not a roar—it was almost music. It struck the Maker with all the force of everything that made it: the life of the human realm. Its claws pierced the hide of the Beast, and the geistlord howled. Its tentacles tore at the Beast, but he could not pierce to the core of its being. Human realm and Otherside wrestled for control of the breach.

Runes flexed on the Living Beast's hide as it drove the Maker of Ways backward, biting and clawing at it with all the determination of life trying to overcome death. It had only a moment to exist and triumph. It only had one purpose.

As its feet gouged deeply in the earth, it gained strength from the blood there. It pushed harder.

When the Maker of Ways fell, it lost everything, connection to the human realm and strength. It could not muster itself again. As the figure collapsed backward into the Otherside however, the Beast also fell.

It landed on the sand and burst for the same reasons the Maker had. Connection was lost. The living could not hold. The Living Beast let go of its brief existence, exploding into a shower of realities that would never again come together.

The Rossin, Merrick and Sorcha were left scattered on the floor. The Maker of Ways had been beaten back, but the breach was still closing, ever so slowly.

Sorcha, her body healed in the Meld, saw the geists racing to escape into the human world while they could. They had stopped the Maker, but there would still be hundreds of lives lost if these geists entered. The gift of the Wrayth flared in her, and Merrick felt her understand what she needed to do. Before he could stop her, she turned the connection she had with the humans on the undead.

I'll hold them, she sent desperately along the damaged Bond to Merrick. *You must stop Derodak!*

She was right. With the breach sealing itself the power of the Ehtia was failing. Their flimsy forms were not like geists; they could not exist beyond the Otherside without bodies. They evaporated like so much mist in the sun.

Derodak smiled and raised his hands still burning with runes to strike.

The Rossin snarled and bunched. The Arch Abbot pointed at him as if he were a house pet. "You cannot even touch me Beast. Remember our pact." His eyes fell on Merrick. "You will be the first to die, and with your blood we will begin again."

The Sensitive was too weakened by the Meld to do anything but watch as Derodak drew a long hunting knife and approached.

The Rossin's roar filled the cavern again, and it was not that of a defeated creature. "Only your blood can kill you," he snarled, and then immediately sprang forward.

This day's events had slowed the Arch Abbot down too. He could not get out of the way quickly enough.

The great pard threw himself toward Derodak, but in mid-leap his flesh changed. It was Raed Syndar Rossin that landed atop him, still full of the strength of the Beast. He bore Derodak to the ground with a guttural yell. The sound of the Ancient man's neck snapping echoed in the chamber, but Raed did not stop there. He tore his head free and flung it away into the shadows. It was the most impressive physical feat Merrick had ever seen, and he was left breathless.

When he levered himself up, Raed was covered in his ancestor's blood. "No," he said to the corpse, "only your blood can take your blood. Not the Rossin. Just me."

Then he turned to Merrick and helped him to his feet. They both looked to Sorcha.

She was burning, as if her whole body lit from within. Her partner shivered at the strength of the connections she was holding to the geists—to the whole Otherside.

Let go! he shot along the Bond, but she was so weakened, so broken that she could not hear him, and he knew, neither could she let go.

"What's happening?" Raed asked, shivering in his nakedness before the breach.

"We're losing her," Merrick replied, dropping to his knees beside his partner, "and gaining geists." Nynnia had been right. If Sorcha held her connection to the geists, then the breach would never close, and they would not need the Maker of Ways to enter. She would be their eternal conduit.

"Do something then!" Raed demanded, and he could not really understand what he was asking.

Yet, Merrick knew what he had to do. The distressed face of Nynnia was close, but she did not press. They both knew what had to come. She had asked him once if he would have the strength to do this very thing.

In the halls of the initiate, in the quiet of the Sensitive training, Merrick had learned along with all his fellows the rune Ticat; the Final Rune. Actives thought it was another level of consciousness—which in a way it was. It was the rune of control, for when an Active became as Sorcha was now; a danger to the human realm.

Along the Bond, comprehension of what he was about to do flowed to his partner. She understood. Her partner felt that instantly. In all the chaos of the moment, there was an instant of clarity. In it, there was only the two of them and the Bond.

It's too much, Merrick. I can't stop it, so you have to stop me.

Her voice echoed in his head, cool and calm, but it held none of the passion he'd come to associate with Sorcha. The world was only her blue eyes and her acceptance. They'd both trained. They both knew the risks. However, Sorcha had to tell him this, and Merrick knew why: she didn't want him to be haunted by guilt, and she wanted to make sure he didn't hesitate.

Silver light flared along Merrick's forehead, running along the Pattern, flooding his vision white. He dived down into Sorcha, became her for an instant. Then he took it from her, ripping away all that made her powerful. It was the cruelest thing to do to a Deacon—to take away all that made them who they were. He flayed the channels of the runes, burning everything out as he plunged through her.

The marks on his partner's arms faded as Merrick wielded Ticat, and he made sure to take all that she had; she would be no conduit for geist or geistlord.

When Merrick opened his eyes, it was to look into Sorcha's blue ones. The breach behind them was sealing with nothing to hold it open. However, in that instant all that mattered was each other.

Merrick had burned everything to nothing. Not just her power, but their connection. They were now just as two normal people who knew each other very well. No Bond lay between them. Not between them or between the Rossin.

He expected hatred, but instead she looked remarkably calm. Pressing her hand on top of Merrick's, Sorcha climbed to her feet, and all three of them embraced. Words were unnecessary between them. They all knew what had been lost, but also what had been saved.

In the silence, they heard a yip. Turning, they saw that the Fensena had entered the chamber. The huge coyote with blood drying on his coat was panting, but when he spoke it was with confidence. "Harbinger Sorcha Faris, while you still hold the title of head of an Order, I need that one favor you owe me."

Sorcha sagged slightly, her arm around both Merrick and Raed. "You . . . you ask me this now?" Even exhausted her voice was outraged. "Have you not seen what we have just done, did you not—"

The coyote tilted his head. "Yes, very impressive, and I am grateful, but I think you will find I have done more than I ever expected . . . but nonetheless you still owe me that favor."

Sorcha's jaw clenched. "Very well, what do you want?"

"A simple thing," the Fensena said, walking in closer. "Take up your partner's cloak, wrap it around the Imperial blood, and tell my master he must be free."

"Your master?" Merrick had a feeling he knew what the answer would be.

The coyote performed a little bow. "Yes, the Rossin. Only a leader of the Order can give my master the freedom he has always wanted."

Raed, who had the most to gain in this transaction, held up his hand. "Hold on! Do you mean that the Rossin would be separated from me, free to roam the world?"

"Yes," the Fensena replied simply.

"No!" Raed turned on Sorcha. "I have always dreamed of being free of the Rossin—but you cannot unleash him on the world. His bloodlust . . ."

"Raed." It was Sorcha who interrupted him. "Did you really not understand the Rossin when we were in the Meld?"

Merrick stopped breathing for just an instant. He understood what she meant. They had been so tightly bound together nothing had been hidden. The Rossin's bloodlust had subsided with the Bond; he had become more a part of the human world than part of the Otherside the longer he was bound to them.

He had not needed to kill to sustain himself for some time. When they had been one, his need for freedom had been theirs. They could still taste it, and what was more, they understood it.

Raed's shoulders slumped, he sighed, and then nodded. "No one wants to understand an enemy," he finally said, "but now I do."

"Be not too worried," the Fensena offered, "the Rossin, I think, will find being bound to one form, one life, not as much freedom as he might think." A sly coyote grin spread on his jaws. "Think of it as the sting in the tail if it makes you feel better."

"Very well then." Sorcha bent and took up the silver fur Merrick had let drop and wrapped it around Raed. "Be free."

It seemed such a simple thing. The pelt of the Rossin was

given back to him by the Harbinger of the Enlightened—as Derodak had made it so.

When Raed staggered back, the Rossin was born anew into the world and ran. They glimpsed only the flick of his tail and heard his roar of delight.

The Rossin ran from Vermillion. His great pads made no noise as he pounded along the cobblestones. The war drums were gone. Citizens of Vermillion, those that still remained on the street that was, hurried to get out of his way.

He did not think they knew what he was, perhaps just some Beast that had escaped the Imperial menagerie in the tumult. He took no more blood from them, because he did not need to. The mad lust for it was gone, and it was another thing he was free of.

The sudden realization hit him as he bounded over a man tugging a recalcitrant donkey pulling a cart—he was free. He heard the donkey's frightened bray, and the howl of the man, but they were suddenly a long way behind him.

He had his own body. The flesh he wore was his alone now. He was no longer geist, since that had been ripped away from him when Sorcha Faris broke all Bonds. She'd freed him, and in doing so fulfilled her promise to the Fensena.

His longs strides slowed, and the great pard looked around. He was standing at the very edge of Vermillion again, looking out over the swamplands, and it was as if he were seeing them for the very first time.

The Fensena's warning now came to him. Without the powers of the geist or any connection back to the Otherside, the geistlord was nothing more than a large, peculiar creature. He had his intelligence, his size and his strength—and that was all.

The Rossin snarled, shaking his thick mane and inhaling the smells of this new world he had literally just been born into. He was indeed no longer a geistlord, but he was certainly no normal lion. He was indeed something new. This world needed something new.

Yet he only had one life now. The Rossin could no longer hide in the bloodline of the Imperial family that had taken his name.

As the Rossin stood there contemplating, he heard a sound in the streets behind him, and turned to see a small child that was staring at him. It was a boy of no more than five, standing in the shadow of one of the shacks that made up the Edge of Vermillion. He had wide brown eyes, and he was staring at the Rossin with not a trace of fear in his face.

The great pard saw himself reflected in those eyes, and he was no terrifying geistlord. He was a shadow-maned wonder with gleaming eyes. The child actually raised one hand and waved at him. He was fearless, and the Rossin wondered if perhaps there was a way that humanity would forget its terror of him.

A sea of possibilities opened up before the Rossin, and even though there was risk waiting for him out there, he was at least free. As the great pard sprang away from the city of Vermillion, he let out a roar. It was a promise of things to come—a promise of freedom.

TWENTY-NINE

Setting Sail

Three weeks after the end of Derodak and his Circle of Stars, four people, respectfully followed by two platoons of Imperial Guard, walked down from the palace to where the remains of the Mother Abbey lay.

One wore a black cloak with bands of emerald green and sky blue, two others thick brown wool cloaks, while the fourth was in a dress uniform of pure white and wore a band of gold on her head.

The Mother Abbey seemed a good place to contemplate what needed to be done and to bid farewell to one another.

Sorcha, Raed, Merrick and the Empress of Arkaym, with the now-confined-to-one-body Fensena trotting at their heels, picked their way over the ruins of the devotional, examining the space where the new Arch Abbot of the Order of the Enlightened wanted to build his new Mother Abbey. Merrick had decided not to call himself Harbinger—that he would leave for his predecessor.

"Are you sure you want to start again here?" Sorcha frowned and pushed some stones through the dirt with her foot. "This ground has seen a lot of death and pain." Her arms were healing, though the marks the Patternmaker had carved on her skin had become nothing more than strange scars. No runic power had flowed through her skin since Merrick had cast the rune Ticat on her. She found she was at peace with that.

Merrick's brown eyes grew distant for a moment, so that she wondered if he were attempting to peer into the future. He shook his head and smiled at her. "It has also seen a lot of laughter, healing and intelligent discourse. The stones we will bury far from Vermillion, but the ground is still solid. I know you wanted to build something new, Sorcha, but the Order is mine now. And besides," he said, shooting her a sharp grin, "this is the place you and I first met. In days to come, it may become holy ground."

In answer, she threw a clod of dirt at him.

Raed was sitting a little distance off, on a piece of finely carved stone, and looking out over the devastation. Zofiya was at his side, and they were talking quietly. Nearby, the Fensena nosed through the rubble.

Sorcha wondered what the humans were saying. In the last few days, the new Empress and the former Pretender to the throne had been deep in discussions.

"He is a clever man," Merrick offered, standing at her side and staring at them with a kind of wistfulness. "Zofiya will have need of clever people in the coming days."

"Well, she can't have this one," Sorcha replied firmly, "and besides, despite renouncing the throne, Raed is still an awkward person for her to have at Court."

"Not if she married him. It's not like she can marry me," Merrick said, his voice wrapping around that little pain.

She wanted to act surprised, but the idea had come to her too. If the Young Pretender married the new Empress, it would certainly tie up some loose threads. "Do you think she will . . ."

Merrick laughed and shoved her shoulder. "How long have you been sleeping in this man's bed, Sorcha? Raed has never wanted power . . . he has only ever wanted his freedom, the sea . . . and now you."

She knew that very well, but somehow it meant more coming from Merrick. He saw so many things true—even at the end. "Then he shall have them," she whispered.

Many of the Deacons had tried to get her to stay. She'd been inundated with tearful farewells, some even on their knees. Merrick did not do that. Even with their Bond broken and thrown into dust he knew her well enough. It would hurt her dreadfully, but so would staying.

"I shall miss you." His hand slipped into hers. "I shall miss you like part of my own soul."

That was when she threw herself into his arms, and cried . . . a little more than she had anticipated. His arms were tight about her, as tight as when he had pulled her back from the edge of madness.

"The Harbinger's job is done," she said simply into his ear. "I miss the runes and the Bond, but also I am just very, very tired."

"You are just going sailing, that is all." Merrick pulled back from her, clasped her shoulders and gave her a little shake as if to reassure himself. "You are going sailing, and you can always come back."

Not quite able to find her own words, she watched as he bent and pushed stones away from a larger piece of masonry. It was the face of an Ancient Arch Abbot of the Circle of Stars—who knew, it could have even been of Derodak himself.

Merrick looked up at her. "You will come back, at least to see what I make of this place, but I can promise you this . . . we will not try and wipe away the memory of the Circle of Stars, or the Order of the Eye and the Fist. When they took away history before, we learned nothing from it." His eyes gleamed with excitement and hope. She could tell he was very much looking forward to the challenge of rebuilding. Her Sensitive had always been a man of ideas and wisdom.

"And the Arch Abbot has no need of a partner." Sorcha smiled and flicked away the remains of her tears. "I know you will make something great, Merrick, and I will come back to see it—I promise." He was the man for the job after all; in his blood ran human, Ehtia and a touch of geist. The Order of the Enlightened, she was sure, would be a great thing with Merrick to lead it. Probably, she had to admit, better than if she had kept her powers and position. Still, she would not stay around here and be a lay Brother. That was not for her.

Merrick swallowed, his eyes bright. "I promise when you come back 'Rise together or fall alone' will be carved on one of these stones."

Sorcha dared not open her mouth to reply to that.

Luckily, Raed and Zofiya were making their way back toward them, and they were laughing. It might have seemed a little odd, the Imperial Guard waiting at the perimeter, but Sorcha knew it was a sound beginning.

The Empress nestled up against Merrick for a moment. Raed took Sorcha's hand. "Looks like quite a job for you, Merrick, but it should at least keep you out of trouble," he said with genuine warmth in his voice.

Merrick kissed the top of Zofiya's head while he could, in the relative solitude of the ruins. "I would be worried if I was you, Captain. It was usually Sorcha that got me into trouble. Are you sure you really want her on your boat?"

It was a fair enough question, the former Deacon thought. She raised one eyebrow and tilted her head at Raed. He brushed aside one copper curl from her face. "Oh, I think I will risk it."

His hands rubbed along the raised flesh where once the runes had run, and she shivered. They were still sensitive, but she hoped that would fade with time. "Then let's be going," she whispered, "and find out if I am worth it."

The four of them, trailed by the Fensena, proceeded down to the docks, the Imperial Guard falling into line around them. The citizens of Vermillion did not treat it as a parade—too busy mending their damaged city and her bridges—but many did call out to the new Empress, blessing her. Very few knew the others who walked with her. Sorcha realized that soon enough Merrick would be just as well-known as Zofiya, and wondered how he would cope with that.

It distressed her a little that she wouldn't be there to see it, but she had her own wounds to lick. The places where the runes and the Wrayth had been still hurt. She could not stay and watch Deacons build Bonds, fight the remaining geists and feel the Brotherhood that had been so much a part of her life before. That would hurt even more than her physical injuries.

Finally, they reached the docks, and there was the *Dominion* sitting among the other ships of the fleet. It had been a long time since Sorcha had seen it, and it made her breath catch in her throat.

"You know, I never imagined seeing her in this port," Raed said, waving to his crew on the decks, "but by the Blood she looks wonderful here."

The colors she was flying were no longer the rampant Rossin. Zofiya had gifted Raed the Imperial colors, so that everywhere the *Dominion* sailed, she would be given the honors of an Imperial Ship.

"Indeed she does, my captain!" Aachon walked down the gangplank to meet them. He too was bandaged, but he strode as confidently as he ever had. "The *Dominion* is all shipshape and ready for you." He looked down at his feet for a moment.

The first mate was no longer the first mate. Like the Fensena, he had chosen to stay in Vermillion with Merrick to help him rebuild the Order. He had, however, organized the return of the *Dominion* and helped find crew to replace many who had died through the course of the land adventures.

Raed smiled and pulled his friend into a tight hug, where they both spent some time thumping each other on the back. When they broke away, both of them were smiling, but their eyes shone suspiciously.

"No more piracy for Raed Syndar Faris," Sorcha said, a little too loudly. She felt a proud swelling in her chest that he had chosen to take her name, to replace the one he had gladly lost. Caught on the wings of that, she spun around and embraced Zofiya and Merrick together. It was a tight, desperate hug that was highly inappropriate to give to the Empress of Arkaym and the Arch Abbot of the Order, but Sorcha was about to run away, so she didn't give a damn.

"Be good to each other," Sorcha told them, and then loosening the startled couple, grabbed Raed's hand and dragged him up the gangway. She knew that they would all be waving; Merrick, Zofiya and Aachon, but she couldn't bear to look back. If she did, she feared she would never have the strength to leave. One thing she did not want to be was some old relic hovering over what those three would make in Vermillion.

For an hour or more she sat near the prow and kept her back to the city that had been home and danger for her. Raed busied himself with his crew and was smart enough to leave her alone. Then, just as the sun was setting he came to find her, wrapped his arms around her, and held her.

"I know this is going to be hard—" he began, but Sorcha cut him off.

"Not hard," she replied, squeezing his hands, "different. I was so long in the Order that I don't quite know how life goes on outside the cloak." She pulled him down and kissed him hard, then gasping slightly, released him. "But I will learn."

The captain stroked her face. "We'll learn it together—I can't recall a time without the Rossin either. Perhaps you'd like to come to my cabin and we can see if everything is where we last had it." His wicked grin sparked a twist of her stomach that said some things had definitely not changed.

She needed him . . . but she wanted to see the sun finally set. It was important to mark the moments of change, to celebrate and reflect. Sorcha fished out one of her Imperium cigarillos—a gift from the Empress' own store. She held it up. "Just a few more moments, my love. I'd like to mark the end of an era."

Raed kissed her again, looked into her eyes and smiled. "Don't be too long, this captain is aging as we speak." Then he turned and left her to her moment.

The sea was silvered blue black, and it smelled clean and fresh—the smell of hope perhaps. Sorcha rolled the cigarillo under her nose, anticipating the moment. Then she realized she had not asked Raed for his flint to light it.

A tingle ran along her arm, the slightest burning sensation. Holding up her arm, Sorcha stared at it for a second. The feeling was familiar. When a tiny blue flame danced on the tip of her right hand, she gasped in surprise and delight.

Hand wavering, she lit her cigarillo with it, and then passed it back and forth in front of her eyes. The sensation retreated, and the tiny flame died with it. It had to be a remnant of the power, like the jerking of a dead man, and yet . . . perhaps it was more.

Sorcha Faris sat on the prow of the ship and smiled to herself. Perhaps there was life and hope left—but for the moment she would keep it just for herself.

ABOUT THE AUTHOR

Born in New Zealand, **Philippa Ballantine** has always had her head in a book. A corporate librarian for thirteen years, she has a bachelor of arts in English and a bachelor of applied science in library and information science. She is New Zealand's first podcast novelist, and she has produced four podiobooks. Many of these have been short-listed for the Parsec Award, and she has won a Sir Julius Vogel Award. She is also the coauthor of the Ministry of Peculiar Occurrences novels with Tee Morris. Philippa is currently in the United States, where her two Siberian cats, Sebastian and Viola, make sure she stays out of trouble. Visit her website at www.pjballantine.com.

M988JV1011